Praise for
The Mud of the Place

"The pacing is perfect, the multiple viewpoints well handled and well distributed, a complicated storyline made easy to follow, and the characters engaging. . . . Really wonderful work!"

–Karen Joy Fowler, author,
The Jane Austen Book Club and *Wit's End*

"From the first gunshot on the West Tisbury–Edgartown Road to the very satisfying ending, Ms. Sturgis draws the reader in with expertly turned phrases and a keen knowledge of Vineyard byways.

"Her well-developed characters reside on the beloved (but oft-misunderstood) island where the alluring beauty belies the reality beneath—one where too frequently 'ambition is useless and apathy a virtue.'

"Ms. Sturgis's seamless transitions keep the reader poised on every page waiting for the twists and turns surely to come—along casual dirt roads or by the shore. Her astute observations lay bare the workings of the five-corners-miasma of island life.

"A must-read that will leave the reader begging for a sequel—and soon!"

–Susan Klein, storyteller and author,
Through a Ruby Window

"*The Mud of the Place* does such a beautiful job of capturing the quality of interactions among people in the small Cape and Islands towns, and the culture and environment of the place. It's all the more precious because the communities and their fragile environment are changing so much. And what memorable characters! As a gay man, Jay faces the challenges of being different in his own hometown, and the fear that coming out will mean losing the family, friends, and job that he loves. He might not have to be so frightened these days."

–Amy Hoffman, author, *An Army of Ex-Lovers*;
editor in chief, *Women's Review of Books*

More praise for
The Mud of the Place

"I thoroughly enjoyed this novel! The characters of *The Mud of the Place* ring true and all the island references have such authenticity. Sturgis speaks with a great awareness of the many and varied aspects of life on Martha's Vineyard. And Pixel adds a warm touch for those of us whose dogs often accompany us on our errands. I feel like I know these people and—who knows?—maybe I do!"

–Mary-Jean Miner, co-author,
Unbroken Circles: The Campground of Martha's Vineyard

"A solid, clever, compelling immersion in the realities of life in a famous, glamorized place, from the working-class level all the way up to island aristocracy. The story is made of real-life challenges, dangers, ethical dilemmas, and warm, true human bonds that kept me reading eagerly even without a murder or a monster to keep me engaged. That's because the writing is excellent—lean, sharply observant, and downright witty. What a good, satisfying novel!"

–Suzy McKee Charnas, author,
the Holdfast Chronicles and *The Vampire Tapestry*

"A sensitive, witty, and tightly plotted portrayal of life on Martha's Vineyard that only a true Islander could have written. Nice going, Susanna!"

–Cynthia Riggs, author,
the Martha's Vineyard Mystery Series,
featuring 92-year-old Victoria Trumbull

The Mud of the Place
a novel

by Susanna J. Sturgis

THE MUD OF THE PLACE
copyright © 2008, Susanna J. Sturgis

Published by
    Speed-of-C Productions
    PO Box 265
    Linthicum, MD 21090-0265

Cover photo by Virginia A. Lobdell

ISBN: 978-1-934754-10-8

First edition: December 2008

Printed in the United States of America

Dedicated to the memory and spirit of
Betty Ann Lima Bryant (1938–1994)
who showed me where to look

If your feet aren't in the mud of a place,
you'd better watch where your mouth is.

Grace Paley

CHAPTER ONE

Amateur sages like to say that when one door closes, another opens—ideally when you've been dumped by your girlfriend or fired from your job, or you've committed a faux pas so terrible that you don't dare go out in public. Sometimes it works the other way: a door opens, you walk through it, and a heavy metal gate slams shut behind you, creating a gust strong enough to part your hair in a new place. What the sages can't explain is why those doors are so hard to see before they move, and why your friends always see them better than you do.

Since the day they met, Shannon Merrick had seen plain as day the door facing her friend Jay Segredo, and she'd been sure that his hand was moving slowly toward the knob, turning it *slowly,* letting a little light and fresh air in from the wider world on the other side. Then fate interfered and he slammed the door shut. True, Shannon might have done the same if one of her own psycho estranged relatives had taken a potshot at *her* car, but she hoped she'd be over it by now. Jay by the sound of it was piling furniture against the closed door and digging himself a hidey-hole under the floor.

Just before eleven o'clock on a Monday night the previous October, Jay had been driving home along the Edgartown–West Tisbury Road, a long and uneventful route that more or less parallels the island's south shore about two miles inland. As he approached the T intersection with Barnes Road, just before the county airport, his right front tire blew out. He managed to wrestle his startled old Volvo wagon across the grassy shoulder to a bumpy halt. Because Jay had lived a big chunk of the previous two decades in the dicier neighborhoods of big northeastern cities, he ducked down instinctively. The woods were silent, there were no other cars on the road. *It was a blowout, that's all it was,* he told himself, *just a blowout,* but he waited two full minutes before easing out of the car. His left ankle protested when he put weight on it, and both knees were banged up, the left worse than the right, but he guessed he could make it to the airport without doing himself permanent damage.

He looked up and down the road: nothing was coming, not even the most distant glow of headlights in either direction. His left hand pressing the car's sides for support, he hobbled counterclockwise around the back. Even in the dark he could tell the right rear tire was fine. The right front was not. He fished the flashlight out of the glove compartment and trained the beam on the tire. Not only was it flat, it was partway off the rim—and even in the dim light and deep shadow he could see what looked like a hole in the sidewall. He crouched down and felt it with his fingers. No nail or sharp object on the road could possibly have done that damage.

Except during hunting season, open hours at the Rod & Gun Club, and private target practice, gunfire on Martha's Vineyard takes place exclusively on TV and movie screens. Jay had lived most of his adult life in places where it was otherwise, but in the three years since he'd moved home to the Vineyard, his city reflexes had faded. Now it seemed they'd only been dozing: it took Jay less than a split second to accept that yes, he had been shot at. In nearly the same instant he knew who had pulled the trigger.

When the roadside trees began to glow with oncoming high-beam headlights, Jay tossed his flashlight onto the front seat and walked carefully around the hood of the car and up to the edge of the pavement. He faced the oncoming car and stuck out his thumb. Being a longtime Vineyard resident, the driver of the aged white Toyota Tercel didn't think twice about stopping in the middle of the night for a man she wasn't sure she recognized. In the short distance between there and the airport, they established a connection: she had been his younger nephew's first-grade teacher at the Oak Bluffs School before she left the school system to work as a mortgage officer for one of the banks. Jay did not tell her how his car had come to be broken down by the side of the road—like the rest of the island, she read it in the *Martha's Vineyard Chronicle* when it came out on Thursday—but she drove him up to the terminal and departed only after he had assured her that he would be fine; he had enough quarters to call not only 911 but most of his friends and acquaintances.

The *Chronicle's* front-page story for October 16, 1997, was headlined "No Leads in Holiday Shooting, Police Say." Also featured on the front page were yet another tale of ineptness in county government, a new installment in the long-running feud between Martha's Vineyard and the mainland town of Falmouth about island-bound traffic, and local real estate brokers crowing about rising prices and complaining about the dearth of "high-end properties." On Martha's Vineyard, political and economic woes are like the weather: annoying, even infuriating, a fertile subject for complaint, but grandly resistant to human intervention. Shootings with human targets are still a novelty: 1998 brought the island's first murder in twenty years, and before the year was out there'd been a second, but in October of 1997, no one knew that was coming. No matter what their interests, no matter how much they'd already learned from the radio, the off-island papers, and the grapevine, every reader of that week's *Chronicle* started with the story about how someone had taken a shot at the Youth Services director as he drove down the Edgartown–West Tisbury Road.

Shannon called Jay from the pay phone at Alley's General Store late Thursday morning, right after she picked up the paper. It wasn't quite warm enough to be sitting on the old porch, but Shannon thought she might delay winter by toughing it out with the *Chronicle,* a large coffee, and a jelly doughnut. "Hey, man," she said, watching the cars and pickups passing by so she could wave to anyone she recognized, and wave back at anyone who waved at her, "what's with all the testimonials? It sounds like you just announced your resignation. You sure you're OK?"

"I'm fine," Jay insisted. "Your friend Leslie wrote the story—why don't you ask her if I'm about to retire? Listen, got to go—meeting in thirty seconds, OK? Talk to you later."

"Weasel," muttered Shannon. As half a dozen Lycra-clad cyclists settled themselves along the long edge of the porch with their designer waters and their Power Bars, Shannon jabbed the number for the newspaper office, though she didn't really want to talk to Leslie. Naturally Leslie answered the phone. "Hey, girlfriend—" Shannon began.

On the other end of the line, air hissed sharply through exasperated teeth. "Don't call—"

"Sorry, Scoop," Shannon said. Jay had started that one; Leslie didn't like it either. Shannon forged ahead, realizing that it was going to be one of those days when she couldn't say the right thing if she tried—a good day to go home and curl up with the computer. "Good story you wrote there, but . . ."

"But it sounds like a eulogy?" Leslie was probably raising both of her eloquent eyebrows. "What can I say? It was a slow news week."

"Slow compared to what? Boston the week before election day? I didn't see much fluff on that front page." Shannon glanced over at her mud-streaked Subaru wagon in the parking lot: Pixel, her half-malamute dog, was slumped against the passenger-side door, obviously bored. Shannon signaled with her fingers: *Two minutes max.* Pixel looked skeptical. She circled around on the seat and lay down. All Shannon could see now was the tips of two fuzzy gray ears.

"All right, all right," Leslie was saying. "The big boss and I are betting they'll arrest somebody in the next few days, and if it's who we think it is, this could turn into a real story."

"Who do you think it is?"

"Same person you think it is."

Duh. Leslie didn't say it, but Shannon heard it in her voice. "Like snipers firing out of the state forest aren't real enough?" she said, somewhat snippily.

"Spot news," Leslie sneered. "Whoever won a Pulitzer Prize for *spot news?*"

The next day, the island's other weekly newspaper, the *Martha's Vineyard News Beacon,* carried substantially the same story.

The following week both papers printed updates that said, more or less, that there was no news, and after that the incident disappeared from the news pages, though not from the island's kitchens, supermarket aisles, and coffee shops. Feeling cheated, Leslie Benaron returned to her regular diet of fincom meetings, zoning violations, and rumors of official malfeasance. The *News Beacon* for October 31 did carry the following notice in its weekly report on district court business:

Monday, October 20
Wayne D. Swanson, reckless discharge of firearm, discharge of firearm within 500 ft. of inhabited dwelling, public intoxication, violating restraining order. Pretrial conference Oct. 27.

The *Chronicle* carried virtually the same entry a week later.

The incident that landed Wayne Swanson in court was not reported in either newspaper. You had to know someone, or someone who knew someone, to know that the dwelling within 500 feet of which Wayne D. Swanson had allegedly discharged his firearm was inhabited by Jay Segredo. And that Wayne D. Swanson was currently separated from Jay's younger sister, Janice, who had filed for divorce four months before. And that Mr. Swanson blamed Mr. Segredo for the failure of his marriage—a belief shared by no one outside his own very small social circle. Mr. Swanson was widely acknowledged to be both a pretty good plumber and an outstanding drunk. Over the years his behavior had gone from erratic to threatening to sporadically violent; before his wife sought help, there had been two incidents of domestic violence that involved the police, and several more that didn't. But Mr. Segredo and his associates at ISS, Island Social Services—particularly the staff and volunteers of the Women's Resource Center—had found emergency housing for Janice Segredo Swanson and her three children; they had found her a lawyer and a crisis counselor and supported her through the court appearances necessary for a separation, a restraining order, and a filing for divorce. Without a doubt their assistance had made it easier for Mrs. Swanson to leave her husband.

Mr. Swanson had responded by making threats against Mr. Segredo's person and personal property. These threats were repeated often enough, and forcefully enough, and publicly enough, that even Mr. Swanson's fellow regulars at the Circuit Avenue bars were a little uneasy. Mr. Swanson, after all, owned several guns and knew how to use them; he had been heard to say that if he had an Uzi, he could wipe out the island's deer herd in a week. A second restraining order was issued, warning Mr. Swanson against any contact with Mr. Segredo, and against coming within 100 feet of Mr. Segredo's office or house.

It didn't take a math whiz to add two and two and surmise that Wayne Swanson had fired the shot that disabled Jay Segredo's car late Columbus Day evening. Jay's friends assumed as much, and so, unofficially, did most of the island's law enforcement officials. But in the absence of evidence, concrete or circumstantial, or a confession, Wayne Swanson could not be charged with the crime. Had there been enough evidence to arrest him for attempted homicide, it is highly unlikely that, at the pretrial conference on October 27, the court, the probation officer, and Dr. Jerome Turner—Wayne's counselor at Island Social Services—would have agreed to send him off-island for psychiatric evaluation and treatment for alcoholism. With considerable misgivings, Jay Segredo and Janice Segredo Swanson concurred with the decision. Janice did not want to appear vindictive. Jay had his own reasons for remaining silent.

Of all the island's residents, only two knew more than the police. One of the two was Jay himself. The Wednesday after the accident—Tuesday morning had brought torrential rain—he left for work early, parked his car in an inconspicuous place, and walked into the corner of the state forest bordered by Barnes Road on the west and the Edgartown–West Tisbury Road on the south. He had not been hunting in more than twenty years, but the woodsmanship his father had taught him was ingrained in all his senses. Starting from where his car had been hit, he paced the likely trajectory of the bullet through leafy brush, between the tall, slender pines and fledgling oaks. Where the ground rose slightly and still offered a reasonably unobstructed view of the road, he found two soggy Marlboro filters, smoked down to the nub: Wayne smoked Marlboros, but then so did a lot of other guys. Using tweezers, Jay picked each one up by its burnt end, dropped them into a plastic sandwich bag, and stored them in the pocket of his canvas field jacket.

Jay's nephew, Kevin Swanson, a high school junior, had also noticed something out of the ordinary. The previous July Kevin's grandfather, Ernie Segredo, had given Kevin his prized .30-30 rifle, a replica of the 1894 Winchester original, for a birthday present. Kevin took it regularly to the Rod & Gun Club for target practice. He was impatiently waiting for Deer Week, the first week in December, to take it hunting. He cleaned it every weekend, whether he used it or not, cherishing the link to his grandfather, who—as everyone could see but no one would admit out loud—was dying of emphysema. At his mother's insistence, Kevin kept the rifle in a locked cabinet in his room, next to the .22 that had taught him to shoot, and its ammunition in a locked file drawer. Tuesday morning he learned that his uncle had been shot at. Not until Wednesday afternoon after school did he dare unlock the cabinet and look at his gun.

It had been fired. It had not been cleaned. His stomach dropped like a falling elevator, but he was not surprised. He couldn't sleep that night. Just before one in the morning he phoned his uncle and reported what he'd found. "Should I tell Mom?" he asked. "Should I tell the police?"

"No," said his uncle Jay. "Keep it to yourself. For now. Can you do that?"

"I can do that," Kevin said. And he had.

Jay had no desire to protect Wayne: he would happily have locked Wayne away for the rest of his natural life for the grief he had put Janice through. Nor was Jay a man who evaded his legal or ethical responsibilities without compelling reason. But the day after the shooting, when he was resting at home, watching TV and catching up on the several professional journals he subscribed to, his friend Shannon had come by with two cups of coffee and some disturbing news: Wayne had been seen hanging around the modest Edgartown neighborhood where Giles Kelleher lived—the friend whose house Jay had left about ten minutes before someone took a shot at his car. Wayne, Jay assumed at once, had been tracking his movements. Probably he had followed Jay when he left the holiday cookout at Janice's, dropped his mother off at her house nearby, and drove not home to West Tisbury but down the Beach Road to Edgartown. For whatever reason, Wayne had guessed that sometime that evening Jay would be driving west on the Edgartown–West Tisbury Road.

What else did Wayne know?

The question was too hot to touch.

Jay had grown up on the island, as had both of his parents and all but one of his grandparents, but his growing up had been both like and unlike theirs. Like them he had gone to the island schools; he had learned the woods as a hunter and the shore and coastal waters as a fisherman; he ate deer and ducks his father shot, and vegetables his mother grew and put up. But unlike them he had gone off-island to college; he had lived off-island for most of two decades. Not for a moment had he ever felt estranged from either the island or his family: he came back often, for Easter, Thanksgiving, and Christmas; for the baptisms, First Communions, graduations, weddings, and funerals of family members and close family friends; and for the Holy Ghost Feast, the celebration that the Portuguese American community threw for the entire island every July.

Only after he moved back to live had it dawned on him that when he'd come home to visit, he'd always left part of himself on the other side.

Shannon, on the other hand, had seen rough weather in Jay's forecast almost from the beginning. Three years before, she had been on the search committee that chose Jay as the new Youth Services director. For several members of the committee, Shannon among them, he was the obvious choice to repair the damage done to the agency's competence and credibility by his disastrous predecessor. An articulate, congenial island native with an MSW, clinical experience, political savvy, and administrative ability? This was more than they had dared wish for. Other committee members, notably those whose fierce devotion to their own turf frequently overrode their commitment to the agency's, and the island's, best interests, were not so happy. Each of them had an off-island contact or two who warned "watch out for this guy, he's a maverick, he doesn't play by the rules."

Shannon, who with her combination of mild persona and steel backbone might have been a native but wasn't, didn't leave the outcome up to either chance or her colleagues' good intentions. When conversations with clients or her volunteer colleagues came around to the Youth Services director search—often thanks to her invisible nudging and prodding—she'd mention how impressed she was with the island-born candidate. She went walking with the *News Beacon* reporter who covered the social services beat—a young man whose Gordon setter was a big fan of Shannon's Pixel—and managed to convey her admiration for Jay Segredo. She introduced herself to Leslie Benaron, then the newest reporter on the *Chronicle.* After one phone conversation with Jay, Leslie stepped up to the plate. As the finalists arrived on the island for their interviews, ministers, therapists, teachers, and even some of his high school classmates were praising Jay Segredo in letters to the search committee, ISS executive director Jack Purcell, and even the editors of both papers; and the bureaucratic diehards realized that it was going to be impossible to appoint anyone else.

Jay didn't know Shannon from Mary Magdalene. She had moved to the island while he was in grad school; he spoke with her twice on the phone and then met her for the first time at the interview. After he was hired, Jay heard enough about the behind-the-scenes machinations to conclude that without Shannon's advocacy, he might not have gotten the job. He was just beginning to settle into that job when he met Shannon for lunch on a sunny, not quite unpleasantly humid afternoon a couple of weeks after Labor Day. They sat on a bench on the bulkhead that ran along the east side of Oak Bluffs harbor, watching day-trippers wander in and out of the trinket shops. Each had ordered suicide buffalo wings from Coop de Ville, along with a large order of fries, which they shared. "You like hot stuff?" Shannon asked, twirling a french fry in the blue cheese dressing.

"Yeah," said Jay. "The hotter the better."

"You will notice," Shannon said, "that the longer you live here, the more unreliable your taste buds will get. They'll start screeching whenever you send some lukewarm salsa their way. They're not lying to you. They just don't know any better. There is no Indian food on Martha's Vineyard, the Tex-Mex is so-so, and the Chinese is only tolerable if you haven't had the real thing in a couple of years. Between May and mid-September, however, you can come to Coop de Ville, order suicide wings, and keep your taste buds in shape."

"So how come you didn't let me try the Three Mile Island wings?"

"Because Three Mile Island is for lunatics. It's so hot you can't taste the celery, never mind the chicken. Don't go there. It's about as much fun as Russian roulette." Shannon sucked blue cheese off the tip of a french fry then dunked it again and ate it whole. A power yacht backed out of its slip and slowly turned to face the harbor's narrow mouth. "So," she said, "tell me the truth. I'm not on the search committee anymore. Why the fuck did you want to move back here?"

"My dad's sick," Jay replied. "As you know. Without a miracle, he'll never get out of long-term care. My mother could use some help. There's also the fact that my sister is married to this—"

After a polite pause, Shannon suggested, "Asshole?"

"In a word."

"In a word," said Shannon, "I'm glad you took the job. The kids need you, Youth Services needs you, Island Social Services needs you, though they'll implode before they admit it—the island needs you, probably, though you know damn well it won't admit to needing anything. But I still think you've got your head up your butt. You're lucky I'm more or less in favor of assisted suicide."

Jay grinned. He had a smile that could only be described as "winning" or "boyish," especially when it was accented by a dot of hot sauce at the corner of his mouth. Shannon pointed at the corresponding corner of her own mouth; Jay wiped the spot clean with a paper napkin. "It's not *that* bad," he said. "The island is a pretty laissez-faire place if you know how it works. Some of the family arrangements around here are not exactly traditional—"

"They do tend to be het, however," Shannon muttered under her breath.

Jay glanced around before replying: "There was that attempted book banning last year."

"There was that," Shannon admitted. "And it did indeed fail, after which all the liberals went into veritable paroxysms of self-congratulation about what a tolerant and mature *community* the Vineyard is. In a word: *feh.*"

"Keep talking," Jay said.

"OK." She extracted the last bit of meat from a drumstick, placed the bone on the lid of her Styrofoam tray, and licked her fingers. Her lips tingled. "One: the daddies who tried to get the dangerous books out of the school library were dimwits. Two: Plenty of people did indeed protest what the daddies were doing—they showed up at meetings, they wrote letters to the editor, et cetera, et cetera. For the most part, however, they were the usual suspects: young people, gay people, arts types, people who hadn't been on the island all that long. There was exactly one organization that went on record against the daddies, and that was the librarians. Everywhere else: silence. It was eerie. I'd be in meetings with ministers, counselors, teachers, people with gay brothers or lesbian daughters, and no one ever brought it up. When I did, they'd say, 'Oh, no one takes them seriously.'"

"So do you think they were a serious threat?"

"In a word: no." She and Jay both laughed. "They were too unclever to realize that they were actually using a clever tactic: seeing what they could get away with, what the community would tolerate and what it wouldn't. It's OK to have books about gay families in the school library. Big deal."

"But it *is* a big deal, isn't it?" Jay sipped his Coke through a straw.

Shannon shrugged. "All the real-life gay families I know on Martha's Vineyard are more or less in the closet because they're afraid that otherwise their kids will bear the brunt of it. If you staked out Main Street, Vineyard Haven, from New

Year's Day till the last of December, you might see maybe three people max holding hands with someone of the same sex."

Until that moment it hadn't occurred to Jay Segredo that there *were* gay families on Martha's Vineyard. Families with kids in the school system, maybe even families who were clients of Youth Services? The realization released such an adrenaline rush that for a moment he felt dizzy. He set his drink down on the bench and felt its chill penetrate his khakis and seep toward his knees.

"So," Shannon was asking, "did you ever bring a boyfriend home to meet the folks?"

For an instant all sound stopped: the breeze, the lapping of the wavelets in the harbor, the cars on nearby New York Avenue. "Jesus Christ!" Jay hissed. "Will you—"

"Don't panic," she said quietly, gazing at a gaff-rigged sloop anchored in the middle of the harbor. "A, there's no one within twenty feet of us, and B, if we were in the back of the class, they wouldn't have heard me in the next row up. The prosecution rests, yes?"

Thrown together by circumstance, held together by the politics, the secrets, and the sense of humor they shared, Jay and Shannon fell into friendship the way some people fall into love: fast and hard, with no looking back. They talked often, by phone and sitting in each other's living rooms, as Jay set about turning Youth Services around, recruiting new caseworkers and slowly mending relationships with all the island teachers, counselors, parents, and young people who had learned over the years that the Youth Services office was not to be trusted. Meanwhile Shannon returned to her freelance graphics business, teaching herself website design to meet the demands of her regular clients and, predictably, getting most of her practice designing free websites for nonprofits and friends. She resumed what she called her "regular volunteer gig": being on call twice a week for the

Women's Resource Center, fielding calls from battered women, arranging shelter for women and children fleeing violent husbands and fathers, filling in sometimes as a court advocate though courtrooms gave her the creeps.

Because crises involving women often affect children, and crises affecting young people almost invariably involve their parents, the Women's Resource Center and Youth Services seemed to be natural allies. Not for nothing did they occupy the same building in the sprawling Island Social Services complex, the most spartan building, the one physically farthest from the agency's executive suites. But in the almost fifteen years of Youth Services' existence, the natural alliance had never developed. Reasons given for this varied. When pressed, and promised anonymity, ISS head Jack Purcell alluded delicately to "departmental priorities" and, a little less delicately, to "personality conflicts." Evalina Montrose, director of Women's Resources, was characteristically more blunt: "Sexism," she said. "What else is new? And while we're at it, let's talk about *Doctor* Jerome Turner."

Dr. Turner headed the Family Services department, which encompassed both Women's Resources and Youth Services as well as the ISS day-care center. Some twenty-five years earlier, Jerome W. Turner had been a prize catch for ISS, with his three advanced degrees, impeccable island connections—his mother and two of his aunts were grandes dames of the African American summer community—and a self-proclaimed "roll up your sleeves" attitude. Over the years, though, he had devoted less and less of his energy to meeting the island's needs, more and more to giving speeches to newsworthy off-island organizations and developing a power base within the expanding agency. His progress had stalled when he tried to bring the Women's Resource Center to heel. Women's Resources had deep roots in the wider community: its volunteer roster was the envy of the other offices, as was its list of annual contributors. Jerome Turner recognized clout when he saw it, so his challenges to Evalina Montrose and her staff were calculated to annoy but not anger; his adversaries took to referring to him as Gerbil Turd, "the Gerb" for short. But Youth Services was his baby, his claim to fame: he had fought for its creation in part to provide a job for one of his protégés, and he had shaped its development ever since.

Or he had until, despite his strenuous efforts to prevent it, Jay Segredo was named its director. Dr. Turner's own clout had been shaky at the time, owing to the spectacular lack of judgment of Segredo's predecessor: Terry Randolph had come to the job with impressive credentials and high praise from his peers, but none of the glowing recommendations had included a hint of his problem with alcohol. Dr. Turner's attempts to get him some help while soothing the feathers he occasionally ruffled had paid off for a while. Then Randolph was arrested for drunk driving, and the offense was compounded by the presence in his car of an intoxicated female high school junior. That had been that.

Jerome Turner hadn't been able to derail Jay's appointment, and it had required considerable patience and self-discipline to bide his time while Jay Segredo's popularity grew both within and without Island Social Services, and while an ever-warmer working relationship developed between Youth Services and the Women's Resource Center. In their building at the back of beyond, Women's Resources was on the second floor—turn right at the top of the metal staircase—and Youth Services on the first, to the left of the stairs. Foot traffic echoed frequently in the stark stairwell as staff from the two offices consulted with each other or attended each other's birthday and holiday celebrations. For the time being Dr. Turner could do nothing. Sooner or later, if he played his cards carefully, Segredo's halo would start to slip. When it did, he would be ready to move.

CHAPTER TWO

By the time Leslie Benaron's mud-splattered Camry slid to a halt inches from a sturdy oak, the fire was out, but bright glare through the trees and the rumble of a generator indicated that there was still some action up the hill. The dark air reeked of sodden smoke, and an assortment of pickups, sedans, and SUVs waited where they had been deserted hours earlier, noses deep in the brambly brush on both sides of the road.

Road, hah! Call this a road? Only on Martha's Vineyard would this string of ruts pass for a road. Reporter's notebook clutched in one hand, rollerball pen trapped in its spiral binding, Leslie picked her way up the muddy track. It wasn't enough that mud season was still upon them the third week of April; runoff from the hoses was gouging deeper and deeper tracks on either side of the slippery median mound. And was Leslie wearing her duck shoes? She was not. Leslie had just come from a dinner date, a precious opportunity to wear her fine black Italian leather boots, the ones that shaped her ankle and lower calf in graceful curves that approached—she hoped—elegance. The ones whose soles were so thin that the cold clamminess of the mud chilled the bottoms of her stocking feet. If she was really lucky, the soles would stay attached to the uppers till she got home.

Damn Roger for turning his scanner on anyway. If his attempts at conversation had been more interesting, she would have insisted he turn it off. Damn herself for being unable to ignore it. Why couldn't this house fire be covered like every other house fire on Martha's Vineyard—after the fact, with phone calls to the police chief, the fire chief, the owner, the neighbors? Damn herself for being her father's daughter.

Of course, when her father was her age, he was digging into the roots of the Bay of Pigs fiasco, on his way to his first Pulitzer Prize, not picking and sliding his way up a mucky excuse for a road to cover a *house fire.* Which was not to say that he hadn't slogged down some muddy roads in his time: the mid-sixties had found him in South Vietnam, where he not only earned his second Pulitzer but also conceived a deep admiration for the medics and doctors and nurses who patched up the wounded and held the hands of the dying—a fascination that had inspired his subsequent, equally successful journalistic career exploring the politics of health care. Leslie's mother liked to say in her more acerbic moments—she had many acerbic moments—that her mother had told her to marry a doctor, but instead she had married a man who made doctors look like idiots.

Leslie's left foot slipped; for a sickening second she thought she was going down. *Wake up, klutz,* she warned herself, and from that moment on, not even her father could have found a flaw in her performance.

Against its backdrop of pines, the house was small, wood-shingled, of indistinct style. The roof might have had lofty aspirations once but it seemed to have encountered its own glass ceiling; the house hunkered down instead of standing tall. The door was a yawning maw under one furrowed brow—a clunky little circumflex of an overhang that might have sheltered, at most, one visitor in waiting. The outline of the structure seemed intact, but Leslie noticed the vacant rectangles where the two front windows had been, and the way the floodlights on the fire engines revealed several feet of brick chimney that should have been concealed by the roof.

"Nothing back here," called a male voice, rising above the

eddy and swirl of male voices. Should she take a walk around the mess, assess the damage? The sagging yellow tape—POLICE LINE DO NOT CROSS POLICE LINE DO NOT CROSS—was less of a deterrent than her indoor boots, her chilly feet. Would she find out anything she couldn't learn by phone in the morning? *No wonder I'm not reporting from Kosovo. What lazy schmuck tries to cover a war by making phone calls?* The firefighting force was dissolving into its constituent parts; most of the guys were hanging around kibitzing, waiting for the OK to leave.

Tom Ferreira leaned against West Tisbury's ladder truck, sipping coffee from a thermos top. His long black slicker hung heavily open, his hat was perched on the wheel well: the picture of a work-weary volunteer yearning to go home.

Speaking of which, it was probably too much to ask for one of the paper's freelance photographers to get his butt in gear . . . Of course it was. Not for nothing was the *Martha's Vineyard Chronicle* called the *Chronic Tightwad* by almost everyone who had ever worked for it, written for it, or taken pictures for it. The paper had one full-time photographer and an ever-changing roster of stringers eager for exposure who got paid by the published print. Leslie had rushed out of Roger's without calling any of them, without asking Roger to call one of them. *Schmuck once, schmuck twice . . .*

"How's it going?" Leslie asked Tom. *And while we're at it, why didn't I stop by the house to pick up my own camera?* Her trusty old Canon single-lens reflex was in its case, hanging from a peg by the front door. Plus, if she'd had a cell phone, she could have pried one of the freelance shutterbugs away from whatever pleasure pot he frequented on a Sunday night and persuaded him to come down here and be as miserable as she was. Why didn't she have a cell phone? Because she didn't want people buzzing her at all hours of the day and night. Finally it dawned on her that with a cell phone *she* could be buzzing people at all hours of the day or night. *A little slow on the uptake there, Dumbo.*

Tom jutted his bristly chin toward the house. "It's gonzo," he said. "Pretty much. We saved the garage."

Leslie followed his gaze up the hill a ways. Indeed, a small square building stood untouched barely twenty-five feet from the wreck of its parent. "Anyone in it?"

"Nope. Good thing. It was one helluva bonfire when we got there."

"Pretty close to the trees back there, isn't it," Leslie offered.

"Pretty close. Never thought I'd be glad of all that snow and sleet and rain we've had, but it sure made our job easier." Tom grinned. "You gonna quote me on that?"

She raised both eyebrows and scowled. "Only if I'm really hard up." Glancing downslope, she noticed lights glowing upward through the tall skinny trees. "Whose house is that?" she asked.

"That's Don Everett's new place. You gotta know his dad."

She did: Jim Everett was a semi-retired builder who served on the town's finance committee; he pushed, prodded, and annoyed everyone with his persistent questions until clarity emerged from fuzzy budgets and bylaw proposals. Leslie liked him. His dogged attention to detail drove some of his colleagues crazy, but when it came to explaining budgets and procedures to a math-impaired reporter, he had the patience of a third-grade teacher. "Sure do," Leslie said, about to launch into a Jim Everett anecdote. The attempt was derailed by an angry voice, rising so fast and high it threatened to crack: "Tomorrow? What are you talking about, tomorrow? I want this investigated now!"

The reply was inaudible. Leslie searched the gloom for the source. "Asshole," Tom muttered.

"Who's that?" Leslie asked.

"The bereaved homeowner." The firefighter squinted up the hill and shook his head. "Couldn't have happened to a nicer guy. Don't quote me on that."

"Not to worry. I should probably go check him out."

"Good ta see ya, Scoop," said Tom, and sent the dregs of

his coffee in a slow arc down the hill. "Can't wait to read all about it."

The bereaved homeowner wore a tweed Irish walking hat with a moderate crown, but even so he barely reached the steel gray mustache of Tay Francis, Tisbury's veteran chief of police. Chief Tay was riding out the verbal torrent with his usual cool, but Leslie noted the rippling in his coat pocket, where an invisible fist was clenching and unclenching.

"In Cleveland that—that sloven would be behind bars by now."

That's what I like, thought Leslie: a man with a vocabulary. His trench coat fit nicely too, despite the sartorially challenging combination of broad shoulders and less than average height. The man couldn't be more than an inch taller than she was.

"I expect they have due process in Cleveland too, Mr. McAuliffe," the chief said mildly. He raised an eyebrow and smiled slightly. "Be right with you, Ms. Benaron."

Ms. Benaron am I now? She beamed at him. "No hurry," she said.

Whether annoyed by the interruption or impressed by her unmistakably female voice, Mr. McAuliffe glanced in her direction. His eyes gave her instant creeps. Pale gray or light blue, they looked like glass marbles in the contorted mask of his face.

"Ms. Benaron is an investigator of sorts, Mr. McAuliffe." Chief Tay's voice slowed almost to a drawl—a habit with him when he had to explain something step by step to someone who probably wasn't going to get it anyway.

"I'm a reporter," she said. "Leslie Benaron, *M.V. Chronicle.* Where can I reach you in the morning?"

Those creepy eyes never left her face as he drew a black leather folder from an inside pocket and passed her a business card. The address and phone number were indeed in Cleveland, but there was a pager number as well, and an e-mail address. "I'll have one too, if you don't mind," said Chief

Tay. When the man hesitated, the chief added, "Not that my officers couldn't find you without it."

Mr. McAuliffe flicked a second card out of its case and held it out. "I'm at the Harbor View Hotel," he said, a little more graciously. "I'm booked on an afternoon flight out tomorrow, but with this—" he glanced over his shoulder at the eerily lit remains of his house "—I'll probably be here till the end of the week."

"Thank you," said the chief. The guy whose dwelling had gone up in smoke stalked up the hill to his surviving outbuilding and, Leslie now saw, a sporty little probably red, probably Mercedes convertible—the floodlights made it hard to tell.

"Any evidence of arson, Chief?" Leslie asked, extracting her pen from the spiral binding of her notebook.

"Well, Ms. Benaron," he said, "it's premature to make any statement about that. We'll be up here in the morning going over this place with a fine-toothed . . ."

"German shepherd?" Leslie suggested, rescuing him from the precipice of cliché. Chief Tay loathed sloppy reports, pompous prose, and all sorts of linguistic imprecision. He loved Leslie's father—"the man can *write*," he had said when he met Leslie for the first time, just after she'd been hired by the *Chronicle* and decided to stay on the island for the winter; he could barely contain himself when Leslie invited him and Mrs. Francis to dinner the following summer when her parents were in residence. The only problem on that occasion had been Leslie's mother, who gushed that she couldn't *understand* why such an *articulate* gentleman who not only held a *law* degree but could sing lines from several Verdi *arias* in a decent baritone was on the Tisbury *police force.*

"Thank you," he said, withdrawing a folded-over half-pound bag of peanut M&Ms from the pocket of his overcoat. "Have a few?" She held out a cupped hand; he filled it with candies. She popped three into her mouth and slid the rest into her pocket.

"So what can you tell me about tonight's fire?" Leslie inquired, all business.

"Got the call from Communications at 4:53 p.m. Neighbor reported flames." His gaze flicked from the ruins to the house down the hill. "Tisbury fire department responded—you'll have to get the details from Chief Robinson on that—called in West Tisbury at 5:20, Oak Bluffs at 5:24 . . ."

Leslie scribbled notes that she probably wouldn't even look at; whatever she wrote down stuck in her head for at least a week. Chief Tay might not be the most quotable informant around, but his details were invariably exact to the second. For a reporter, getting good quotes was easy; it was facts that were hard to come by. *Speaking of which . . .*

"This Mr. McAuliffe . . ."

"Well, Ms. Benaron, you'll have to check with the register of deeds to ascertain whether Mr. McAuliffe is in fact the owner of the property."

"Well, Mr. Francis," she replied, wiping the incipient grin off her face but unable to keep it out of her voice, "I will certainly do that, but—off the record, if you prefer—how did you come to know the man's name?"

"No point keeping that off the record, ma'am," said the chief. "The fire departments of three towns saw the whole sequence of events, and"—here he deliberately consulted his watch—"I expect it will be the talk of Circuit Avenue within the hour."

Most of the Vineyard's year-round watering holes were located on Oak Bluffs' Circuit Avenue. Only two of the island's six towns were wet—Oak Bluffs was one, Edgartown the other—which considerably limited the options for public drinking. When Leslie needed the scuttlebutt on a drug bust, a fire, or a serious motor vehicle accident, she headed for the bars. It beat tracking down informants the next day, when they were likely to be scattered all around the island, and much more cautious about what they said to the press.

"Mr. McAuliffe introduced himself to me while I was

taking a radio call from Sergeant DeBettencourt, who was stationed at the end of the Hoft Road to direct incoming personnel. He advised me to 'immediately put out an all-points bulletin for the apprehension of Alice Chase'—that's a direct quote—who, he seems to believe, had something to do with the fire. I'm sure he'll give you the details when you call him." The chief actually winked at her. "I explained that we were trying to save what was left of his house, and if we were real lucky and the wind didn't blow, we might be able to keep the woods from going up too. He wanted me to know that he was Nick McAuliffe—*the* Nick McAuliffe—the Nick McAuliffe whose first novel had just been optioned by . . . I don't remember. Miramax, DreamWorks, one of those guys."

Couldn't have been much of a sale, Leslie thought, if this was all he could afford. Or maybe he just didn't *want* waterfront property, or waterview property, or property in a town that had its tax rate under control. "Did he say who this Alice Chase was?"

The chief regarded her oddly for just a moment too long before he said, "Tenant. The former owner's tenant, that is."

"Oh yeah," said Leslie, "Alice Chase." *I'm supposed to know who Alice Chase is? Who's Alice Chase?* "I won't keep you, Chief; as usual, you've been extremely helpful."

Tay Francis touched the brim of his cap. "As usual, it has been my pleasure."

"Thanks for the M&Ms," she added, fishing one from her pocket and tucking it under her tongue.

"Thank *you*," he replied. "Can't have the wife find them in my pocket when I get home."

She started carefully down the dark dirt road toward the neighboring house. It was all lit up: plainly the Everetts were still awake. But the mud had long since managed to ooze into both her boots; her feet were clammy with cold, and Leslie was beginning to shiver. Whatever the Everetts knew would keep. She continued down the hill, grateful for the bright following headlights that now lit her way. Stepping off the road onto the less traveled track that led to her car, she turned to blow a kiss to her benefactor, which turned out to be the West Tisbury pumper truck. It tooted acknowledgment, and the firefighter riding on the rear platform tipped his hat.

Once the truck passed, the trees were indistinguishable from the dark; twice she stumbled off the dirt road and into the scrubby undergrowth. *Did I really come this far?* She halted, her hand resting on the driver's side door of an old Ford 150. Her eyes, now accustomed to the dark, picked out no more metal glints, no carlike shapes among the slender trees; just ahead, the rough road dwindled to a path barely wide enough for a car to pass without scraping its sides. Turning around, she immediately spotted her Camry, bumper to bark with a sturdy oak and farther off the road than she remembered. *Whew.* She slid into the driver's seat. The starter responded to a turn of the key; the headlights illuminated tree trunks, undergrowth, and sodden leaves. She drew two deep breaths and dared meet her own eyes in the rearview mirror. *Journalist in the rough doesn't look half bad.* After a hot shower and a glass of wine she'd be ready for prime time—not that anyone would be around to applaud.

She shifted into reverse, released the emergency brake, and hit the accelerator. The wheels spun to a high whine before she realized what was happening and lifted her foot. Her heart was already thudding in alarm. Beyond the rear window the brake lights threw a dying-ember glow against the trees. Cautiously this time she pressed the gas pedal. Again the tires whined. *Shit.*

Of course she kept a flashlight in the glove compartment for emergencies, and equally of course the batteries were weak: a dim orange beam was the best it could manage. She grasped it anyway as she stepped out to survey the situation, leaving the engine running and the headlights on. The situation was not good: the Camry's trunk was now noticeably higher than the hood, and already the front tires were sunk up to their rims in slurpy mud. Worse yet, Shannon Merrick was laughing in her head: *Scoop, why doesn't a smart girl like you know how to drive a standard?*

Leslie cut the engine, turned off the lights, and trekked back up the hill to the Everetts'. A couple of lights remained near what remained of Nick McAuliffe's house; voices drifted toward her, but she couldn't make out what they were saying or who they belonged to. Besides, it was uphill to them and downhill to the Everetts' front door. Downhill was good, and the glow from the windows of the new-shingled house was so inviting.

While Don Everett was pulling on his boots, his wife, Sophie, plucked the near-useless flashlight from Leslie's hand and replaced the batteries from a kitchen drawer. After a longer look at Leslie's coat, lack of hat, and sodden boots, she pressed the visitor to accept a cup of hot tea. Don laughed. "Next she'll be heating up leftover macaroni," he told Leslie, who truth to tell wasn't eager to leave the warmth and bright light of the Everetts' kitchen. "Some other time, Soph. All this lady wants is home, a hot bath, and a bottle of beer."

Walking down the hill by the bright beam of his industrial-strength flashlight, two pieces of plywood tucked under his arm, Don Everett noted that if Leslie covered Tisbury, she must know his dad, Jim, "self-appointed scourge of the selectmen." Leslie laughed. "I thought you might be related," she said.

Don raised his light-bearing hand to his generous head of dark blond hair. In mock terror he asked, "I don't—I'm not beginning to *look* like him, am I?" The senior Everett's hairline had receded to the top of his head, a sad fact that he concealed, outdoors at least, with his signature navy blue captain's hat.

Leslie studied the situation. "Nah," she replied, though she'd been struck by the filial resemblance as soon as Don Everett opened his front door. "You talk like him, though."

Don chuckled. "You're not the first to say so," he said. "A

man could do worse, I guess."

After a pause, Leslie asked if he'd called in the alarm. "Yeah," he said. "The kids saw it first, though. They were out playing fetch with the dog."

By the time they reached the car, Leslie had learned that Alice Chase, accused sloven and possible arsonist, had moved out the previous Tuesday, after living in the house for more than two years with her son, Mitch; that Mitch went to the Tisbury School—"fourth grade," Don thought, "but don't quote me"—and that Alice was related by a previous marriage to the house's former owners, Zack and Ruth Butler, who had moved to Maine maybe three years back.

Don circled the car, training his light on the wheels one by one. "Standard?" he asked.

"Automatic," Leslie apologized.

Don handed Leslie the flashlight, placed a plywood rectangle behind each front tire, and climbed with some difficulty into the front seat; Leslie wasn't short, but Don had to be six-foot-two at least. Once the engine was running, he rolled the window down. "You think my dad's tight with a buck, you should meet old Zack. Soph and I bought our lot from him. Spins a good yarn, though, if he doesn't think you're out to fleece him."

Leslie managed a smile. Her car eased backward one inch, then another, slowly, oh so slowly. The plywood held; the tires rolled back and up out of the mud. Leslie released the breath she didn't know she was holding. "Wow," she said, stepping out of the way as Don backed the Camry around and pointed it in the right direction. "Thank you so much."

Don left the motor running and climbed out. "Nothing to it," he said, picking up the two filthy pieces of plywood.

Handing back the flashlight, Leslie asked Don if he'd met Nick McAuliffe before tonight. An involuntary narrowing of the eyes not only answered her question but eloquently conveyed that he didn't think much of the best-selling author. "Couple of times, just in passing," he said. "Soph got to know

Alice pretty well. You might want to talk to her."

"I will," Leslie said. "Yeah. Thanks." She got into the car. Her little flashlight, with its fresh new batteries, went back into the glove compartment. "Thanks again. If I can return the favor—"

"Hey, who knows?" He smiled. "If I get busted for disturbing the peace, maybe you can keep my picture off the front page."

CHAPTER THREE

Shannon was rushing, Shannon was always rushing. She invariably got to where she was going close to on time but with hair rumpled, shirt misbuttoned, or missing the envelopes she meant to drop off at the post office. It wasn't that she was unaware of time; like any freelancer, she tracked hours like a hawk and measured her life in deadlines. It was more that she couldn't bear to waste a minute, and the tasks she tried to squeeze into available pockets of time had a way of spilling over. Procrastination, ever helpful seductress that she was, assured her that *of course* she had time to read e-mail or make a quick phone call before she had to be where she had to be. She'd known since last Thursday that she had to be at the high school at 9:30, because the computer graphics guru she wanted to do a little brainstorming with had only a small window of free time between classes. Here it was 9:16 and she was still printing out samples of what she wanted to show the guy.

And no, she couldn't blame the fact that she'd had to deliver a nine-year-old to the Tisbury School because his mother got picked up early for a demanding day of house-cleaning jobs. She'd been home by eight; she rarely got any work done before eight. Then she'd run the dishwasher—never used when she had the house to herself—and zapped a lukewarm mug of coffee, taken it to the computer, and downloaded her e-mail. Which included an interesting software question that she just *had* to drop everything and solve for someone on her MacGraphics list. The answer safely posted, she remembered a couple of sample layouts that she wanted to take along to her 9:30 appointment. While they were printing, she called up Tetris, her favorite computer solitaire. Blocks in various shapes and bright colors fell from the top of the screen and had to be built into a solid wall. This satisfied her desire for clean design, but as the wall, and her score, got higher, the blocks fell faster, releasing an adrenaline rush that was like trying to get a job done in the last minutes before the FedEx lady showed up. Her first score was embarrassing, the second not much better, and Shannon was well into her third game before she realized that there was barely enough time to get to the high school by 9:30.

Shannon ignored the ringing phone, grabbed her brown corduroy jacket off its hook, and shrugged her way into it as she hurried down the stairs, Pixel leading the way. Ben Wharton, her neighbor, was washing his old Ford pickup in the driveway. Shannon groaned: Pix was already squeezing under the post-and-rail fence to play in the spray of water. Ben was no help at all: he directed the hose just over the dog's head, and sixty-five pounds of dark gray and white fur leapt into the air to catch the stream.

"Pix!" she yelled, strictly for form's sake. Pixel came when the fun was over and not a moment before.

"She's all right," said Ben, also as usual. He flicked the hose in the opposite direction; Pixel twisted in midair and dashed after it. Ben had become Pixel's foster dad even before his and Mary's old yellow Lab died a couple of years back. Mary insisted that they were too old for a puppy, and Ben didn't want a dog from the pound—"either they're one foot in the grave or they're nuts," he opined—so Pix filled the gap. Shannon thought Mary's resistance to a puppy was softening, what with the occasional remark to the effect that "you just can't keep dogs away from that man," but Mary was Old Island to the core and not to be pushed. Pixel was now sitting all ears and eyes in front of Ben, her bushy tail wagging in the mud. Ben held the nozzle at mouth level and the dog slurped.

Shannon glanced up at what sky was visible through the surrounding pines. It was glowery gray, a distant shadow of Pixel's outer coat. "Washing the truck when it might let loose at any minute?" she wondered aloud.

"Carried two loads of manure for Mary's flower garden yesterday," said Ben, glancing beyond the house to where his wife's gardens were, foot by foot, taking over the sunny south side of the lawn. He reached into the pocket of his overalls and handed the dog a biscuit. "It was pretty ripe."

Shannon's summer and fall diet was brightened every year by Mary's voluminous vegetable harvest. In return she helped Mary with weeding and watering—not that Mary wouldn't have come by anyway with frequent baskets of peas, strawberries, lettuce, broccoli, eggplant, peppers, and tomatoes, an astonishing bounty from a plot that wasn't half the size of a basketball court, but Shannon would have felt guilty if she hadn't exerted at least some effort. "Looks pretty good now," she said, leaning on the fence and peering into the truck bed. Cleaner than the back of her Subaru wagon, that was for sure.

"Some fire last night," said Ben.

"Yeah?" Shannon prompted.

"Tom was there start to finish," he said, one gray eyebrow rising almost to the brim of his duckbilled cap and taking his eyelid with it. Tom Ferreira, husband of Mary and Ben's younger daughter, Sally, was a volunteer with the Tisbury fire department; Ben had retired two years before, after several decades' service on the West Tisbury squad. One way or another, he got up-to-the-minute intelligence on all the island's fire news. "Sally says it was quite a crowd. They called Oak Bluffs and West Tisbury in. House was a total loss, I hear."

"Where was it?"

"Zack Butler's old place," Ben replied. "You ever meet old

Zack? A real cuss and a half."

Christ on a moped. "Zack Butler's old place" was where the mother and son currently sheltering in her house had been living till last Tuesday. "Yeah," said Shannon, glancing up the stairs she'd just descended. "I saw a fair amount of Zack in my scalloping days." She had to call Jay. Right now. Even if she got to the high school later than she was running already.

Ben opened the door to the truck's cab and looked around. "Clean enough," he decided out loud. "Owner was on the scene, Tom says. Says he's a banty rooster." Ben grinned, half to himself, half to Shannon. "Your friend there," he said, nodding toward Shannon's house. "Married to Zack's family, wasn't she?"

Mary and Ben didn't miss a trick. "Yeah," Shannon said warily. "His nephew. Bobbie's second son."

"Lenny," Ben remembered. "Runt of the litter," he said, tapping his forehead to indicate this was a judgment of the man's mental capacity. "Gotta feel for his mother. Mary keeps telling me it's lucky I don't have a taste for the hard stuff. Just beer. Can't do as much damage with beer."

"Damn," said Shannon, hoping her lie wasn't too transparent. "I totally forgot—could you keep an eye on my buddy for a moment? I forgot to make a phone call."

"Take your time," Ben advised, shooting a spray from the hose just above Pixel's head. The dog leapt for it and managed to catch a few drops in her mouth.

Shannon punched in Jay's number. Now Procrastination was nagging her to respond to the blinking red "1" on her answering machine, and put her mug in the sink while she was at it. She told Procrastination to shut up. Jay picked up the phone after the first ring. "Jay, my man," said Shannon, "we may have a problem."

"May?" Jay barked. "We *may* have a problem? You got my message?"

Shannon stared at the blinking "1." "Is that you?" she

asked. "Did you just call?"

Jay was exasperated. "Damn right I just called. What—"

"Ben next door says Zack Butler's house burned down."

"Damn right it burned down," said Jay, "and about two dozen firemen, cops, and EMTs from three different towns heard the owner screaming at Chief Tay to go arrest Alice."

"No way," said Shannon. "He thinks—?"

"He thinks she torched his house."

The thought of Alice torching a house was so ludicrous that she burst out laughing. The thought of Mitch, her nine-year-old son, torching a house wasn't quite so funny: until recently Mitch had been what is politely known as a "troubled child." Shannon mentally flipped through yesterday, looking for alibis.

"I know it's insane, but listen, Shan, this could mean big trouble."

"Don't think so, buddy," said Shannon. "We all slept in yesterday morning, then I made pancakes. Then we hung out; Mitch played computer games and Alice and I pretended to read the paper while speculating about what planet men *really* come from. Then I drove us all down to Sepiessa and we walked all the way out to Tisbury Great Pond—left here about one fifteen or so. We were back here by three o'clock, playing games and eating supper and watching TV shows I didn't know existed. Unless she swiped my car out from under my nose in broad daylight—my car with the muffler that will flunk inspection if I don't get it fixed before the end of June—there is no fucking way—"

Jay took an audible breath. "My morning just took a turn for the better. Listen," he said, "I don't suppose there's any chance you could drop by, like before lunch?"

"Sure," she said. "I was just heading out for an appointment with my cyber-geek buddy at the high school. We'll be done by 10:15 because he's got a class. That sound OK? I'll be right over."

"I'll be here," he said.

Shannon clattered down the front stairs for the third time that morning. "Now I really am leaving," she called to Ben, who was over by the house turning the water off, assisted of course by Pixel. "C'mon, Pix!"

The dog acknowledged Shannon with a perfunctory glance then gazed up at Ben, her tail waving slowly back and forth. Shannon started for the car. Ben pointed in her direction. Pix warbled a hopeful "Rrrr-RRRR?" At the sound of the opening passenger-side door, the dog gave up on Ben and trotted toward the car.

When old Zack Butler told his nephew's ex-wife that she and her son could live in his house, he had both provoked a deep undercurrent of muttering among his family and offered Alice respite from an ongoing nightmare. Her marriage to Lenny Chase had been a trial almost from the beginning, but it wasn't till their third anniversary that he hit her hard for the first time. Lenny was profusely repentant after that and actually sobered up for several months, a pattern that continued for almost four years, with escalating violence and diminishing periods of repentance. One Thanksgiving he fell hard off the wagon, sending Alice to the emergency room with a dislocated shoulder; Alice went from the hospital straight to a Women's Resources safe house.

Not long after, she was lucky enough to find a year-round room in West Tisbury, in the house of an older couple, and there she lived while she filed for divorce, and while her six-year-old son told a lawyer, two social workers, a psychiatrist, and a judge that he didn't like his mother and didn't want to live with her. And it was to that house that her son, by then seven, hitchhiked after slipping away from school and there that he told her he didn't want to live with his dad anymore because sometimes he "starts yelling and breaking things and I'm scared he won't stop." Barely two months later the owners had asked her to leave that house because, although she was welcome, her son was not: he was pilfering money, food, jewelry, and other small objects and denying it even when caught red-handed. Zack Butler had solved this dilemma with a gruff "You and the boy can live in the house."

The house was on the market, but Alice and Mitch lived there without incident for more than two years. Then Zack finally came down on his asking price; an offer was made and accepted, and last fall the sale went through. After prolonged discussion with Jay Segredo and Evalina Montrose, the new owner agreed to let Alice and Mitch stay on until the child custody hearing scheduled for late January: Alice wanted nothing more than to take Mitch off-island, to the New Bedford area, where her mother and two of her sisters lived, but under the current custody agreement this could not happen without Lenny Chase's permission—which was not forthcoming, though he rarely tried to contact his son and was far in arrears on child support. Lenny didn't appear at that hearing, or at the one rescheduled for the first week in March. The new owner went along with the first postponement, after considerable pressure from Jay and Evalina, not to mention a friendly lunch with a family court judge. After the second, he filed to have Alice evicted. Jay and Evalina decided to tough it out until the new hearing date on May 19: eviction proceedings could take months, especially where hardship was involved, and the odds were excellent that after the nineteenth of May Alice Chase would have sole custody of her son and freedom to leave the island.

A few days after the second postponement, the harassment started. First it was the owner's real estate agent bringing tradesmen and landscapers by at odd hours; Alice would come home to find furniture pushed out of place, windows open that had been closed, lights on that had been off. Alice started locking the doors, but that made no difference: the agent had keys. When Alice complained to the agent, the agent smiled and said that the owner might change the locks any time he wanted and we wouldn't want that, would we? Since the case was in the courts, trying to shut Alice out was illegal; presumably the real estate agent knew that, but the implicit threat exacerbated Alice's already high anxiety. If she'd had anywhere else to go, she would have gone. The anonymous phone calls started a few days later; they came at suppertime, in the middle of the night, or when Mitch was getting ready for school. Alice watched her son turning back into the angry, hyperactive, sneaky kid he had become during the collapse of his parents' marriage. The ordinarily mild-to-the-point-of-mousy Alice became adamant: if ISS couldn't find them somewhere to live until the custody hearing, she was taking Mitch to her mother's and the cops would need guns and shackles to drag them back to Martha's Vineyard.

It was a reasonable request, and in most places it wouldn't have been hard to fill. On Martha's Vineyard, though, despite the rain and chill weather, approaching summer was already calling the shots. Winter renters were preparing to crowd in with friends or relatives lucky enough to own their own houses or to have snagged year-round rentals; the hardiest and least encumbered got ready to camp in tents or trailers or garages. Hired off the books by a friend with a cleaning business, Alice helped ready house after house for summer residents and summer tenants. If she didn't have a kid, Alice thought, she might squat for a week or a weekend in whatever house happened to be vacant then move to another when the owners showed up. But that was no life for a fourth-grade boy who needed a place to do homework and a phone number where his school friends could call him. Thank God Mitch finally had a few friends to play with.

The Women's Resources volunteers who offered shelter to women in crisis were as strapped as everyone else. If they weren't already sheltering someone, they had to keep the spare room free for the child off at college who came home for the summer or the loyal employee who last fall had managed to find only an October-to-May sublet. Evalina, Jay, and their co-workers were almost out of options, and to make matters worse, the Big Boss, "the Gerb," Dr. Jerome Turner, was threatening to take over: the eviction proceedings, he hinted, were clear evidence that his subordinates were bungling the case. "If he's got housing for Alice and Mitch," sputtered Jay, "why won't he tell us?"

"Because," Evalina responded, tongue half in cheek, "I'll bet you my next vacation it's with Bobbie Chase—where son Lenny seems to be spending a good deal of his time when he isn't dodging warrants. Besides, if Dr. Gerbil can make us look bad by dicking with some woman's head, you don't think he'll take the chance?" Jay couldn't help grinning when that kind of vernacular came from such an impeccably dressed woman with silvery gray hair.

Exactly one week ago Shannon had appeared in the right place at the right time—or the wrong place at the wrong time, depending on how you looked at it. Actually it was Pixel's doing: while Shannon kibitzed overlong with Evalina at the top of the stairs outside the Women's Resources office, the dog had descended the stairs, deliberate as a Slinky, trailing her leash, and wandered toward the Youth Services office, whose main door was, as usual, open. Jay Segredo, agnostic though he was, took it as a sign from heaven. Despite the urgency of the need, he had resisted calling Shannon: her last shelter assignment, almost exactly a year ago, had been his sister, and that had ended badly. But buoyed by such a favorable omen—Pixel was wheedling treats from Becca Herschel, the office manager—Jay emerged into the stairwell and beamed up at Shannon. "You got a minute?" he asked.

"Sure," she replied. She never saw the thumbs-up Evalina gave Jay behind her back. Alice and Mitch moved in the next afternoon.

After a truncated but productive session with her colleague at the high school, Shannon crossed the Edgartown–Vineyard Haven Road and drove slowly around to the back of the Island Social Services complex. She squeezed into a parking place not far from the door. "I'll be right back," she promised

Pixel. "Rr-RRR, rr-RRRR," the dog insisted. At their last stop, she'd been left in the car; this was not going to happen again. No dogs were allowed in the ISS complex, of course, but Shannon clipped the brown leather leash to its matching collar and let her come along.

Closing the door behind her, Shannon skirted the stairway—from the back its ladderlike steps reminded her of bars in a holding tank—and opened the Youth Services door behind it. "Shh," she told Pix in a whisper, in case any high-mucks were wandering the downstairs halls. This was not likely. Shannon wasn't convinced you could even get down here from up there.

A whiff of tobacco embraced her at the door. Smoking, like dogs, was prohibited everywhere in the complex, but Jay Segredo kept a small Welcome to Worcester ashtray in his top desk drawer and produced it whenever enforcing the rules seemed less important than winning the trust of a distraught young person.

To Shannon's right a raised voice and a burst of laughter signaled a conference going on behind Becca Herschel's closed door. To the left, Jay's door was cracked open. ". . . free from two twenty," she heard him saying, "till the department heads' meeting starts at three—make that three fifteen. Today probably won't be the first day in recorded history the Gerbil gets there on time. No, take that back: punctuality is his new shtick . . ."

Holding the door steady with her leash hand, Shannon rapped lightly on it with the other and peeked in. Her eyes took a few moments to pick Jay's plaid flannel shirt and dark brown hair out from the backdrop of floor-to-ceiling bookshelves. He held up two fingers then jabbed one of them toward the coffeemaker, which sat on a movable table in the hall behind her. Pixel, obedience paragon that she was, pushed into the office. "Rrrr-rrrr," she said, white tail waving, her gaze riveted on Jay's face. Jay, sucker that *he* was, scratched between her ears and reached for the top right drawer of his desk, where he kept a stash of dog biscuits, mini Hershey bars, and Doublemint gum.

Shannon, resigned, helped herself to coffee.

Jay's office was reputedly smaller than what the Geneva Convention prescribed for prisoners of war. Because this side of the building was nestled into a hill, the only windows were two oblongs near the ceiling above Jay's desk; what light they admitted barely grazed the top of his head, and that only if he sat up very straight. The grass outside was past due for mowing, so the incoming light was tinged with green.

Shannon dropped into one of the two armchairs behind Jay, listening with one ear as he wound up his conversation, and put her coffee down on the two-drawer file cabinet that doubled as an end table. "So," she said, resting one calf on the opposite knee, "what's up?"

The phone rang again. Shannon shrugged. Pixel, having sniffed at the wastebasket, Jay's chair, and the stack of magazines on the bottom bookshelf, stretched out for a snooze on the only squares of linoleum left exposed by the gray-brown institutional carpet. Shannon tried hard not to think about her last assignment: Janice Segredo Swanson, client from hell. No one thought the match had been made in heaven—Janice never acknowledged that Shannon had been instrumental in enabling Jay to return to the Vineyard, and Shannon tended to blame Janice's less-than-enlightened attitudes for Jay's being such a closet case—but how could Shannon have said no? It was June, a dreadful month to be seeking emergency housing, and the previous night Janice had been hiding in her locked bedroom with her younger children, Danny and Amy, while her husband tried to beat down the door and her eldest, Kevin, called 911 on his private line. Wayne vanished before the police showed up; Jay and Connie, one of the Women's Resources counselors, arrived moments later. The next morning they called every safe-house provider they could think of, but no one had even floor or sofa space free for a family of four. Finally Jay had called Shannon and

Shannon had said yes. Janice and her younger kids moved in that morning. Kevin went to his uncle's, an easy two-mile bike ride from the rest of his family.

Danny, Amy, and Pixel loved the arrangement. By lunch time Danny, the third-grader, had taught the dog to shake paws and roll over, two things she'd never been willing to do for Shannon. Shannon kept an eye on both kids, who stayed out of school for the day, while their mother met with the police, a crisis counselor, a lawyer, and a court advocate and spoke by phone with the children's teachers. Cleaning up after a pleasant supper, Shannon was beginning to believe that this might actually work out until the Swansons could get back into their own house. Kevin had returned to Jay's, Amy was watching TV in the living room, and Danny was trying to lure Pixel out from under Shannon's bed, where she was hiding with her stuffed hedgehog. Janice went in to coax him into a bath before bedtime. Shortly thereafter, Shannon noticed a perceptible chill in the air.

After the kids were asleep—Danny on the rollaway bed in the guest room, Amy on the living-room sleep sofa—Janice cornered her in the kitchen. "Would you please," she said, the tendons in her neck gone rigid with tension, "take that poster down?"

Shannon stared at her blankly. "Poster?"

"Dan and Amy are *children,*" Janice said. "Maybe you don't often deal with *children*—"

Hell no, Shannon thought. *I helped start a project to help protect kids against child abuse and incest, I've run a few gazillion workshops in elementary school and preschool classrooms, but I guess that doesn't qualify as "dealing with children."*

"They are *impressionable.* This is not an easy time for them. They don't need to have—*that* rubbed in their faces."

At last Shannon got it: the framed Lesbian Herstory Archives poster that hung beside the mirror above her bureau. It featured a Depression-era photograph of a dignified young black woman and under it the archives motto, "In memory of the voices we have lost." Shannon said she'd take it down. She had been doing crisis intervention for too many years to get into a political discussion with anyone under this much stress.

The case, she thought, was closed.

It wasn't. Just after two o'clock the next afternoon the phone had rung. Shannon thought it might be Janice asking her to pick the kids up at school. But it was Jay, telling her that the next day the Swansons would be moving to Randall and Kate Hammond's in Oak Bluffs: the Hammonds had plenty of room, the kids would be close to their school . . .

Shannon liked the Hammonds, but she smelled a rat. "It's about the poster, isn't it?" she said.

Jay's pause was a beat too long. "Poster?" he asked.

"Jay, don't bullshit me," said Shannon.

"Yeah," he admitted, "it has to do with the poster."

"Exactly what," Shannon demanded, hearing the dangerous tone in her own voice, "is the problem with the poster?"

"Shan," he said, "these kids have been through a lot—"

"They've watched their father hitting their mother, throwing dinner in her face, ripping the phone out of the wall—they've seen cops show up at the front door. Twice. And I'm supposed to believe they're being traumatized by a poster that has the word 'lesbian' in it?"

"Shan—"

"OK, OK—just don't tell me that it's about 'the kids.'" She stopped short of adding, "It's about your homophobic sister." For this she gave herself a gold star.

Jay seemed to know what she was thinking. "Janice is under a lot of stress right now," he said. "For her, admitting that this marriage can't be saved is a big deal. It's like—it's like . . ."

Like coming out? Shannon didn't say it out loud: another gold star. "Like the First Step?" she suggested. "Admitted we were powerless over our fucked-up husband, that our lives had become unmanageable?"

"Yeah," said Jay, obviously relieved. "Exactly."

"OK, fine," Shannon replied. "Cool. But next time you want to place someone in my house, do me a favor and get their homophobia quotient first. If it's over five on a scale of one to ten, stick them somewhere else."

Jay didn't tell her to stuff it: Jay never did. She stripped the two gold stars off her invisible epaulets and told herself to shape up. She might have eight years of sobriety under her belt—eight years, two months, and two days—but at a moment's notice she could lapse into the pugnacious teenager who wouldn't take lip from anybody. *Progress, not perfection,* she reminded herself. All the same, sometimes the progress was too damn slow, and perfection too damn far away.

Compared to Janice, Alice and Mitch were easy. Shannon admired Alice. Shannon could so easily have *been* Alice, if she hadn't run away from home, if she hadn't found Boston's women's community, if it hadn't been 1971, a few years before any of the radical women started to worry about sheltering "jailbait." And what if her first lover had turned out to be like Lenny Chase, a handsome, sweet-talking, charismatic drunk? She wouldn't have finished high school, that was for sure, and no one would have recognized her artistic talent and introduced her to Ingrid, who had helped her apply to the Rhode Island School of Design (and paid the application fee), and she wouldn't have met Annette, who had dragged her kicking and screaming to Martha's Vineyard, where she had been ever since. Annette herself couldn't hack island living; she had left after two years and now came only for occasional R&R.

Finally Jay jabbed one forefinger in the direction of the coffeepot and, phone nestled against his shoulder, pressed hands together in supplication. Shannon plucked the mug off his desk and went to refill it, keeping one ear on the phone conversation. It seemed to be winding down. She had barely set the steaming coffee down on Jay's desk when he said, "Sounds good. Let's talk tomorrow, OK?"

"So," she said after he replaced the receiver in its cradle, "about this fire."

"About this fire," Jay echoed. He linked his fingers, pushed his palms toward her, and cracked his knuckles. She rolled her eyes. He apologized. "Our friend Leslie was on the scene, I'm told. I expect to hear from her any minute now."

Shannon grinned. "She'll be all over it. She's hungry: she hasn't had a good story since—" *Since the shooting last Columbus Day weekend,* she was about to say, but she and Jay couldn't even tiptoe past that one without snarking at each other. "In a long time," she finished.

Jay played along. "I've talked to Tay," he said. "He says, off the record *of course,* that there's no reason at this point to suspect arson, but he can't rule it out till the investigation is complete."

"That's my man." Shannon relaxed, relieved that Tay Francis was in charge. Chief Tay had been so competent for so long that he had nothing to prove by trying to score points with the press, the town, the public, anyone.

"However," said Jay, "the owner of the house, one Nick—" he leaned over to glance at a paper on his desk "—Nick McAuliffe, was accusing Alice of causing the fire, so they're going to have to at least look into it. You know anything about this guy? Supposedly he's written a best-selling novel."

"I hear he's an asshole."

Jay tipped an imaginary cap in her direction. "I believe the chief agrees, though he's far too polite to say so. McAuliffe bought the house last October, presumably with the proceeds from his best-selling book—"

The phone rang yet again, its nasal blat bouncing off the walls. Jay glanced at his watch, then scooted his chair back to his desk. "This is Jay Segredo," he said into the receiver. "If I can—you know I exist only to serve." He was bantering, evidently with someone he knew pretty well. "I do remember the name."

Tuning out the conversation, Shannon glanced around the office. No remarkable changes since she was last down here, maybe a month ago. A poster featuring a pensive portrait of Robert Kennedy still hung to the right of the bookshelves, with Tennyson's line from "Ulysses" printed under the image: "Come, my friends, / 'Tis not too late to seek a newer world. . . ." The bookcase itself was crowned by a large framed color photograph of a dozen young men and boys on a basketball court—some of the guys Jay had worked with in Worcester, before he accepted the Youth Services job and returned to the island. *I heard from Nate yesterday,* Jay would say, *that's Nate in the back there, trying to grow a beard. Now he's doing substance abuse counseling. Still takes his basketball* very *seriously.* Shannon knew more about those guys than she did about most of her relatives.

Next to the basketball photo was one she had taken at last year's Segredo family Labor Day cookout: Segredo aunts, uncles, in-laws, cousins, and cousins' kids, spilling off the porch of the house Jay and Janice had grown up in. In the center Mama's arm was around her husband's frail shoulders. Ernie had insisted on leaving the island's long-term care facility for the occasion, accompanied by the portable ventilator that was visible in the picture. Ernie had finally slipped away in February, surrounded by his immediate family.

"Sounds like a matter for the police, don't you think?" Jay was saying into the phone. "Where was it, Tisbury? You talk to the chief yet?"

Shannon tried not to listen, but in a room this size how could she help eavesdropping? It had to be Leslie Benaron; who else could it be? She tried to concentrate on the small photos on Jay's desk, familiar all of them: Jay and his sister Janice with their arms around each other; a triptych with baby pictures of his niece and two nephews; Jay and Kevin, the eldest, now a high school junior, playing beach volleyball last summer; the middle child, Amy, playing the Wicked Witch of the West in a school production of *The Wizard of Oz* . . .

Shannon's stomach lurched. A new photograph had assumed pride of place in the center: a woman grasping the top of a pair of cross-country skis, wearing a snowflake-patterned ski sweater and matching cap. She was smiling a "you aren't really going to take my picture" smile. The frame was dark-stained wood, not something you bought on the fly at the hardware store. Lorraine Silvia, née Corbett, known to all as Rainey since she was a small child—a classmate of Janice's at the regional high school. Rainey had been widowed by a car accident in '92; after a couple of rough years, she had settled into single motherhood and didn't seem desperate to find a stepfather for her young son. Jay's mother and sister, however, had been playing matchmaker with a vengeance since the day Jay moved back to the island. For the first couple of years Jay and Shannon had poked fun at their efforts. "How come they aren't trying to fix you up with *me*?" Shannon would grumble, and Jay would retort, "Don't worry, you can be Dyke of Honor at the wedding." After the shooting, however, Shannon got no more uptake for her wisecracks and Jay had started bringing Rainey Silvia to ISS functions. Rainey's son, Steve, and Jay's nephew Danny were best buddies, so on the surface it wasn't strange that Rainey and Jay often appeared together at ball games and other school events, but, as Shannon quickly noted, the *News Beacon*'s Oak Bluffs columnist—Janice's godmother, as it happened— seemed bent on encouraging the "couple" at every opportunity.

Gazing at the framed photograph, Shannon couldn't help wondering if the "romance" was heating up. She didn't dare ask. She just watched for symptoms and worried whenever she found one.

"You know I couldn't give you that information," Jay was saying, "even if I knew—and, seriously, Les, how likely is it that I'd know what the police can't find out?"

Plenty bloody likely, Shannon almost said aloud. It was Leslie, all right; if it wasn't, Shannon would eat a dozen raw oysters (she loathed raw oysters), and if this conversation didn't have something to do with Alice and Mitch, she would eat an additional six. The matter of Rainey Silvia retreated abruptly to the back burner.

"Listen, Les, I can't talk now, I've got someone here. . . . No, if you drove over right now, you'd be wasting time and gas."

"How am I supposed to take *that?"* Shannon whispered. Jay raised his eyebrows and pressed a forefinger to his lips.

"I will do that, but not right this minute. A pleasure as always, Ms. Benaron. Talk to you later." He replaced the receiver gingerly in its cradle. "Whew," he said. "Give the woman an A for tenacity."

Shannon managed a grin. "What does she know, do you think?"

"This guy McAuliffe was in everyone's face last night, she says. She saw him in action. She heard him demand that Chief Tay arrest Alice." Jay shook his head. "She didn't hear him explain why he should do this. When she talked to Tay this morning, he was noncommittal."

"Of course," said Shannon.

"Of course," Jay agreed. "She's got McAuliffe's card—"

"Of course," Shannon muttered again. "What do you bet she knows his life story by tomorrow night?"

"You think I'm crazy?" Jay smiled. "No way I'm betting on that."

"How much does she know about Alice?"

"I didn't get the feeling she knows much—yet," he said thoughtfully. "It won't take long, though. Lenny Chase has been a swashbuckler for a *long* time. As soon as she connects Alice to Lenny—"

"And Lenny to Zack—" Shannon added.

"Yeah, she's going to know a lot. Does Alice know about the fire?"

Shannon shook her head. "I didn't find out till after she left the house this morning, and you know, I don't know where they're working today. Shit, I hope it's not all over the school . . . I should probably pick Mitch up at school. What do you think?"

"Do it," said Jay.

"And I could probably talk Alice into doing a pre-emptive strike on the police department. 'Here we are, Chief, ready to answer all your questions.' Good idea?"

"Very good idea."

Goddamn, Shannon thought, *it's great to be working with you again.*

"So," said Jay, "how are you and Mitch doing?"

"Me and Mitch," Shannon repeated thoughtfully. "Me and Mitch aren't doing so bad, surprisingly enough. He's got about as much memory for past unpleasantness as Pixel. Wag wag, smile smile, aren't I cute?"

"Well, he *is* a kid."

"Yeah, he's a kid. He also likes my computer. As long as I let him play with my computer, he likes me. All the same," she said, "the idea of housing the two of them till the nineteenth of May . . . It's not that I *can't* do it—" She'd never kick anyone out with summer coming on; Jay knew that, but he also knew that she worked at home.

"Randy and Kate Hammond," said Jay.

Shannon stared. She beamed. "You're brilliant, you're goddamn brilliant!" she said. "Are they free?"

"They've got houseguests this week, but they're leaving Friday. Saturday sound OK to you? I'll be off-island. Think you can handle it?" He smiled rather slyly.

"In my sleep. And where are *you* going?"

Jay looked slightly embarrassed. "Another well-funded, semi-state-sponsored conference on at-risk youth." He brightened. "One of the Free Radicals is pretty much running the program, because the titular head is out promoting his new book. So I got to organize a panel of teenagers telling the state how to do its job better. It's going to be dynamite." Jay rubbed his palms together then did a short Muhammad Ali imitation: jab, jab, *whap.*

"Oooh, fun! You going to wear your tie?" Shannon's snarkiness had dissipated. The Free Radicals were a loose association of Jay's old colleagues from Worcester, mostly social workers and community activists. When the first core group had started meeting, way back in the mid-1980s, most had been in their late twenties, not long out of school and already disgusted by the social service bureaucracies that employed them. The initial objective had been modest: to "process the week" every Friday over beer in a local saloon. Processing had evolved into plotting, and within a year the group had become a grapevine for upstart social workers in southern New England. Members who moved on to other regions and other jobs—"bonded with new molecules"— remained part of the network, and new Free Rads were recruited from among the disgruntled electrons in city or state agencies, college departments, and nonprofit organizations.

After learning about the cabal—not from Jay, of course, but from one of his old buddies who came to visit—Shannon had said, "You need a secret handshake, a decoder ring, something like that. How about a tie?"

"I hate ties!" Jay snapped back. He only wore a tie when protocol or his mother insisted, and he probably lost a half dozen a year by abandoning them on restaurant chairs or convention podiums. But Shannon doodled a design on a restaurant napkin, and Jay's visiting friend had an ecstatic experience. "That's it!" he cried. "I don't care what it costs: make me three dozen."

And Shannon had. On a pale lavender tie was silk-screened a steel-gray replica of the old atomic energy symbol. Flying around the outer orbits were two oversized electrons, one in blaze orange, the other in vibrant green. Shannon had yet to attend a gathering where the ties were worn en masse, but she was regularly assured that yes, they *were* worn, by both men and women. Jay had two: one at home, the other at work. He hadn't lost either one yet: the ultimate compliment.

"Of *course* I'm going to wear my tie," Jay protested.

"You better," Shannon said. She stood up and stretched, then asked, "Can I use the phone?"

"Be my guest."

She punched in the newspaper's number. Leslie Benaron serendipitously answered the phone. "Hey," said Shannon, "I'm free, I'm down-Island—got time for an early lunch?"

CHAPTER FOUR

"Alan! Atlantic Connection on line two!" Natalie Carter, the *Chronicle*'s veteran features editor, had been a semiprofessional actress before she married and moved to the Vineyard. She still had a carrying voice.

"Will you shut up!" yelled Steve DeKuyper, the reporter at the next desk over, who was trying to talk on the phone.

"Or use the intercom?" Leslie muttered, her right hand pausing over the telephone's number pad.

Alan, display ad sales rep, hollered back from the kitchen, "Be right there!"

Leslie waited to make sure that the shouting was over, then carefully punched in the listing for Everett, Donald & Sophia.

"Alan! Seriously! Winston needs to talk to you!"

Alan appeared in the hallway, apologizing to the news section with open palms, and disappeared behind the tall bookshelves into the area the reporters called Golden Gooseland. Money was made on the west side of the building and spent on the east; if the business manager were to be believed, the east was a stove-in keel that continually threatened to sink the ship and she, only she, was keeping the enterprise afloat. At least once every staff meeting she leaned forward in her chair and adjured her colleagues to "keep those sails trimmed."

"Trimmed sails" explained the vast overstock back in the supply closet of cut-rate sticky notes that wouldn't adhere to a sheet of paper, not to mention the word-processing software that hadn't been upgraded in seven years.

Sophie Everett picked up on the fourth ring, sounding out of breath. "Sorry, I was down in the basement," she explained, "painting drywall. My niece is going to be living down there this summer. Don said you'd probably call. About the fire?"

According to Sophie, Alice Chase and her son had moved out without warning. "I didn't know they were gone till it got dark Tuesday night and no lights came on," she said. "I went up the hill after supper. Mitch's bike was gone—he always kept it locked on that funny little porch. The door wasn't locked"—Leslie could hear her smiling a tad sheepishly—"so I poked my head in the living room. Alice didn't have much in the way of furniture, but she had lots of family pictures, on top of the TV, on the mantelpiece, the end tables . . . They were all gone, every one."

Sophie wasn't completely surprised by the abrupt disappearance. The new owner was determined to use the house this summer; his impatience grew each time the custody hearing was postponed. Alice had recently confided about the all-hours phone calls, hang-ups at first, and supposed wrong numbers, then, more and more, whispered allusions to her boyfriends (she didn't have any) and Mitch's psychological problems (which had all but disappeared during their two years in Zack and Ruth Butler's house). Alice was sure the new owner or even his real estate broker—the whisperer's voice could have been male or female—was responsible, Sophie confided to Leslie that she thought Lenny Chase—Alice's ex, Zack and Ruth's nephew—a more likely culprit.

"Sounds like he wasn't on great terms with his uncle," Leslie prompted.

"He never was," Sophie said. "The sad thing is how it drove a wedge between Zack and Bobbie, Lenny's mother—Zack's sister. I hear they'd been close since they were kids—at least Zack was closer to her than to any of his other kin. She let Lenny run wild after his dad left, that's what Zack thought. He tried to intervene a few times; she wouldn't have it, and he started keeping his distance. More and more distance. He let Alice caretake the house pretty much for free. He didn't tell her when the house sold—I guess he didn't know how. She heard from the real estate agent."

"Just between us," Leslie said, "do you think there's any chance Lenny Chase could have—?"

"Burned Zack's house down?" Sophie laughed. "He's never put out that much effort in his life. Obnoxious phone calls are much more his style."

"How about Alice?" Leslie asked.

"Alice?" Sophie's voice was incredulous. "Set a fire? Alice? No way. I doubt she'd know how. She just wants to move off-island and take Mitch with her. That's all she wants."

That's all she wants. Leslie felt the story taking shape: plucky young woman struggles to do right by her son, thwarted by some—her wastrel ex-husband, for one—and aided by others, like her ex's crusty Old Island uncle. Accused of arson by famous author; defended by police chief unimpressed by fame . . . Alice's story could make up for the fizzle of last year's most promising lead, the officially unsolved shooting on the Edgartown–West Tisbury Road. It might even grow into a book. She closed her eyes and imagined: a review in the *New York Times* hailing her as a new Tracy Kidder for her vivid evocation of Martha's Vineyard in the late 1990s . . . ?

First she had to find Alice Chase. Her fingers jabbed the general switchboard number for Island Social Services, and when the receptionist answered, Leslie, all business, requested extension one-six-eight.

"Youth Services, Jay Segredo," said the man she'd been trying to reach off and on for the last hour.

"Hi, Jay—this is Leslie, calling from the *Chronicle*." That was how she established that this was a business-not-personal call, with all the cautions that implied. Keeping the two separate in a place this size, where you regularly ran into your sources—not to mention the people you had ridiculed in print, or were intending to ridicule in the future—on the street or at the supermarket, took a certain amount of mental dexterity, not to mention chutzpah. "I wonder if you can help me with something."

"If I can," he said. "You know I exist only to serve."

"I'm looking for a woman named Alice Chase," she said. "I have this hunch you might know her."

A pause on the other end of the line. "Alice Chase?" Jay said carefully. "The name rings a bell. What's up?"

"Anyone know where the Queen Mother went?" called Diane, who played receptionist while selling classified ads in Gooseland's hot corner. The Queen Mother was Arabella Roth, publisher of the *Chronicle* and mother of the editor in chief.

"Dentist appointment," answered George, whose desk was just behind Leslie's. "Back by noon."

"A house burned down last night, off Lambert's Cove Road," Leslie said. "Alice Chase was the most recent tenant."

"I see," said Jay. "Anybody hurt?"

"Nobody was in the house," Leslie replied. "Alice Chase moved out last week." *As if you didn't already know.*

"So whose house was it?"

A moment too late, Leslie realized that Jay had dodged her question. "Till last October it belonged to Zachary Butler and his wife, Ruth." *I bet you know all that too.* When would she learn that she couldn't surprise, trick, or flirt information out of Jay? "Jay, I'll cut to the chase—so to speak," she said, groaning inwardly at her own stupid and totally unintentional pun. "The new owner, off-Island guy named Nick McAuliffe—famous novelist, so I hear—is on the warpath. I was at the scene. Before the fire was even out, he was buttonholing Chief Tay and demanding that Alice Chase be arrested immediately if not sooner."

"Why would he say that?"

"That's what I want to find out. McAuliffe was off the

wall—here's hoping he's settled down by now—but it still might mean trouble for Alice."

"Sounds like a matter for the police, don't you think?" Jay said. "Where was it, Tisbury? You talk to the chief yet?"

"Once, but we got interrupted. Alice isn't charged with anything, yet. I got the definite impression they don't even know where she is. Listen, Jay—there's some possibility McAuliffe was pulling some shady stuff to force Alice out of the house. I'd like to talk with her about it. Do you have any idea how to reach her?"

"What," asked the Youth Services director, "makes you think I'd know how to reach her?"

Leslie was getting exasperated. Didn't she deserve a *little* cooperation? True, he didn't exactly *owe* her anything, but she had been directly or indirectly responsible for some pretty favorable Youth Services coverage over the last three years . . . "Come on, Jay," she pleaded. "If you and Women's Resources haven't got thick files on Alice and Mitch Chase, I'll—I'll shave my head." She twisted a dark brown curl around her right forefinger. *Don't worry, hair; I'd never do it.*

Jay laughed. "OK, OK," he said. "I know Alice, and I know Mitch. Note that I'm saying nothing about how? But if I knew where they were right this minute, you know I couldn't give you that information, right? Even if I knew? And, seriously, Les, how likely is it that I'd know what the police can't find out?"

"Seriously, Jay, it's so likely that I can't believe you said that."

"Listen, Les, I can't talk now, I've got someone here—"

The schmuck is blowing me off. "Let me guess: Alice Chase is sitting in your office right this minute!" Leslie's heart leapt. *She could be, she might . . .* "What if I drove over right now? You wouldn't be violating any principles, and I'd get to talk to—"

"No, if you drove over right now, you'd be wasting time and gas."

"Oh, hell," said Leslie, "you win. Let me know if anything comes up, would you?"

He said, more or less, that he would and then hung up the phone. Leslie stared at the blank page in her notebook and wondered what to do next.

The immediate issue was settled when Chet Roth dropped into the chair alongside her desk. "You've been on the phone all morning with that thing," he said, in the I'm-prematurely-gray-and-on-blood-pressure-medication-because-of-you tone he reserved for his reporters. "Haven't you got other stories to write?"

She started to say, "This could be important—" but he hadn't finished: "I know," he said, oozing with sympathy, "that a West Tisbury zoning board of appeals hearing isn't as sexy as a fire in some falling-down dump—"

"It's important," Leslie repeated, looking Chet right in the eye and trying not to whine. *It's true: the man is dyeing his hair!* "I just have this sixth sense . . ."

"Les, Les, Les," said Chet, shaking his head, rubbing his temples, sliding his sturdy fingers back into hair that, even in the perpetually inadequate light of the newsroom, now glowed like an ad for Clairol for Men. "It's not arson. Believe me. It's your typical island fucked-up wiring job."

"Maybe you're right," she reassured him with a warm smile. "I'm sure you're right. But I have a feeling . . . Meanwhile, I've got a call in to the zoning board on the tennis court thing you told me about, and Quincy Hancock the Third is coming in to tell me his side of the story at two thirty. With any luck, Prudy'll get back to me before Q.H. shows up."

"Eeewww," Chet said, pursing his lips. "I think I'll take a late lunch." Reporters were just appetizers to Quincy Hancock; the main course was in Chet's upstairs office. Once, just once, he'd tried to go higher, ambushing the publisher on her way to lunch. The Queen Mother had almost devoured him whole, within easy hearing of most of the staff. "OK, you follow up on this fire, but you don't let it get in the way of the other stuff. Got that?"

"I got it, chief," she said, extending her hand for a shake.

Chet raised one eyebrow, shook her hand, then went off to see what Steve DeKuyper was discussing so intently with the head photographer. Poor man. Leslie felt guilty for pulling hunches on him again: during her years at the paper, she had scored on several stubborn certainties. The most spectacular had been the first. Terry Randolph, Jay's predecessor at Youth Services, had had stellar credentials: the island's social service and educational elite thought the guy had skipped the ferry and walked from Woods Hole to Vineyard Haven. Then Leslie wrote a story about high turnover in his small office, alluding to similar problems in his previous, off-island position.

Two Island Social Services board members and Dr. Jerome Turner had blown a collective gasket in Arabella's office. Three letters were published, one by a psychiatrist, one by a PhD, and one by a retired minister, all defending the Youth Services head as a paragon of professionalism. Leslie followed up with a report focusing on clients' experiences with the agency, and another that critically examined the man's previous career, discovering in the process that one statement in his CV was false and two others misleading. In public Chet backed his reporter to the hilt; in the office he clutched his shirt right over his heart and speculated about his blood pressure. Leslie lay awake night after night hoping she hadn't misjudged her evidence. What did she really know about Shannon Merrick, whose leads all turned out to be golden? What if one of her key informants was grinding an ax against her quarry? At least no libel suit had materialized—yet.

Then, early one spring evening, the stellar Youth Services director crashed the barrier on the Beach Road drawbridge just as the bridge was about to go up, and led police on a merry chase before he lost control of the wheel en route from Oak Bluffs to Edgartown and came to a halt just above the low-water line on Joseph Sylvia State Beach. Not only did his blood alcohol level test out at a spectacular .16, he also had an almost equally intoxicated female high school student in the car with him.

The series had won her two major regional awards, the *Chronicle* one for community service, and Chet yet another for an editorial analyzing the bureaucracy's resistance to his reporter's discoveries; it had earned her the undying loyalty of the local Mothers Against Drunk Driving chapter, and prompted a shake-up at Island Social Services. Best of all, her father had FedExed a decadent assortment of chocolate truffles, accompanied by a card that said WOODWARD & BERNSTEIN GOT NOTHING ON YOU. Without a doubt it had been Leslie's finest hour.

It had also been three years ago.

The phone rang. No sooner had the blinking green light on her phone turned red than a call came in on another line. "Leslie, you still there?" called Alan.

"Still here," Leslie answered. Chet, Steve, and Jules the photographer had been joined by the production manager and one of the typesetters. Chet glanced in her direction; she hoped it was Prudy Winchester, West Tisbury zoning board chair, returning her call.

It wasn't; it was Roger, calling partly to hear how the 911 had gone last night but mostly to see if she wanted to go out for a drink after work and continue the enjoyable conversation they'd had over dinner. *What the hell had they talked about?* She begged off, citing deadline pressures and dangling "after we get the paper out" as a vague alternative. "Call me on Thursday," she said, "I'll be here." On Thursdays she usually escaped as soon as the weekly staff meeting was over. With any luck Roger would forget to call.

The next call was from Prudy: Yes indeed, Quincy Hancock III and his equally annoying brother-in-law had a permit to build two tennis courts and a small equipment shed on their ancestral holdings; the permit included landscaping and a bluestone parking area for four cars. Yes, the abutting Fitch Family Trust had gone along with the plan once the outdoor shower was dropped and the height of the chain-link fence was decreased by three feet, but no, they were not at all pleased with the unpermitted floodlights that had appeared at each corner of the court or with the large horizontal window and counter on the equipment shed that made it look "very much," according to one Fitch family member, "like a cheap hot-dog emporium." And the family was outraged by the "horticultural windbreak" that had turned into an eight-foot-high wall facing their property.

"Off the record," said Prudy, "I don't know what the Hancocks were thinking. Cassandra St. Christopher Fitch and her sisters are at least as stubborn, and twice as rich, as the Hancocks, and they definitely have smarter lawyers. Not to mention a newspaper in the family." Arabella, publisher of the *Martha's Vineyard Chronicle*, had been a Fitch before she married Chet Roth's father, whose family had owned the paper for three generations.

"Tell me about it," Leslie said, scribbling down the names of the lawyers, the surveyor, the off-island tennis court specialist, and the island contractor who had handled the landscaping. "That's why I have to make extra nicey-nice to Q.H. Three, so he won't start his infernal yammering about conflicts of interest." Something cool and moist burrowed unexpectedly into her lap.

"Yeow," she said.

"What's that?" asked Prudy.

"A wolf just stuck its nose in my crotch. Don't mind me. Listen, Pru, can you fax me a copy of the permit application? Not the permit—I've got that. The original application and any amendments you've got."

"Done. Let me know if Q.H. Three has anything interesting to say, will you?"

"I'll let you know. Thanks, Pru."

Leslie opened her bottom drawer, withdrew a large Milk-Bone, and handed it to Pixel, who padded over to the big front window and settled down for a nosh.

"Hey, girlfriend," said Shannon, coming up behind her. "How's the pyro beat?"

Leslie gritted her teeth. "Don't call me that," she hissed. Shannon dropped into the desk-side chair, looked contrite, and pressed the palms of her hands together in a caricature of a Buddhist bowing. "What's this pyro beat?"

"There was a fire in Tisbury last night, Tisbury's your beat. Q.E.D." Shannon grinned at her. "Besides, I was in Jay's office when you called."

Leslie thanked the hunch god that she'd accepted Shannon's invitation. "What were you doing there? I thought you'd retired." *Not to mention that on occasion it's looked as if it was going to be "pistols at ten paces" if the two of you spent too long in the same room.*

"Nah, I just pulled back. I still do two shifts a week on the hotline for Women's Resources."

"Speaking of which—" Leslie glanced around. "What's the word on his meshugge brother-in-law?"

"No longer his brother-in-law," said Shannon. "Still meshugge, I'll bet on it."

"Yeah, but isn't it about time he came back to the island?"

Shannon stared at her, one eye open and one eye closed. "You're good, Benaron." She counted on her fingers: "November, December, January, February, March, April—six months almost to the day. Psychiatric evaluation never lasts longer than that, even when accompanied by residential detox. I might have to check it out."

"Listen," Leslie said, "I've got to transcribe these notes while I can still read them. Can you keep busy for five minutes? Why don't you go sit down with Chet and Laura and redesign the news section or something."

"All pictures, can the prose," Shannon said darkly. "B-i-g margins."

"Whatever." Leslie propped her reporter's notebook against her brown leather handbag, squinted at her own scrawl, and started typing.

* * *

While Pixel made the rounds looking for handouts and scritches, Shannon sank into the comfortable easy chair by the big picture window with the morning's *Cape Cod Times* on her lap. Wayne. How to find out about Wayne? She could always call Jay. *Oh no, I couldn't, not without dragging a whole lot of other crap into it.* Or Janice. *Right: the sound you hear is her hanging up on you.* The county parole officer was the obvious choice, but he was a by-the-book kind of guy, and she'd antagonized him more than once; he wasn't going to break confidentiality on her account. She started skimming the newspaper; the Bosnian crisis, the Russian ruble crisis, and the collapse of another Asian economy crisis flashed by before her eye settled on a short account of last night's fire. Evidently it had been written from phone reports from the Tisbury police and fire departments; both chiefs stated that there was no evidence of arson. The news editor had managed to scare up a jacket photo of Nick McAuliffe. He had a pleasant enough face, but the Irish tweed cap that shadowed his brow was a literary cliché. Shannon didn't hold out great hopes for his novel.

With the heightened sensory perception of a dog mama, she heard Pixel stealing up the stairs at the back of the building. Arabella Roth kept an assortment of treats in her second-floor office; Pixel had a long memory. All around the office *Chronicle* staff members were talking on telephones, typing on keyboards: it wasn't a good time to bellow, "Pixel Merrick! Get your pointy-nose face back here *RIGHT NOW!*" Quietly she rose, set the paper aside, and followed. She nabbed Pixel's collar on the top step and escorted her back down the stairs.

She didn't see the visitor come in; it was his voice that caught her attention. Faux English, or just an out-of-work stage actor? Observing the fellow surreptitiously from the opposite end of the room, Shannon decided that he was neither, only that he was unnaturally precise with his consonants—and he dressed much too nattily for Martha's Vineyard in mud season. Pale gray trench coat, dark gray tweed cap, black cashmere (she'd bet on it) muffler, and black dress shoes, not Reeboks or chukka boots or L.L. Bean duck shoes: he was smiling politely at Diane and asking for Leslie Benaron.

"Just a moment," said Diane. "I'll see if she's in."

Obviously Diane didn't like the guy: *Chronicle* staff tended to holler across the room rather than use the intercom, unless someone was conducting an interview or trying to impress an advertiser. A phone rang on the news side. A moment later Leslie got up and went to greet the well-dressed man, who turned to greet her with a professional smile on his face. Shannon already disliked him intensely. "Ms. Benaron," he said, with a hint of self-effacement, "we met last night under rather fraught circumstances."

"Fraught"? thought Shannon. *Fraught?*

"Mr. McAuliffe, what a pleasant surprise," Leslie was saying, sounding a little flustered. *Faux flustered,* thought Shannon. "I was just about to call the hotel . . . I'm sorry, I'm in the middle of a dozen things."

As he turned to follow Leslie, Shannon saw the resemblance between the actual face and the grainy newspaper photograph. It was almost certainly the same tweed cap. As Leslie led the visitor over to her desk, Shannon slipped through Golden Gooseland and back to her chair, maintaining her grip on Pixel's collar. Naturally she kept an ear open for the conversation behind her left shoulder.

"Of course. My apologies: I should have called. But I was in town—I keep hearing about island informality; I thought I'd give it a try." His chuckle sounded like a feeble attempt to be charming, but maybe Shannon wasn't giving him enough credit: she didn't cut much slack for literary celebrities who kicked single mothers out of their homes.

"Are you free for a drink after work?"

Oh jeez, he's putting the make on the girl.

"Business or pleasure?" asked Leslie coyly.

I'm going to throw up.

"No reason it can't be both, is there?"

Yeccchhh.

"Of course not." Big beaming smile. "You're at the Harbor View, right? There's a pub called the Yankee Clipper within walking distance, up North Summer about a block from Main Street. What say we meet there around five thirty."

"I look forward to it. Five thirty it is."

Watching the man exit and pass before the big front window, Shannon realized that he had never removed his hat. "Nick McAuliffe, I presume," she said.

"The same. He's looks better in broad daylight, that's for sure. He was a wild man last night. Maybe he talked to his shrink."

"Or his lawyer, or his agent? Maybe he upped his Prozac for the duration. Get your jacket," said Shannon, "while I put Pix in the car."

Meg Hasbro, senior broker, Burnham and Wood Realty, sat on the edge of her desk, taking care not to dislodge the inbox, the outbox, or any of the stacks of folders and loose papers that hadn't made it into any box yet. She smoothed her blue tweed skirt down her thighs and over her knees. Past her prime she might be, but her legs were still impressive.

"Hello. You have reached . . ."

No no no. She pressed PAUSE. Man Boss was chuckling in her ear: *Don't be so grim, Meg, you're scaring the clients away.*

She started again, in her smoky whiskey voice with barely suppressed amusement rippling underneath: "Hello. You have reached the office . . ."

Girl Boss, one-time Miss Third Runner-up Connecticut, would hit the roof. She really thought Meg was after her husband, who was indeed closer to Meg's age than her own. The suspicion was so preposterous that Meg had half considered seducing the poor fellow. She didn't think it would be hard.

"Hello. Hello? Hello!" She tried a dozen hellos at as many different pitches. Outside, cars made their way around the horseshoe-shaped driveway of Martha's Vineyard's most tasteful mini mall. Sixty seconds of nothing would be followed by car car car, ninety seconds by car car car car car. Probably chaos theory had something to say about that, but she didn't know what. She took a deep breath and hit RECORD.

"Hello! You have reached the ugliest real estate office on Martha's Vineyard. We're sorry we're not here to take your call, but if you are interested in listing or buying a property assessed at a minimum of eight hundred thousand dollars, please leave your name and number and we'll get back to you as soon as possible."

The red light went off. Had she really said that? She pressed PLAY.

"Hello! You have reached the ugliest real estate office on Martha's Vineyard. . . ."

Meg stared enthralled at the shiny black machine as the message played all the way through.

RECORD: "Hello! You have reached the ugliest real estate office on Martha's Vineyard. How ugly, you ask? Well, directly in front of me are two plate glass windows better suited to a saloon. In the town of Tisbury it is all right to look like a saloon, but it is not all right to act like one. A pity, because a scotch on the rocks would be lovely right now, and the nearest scotch is three miles away."

The red light went out, marking the maximum length of the outgoing message, just as she was hitting her stride. After playing it back, she started again:

"Hello! You have reached the ugliest real estate office on Martha's Vineyard. How ugly is ugly? Imagine a floor whose dimensions are identical to those of the bays at your local service station and a rug that is approximately the color of the oil splotch in the middle of one of those bays . . ."

STOP. She did not want to talk about gas stations.

"Hello. Although you have reached the ugliest real estate office on Martha's Vineyard, you are fortunate enough to be listening to the voice of Meg Has-been—oh, excuse me! Did I say 'Has-been'? I meant Hasbro. I took the name from my ex-husband and never gave it back."

Uh-oh, that nasty old self-hater is staging a comeback. STOP. It's 11 a.m.—do you know where your therapist is?

"Hello! You have reached Burnham and Wood, the ugliest real estate office on Martha's Vineyard. Yes, that really is our name, and do you want to know something astonishing? Neither Burnham nor Wood, his married adult daughter, understands why I find it hysterically funny! 'We move forests to find your dream home,' I suggested once, and they stared at me with blankly identical blue eyes. 'Birnam Wood,' I said helpfully. *Nada*. 'It's from *Macbeth*—you know, Shakespeare?' Then Andy Burnham burst out laughing. He understood! I dared to believe it, I really did. But he didn't. 'Is that what they taught you at Columbus College?' he wanted to know. Did I correct him for the twenty-fifth time? Did I say, 'No, actually, I went to Barnard College of *Columbia University*, but I learned that at Concord-Carlisle Regional High School'? Did I throttle him with my bare hands? I did not. I said, 'I'm going to order Chinese. Want anything?'"

The red light had long since flashed on, and in any case she had moved to the front windows, several yards from the answering machine's microphone, and was peering through the letters of BURNHAM & WOOD REALTY at the parking lot. She still had to record a new message. So what? She felt better. Lots better.

Then some idiot in a hotrod hung a sharp right off the Beach Road and roared into the driveway in a genuine cloud of dust. Only it wasn't a hotrod, it was a snazzy red Mercedes convertible, and it wasn't just any idiot, it was Nick McAuliffe.

* * *

As Chinese food went, the Golden Dragon's tasted best if one hadn't been off-island for six months or so, but the Five Corners restaurant possessed two great assets: its convenience and its lunch specials, which were a great deal by Vineyard standards. Five bucks got you a half-size entree, a generous dollop of fried rice, and a cup of soup, hot and sour or wonton—enough to satisfy an average appetite for both lunch and supper—and you could either take it out or eat at the kitchen-style tables up front. Shannon stepped up to the counter, ready to order, but Leslie nudged her toward the dim, nearly empty dining room around the corner.

"What's this?" Shannon whispered. "The *Chronicle*'s sky's-the-limit expense account?"

"Don't make me laugh," Leslie whispered back. "My treat. You want to sit in the cheap seats where every passerby can see you?"

"Why not? Being seen with a reporter isn't going to sully *my* reputation." But she let herself be pushed. She also, once the waitress had brought menus and a pot of hot tea, let herself ask the first question: "So who's your hot date?"

"Date, schmate," said Leslie, in a tone that said *Get off my case.* "It's work-related. His house burned down last night. I'm on the story. Period."

"Sorry, Scoop." By way of apology, it was less than convincing, but Shannon held the high hand and they both knew it: Leslie wanted to know about Alice Chase a lot more than Shannon wanted to know about Nick McAuliffe. "So does it really look like arson?"

"Nope, at least not according to both Tay and Slater Robinson and what I hear about the scuttlebutt down at the Ritz last night."

The Ritz was a year-round, no-nonsense bar in Oak Bluffs. "Best hearsay on the island," said Shannon. The arrival of her hot and sour soup and Leslie's egg roll softened her up, so she lobbed one into Leslie's forecourt: "So who's this tenant?"

"Woman named Alice Chase. Single mother, has a fourth-grade kid named Mitch. Does the name mean anything to you?"

"It might."

Leslie used a forkful of egg roll to push duck sauce around on her plate.

"Off the record?"

"Way off the record."

"I knew her," Shannon said, "once upon a time." From this Leslie would infer that Shannon had been involved in Alice's case at some point. "It's the same old story: came here summers to wait tables, met an island guy named Lenny Chase, married him, had a kid, guy turned out to be an asshole with an alcohol problem."

"Domestic violence?"

Shannon preferred to call it "wife battering," but she let that one pass. "Yeah. Started off bad and got worse. Alice wound up in the hospital a couple of times. That's where the story gets a little unusual: she left him, and she stayed gone."

"And eventually," Leslie said, "she wound up living in a house that belonged to her ex's uncle Zack."

"Good sleuthing there, Scoop." Shannon grinned at her soup and raised both eyebrows in Leslie's direction.

Leslie resisted the impulse to scowl, or to kick Shannon's shins under the table. "Word is," she said, "McAuliffe agreed to let Alice stay till she could get her custody agreement changed and get off the rock for good. The hearing date's been moved back at least twice. Mr. McAuliffe was getting impatient. Alice was getting harassing phone calls. Maybe there's a connection."

"So?"

"So I want to talk to Alice."

"You want to ask her if Mr. Author was making anonymous phone calls?"

Leslie set her fork down very, very deliberately. "You," she said, "are the most infuriating person on the planet."

Shannon made a time-out sign with her two chopsticks. Leslie had to laugh. "OK, you want to talk to Alice."

"I want to know why she moved out so suddenly—"

"How do you know it was sudden?"

"The neighbors didn't realize she was gone till after she left." Leslie barely managed to keep the smugness out of her voice. *See? I do know a few things, even without you telling me.* "Mr. Author was on a tear last night. I heard him. Sure, he was stressed because his house just burned down, but why would he jump to the conclusion that she did it?"

Shannon snorted. "Maybe he's got Martha's Vineyard mixed up with his book. What is it, some kind of thriller? Probably he hasn't been around long enough to know that renters on Martha's Vineyard are so used to being pushed around that revenge doesn't occur to any of them. Unless they're stewed to the gills, of course, in which case they talk big but still don't *do* anything."

Leslie rolled her eyes. "So I need to talk to Alice." She held up both hands to forestall whatever protest Shannon might be thinking of making. "I don't think Chief Tay knows where she is. Maybe you really don't know where she is. Jay Segredo *says* he doesn't know where she is—correction: he strongly *implies* he doesn't know—but if I took that to the bank, the tellers would laugh at me."

"Well, he can't exactly—"

"I know that." Leslie fixed her most earnest gaze on Shannon. "All I want you to do is put the word out. Leslie wants to talk to Alice. Off the record or on, location of her choice."

Just before Shannon flinched, their lunch arrived, kung pao shrimp and an order of the marinated green beans that were Shannon's favorite item on the menu. "So," she asked as she filled her plate with green beans, white rice, and stir-fried shrimp with peanuts and vegetables, "what's so hot about this particular fire?"

"Groan," said Leslie.

Shannon made a face. "Sorry," she said. "Make that 'newsworthy.' Young family burned out of house on Christmas Eve didn't grab you last year, and neither did the bedridden old lady who actually died in a house fire a couple years before that. What's with this one?"

"Because I haven't had a good story in *forever,*" Leslie said. "The shooting last fall *looked* good, but then—a big fat nothing. Everyone knows Wayne Swanson did it, but what good does that do? He'll come back cleaned up and sober and spouting Twelve Step slogans."

"Aw, who knows?" Shannon said. "Maybe you'll luck out: he'll come back and try to kill Jay again."

"That's *not* what I *meant,*" Leslie retorted. "I want a story I can get *into.* What have I got at the moment? Town meeting crap, town election crap, and this zoning board crap about Quincy Hancock's fucking floodlights. Chet's all over that one, and we're supposed to pretend it's not because Queen Mother Arabella *Fitch* Roth is a beneficiary of the Fitch Family Trust? Give me a break."

"Hey," Shannon suggested, "do a story on Cassie Fitch. Arabella's eldest sister, Cassandra St. Christopher Fitch—now there's a name to die for."

"Oh, come on!"

"Seriously. Everyone thinks she's just another grande dame from West Chop—that's how she wound up chairman of the ISS board, the classic compromise candidate. But she's good. Politically astute, tactful—she got re-elected for the second time at the last annual meeting, with no opposition. She'd make a great story. Plus it would get Chet off your case."

"OK, OK, maybe I'll check it out," said Leslie.

Shannon knew she wouldn't. She shook her head. "Just don't tell me I never do you any favors."

"I won't," Leslie said. "Don't worry, I won't."

CHAPTER FIVE

After lunch, Shannon figured that Pixel wouldn't mind waiting a while longer in the car, so she turned left and headed across the A&P parking lot toward Main Street and the Bunch of Grapes bookstore. For sure they'd have Nick McAuliffe's first novel, the one that was supposedly making it big. Shannon hoped it was a lurid male fantasy, like *Politicians of Gor.*

No such luck. Its title was *Devoted to Her Duty,* and it was featured in a bold but tasteful display in the bookstore window. Leaning against the base of a pyramid of books was a placard that featured a larger, glossier, more flattering print of the *Cape Cod Times* photo; in this version Nick McAuliffe seemed more boyishly attractive and—thanks to some tasteful cropping—his tweed cap less of a literary statement. Accompanying the image were blown-up excerpts from apparently rave reviews in *Publishers Weekly,* the *New York Times,* and the *San Francisco Chronicle.* Nothing, however, alluded to the author's Vineyard connection, which had to mean that neither store nor publisher knew about it. Any author who ever set foot on the island, or buried a two-line mention of the place somewhere in the book, the smart publicists were all over it.

Inside, the book was the first to catch her eye on the New Arrivals shelf. Shannon picked up the top copy, her designer's eye noting with approval the moody monochromatic cover, the bold serif font, dark green edged in gold, used for both the title and the author's name. The first few pages passed muster as well: readable type, adequate margins, no obvious typos, and appropriate use of serial commas and semicolons. The author's face filled the back jacket. His bio, on the inside back flap, did raise her eyebrows:

> Nick McAuliffe worked in the health-care field before turning his hand to fiction. He lives in the Cleveland area. This is his first novel.

Well, that's vague. Shannon flipped to the dedication page, expecting an effusive paean to "my wife, without whom this book would still be a glimmer in a lazy man's eye." No dedication at all. She turned her attention to the front cover flap.

> Life dealt Georgia Duvall a lousy hand, but she's played it brilliantly, scheming and gambling her way to success in a prestigious Chicago law firm. Now the senior partners have handed her responsibility for what the press is already calling "the case of the decade," the defense of a controversial state politician fingered by police as the mastermind of a brilliant drug ring—an assignment that at least one colleague swore he'd kill to get. . . .

Beautiful, brilliant, reasonably young woman survives adversity and works her way (almost) to the top, where (Shannon had this hunch) a handsome, brilliant, unbelievably *sensitive* man would rescue her from dastardly enemies and—worse, far worse—from the curse of loneliness. So if Nick McAuliffe was so into plucky heroines, why hadn't he given Alice more of a break? Could such a boor actually write a decent book? Shannon plunked down good money to find out.

While the cashier tucked her receipt into the book and slipped the book into a bag, Shannon was thinking that maybe she could help Leslie out—get some background for her story, or at least let her know if she was dating a bigamist or an ax murderer: *OK, OK, so she wasn't dating him yet, but "business or pleasure?" Yee-uck. Cleveland, Cleveland—who do I know in Cleveland? Who do I know who knows anyone in Cleveland?*

Halfway across the A&P parking lot, headed toward the newspaper office, where she had left her car and her dog, she stopped short. Giles Kelleher, of course. Not only had Giles lived in Cleveland, not only did he have friends in Cleveland, but he was up on every celebrity great or small who ever set foot on Martha's Vineyard. She could call him from the *Chronicle* office . . . where Leslie would pluck the name, the number, and the subject of the conversation out of her mind? No way, José. Shannon spun on her toes and headed back to Main Street, to the nearest pay phones.

The phones were attached to the outside of the jewelry store, the last of a short row of shops in the block anchored by the Capawock movie theater. They were surrounded by a small brick plaza that in warm weather was a lively place indeed. Friends met there, tourists set down their burdens there, musicians practiced their tunes there, Girl Scouts sold their cookies there. From time immemorial—which was to say, since before Shannon moved to the island—the plaza had been dominated by the Linden Tree. Then the tree died and brought forth no summer shade. Still, it remained the historic and beloved Linden Tree; some residents yelped when town officials proposed removing it, and others gathered to collect relics when the town finally had its way. Volunteers rallied to purchase and plant a replacement.

Throughout the process, when the Linden Tree was dead, then departed, then replaced by a hopeful youngster, islanders continued to meet "at the Linden Tree." It was one of the things Shannon secretly loved about Martha's Vineyard, even while she railed against its ingrained unwillingness to look unpleasantness in the eye. Linden Two *would* grow into a noble tree, and not because of rain or sunlight or conscientious pruning; it would grow because Martha's Vineyard *assumed* it would grow. Even Shannon, who took little on faith, believed it.

There was no one within earshot as Shannon punched in Giles's number. The first two pedestrians made a conscious effort not to glance toward the phone bank; the gaze of the third, a carefully coifed woman of sixty or so, met Shannon's and ricocheted guiltily away. No one saw Shannon stamp her foot as Giles's answering machine kicked in: "Giles can't come to the phone right now, he's romancing two paintbrushes in the alcove . . ." Shannon waited for the *bip bip bip beeeeep* before saying, "Hiya, Giles, this is Shan, desirous of picking your brain . . ."

"Wait, don't hang up! I'm here, I'm here!"

She visualized her buddy with his thick curly reddish-brown hair uncombed, probably unshaven, wearing air-conditioned paint-flecked jeans and a black sweater made for a stockier, taller man, standing barefoot in his tiny kitchen. Giles, who ordinarily didn't leave his house with a hair or a thread out of place, was a total slob when on a painting jag, and he had been on the current jag since the middle of January, when he had been invited to be part of a two-man August show with the eminent landscape painter Erasmus Stanley. Shannon, of course, had been the first to know about each small step on the way: how "Razz" Stanley was a summer regular at the restaurant where Giles worked; how Giles had worked up the nerve to initiate one of those potentially hope-crushing "I'm an artist too" conversations, and been invited to bring some of his paintings to Mr. Stanley's studio the following Sunday afternoon; and how a few weeks later the owner of the prestigious up-island gallery where Erasmus Stanley showed every summer had encouraged Giles to submit slides of his work, and finally, gloriously, offered him a slot in *August,* the primest of prime time for the island's art scene.

"That's fair, isn't it?" Giles worried. "You don't think it's nepotism?"

"Nepotism?! The man admired your work and gave you an intro. Where's the nep—" Shannon stopped. "You didn't sleep with him, did you?"

"Girlfriend! I would *never!* The man's an avowed heterosexual!"

Determined to hang no work that was more than one year old, Giles had been painting like a madman ever since.

"Girlfriend," the madman was saying, "I cannot *believe* you got my message already!"

"Message? What message? I'm calling from the pay phone at the Linden Tree."

"What are you doing there? Get your butt over here, girl. I have to show you something, and we have to talk—in a program sort of way."

Shannon had been Giles's sponsor in Alcoholics Anonymous for almost three years now; she'd given him the coins that commemorated his second and third years of sobriety and fully expected to give him his fourth-year token in July—*provided,* she thought, to ward off misfortune, *we both make it that far, one day at a time.* "You want me to drive all the way to *Edgartown*?" she demanded. "You want me to drive all the way to Edgartown *now*?" Edgartown was six miles away. People who didn't live there acted as if Edgartown were somewhere near the New York state line. It drove people who did live there crazy.

"I'll make a fresh pot of coffee, and . . . and I stole some croissants from the restaurant. Their day-olds are better than most places' fresh. How can you possibly turn me down?"

Shannon couldn't. She couldn't tell him that she'd just had lunch; Giles's circadian rhythm was completely perverted by working nights and painting at weird hours all day, and as far as he was concerned any time was a good time to eat. "Be there in a few," she said, and hung up the phone.

Pixel's put-upon face gazed at her over the back seat when she got back to the car. By the time she opened the front door, the dog was sitting hopefully in the passenger's seat. Shannon fished a biscuit out of her jeans pocket and handed it over. "We're going to Edgartown, kid. OK with you?"

Pixel seemed up for it. Cussing as she shifted into reverse, first, reverse, and first again, Shannon maneuvered her way around the pickups, sedans, and bloated SUVs that jammed the *Chronicle*'s substandard parking lot. After a five-minute wait, she sprinted across the bow of an oncoming taxi van and headed for Edgartown by way of Oak Bluffs.

During her first four or five years on the Vineyard, except in summer of course, when traffic made the beach route unbearable, Shannon had taken advantage of every opportunity to drive this way. She loved it still, long after she'd become islander enough to skip the scenics. To the left Vineyard Haven harbor, sheltered by the West Chop headland on one side and East Chop on the other, opened into Vineyard Sound. To the right stretched Lagoon Pond; a few intrepid sailboats were already at their moorings, but nothing moved on the sheltered water. Spanning the narrow channel between harbor and pond, separating Vineyard Haven from Oak Bluffs, was the drawbridge, where stood the island's only stoplight. Kids loved to watch the bridge go up and boats pass from pond to harbor and back again. Adults groaned at the sight, because it meant backed-up traffic and a ten-minute wait. Some took the amber warning light as a signal to floor the gas and make it across before the barriers came down and the bridge went up.

On this April Monday afternoon, no boats waited on either side of the bridge, and Shannon passed smoothly from one town to the next. Once past the Oak Bluffs police station, it was again water water everywhere, all the way to Edgartown: Nantucket Sound on the left, Sengekontacket Pond on the right. Today the blue-gray water mirrored the undecided sky, but it still gave the land-bound driver a glimpse of infinity before the scrub pines and oaks concealed it from sight. Shannon hung a hard right after the liquor store, and headed into the unpretentious year-round neighborhood where Giles lived.

If not for the gravel area occupied by Giles's ancient Mitsubishi pickup, a casual pedestrian probably wouldn't have noticed that a house, a very small house, was hidden behind the pines. Trailed by Pixel, Shannon followed the flagstones around to the right and peered through the screen door before she rang the little bell mounted on the jamb. Giles, brush in hand, was contemplating a large horizontal canvas. After a pause, Shannon rang again. "Enter, and sign in, *please*," he called. Scowling at the canvas, he set his brush in a nearby glass and maneuvered easel and painting around so they faced the far wall. The little alcove, probably intended as a breakfast nook, was Giles's studio cum laundry room. The lid of the washer doubled as a shelf for brushes, palette knives, and other tools; a three-tier rack of paints hung from the top of the dryer stacked above it.

Shaking her head, Shannon entered. "So where do I sign, huh?"

Giles sat her down at one end of the narrow kitchen table. Had it been one inch wider, the oven door wouldn't have opened all the way. With his customary flourish he served up fresh french roast coffee (in white mugs borrowed from the restaurant) and warm day-old croissants (on souvenir plates, one from San Francisco, one from the White Mountains). "So what's up?" asked Shannon.

"You first," Giles replied. "You're the guest."

She grinned, and licked a bit of buttery pastry off her lip. "OK. I want to know about a nouveau best-selling author. The dust jacket is, shall we say, vague. It does say that he's from the Cleveland area."

"I am *so* sorry," said Giles.

"His name is Nick McAuliffe. The book is *Devoted to Her*

Duty . . ."

He wagged his finger at her and gave her a lascivious look. "Is this one of those latter-day Marchioness de Sade sex manuals?"

She started laughing. "Will you shut up and let me finish? It's in the window at Bunch of Grapes."

"Yes, mistress," he said, contrite.

"OK, so his book's a hit, movie rights have been sold, blah blah blah." She read him the less-than-forthcoming dust-jacket bio and went on: "Last fall he bought a house way back in the woods off Lambert's Cove Road—*not* the kind of house you'd expect a high-flying author to be buying . . ."

"A dump, in other words?"

"Our sisters and brothers in real estate would probably prefer 'Old Island Charm.'"

"Straight writers from Cleveland are rarely known for their impeccable taste," Giles opined. "So the famous writer is stuck with a dump."

"Not quite. Last night the house burned down."

"My opinion of the man has just gone up seventy-five points."

"I don't think he torched the place himself."

"Down forty-five."

Shannon snarfed her coffee. "See what you can find out, will you?"

"I will. Did Brenda Starr put you up to this?"

"Nope. She is working on the story, however, but calling you was one hundred percent my idea."

Giles tossed back the last of his coffee. "Insatiable curiosity isn't your style, girlfriend. You mind sharing *why* you have to know about this dude?"

Uh, because Leslie's meeting him for a drink after work? "It's complicated," she conceded at last. She described Alice, and Alice's abrupt departure from the house, and the rumor that Mr. Best-Seller had forced Alice out. She implied that Jay—"our conflicted friend"—was involved in the case without mentioning that she herself was. When Giles started to look interested, she punched the table emphatically with her right forefinger. "Mr. Best-Seller was out there last night, insisting that Chief Francis arrest Alice for arson."

"Guilt," Giles intoned sagely, "turns to hostility."

"No shit," said Shannon. "Did you make that up?"

"I stole it from Harold."

Shannon looked blank.

"*Boys in the Band,* of course," he said, shaking his forefinger. "You should know that. I'll lend you the video. OK, so Mr. Best-Seller is a moral cretin. I'll see what I can find out. My turn!" He stood up. "More coffee? I want to show you something."

She placed her hand flat over her mug. "I'm liquid-logged," she said. Her eyes tracked him around the table to the easel and watched him maneuver it so she could see the painting resting on it.

"Oh," she said, a drawn-in breath. She exhaled softly: "Oh, *wow.*"

Rendered in night colors a man slept, face turned toward her, head cushioned on his bent right arm. Ambery light from an unseen source beyond the upper-right corner warmed the rise of shoulder, the fall of back, and limned the edge of a blanket that might, in bright light, have been red. It was masterfully done, her art-appreciative left brain told her with absolute certainty, only to be swept aside by her heart, which understood in an instant how much love, how much loss had gone into every brush stroke. *Would Jay ever see it?* Her eyes watered. A drop of water trickled toward her upper lip. Giles handed her a paper napkin.

Shannon dabbed at her eyes. She reached for her mug, held it to her lips without sipping, and set the mug between her knees. Giles put his hand on her shoulder; she put her hand on his. Her gaze never left the painting. "I don't need to say," she said, "that it's the best thing you've ever done. And I don't need to say that *doesn't* mean that what you've been doing is less than excellent. Jesus Christ, talk about quantum leaps."

"By George," murmured Giles, "I think she likes it."

"You goddamn drama queen, you're goddamn right I like it. What's not to like?" Shannon took a deep breath. "Seriously, it's . . . it's . . . gorgeous, heartbreaking, awesome, what the fuck, I don't know the right words. It's *really good*."

Giles dragged his chair around to her side and sat down. "So. Do I put it in the show?"

"Of *course* you put it in the show." *No. Wait a minute.* "Oh," she said. And again: "Oh." Then "Now I get it."

"Of *course* it's the best thing I've ever done," he said, "but *can* I hang it? In a program way, what do you think? 'Check your motives,' right? Well, when I started, my motives *sucked.* 'I'll show you, you cowardly hypocritical shithead.' The first sketches looked like Goya meets Godzilla in the ninth circle of Hell. But it . . . changed."

"I guess." Shannon studied the face in the painting: shadowy, serene, the resemblance didn't hit you all at once—well, it did hit *her* all at once, but she wasn't your average summer gallery goer. "You think people will know?"

"I'll know. You'll know. *He'*ll know. If he comes to the show, that is, which he won't. But that's not the issue. The issue is that deep down my motives still reek big-time. Deep in my heart I am absolutely positively certain he'd be much better off if he'd smash that closet door off its hinges. And I am dying to get in the first kick."

Shannon recalled the photograph in Jay's office: Rainey Silvia, the sister-in-law that sister Janice always wanted. *And you think your motives suck,* she thought. So far she'd spared Giles any mention of that situation. Given the circles he moved in, it was unlikely he'd hear of it from anyone else. Now she wished she'd been less discreet.

"Well, I don't need to make up my mind right now," Giles conceded, "but think about it, will you? What would Bill W. do in my shoes?"

"Jump into bed with Doctor Bob, what do you think he'd

do?"

Bill W. and Doctor Bob were AA's most revered ancestors. Giles whooped, he hooted, he crowed with laughter. "Did you make that up?"

"Nah, I heard it somewhere," Shannon conceded. "Careful where you tell it, though: I told my sponsor and she was *shocked*. So, what's your higher power say? About this?" She glanced at the painting and couldn't look away.

"Same thing she always says: 'Shut up and paint.'"

"You know," said Shannon, "my motives are having a little upheaval of their own. I think I need to take my own inventory on this one. Let's talk about it later, OK?"

"It's a date," said Giles.

Shannon kept gazing at the painting. Where *was* that light coming from? For sunlight it was too gentle; for moonlight too warm. "I don't suppose your HP would be willing to move in with me for a couple of weeks, would she? Mine just says stuff like 'It's OK if you paint, and it's OK if you don't.'"

Giles aimed his forefinger at her. "That *doesn't* mean 'don't do it.'"

"I know," she said. "I *should* have the time, but somehow I just don't."

"OK," said Giles, "here's an idea. Make yourself some time. An hour a day, two hours every other day: something realistic. When the bell goes off, it's Painting Time. You will spend this time in your studio. You don't have to touch a brush or a pencil, you just have to be in your studio. See what happens, OK?"

"OK," she said, carefully examining the idea for traps and snags. The most obvious was that she hadn't opened the door to her studio in at least four—five? could it be six?—years. At one point she'd even considered junking the paints, which had probably turned to rock by now, and selling the easels, the paper, the salvageable equipment, then turning the studio back into the bedroom it had been when she bought the house. She could rent out the room, or maybe have it available for emergency shelter: if the studio were a bedroom, Mitch wouldn't be sleeping on the sleep sofa. The only problem she could see with Giles's plan was that she couldn't make herself open the studio door. How could she paint if she couldn't open the damn door? "Does it have a name?" she asked. "A title, I mean. Does it have a title?"

Giles studied his painting. "I'm thinking of calling it *The Hanged Man.*"

In her pre-Vineyard life Shannon had known the Tarot very well, could still vividly recall the twelfth card of the Major Arcana from the popular Waite-Smith deck. In her mind she rotated Giles's masterpiece ninety degrees to the left, so that the figure hung suspended by its (barely suggested) feet. It worked. Waite-Smith's Hanged Man was remarkably serene for a person hanging upside down by one foot. Jay Segredo couldn't manage that kind of serenity unless he was asleep—Shannon didn't know for sure, she'd never watched him sleep. "Perfect," said Shannon. She took a deep breath. "Giles, you *have* to put it in the show."

He grinned. "And that is Shannon Merrick the artist speaking. Glad to meet you, my dear." He looked at *The Hanged Man* and shook his head. "What does Shannon M. have to say?"

"She says she's very glad that she hasn't painted anything worth showing in the last nine years."

Standing at the store-front windows of the real estate office, Meg Hasbro stared at the wretched little red car until it disappeared down the Beach Road. Her mind spun a story: *Novelist Nick McAuliffe was killed earlier today when his blood-red Mercedes convertible plunged off a bridge on Martha's Vineyard, Mass. Police in Oak Bluffs, one of the island's six towns, said that Mr. McAuliffe was going at least seventy-five miles per hour when his fifty-thousand-dollar car ran a red light, crashed through a wooden barrier, and dove off the end of a drawbridge that was rising to let a large*

sailboat pass from Lagoon Pond into Vineyard Haven Harbor.
Mr. McAuliffe's celebrated first novel, Devoted to Her Duty, *has already sold more than one hundred thousand copies in hardcover.*

Meg stuffed the wrappers from Nick's meatball sub and the disposable plastic container that had held her feeble-excuse-for-Greek-salad into a grease-stained brown paper bag and dropped it into her wastebasket. So his house had burned down, so he wanted to nail sad little Alice for arson, so his next novel was coming along well: Nick McAuliffe was still a jerk.

"It was like watching a roller coaster fly off the track," said a Vineyard real estate agent who witnessed the accident. Prescott Gotrocks, captain of the ketch Lucky Break, *which was passing under the drawbridge at the time, said that the falling car missed his boat by "a scant two feet."*

"The wake nearly swamped us," he said.

An avid reader all her life, Meg had only met authors at book signings and readings. She stopped going to those because it was invariably such a letdown when the writers she admired couldn't recall her name two seconds after she pronounced it for them, or, worse, when they misspelled it on her copy of the book she had loved so much. Then Nick McAuliffe, *the* Nick McAuliffe, the author of *Devoted to Her Duty*, had appeared at Burnham and Wood at the end of last summer. "A real estate office named Burnham and Wood?" he had asked, dimples appearing at the corners of his mouth before he smiled. "How could any writer resist?"

She probably would have fallen in love with the guy had he written nothing more ambitious than *The 30-Day Chocolate Mousse Diet* or *Make Friends with Your PC*. But this Nick McAuliffe had written a novel that illuminated her own soul. A novel she probably wouldn't have discovered on her own, because she rarely read political thrillers, but one day last summer Abby Wood had been filing her nails and telling her father how she had tried to read the new best-seller everyone was talking about and she absolutely couldn't "get into it" no matter how hard she tried, because the main character was *so* unsympathetic. So Meg had drifted over to Abby's desk during the next dead stretch and picked up the book.

The jacket copy intrigued her, and before she'd finished the first chapter she was hooked. She was Georgia Duvall, Georgia was she—except of course that Georgia, in the throes of a difficult divorce, hadn't made the foolish decision to run away to Martha's Vineyard. Georgia had toughed it out in the big city, Chicago in her case, working for a top-flight law firm, not a second-rate real estate office.

At the end of the day she asked, as diffidently as she could, whether she could borrow the book. "Keep it," said Abby. "Pass it on. Whatever."

Meg felt as if she'd been invited to steal the crown jewels. Silly Meg, pathetic Meg; why hadn't Meg played it cool when Nick showed up, pretended she didn't recognize the name, hadn't heard of the book?

Literary critics from New York to San Francisco were united in their opinion that Nick McAuliffe was a "one-book wonder." Said one reviewer who asked not to be identified, "Harsh as it sounds, it might even be a blessing that Mr. McAuliffe died at the height of his fame. Devoted to Her Duty *is an exemplary novel, but nothing in Mr. McAuliffe's previous career suggests that it was anything but a fluke. No matter how much it sold for, his second novel is bound to be a disappointment."*

A smile played around Meg's lips as she reached for the ringing phone. It was Douglas Trumbull; he and his wife, Maryellen, had just flown in to Martha's Vineyard Airport, having decided that they wanted to see the house on Makonikey that she'd mentioned last week. Pardon the inconvenience, but was she free to show it now?

She surely was. Burnham and Wood decreed that the office not be left unattended, unless the officer of the day had occasion to show a property priced at eight hundred thou or more. The Makonikey house qualified: it was listed at one-point-nine million and expected to go for at least one-point-six. She couldn't help calculating, though she tried hard to avoid it, that if she sold the house at one-point-six her commission would be forty-eight thou, give or take, and if it went for the whole one-point-nine, she could expect something in the vicinity of fifty-seven. With that kind of nest egg, even a woman of fifty-three could dream of getting off this wretched rock for good.

More immediately, if Meg didn't get away from the persistent smell of meatball grease, she was going to have to either faint, throw up, or take out the garbage. She told the Trumbulls that she'd meet them at the airport in ten minutes.

Shannon headed home on the long straightaway that was the Edgartown–West Tisbury Road. The patches of blue sky had almost disappeared; the heaviness in the air suggested rain. Would Alice get home before she did? Were Mitch's classmates already giving him grief about the fire? How the fuck much should she tell Leslie? Would Picasso hide *Guérnica* in a closet? Giles *had* to hang *The Hanged Man* at his show! Jay probably wouldn't have the decency, or the guts, to show up at the opening, and you could bet none of his relatives would; they weren't exactly art aficionados. Dr. Jerome Turner? Hmm. He might be a problem. His wife was on the board of a year-round arts center; one sister, a successful Atlanta attorney who summered in Oak Bluffs, was often called upon to moderate erudite public forums on Significant Issues. Jerry the Gerbil, aka Dr. Turner, might want to be seen at Erasmus Stanley's opening, if only to stay in the good graces of his womenfolk. If he did, would he recognize the subject of the painting? Not likely—unless he already had suspicions?

Unfortunately, that was a serious possibility. The Gerb had been counseling Wayne, Jay's homicidal ex-brother-in-law, and the unsettling, unsettled question in the whole mess was

How much does Wayne know? If Shannon and Giles had noticed Wayne's van in Giles's neighborhood, Wayne might well have noticed Jay's Volvo outside Giles's house on more than one occasion; he might have seen it on that memorable night last October and gone to lie in wait off the Edgartown–West Tisbury Road for Jay to drive by on his way home. Could he have put two and two together? If Wayne had the slightest idea that there was "something going on" between the brother-in-law he loathed and another *man,* was Wayne capable of keeping it to himself while shooting off bullets in front of Jay's house, or while sitting in his counselor's office or in judge's chambers at the Dukes County Courthouse? Unlikely, but she wasn't about to underestimate the guile of a grudge-bearing raving alcoholic with nothing to lose. The statute of limitations hadn't run out, either. There *was* no statute of limitations. Wayne had the rest of his life to put two and two together.

Had that Sword of Damocles been hanging over *her* head, Shannon would have come out and gotten it over with. Not Jay, of course. Jay had to take the devious route: dump Giles, freeze out Shannon, romance Rainey, all because he didn't want to come out to Janice and his mother. Not for the first time, Shannon thanked the universe for not giving her any relatives whose opinion she gave a rat's ass about.

Her hands gripping hard on the wheel, Shannon passed the T intersection with Barnes Road. Once again she had driven right by the place where Jay's car, its right front tire punctured by a bullet, had come to rest on the grass between the pavement and the woods. The Edgartown–West Tisbury Road looked the same from one end almost to the other. Jay had pointed it out a few days after "the accident," but she had never been able to pick it out for herself.

After making the turn on to her road, she glanced at her dashboard clock. Almost time for Mitch to get out of school. Shit. Was she supposed to pick him up? Had she told Alice she could use the car? How was he getting home? Was she losing it or what?

Pulling into her driveway Shannon remembered: Mitch was going home with a friend; Alice was going to borrow the car to pick him up later. Satisfied, she clattered up her front steps; Pixel stopped to lap water from the metal bowl at the foot of the stairs, then headed off into the woods to pee.

No extra jackets hung from the pegs in the mud room. She let herself exhale. There were no sounds of human life in the house, but just in case she called out, "Alice? Mitch? You here?" No answer. Thank heaven for small favors. She could call Tay Francis in peace.

The police chief wasn't in his office; his calls were being routed to the department secretary. The department secretary knew Shannon; she reported that the chief had a dentist appointment and planned to head home afterward to prepare for a talk he was giving to the Parent Teacher Student Organization that evening. "Is it a root canal or something dreadful?" Shannon asked. "Just a routine cleaning," said the secretary, "although the way he was carrying on you might think that was pretty dreadful." Shannon hedged: "I'll probably catch him at home," she said. "Thanks." She and the chief went to the same dentist—at least they had two or three years back when they crossed paths in the waiting room. It was worth a try: she checked the number in the phone book and called.

Bingo. Rosalie said the chief was in the hygienist's chair. "Do us all a big favor," said Shannon. "Tell him it's me, tell him it's urgent, tell him I'll buy him a hot fudge sundae as soon as Mad Martha's opens for the season." While she waited, she stretched the phone cord to its limit so she could see out the window. Pixel was rooting around the laurel bushes at the edge of the woods. The birches and maples were just starting to leaf out; the bend in the road was still mostly visible. Spring really was coming. Viva spring!

"Ms. Merrick," said the chief's courtly baritone, "to what do I owe this unexpected pleasure?"

"May I be blunt?"

"I am speaking from Dr. Lombard's private bathroom."

Shannon stifled a guffaw. "Chief, there was a fire in your town last night," she said carefully. "There were— complications."

"Complications are not uncommon in my line of work," said Tay Francis. "A policeman's lot is not a happy one."

"Tarantara," said Shannon. The tune to "When the Foeman Bares His Steel" started marching through her head. "One of your complications is indeed staying at my house. Right this minute she's at work, but I think she'll be willing to talk to you, you personally. She is also scared to death that her, shall we say, erratic ex-husband will track her down, and her experience has made her, shall we say, a little jumpy around uniformed officers. Do you think we can set up an appointment?"

"I think that could be managed."

"What's a good time?"

"Well, Ms. Merrick, since I am speaking from Dr. Lombard's private bathroom, I do not have my calendar in front of me, but I believe that I'm free at nine fifteen tomorrow morning. Would that be suitable?"

"I think it would. If my guest has other plans, can I call you at home this evening?"

"That would be fine. If I'm out, leave a message with my wife. Oh, and Ms. Merrick?"

"Yes?"

"I do intend to take you up on your kind offer of a hot fudge sundae. But if I could prevail upon your discretion, might I ask you to say nothing about this to either my wife or my dentist?"

"But I told Rosalie—"

"Rosalie has graciously agreed to keep our little secret," said the chief.

CHAPTER SIX

Jay stretched out his arms, cracked his knuckles, and took a deep breath. All in all, he'd accomplished plenty since he showed up at work this morning. He'd arranged a longer-term safe house for Alice and Mitch Chase; with any luck, they were set till the custody hearing. He had managed not to disclose any confidential information to the press, and without telling any lies either. He'd picked Shannon's brain without getting into an argument about his private life. Tay Francis had strongly implied that the Butler house fire wasn't arson, and Shannon had volunteered to get Alice officially off the hook. The rest of the afternoon promised a smooth coast toward home sweet home, interrupted only by the department heads' meeting—a waste of time, but what else was new?

He let his mind drift forward, to the conference this weekend, an eagerly awaited opportunity to share experiences with his peers and spar with a few longtime opponents, to hang with some of the Free Radicals—to get out of the fishbowl for a couple of days. He needed the break. Shannon was on his case, Janice was on his case, and Doctor Jerome Turner was an ongoing source of frustration. The only one who wasn't giving him grief was Rainey, and he loved her for it. But his mind was tethered to Wayne Swanson, his sister's loathsome ex. Did he dare leave the island if Wayne might be back? All morning he'd been doodling on the yellow pad on his desk. Now the black ink marks gazed back at him:

WAYNE.

W, with an M set on top, forming two side-by-side diamonds.

A turned into an H with a bar across the top. A stick figure was trying to chin itself on the middle crossbar, only it looked as if the stick figure were hanging itself.

Y, with a line turning the uplifted arms into a martini glass.

N, a circle trapped in the downward angle.

E, turned sideways: a devil's fork without a handle.

Why did Janny ever marry the guy? Jay had hated him from the beginning. Sure he seemed friendly, sure he was reasonably good-looking, but was "friendly and reasonably good-looking" enough to make a smart woman promise "till death do us part"? Wayne's idea of "going out" was getting blitzed at the Ritz. He thought minorities—he kept an arsenal of less complimentary names—had too many rights already. Ushering at the wedding, at Our Lady Star of the Sea, where he and Janny and both their parents had been christened, learned catechism, and received First Communion, Jay had so wanted to disrupt the nuptial mass by bellowing "Stop!" But bellowing in church was not his style, and maybe he was making much ado about nothing. With Janny's help maybe Wayne would grow up.

More than once, though, in the days after the wedding, Jay had heard his mother say, "I hope she will be happy," in a tone that suggested she found the prospect doubtful. Even his father acknowledged some reservations: "We go hunting and all he talks about is guns. Says fishing takes too long." What Ernie was saying was that Wayne didn't understand the important things.

Who would know about Wayne's current whereabouts? Jay ran down the list. It wasn't long: three names. None of them—the Dukes County sheriff, the parole officer, and his very own boss, Jerry the Gerbil—were on his short list of preferred dinner companions, but the Gerb was both the easiest to reach and the most likely to know. Jay dialed his private number, the one that didn't go through the agency switchboard. "This is Doctor Jerome Turner, director of Family Services. I'm so sorry I can't take your call right now. If this is an emergency . . ."

Jay listened through to the beep at the end of the message. Mr. Boss still didn't pick up. Jay hung up and dialed again. Same result. Jay went outside to scan the parking lot: the boss man's snappy new white BMW convertible, which must have set him back at least $35,000, was parked just to the right of the walkway. He returned to his office; he dialed again. Same result.

Jay checked his clock: less than half an hour till the department heads' meeting. The Gerb would be there, of course: he had taken to showing up on time, so he could reprimand anyone who didn't and ridicule anyone who didn't show up at all. Jay decided to ambush him in his office. Unfortunately, Doctor Jerome Turner, BA, MPH, EdD, was a stickler for what he called "professional presentation," and Jay was seriously underdressed in a red plaid flannel shirt, beige chinos, and running shoes. He pulled on his tailored brown herringbone blazer—a birthday gift from his sister the previous June. Not quite enough, but he didn't know what would help. He opened his office door, took three steps down the hall, and barged in on Becca Herschel. "I'm going to pay a call on the Gerb. Am I ready?"

Becca scowled. "You need a white, blue, or blue-striped shirt. Got one? Dark pants wouldn't hurt either."

"Not in my office. You got a stash?"

"Sorry, no." She studied him long and hard. "You *might* pass," she said. "You definitely need a tie. If you're wearing a tie, Gerbil T. might not notice the plaid."

"You're a honey," said Jay.

Becca rolled her eyes.

The only tie in his office was his limited-edition Free Radicals membership tie, which hung on a hook on the back of the door. Better than nothing: Jay tied it, adjusted the knot, buttoned up his blazer, and returned to Becca's office. "What do you think?"

Becca looked. "Not bad," she said at last. "Pale lavender and bright red look better together than my mother might think. Just keep your jacket buttoned: I can see the thingmajiggy every time you lean forward."

Jay bowed deep. "One more time, I am in your debt."

On his way upstairs, he stopped by the Women's Resource Center office. Connie, the newest staff counselor, was sitting on the couch in the reception area, sorting papers on a coffee table that wasn't big enough to hold them. Connie, as always, looked impeccable: pale orange sweater dress, two contrasting but complementary necklaces, and pumps with two-inch heels. At odd moments Jay fantasized about fixing her up with Shannon. If Shannon had a love life worth the name, maybe she'd be less interested in meddling in his? Despite extreme differences in *professional presentation*—Shannon's dressing up was less formal than Connie's dressing down—she and Connie had plenty in common. "Hey, Mister Jay," Connie drawled. "How's it goin'?"

"Going, going . . ." He grinned. "Evalina here?"

"She's in court. You notice how she always manages to be in court or off-island every Monday afternoon?"

"Now that you mention it . . ."

"Uh-huh. And today the fortunate yours truly has been designated to attend the meeting." She wrapped the top sheet of paper into a spyglass and glared at him through it. "But I will *not* sit next to you, not after what happened *last* time."

Last time Jay had kept her amused by doodling caricatures of their stuffiest colleagues on his agenda sheet; she had returned the favor by whispering pithy phrases to go with the pictures. Finally Gerbil Turd had fixed them with the evil eye and asked if their business could possibly wait until after the meeting. Now Jay looked properly apologetic and said he'd try to be good if only she'd give him a second chance.

"My mama warned me about men like you," she muttered,

her face glowing with an unsuccessfully repressed grin.

"You have a smart mama," he said, hoping the lurch of his stomach didn't show in his face. *What exactly did she mean by that?* "See you up there. I've got to buttonhole The Man before the meeting starts."

He ran up the steps to the main floor. What *had* Connie's mama warned her about? Did Connie's mama know Connie was gay? *Was* Connie gay? He had a hunch, but she hadn't dropped any real hints, and he couldn't exactly come right out and ask. Better not let Connie's mama cook in the same kitchen as his mama . . .

Anne-Marie Kincaid, the formidable Family Services secretary, was away from her desk. The department's entire suite was so silent that Jay caught himself tiptoeing across the utilitarian gray carpet and down the hall, past two closed doors and a vacant cubicle. The director's door, at the end of the hall, was three-quarters open. Beyond it, Dr. Jerome Turner sat at his desk, concealed from view by the *Boston Globe.* Jay rapped on the door jamb. Newsprint snapped and shook; Dr. Turner looked like a jacklighted rodent. "You don't believe in knocking?"

Jay gazed involuntarily at his slightly reddened knuckles. "I thought I did. Sorry. Didn't mean to startle you."

"I wasn't startled." With exaggerated care, the Family Services director folded his paper and set it to one side of his desk. His desk, as always, was bare except for a black-leather-framed blotter and a black marble pen stand that looked solid enough for a murder weapon. "I wonder why Mrs. Kincaid didn't buzz me."

"Ms. Kincaid wasn't at her desk."

Jerry the Gerbil finally remembered his manners. Half rising from his high-backed leather-upholstered throne, he waved toward the modest gray and black chair to the right of the desk. "What can I do for you, Mr. Segredo?"

Jay sat down, leaned back, and crossed his right foot over his left knee. Immediately his boss's beady eyes pounced on the running shoes, the bright red socks. *Oops.* "I'm trying," Jay began carefully, "to find out the current whereabouts of one of your clients. At a pretrial conference almost exactly six months ago, Wayne Swanson—"

"Ahem," said Dr. Turner. "Is Mr. Swanson related to your current caseload, Mr. Segredo?"

Jay stared at him. "Uh," he said, scrambling hard to keep his cool, "the charges against Mr. Swanson included discharge of an unlicensed firearm within five hundred feet of an inhabited dwelling. Need I remind you that the inhabited dwelling was *mine?* Or that Mr. Swanson is my sister's ex-husband?"

The Gerbil settled back in his chair, whiskers twitching. The tops of his ears seemed more prominent than usual. "Of course not, Mr. Segredo. Need I remind *you* that your personal involvement in the case does not give me license to violate the confidentiality of the client-counselor relationship?"

Jay's mind went sluggish, as if a gallon of molasses had been poured into the works. He struggled to recall any rules, laws, or regulations pertaining to disclosure, but the only ones that came to mind applied to sex offenders. Wayne, bless his withered little heart, had not stooped so low. "The current whereabouts of Mr. Swanson is relevant to my safety," he said, "and, more importantly, to that of my sister and her children."

"I can understand why you might think so," said Dr. Turner in his best placate-the-distraught-client voice. "Mr. Swanson has certainly had his share of troubles . . ."

Mr. Swanson has caused *his share of troubles,* Jay thought. *More than his share; way more than his share.* But Jay's training and long experience as a consummate listener served him well: his eyes didn't narrow, his mouth didn't tighten, his weight didn't shift in his chair.

"And Mr. Swanson," Dr. Turner was saying, "would be the first to admit it. But Mr. Swanson has endured his forty days in the wilderness. He has mastered the demons that threatened to destroy him and all he holds dear . . ."

Which would be—what? Does Wayne hold anything dear beyond his warped view of the world? Jay maintained his attentive posture, though his boss seemed to be playing to an unseen congregation between the desk and the door, and was rewarded for his effort when Dr. Turner swiveled abruptly in his direction:

"People *change,* Mr. Segredo," he said, his voice dropping theatrically to a awe-filled hush. "The prodigal returns, the sick man is healed, the sinner sins no more. Even people we hold in contempt are capable of change."

Jay had had enough. He gazed steadily at his boss. After ten seconds, the man had the decency to appear ill at ease. At fifteen seconds he shifted his weight. At twenty Jay was ninety-five percent sure that Gerbil Turd knew when Wayne would return to the island. Maybe Wayne was already back. Jay relaxed. Jay took a deep breath. "It is reassuring, of course," he said, "to hear that Mr. Swanson is making progress." He stood up. "Perhaps you would consider informing me—if, in your assessment, Mr. Swanson might pose a threat to me, my sister, or her family, you might consider telling me, or her, where he is?"

"But of course, Mr. Segredo. If anyone's safety is in jeopardy, then that becomes my primary obligation."

But of course. If Jay had been packing a pearl-handled Colt .45, he would have drawn it and spun it on the shiny surface of Dr. Turner's desk. It might give the man a new perspective on safety. "I appreciate your concern," he said.

"We all labor to reconcile conflicting interests," the good doctor pontificated. "I must say, Mr. Segredo, that I am surprised by your tie. That is the atomic energy symbol, is it not? I did not take you for a fan of nuclear power."

En route to the airport, Meg Hasbro pulled in at the car wash, then pulled out again without stopping: better to ignore the road-weary exterior of her aging Caravan than to allow the Trumbulls to languish at Martha's Vineyard Airport. Apart from the restaurant, which served decent coffee and diner-style food with a glorious view of the runway, the amusements at the state's only county-owned airport were scanty. Meg herself enjoyed listening to the idle cab drivers swap tall tales about their most recent Fare from Hell, but for non-locals the only entertainment was slipping a quarter into the M&M machine and hoping your hands would fill up with candies. The Trumbulls would get bored quickly.

Douglas Trumbull she had already met. At Andy Burnham's urging, she had shown him a sprawling modern mansion on Chilmark Pond and been impressed when he hated it as much as she did. He was "Good Rich"—he wore his wealth lightly and seemed to appreciate what Martha's Vineyard was really about. "Bad Rich" bought property and immediately started applying for zoning variances for extra bedrooms, extra stories, and guest houses big enough for a family of six. She had tried to encourage Nick McAuliffe to aspire to the status of "Good Rich," but the casual elegance of the Makonikey house had been lost on him. "One best-seller does not a millionaire make," he kept insisting.

Douglas Trumbull was the perfect buyer for Makonikey. It was a gorgeous property, a beautifully designed and livable house with private beach and panoramic views of Vineyard Sound; the sellers, Moe and Dot Switzler, had come down twice on the price and would entertain any reasonable offer. But Meg had already been carrying it for more than two years. She'd shown it to dozens of hand-picked prospects, resulting in several serious offers, three of which had reached the purchase-and-sale agreement stage before falling through. Trouble was, the house was jinxed. One stormy summer evening four years before, the Switzlers' nineteen-year-old daughter, Vida, had had a fight with one or both of her parents; the stories differed on who was in residence at the time. She had rushed headlong down the steep staircase to the beach, apparently tripped and tumbled down the steps, breaking her neck. According to another version, she had gone out to meet a boyfriend her parents didn't approve of; she'd been sitting on the railing, lost her balance, and tumbled over backward. Either way, she was dead before anyone reached her. Meg never told anyone the sad story herself, but all her prospects learned about it somehow, with occasional variations and embellishments that Meg hadn't heard before. Meg had resolved to tell Douglas Trumbull the story right upfront. Maybe that would lift the curse.

There he was, making genial small talk with the only clerk on duty at the rent-a-car counters. He noticed her as soon as she passed through the glass doors; he smiled, then glanced about, his eyes finally settling on a slender blond woman of, at the very most, thirty-five who was sitting rigid in one of the blue plastic bucket seats in the waiting area. Impeccably coifed, made-up, and dressed. Mrs. Trumbull, of course. Meg's eyes narrowed. Twelve years before, her own dear ex had left her for a woman of twenty-eight. When he asked for a divorce, she had raged to friends, co-workers, her older sister, even her mother, and most had responded with tales of how they'd discovered and dealt with their husbands' similar infidelities. Her own father had committed a few—her mother said one, her sister was sure there had been at least four. The whole older man–younger woman thing was one big sick cliché.

Meg picked up immediately that Mrs. Trumbull did not want to be there. Indeed, Martha's Vineyard Airport was tackier than a rundown bus station, but Mrs. Trumbull's body language suggested that decor was not the issue. Had they been quarreling all the way from New York? Was the seven-figure Island getaway strictly her husband's idea? No way was Meg going to tell "The Sad Death of Vida Switzler" in front of her. Meg felt her commission prospects leaking onto the scuffed linoleum floor.

But fifty-seven thousand dollars, or even forty-eight, was worth fighting for, and hadn't she snatched numerous sales from carpenter ants, dismal weather, boorish town officials, stubborn tenants, and jumpy lawyers? "You must be Mrs. Trumbull," she said in her most cordial voice. "I'm Meg Hasbro, from Burnham and Wood Realty."

Mrs. Trumbull mustered a smile and stood, taking Meg's proffered hand. "Please, call me Maryellen," she said, as her husband came over to join them.

Douglas Trumbull chivalrously yielded the front seat to his wife, then leaned forward between the two women as Meg pointed out the sights, such as they were, between the airport and Makonikey. The fields were fallow, the trees leafless, the houses dingy: it was April, the tail end of a long, cold, and especially rainy mud season; what did anyone expect? Along the way Douglas made comments and asked questions; Maryellen gazed stiffly out the window.

Meg drove the dirt road out to Makonikey Head as gently as she could, but Maryellen punctuated every bump with a mutter and finally asked if there wasn't enough money to pave it. "It's a little rough after the winter," Meg explained, "but it'll be graded after the last frost. It's quite a good road, actually."

"I'd hate to see a bad one," said Maryellen.

"No need to build speed bumps to slow people down," Douglas said cheerfully.

Meg pulled up in front of the house; the car skidded forward a few inches after the brakes caught. She pulled forward a little more to get out of the mud puddle, then cut the engine. Douglas helped his wife from the car; Meg went ahead to unlock the door to the main house.

The showing was a disaster from start to finish. The first thing Maryellen Trumbull noticed was the bat mitzvah painting of Vida Switzler, a heartbreakingly beautiful girl with a floral tiara in her long dark hair. "She looks Jewish," said Maryellen. "Are the owners Jewish?" Douglas shushed his wife, while Meg recovered enough to proudly present the state-of-the-art gourmet kitchen. At once Maryellen compared cooking to breaking rocks on a chain gang, and Douglas launched into a reminiscence of delectable bite-size hors d'oeuvres created from feta cheese and phyllo pastry, remembering too late that these were the specialty of his first wife. A tour of the four ground-floor bedrooms revealed that Maryellen didn't care if Douglas's three children by his previous marriage ever came to visit, and during their sojourn in the master suite—possibly the only place where Nick McAuliffe had lived up to Meg's expectations—a tense conversation between husband and wife disclosed that she wanted to get pregnant and he was not enthusiastic.

Meg sided with Douglas one hundred percent and might have blurted out her opinion had not Douglas, prescient Douglas, suggested a stroll down to the private beach. Maryellen consented with surprising alacrity, and Meg begged off with a mumble about needing to check in with her office. She stood by the sliding door and watched Douglas help his wife down the steps that led down from the broad deck to a footpath, which took them to the long zigzagging flights of wooden stairs that descended the steep bluff to the sandy beach. It was obvious what she'd seen in him, but what on earth attracted him to her? Anyone who shared a bed with Maryellen risked being clawed to death in his sleep.

In the oak-paneled, velvet-curtained library that was part of the master suite, she retrieved a opulently illustrated book on America's Cup racing that she had noticed the last time she showed the house. She kicked off her shoes and sank into the sofa to read, confident that she would be aware of the returning couple in time to step back into her professional persona. But as she flipped through the dramatic photographs, the detailed diagrams, her disinterest, or perhaps her anxiety, increased. How could Nick McAuliffe possibly think Alice had burned down his house? Hadn't it dawned on him that now the police would talk to Alice, and that Alice might have figured out . . . The stirring in Meg's belly was not at all pleasant. Mud had a way of splattering farther than you expected. She was actually relieved to hear the Trumbulls climbing the steps to the deck.

Douglas was spinning fantasies of tying his boat up at a mooring off his own beach—doctor that he was by training, of course it was called *Caduceus*—and going for sunset sails, while Maryellen complained that she'd never been so scared in her life, she thought those old stairs were going to collapse and send her hurtling to her death. Meg rushed headlong into the jaws of defeat, asking Douglas about his boat. In moments he was telling stories about his wooden schooner and asking her about the world-famous wooden-boat yard on Vineyard Haven harbor. Maryellen, bored, wandered around the room and back to the kitchen.

"Since I was a little girl," Meg confided, "I've wanted to sail around the world. I'd stop wherever I wanted, and stay for as long as I wanted."

"So have I!" Douglas Trumbull beamed at her with boyish exuberance. "My first wife loved sailing, but my kids can take it or leave it."

Immediately they started comparing dream itineraries, so passionately that neither one noticed that Maryellen Trumbull was back, dropping acid comments into the conversation. "My husband," she confided with a saccharine smile, "has an almost pathological interest in sea stories. You can't imagine his library! He even has an inscribed first edition of *Moby-Dick*. It's in mint condition. It cost a simply *terrifying* amount of money at a London auction, but does he take proper care of it?" Maryellen's voice was rising faster than an oncoming hurricane; Meg, astonished, wondered if she was going to start shrieking. "Of course not. He *reads* it. Can you believe that? He *reads* it, without even washing his hands!" At that Douglas propelled his wife into the kitchen, closed the door behind them, and Meg kissed her commission goodbye.

Marry me, Meg thought. *Dump her. We'd be perfect for each other: I love the house, and we could sail around the world together. Marry me.*

* * *

Light heart jousting with dark resentment, Jay returned to his office after the department heads' meeting. The good news was that Jack Purcell, executive director of Island Social Services, had been called away at the last minute, which meant that the meeting was brief, which meant that he and Connie didn't get into trouble and he didn't get exasperated enough to say something rash to his boss. The bad news was that Wayne might already be back on the island and the Gerbil was playing confidentiality games. Jay was less worried about his own safety than about his sister's peace of mind: Janny had a job she liked, the kids were doing great, but if anything could mess things up, it was the return of her ex-husband. What would it take to get the Gerbil to take early retirement and move to Australia?

"You're back awful early," said Becca as soon as Jay looked into her office. "Your sister called. Call her at home. Everything else can wait. You mind if I take off?"

He couldn't help noticing that her desk was clear, and that she already had her black leather jacket on. "Go. With my eternal gratitude."

"Can it. I'm bringing congo bars tomorrow."

"Good woman," said Jay, grinning. "Have a good night."

There was only one message on his private line. He punched the Play button and started dialing his sister's number. Shannon spoke from the machine. He stopped dialing and hit the disconnect button. Shannon: "I talked to the chief. Everything's cool. We've got a date for tomorrow morning. I can see Mitch out the window. He's playing soccer with Sean from up the road. I think they're about to hit me up for cookies. How do I explain that I have no maternal instinct? Talk to you later."

Jay shook his head. Shannon was a bona fide original and deep down he adored her to death. If only she didn't get so prickly. Maybe he should get her a LIVE AND LET LIVE sticker for her car? He called Janice's number; his niece, Amy, picked up the phone. "Hey, Mister Blue Jay," she said, "you don't have to talk to Mom—she called to invite you to my birthday party on Wednesday. It's my real birthday, but it's not the real party—that's not till Saturday. Kevin and creepy Danny'll be here, and Aunt Rainey and Steve, and *angel food cake*. With chocolate frosting. I'm gonna be *thirteen*. I'm almost a teenager! Mom's scared to death. Be here or be queer!"

Jay got the creeps. "Don't you worry, Amy-o, I'll be there."

"Aren't you going to ask me what I want?"

"Nope. I already got your present."

"I *can't wait*," said Amy. "You're my *favorite* uncle."

After he hung up, Jay dropped into his chair. Amy had three uncles, but Jay was the only one she ever saw. He loved kids. He loved the kids he worked with, even the hostile, seriously messed-up ones; he loved his sister's kids most of all. But *Be here or be queer?*

The Yankee Clipper was, as its signage and advertisements emphasized, a pub, not a bar. To the discerning eye its decor, from the scuffless checkerboard floor to the uniformly framed and unfaded celebrity photos in the foyer, suggested that it was frequented by summer people and new arrivals, not longtime locals, and that it probably served as much scotch, gin, vintage wine, and high-end brandy as it did beer. Leslie was only five minutes late, but Nick McAuliffe was already there, holding down a four-person booth along the left wall. Not that the place was crowded: the Clipper had only reopened for the season at the beginning of the month, and its core clientele didn't arrive in earnest till Memorial Day weekend.

McAuliffe rose to greet her with a genial smile and an outstretched hand. "I hope this is all right," he said.

"Perfect," said Leslie, noticing the brown-bagged book-size parcel on the table and the fizzy, lime-garnished drink that the man had already half finished.

"What's your pleasure?" he asked once she was seated.

"Just coffee for now," she said, rummaging through her shoulder bag for notebook and three identical black rollerball pens. At his raised eyebrow, she smiled. "I'm a working girl, Mr. McAuliffe. Half a glass of wine and I'd be talking twice as much as you." Leslie could hold her liquor better than any woman she knew and most of the men. "Oh, go wild: how about a double cappuccino."

"No tape recorder?" he inquired, catching the eye of the sole bartender at the back of the room. Almost immediately a waitress appeared to take their order, wearing a stark black and white skirt, blouse, and vest combo that matched the floor. At the last moment he added an order of nachos to her cappuccino and his second gin and tonic.

"I prefer pen and paper, unless I'm doing Q-and-A and the point is to let so-and-so talk on the record. Then I whip out the trusty Panasonic." She smiled. "My father's a newspaperman from before the Age of Tapedecks. I started memory training before I hit first grade. Let me tell you, the fastest way to lose a fight in my family is to misquote a source."

"Of course," said Nick McAuliffe, as if realizing this for the first time. Leslie knew for sure that he was faking. "You must be David Benaron's daughter."

"Guilty as charged," she said lightly, and braced herself for the look that said *What's the daughter of a Pulitzer Prize winner doing working for a two-bit weekly on Martha's Vineyard?* It didn't come. Maybe McAuliffe really had done some time on the stage.

"The advance I got for the novel," he said, his fingers briefly touching the brown paper bag, "enabled me to quit my day job. Until then I edited *The Asclepius Report.* Not exactly," he added, with a self-effacing smile, "a mass-circulation magazine, but—"

It was Leslie's turn to play the actress. "I've heard of it," she said, returning his smile. *The Asclepius Report* was a well-funded weekly newsletter for top executives in the health-care industry. Managers at insurance companies, HMOs, big hospitals, and pharmaceutical companies read it to learn more about fighting proposed consumer-protection legislation, circumventing rules already on the books, discouraging unions (as legally as possible), helping large corporations devise benefit packages that cost employees more while offering them less, persuading doctors that Brand Name Drug XYZ would quiet their patients' complaints about mysterious pain . . . David Benaron skirmished frequently with *The Asclepius Report.* Leslie definitely knew the name.

"Please," he said, with all the charm of a freckle-faced kid who's just hit a baseball through the garage window, "don't hold it against me. We all have to make a living, right?"

The interview was off to a good start. Leslie lobbed him an easy one: "So what brought you to the Vineyard? Am I safe in assuming it wasn't President Clinton?"

"You are." He grinned at her over the rim of his glass. "I came here a few times in the eighties and early nineties, visiting friends. I loved it. I like to think of myself as a primarily left-brain person, but on one of those visits I had a very powerful experience that I can only call 'spiritual' at the Gay Head Cliffs. The underlying message was *Take up your pen.* Well, keyboard," he amended, with a slightly sheepish smile that Leslie found not quite genuine. How many times had he told this story anyway? "I'm your basic literary cliché: after college I was all fired up to be a famous novelist, but nothing I wrote went anywhere, so I gave it up. After that morning at the cliffs, I started working on what became *Devoted to Her Duty.* So it's come full circle: Georgia Duvall brought me back to Martha's Vineyard."

"Georgia . . . ?"

"The protagonist of *Devoted to Her Duty.* I apologize: here I am dropping names from a book you haven't read." He pushed the brown-bagged package toward her. "I brought you a copy, in case you hadn't seen it. You don't *have* to read it." His smile suggested, however, that he would be ever so pleased if she did.

"Thanks," she said, slipping the volume from its bag. "I've seen some of the reviews—I look forward to reading it. Sign it for me, would you, before I forget?"

"But of course."

While he scribbled, she continued the interview: "So in a way Georgia bought you a house on the Vineyard."

"That's pretty much it. I started looking early last summer, after we closed the movie deal—my financial planner was telling me I *had* to shelter some of that money," he explained, "and for a variety of reasons property seemed the best way to go. My broker showed me the Butler house at the end of August."

Leslie squeezed "Realtor?" into the margin of her notebook.

"It needed some work, of course," he went on, "but structurally it was sound and the location was perfect for a getaway. Off the beaten track, not too many neighbors . . ." He nudged the book toward her.

"Was the house occupied at the time?" Leslie asked, slipping *Devoted to Her Duty* back into its bag.

"It was," he said, glancing at her notebook. "Alice Chase was living there. My understanding was that she was caretaking, so I didn't think twice. She'd get another job, right? On my broker's advice I had my lawyer give her written notice that she had till the end of the year to find a new situation."

Leslie was profoundly if somewhat guiltily grateful that she didn't have to worry about housing. Did Nick McAuliffe know that there was no good time to be house hunting on Martha's Vineyard, unless price was no object? "What was your broker's name again?"

He hesitated a moment before replying: "Meg Hasbro, of Burnham and Wood Realty. Meg was a great help navigating the troubled waters, so to speak. She got a call from your social services outfit—"

"Island Social Services," Leslie said, her hand moving steadily across the narrow pages of her notebook. Not until her source reached for a tortilla chip liberally coated with cheese and salsa and dipped one corner into the sour cream did Leslie realize that their nachos had arrived. The platterful could easily have satisfied a table of four, though the accompanying green-glazed bowls of sour cream and hot sauce were rather small. "How hot are they?" she asked.

"By Cleveland standards? Hot. By San Antonio standards, not very."

Leslie plunged a chip into the hot sauce and transferred it to her mouth. Instantly her tongue began to glow, though her eyes stopped just short of watering. No wonder the bowl was small! "That's real," she said.

"Are you sure you don't want a beer with that?" he asked. "Or a medic?"

She was, almost, charmed. He caught the eye of the waitress, who was standing behind the cash register listening attentively to the bartender. When the young woman arrived, he said, "Dos Equis, please," and glanced at his companion.

Leslie shook her head, sipped her cappuccino, then helped herself to the cheesiest nacho in the heap, even though it meant some tugging and twisting that her mother wouldn't have approved.

"Well," he said, "to make a very long story short, Ms. Chase had left a bad marriage. The caseworker said she wanted to move off-island with her son but first the custody agreement had to be changed. There was a hearing set for January. I said fine. Then the father didn't show. I had a judge call me personally to ask for another extension, till the beginning of March. I said OK again. Again the father didn't show. The next date wasn't till the middle of May. Meanwhile the house needed work, my contractor still hadn't seen the inside of it, and I was counting on using the house this summer. This court thing could have gone on forever. My lawyer filed to have her evicted. As it turns out, eviction proceedings can go on forever too." He shook his head ruefully.

Leslie stirred up the last of the froth from her cappuccino. Should she have another, or should she spring for beer? "But Ms. Chase did move out before the fire."

"She did. Meg went by Monday morning a week ago, and she was there. Wednesday morning: not a trace. Gone. The place was a mess, of course, but—don't look a gift house in the mouth, I said, and immediately made arrangements to come down and get the renovations started. I flew in Friday morning—Meg had already talked to the contractor, and I met with him at the house early Friday afternoon. The carpenters started on Saturday, I walked the site with the landscaper on Sunday and met with the electrician—things were starting to move." He paused for a long swallow of beer, and another nacho.

"And last night your house burned down," Leslie prompted him.

"Last night the house burned down," he confirmed. "You understand why my first thought was that Ms. Chase had something to do with it. Not necessarily that she literally set it herself—she seems a mousy little thing, but she wouldn't be the first mouse to have friends among the rats."

Leslie watched his face as she scribbled "friends among the rats." She looked serious, all the while thinking, *Oh? Is that how they do things in Cleveland?* "You've actually met Alice?" she asked.

Oh, yes, he assured her: when he first bought the house, he'd even paid her a visit; she'd been hanging laundry and hadn't stopped to invite him in. Then they'd had several phone conversations, each more unpleasant than the last, till all he got was her answering machine. He looked deliberately at her notebook and then directly into her eyes. "If I might say something off the record?"

Immediately Leslie laid her pen down on the table. "We're

off the record," she said. "The mental tape recorder is on pause."

"Last night was, shall we say, very upsetting," he confided. "This morning—well, I won't go so far as to call the fire a blessing in disguise, but today I've been meeting with people—insurance adjusters, town officials, architects, landscapers, that sort of thing. My insurance will enable me to rebuild without unnecessary delays, and well—the house was solidly built, but it was old-fashioned: small rooms, not many windows, low ceilings, jury-rigged wiring . . . There's something to be said for starting fresh, if you get my drift. I'm not glad that the house burned down, and I'm very grateful that no one was hurt putting out the fire—"

"You might want to put that on the record," Leslie advised. "Starting with 'I'm very grateful.' Then add something about the dedicated volunteers."

"Do it," he said, with a friendly, slightly conspiratorial smile. "Put something in there, make me sound good. At any rate, I'm staying till Friday. I don't suppose you'd be free for a non-working dinner?" He turned in his seat and caught the waitress's eye.

"I might," she said. Should she or shouldn't she? Would it help the story, or would it make it impossible? Her father might be interested in hearing more about Mr. Asclepius Report. "Give me a call Wednesday morning. Paper goes to bed Wednesday afternoon. Sometimes by then I'm too wasted to think."

The check arrived in a leather-bound book embossed with a gold clipper ship. Leslie laid her hand on it, then, an instant later, his hand covered hers. It withdrew at once. *Smart man,* she thought. "I'll take care of it. Newspaper business." *And if you believe that, I'll sell you shares in the bridge from Woods Hole to Vineyard Haven.* Leslie laid down four tens, and closed the clipper book. "That's all set," she told the waitress, who glided up an instant later.

To avoid a possible "let me help you with your coat" scene,

Leslie slid out of the booth while Nick finished off his beer.

"Call me if you can't decipher your handwriting," he teased.

"I'll do that," she said.

"And don't forget your book."

CHAPTER SEVEN

It was almost 6:30 when Leslie reached the *Chronicle* office. Vineyard Haven was dark and mostly deserted. Under its overhanging roof, the newspaper's front window glowed, light spilling across the concrete patio but stopping well short of the gas station across the street, a seedy oasis in the night where characters rarely seen by the light of day took refuge, buying scratch tickets, drinking Coke and rotgut coffee, smoking endless cigarettes. A gas jockey in khaki overalls kept a one-sided conversation going while a gaunt blond woman in a Ford Explorer signed a credit card slip; another guy sat on a milk crate, smoking.

As Leslie pulled into the parking lot, the *Chronicle*'s front door opened, discharging Laura, the production manager, who looked both ways and sprinted across the empty street. She skirted the Explorer and disappeared into the convenience store, almost certainly on a quest for chocolate.

Leslie entered the office through the side door. Immediately her nostrils filled with the smell of popcorn and the newspaper's own scorched coffee. In the production room, two ad typesetters stared at their Mac terminals; one moved his lips, probably begging Great God Quark not to send fire or flood or electrical outage before the ad in progress came out of the printer. Against the far wall, the art director perched on a stool and studied a page on her drafting table. As usual, she didn't turn to greet Leslie; also as usual, the nearer typesetter made a monosyllabic mumble and his neighbor smiled hello. The proofreader—a squirrelly guy who might reach five-foot-ten if he ever stood up straight—hunched over a small stack of ads and didn't acknowledge her as she passed his desk. This did not surprise her: the relationship between the reporters and the proofreader had been tense since the staff meeting week before last, when Steve DeKuyper blew up about an error that the Squirrel had introduced into one of Steve's front-page stories.

The lights were on in the news section, and so was Steve's terminal, but no one was home. Leslie sat down at her desk with her shoulder bag on her lap. Phone pressed against her left ear, she checked her messages while her computer booted up. Quincy Hancock III, sounding suspiciously conciliatory, wanted her to call. Her father was back from San Francisco and thinking of coming to the Vineyard this weekend—how did her schedule look? Roger wondered how her day was going, wanted her to give him a buzz when she had a chance. Sophie Everett, Alice Chase's former next-door neighbor, had thought of something that might be important, sorry she hadn't remembered it this morning; could Leslie call her back?

Leslie was tempted to return the call at once, but it was suppertime, when parents with school-age children were easy to reach but unable to talk. She jotted the Everetts' number on the cover of her notebook. Once the computer woke up, she downloaded her e-mail. This took long enough that she became engrossed in pushing back her cuticles, thinking all the while *Home, I should have gone straight home.* Laura returned, peeling a Snickers bar. *Maybe chocolate would help?*

The e-mail in her inbox didn't change her mind. Make $$$ Writing at Home. My Award-Winning Cartoons Will Enhance Your Op-Ed Page. Squelch Union Activity Before It Starts. Dear Mr. Chester Roth: I am a journalism student, please tell me are there any openings for summer interns at the *Martha's Vineyard Chronicle.* DELETE. DELETE. DELETE. Her forefinger paused just before it zapped the post from pixelprod@capecod.net: "The book's not bad. What's the scoop on the author? Catch you later. Shannon." Shannon was smart, Shannon was reliable. If only Shannon weren't— sometimes—such a self-righteous pain in the tuchas.

Shannon was the one who had told her, as rising floodwaters overtook Jay Segredo's predecessor, that Arabella Roth was a Fitch. Leslie never would have guessed: the Fitches were rich la-di-dahs from West Chop, Arabella Roth was a very canny newspaper publisher—how could they possibly be related? But as soon as Shannon said it, puzzle pieces fell into place. At last Leslie understood why people kept telling her how amazed they were that the *Chronicle* was letting her pursue a story that threatened to sink certain Island Social Services administrators in mud up to their hairlines. Everyone else, it seemed, knew that the Queen Mother's eldest sister was on the ISS board, that the Fitch family threw a big fundraising party for ISS every Fourth of July weekend, and that the Fitches rubbed elbows with—and wrote checks to—those very same administrators.

Martha's Vineyard was like that: tectonic plates were always shifting under the terra apparently firma you walked on, reminding you that no matter how much you found out, you didn't necessarily know a damn thing. An islander might have exactly the information you were looking for, but would they ever tell you? They would not—not unless you phrased your question in the precisely the right way, in which case they couldn't avoid answering without becoming, by their own elevated but esoteric standards, liars. Leslie had never lived in a place where everyone knew everything but the truth was so hard to pin down.

Thank God her dad was back: he'd probably take her some place nice for dinner, where she could pick his brain about Nick McAuliffe and he could pick hers about how to deal with her mother.

She retrieved her notebook and propped it up on the typing stand while Word loaded. Glancing up, she couldn't help noticing that the Squirrel was staring at her. Immediately he stood up and carried a stack of ad proofs over to the corrections basket. "Oh no!" cried Laura. "I bombed again."

"Are you saved?" came a voice from beyond the wall. The friendlier of the two typesetters had just enough drawl to make Leslie suspect that he'd done considerable time south of Washington, D.C.

"I'm saved."

Praise the Lord, thought Leslie. She didn't say it because she'd done so on two different occasions and gotten very blank looks.

She wasn't going to get much done here tonight. It was time to go home.

Home was off the lower end of Lambert's Cove Road, on the west shore of Lake Tashmoo. The gravel of the semicircular driveway crunched under Leslie's car tires as she rolled to a stop under the pines. When she killed the Camry's headlights, the trees, the driveway, even the house disappeared. Her first winter here, the dark of the off-season nights had made her jumpy. She always locked her car and took the keys inside. She locked the front door but still worried that anyone with strong fingers could open the latchable but unlockable windows from the outside. No one tried. By spring she was no longer locking the door.

She no longer locked her car either, though she did drop the keys into her shoulder bag. Shannon rolled her eyes at this; Leslie retorted that if Shannon's Subaru were less than ten years old she might be a little more protective. Leslie picked her way along the right side of the house, where the winter rains and melting snow had worn their annual gully down the slope to the lake, down to the brick patio outside her front door.

She lived in the so-called "in-law apartment" that occupied one end of the ground floor of the house her parents had bought more than twenty years before. The real front door was upstairs, an elegant portal of carved mahogany and beveled glass; her own discreet entrance went unsuspected even by Jehovah's Witnesses. Her first winter on the Vineyard she had done almost no entertaining. It wasn't just that, as her mother was forever telling her, she was a hopeless cook, though this was true: she'd rather give a speech to five hundred than prepare dinner for four any day of the week. She was also afraid to let anyone see where she lived. At twenty-six she'd been making enough in the ad biz to have her own apartment in Brooklyn, and here she was three years later, getting paid peanuts by the *Chronic Tightwad* and living almost rent-free in a house owned by her parents. Can you spell "L-O-S-E-R"?

Pretty soon she'd caught on that on Martha's Vineyard this was no big deal. Scruffy just-folks carpenters turned out to have MBAs from Harvard; farmhands working for not more than minimum wage built houses in nice subdivisions with money from the family trust. Besides, the housing situation was so absurd that hardly anyone ever looked a gift horse in the mouth. People who spent the summer in tents were grateful if the tent didn't leak, and if it came with access to someone's outdoor shower, so much the better. If you lucked into a cheap year-round deal with a view of the water—count your blessings, and don't rock the boat.

What nagged at her these days wasn't her living situation, it was her job. The problem was that she loved it. Worse, she was good at it; as a copywriter for the ad agency, she'd been a rising star, but she'd come to loathe most of the clients so passionately that she could barely drag herself out of bed in the morning. Well, duh: writing clever one-liners and developing ad campaigns had never been her supreme goal in life, but she'd wanted to be a reporter since she was picked to be editor in chief of the fifth-grade newspaper.

"Reporter," however, was absolutely the last thing that David Benaron's eldest daughter could sensibly aspire to be. By the time Leslie graduated from high school, her father was widely acknowledged one of the most eminent journalists in the country. He might not be a celebrity on the order of Bob Woodward, Studs Terkel, or the late I. F. Stone, but in households that watched *Meet the Press* and *Firing Line*, that read the *Washington Post* or kept up with foreign affairs or health issues, his name was well known and highly respected. Wherever she lived, wherever she worked, Leslie was approached by pleasant middle-aged women who wanted her father to give a guest lecture, contribute an autographed book to a fundraising auction, or judge an essay contest at the high school. She gave his office phone number to all who asked, knowing that Catherine Lee, his office manager, editor, and social secretary, would decline most of the requests with unfailing tact. Only her newspaper colleagues and her favorite sources, like Chief Tay, got to spend quality time with David Benaron, and that mostly in the summer, when her mother did the cooking.

She let herself into the apartment. Gradually her ears adjusted enough to pick up the purr of the refrigerator in the kitchen, which was separated from the dining-living area by a long counter. A flick of the door-side switch lit the pole lamp by the sofa and the table lamp in the corner, which revealed all the clutter she had closed the door on that morning: the *Boston Globe* and the *New York Times* strewn across the coffee table, garnished by a half-empty mug and a plate with a smear of raspberry jam on the side and a knife lying across it. She dumped bag and jacket onto the wingback chair next to the phone, noticing in the process the red "4" on the answering machine. Hitting the Messages button, she set about straightening the papers.

"HelLO, Leslie, it's me, Roger. Did you guess? I'll try you at the paper."

Beeeep.

A story on the front page of the *Globe* business section caught her eye: NANTUCKET EXPLORES AFFORDABLE HOUSING. Affordable for whom? Bill Gates? But she folded the section and set it aside to be studied later.

"Hi, Les, it's your hypertensive dad calling . . . "

She stopped rustling newspapers.

"I am planning on coming down this weekend. Things are—a little tense up this way. Can you meet me at the airport at four p.m. Friday? Leave a message with Catherine, would you please? I hope this doesn't throw a monkey wrench in your plans."

Beeeep.

Plans? Oh, you mean the hot sex-and-cocaine orgy I had planned for Saturday night! So her mother was on the warpath and her father was ready to get out of Dodge for the duration? Even though he was barely back from San Francisco? What had set Mom off this time?

She continued on her way to the kitchen, put mug, plate, and knife in the sink, grabbed the kettle off the stove, and held the spout under the faucet.

"Hi, Leslie, this is Marian McKern. I'm the new chair of the League's media task force, and we were wondering if you might be willing to speak at one of our meetings. We have quite a few new members who have little experience dealing with the press, even the island press, and I thought you would be the perfect person to explain the whys and wherefores. I'm sorry we can't offer an honorarium, just coffee and cookies, but I hope we'll be able to arrange a date."

Beeeep.

Marian, you call me "perfect" and I'll speak for nothing; I'd offer to bring cookies, but they'd probably break your teeth. Marian McKern had to be new to the Vineyard; only a recent arrival would apologize for not offering money.

Beeeep.

Caller number four was a hang-up. Leslie set the kettle on the lighted burner, and opened the freezer. The freezer contained an automatic ice maker and enough frozen dinners to warm a survivalist's heart—if the survivalist were into Weight Watchers and if electricity could be expected to survive whatever apocalypse the survivalist was waiting for. Leslie pulled eggplant parmesan from the bottom of one stack and stuck it in the oven.

So her father was coming down for the weekend. Good. That made it easier to deflect whatever fantasy Roger had about a weekend date. David rarely got in his daughter's way—he eschewed the inside staircase that led from the main house kitchen down to her apartment, and instead came around outside like any other visitor. This weekend she was far more likely to be bugging him, soliciting his input in the Chase Case. Maybe he'd have some tips on how to trick Zip-Lips Segredo into stretching his professional scruples. *Sophie Everett, I've got to call Sophie Everett.* It was ten minutes past seven: twenty more minutes and she would try.

After retrieving her notebook from her leather bag, she went around the corner and down the hall to her office, where her PC's screen saver was tirelessly cycling through Vineyard sunsets, Vineyard meadows, Vineyard stone walls, Vineyard beaches, and Vineyard boats. In daylight the view through the glass slider rivaled any of these: sparkling in the sun, Lake Tashmoo filled the window, framed by grass on the bottom, pines on either side, and the opposite shore at the top. Across this shimmering canvas, the occasional boat would glide, bright-sailed Sunfish, silent kayaks, business-like Boston Whalers. At night scattered lights from the houses across the water reassured her that other humans were not that far away.

Now she started Word and did some stretches while it loaded: reach for the ceiling, bend right, bend left, touch toes, stretch up, twist right, twist left. *I should join the health club, I should do Jazzercise, I should ride my bike to work . . .*

She sat down, propped her notebook open, and started transcribing the notes from her interview with Nick McAuliffe. As usual, she typed the direct quotes strictly from her scribbles. Important points and follow-up questions were bolded, which yielded this list when she was done:

CASH TRANSACTION—how? oversight?
WHERE IS ALICE??
Meg Hasbro, Burnham & W. Involvement???
JAY
"friends among the rats"?
fucked-up island wiring job—bldg. insp.? renovations?

While her printer was cleaning its print head and otherwise psyching itself up to spit out the list, she logged on to her ISP then went to fix herself some peppermint tea. With the steaming mug beside her she did a Web search on "Nick McAuliffe". She skimmed his publisher's press kit and interviews from three different newspapers, then noted that her computer's status bar was informing her that it was 8:16 PM: it was fast approaching the hour that it would be too late to call Sophie Everett. She logged off and dialed the Everetts' number. The girl who answered called out, "Mo-o-om? It's for you!"

"Hello?"

"Hi, Sophie? It's Leslie, from the *Chronicle*."

"Oh, hello." Sophie Everett sounded a little flustered. Maybe she hadn't expected Leslie to return her call? "This may not be anything important, but—it's just that, well, Don and I were talking this noon—we can't believe that anyone set the fire."

Leslie grabbed for her notebook and opened it to the next clean page. At the top she wrote: "S. Everett, 4/20 eve."

"Don used to go up there and help out from time to time. Replacing a shingle here and there, rehanging a door that wasn't plumb, that kind of thing."

"Yeah, I know," Leslie murmured.

"He said the wiring in that place was really old. Alice got a little space heater—it blew a fuse. Last summer when it was so hot she got an air conditioner for her son's bedroom—it blew a fuse too, and that was the same circuit that the washer and dryer were on, so it should have been able to deal with a small air conditioner. What we mean is, no one had to set that fire. It could have just happened."

"I know what you mean," said Leslie. "Know what my editor said? He thinks it was a, quote, 'typical fucked-up wiring job.'"

Sophie's voice was smiling. "Don's seen some of them. Some guys can't admit they can't do it themselves."

"Don't I know how that works," Leslie said. "You think Zack Butler's the kind of guy who would have done it himself?"

"Did you ever meet him? Heart of gold, he'd give his last cent to help you out if he thought you deserved it, but he could be downright ornery when it came to hiring people to do things. All these young wash-ashores lived for one reason only: to part him from his hard-earned money. Plumbers, electricians . . . Zack didn't trust a one of them. Once Don told Zack he'd help install a couple of windows, and they were talking about how to do it, and all of a sudden Zack clammed up and just stared. Then he said, 'What you gonna charge me?' Don said, 'Who said anything about charging? I'm not gonna charge you one red cent.' Zack stopped staring and started acting like himself. Don said, 'How 'bout you take me out fishing one day during the derby?' Zack said, 'Deal.'" Sophie laughed. "I'll never forget it."

"Sophie," Leslie said, "you have been a major help. Have you said anything to the police?"

Pause. "You think we should?"

Leslie thought fast. "I'll be talking to Chief Tay tomorrow. I'll pass it along if you want."

"That would be great."

"Thanks again," said Leslie. "If the chief says anything, I'll let you know." She hung up and punched in Shannon's number. Shannon, who was always saying, "I haven't been here all that long," though she'd lived here at least twenty years and wormed her way into the confidence of people who'd been here a lot longer. She was probably on a first-name basis with Zack Butler.

Shannon's answering machine picked up: "You have reached the number for Pixel Productions and Shannon Merrick . . ." A live voice interrupted: "Don't hang up, Les, I'm here."

"You got Caller ID!" Leslie gasped.

"Couldn't help it," said Shannon, sounding almost embarrassed. "Brother Logan has fallen off the wagon, and he's calling me every other minute—like he can find my number when he's sober? When it's not him, it's one of his kids or his wife wanting to know where he is."

"You're so sympathetic."

"Yeah, well, when last heard from, Margaret was shipping back the unopened box of Christmas presents I sent my nephew and niece, telling me I was 'bad seed' and if I tried to contact the kids, she'd get a restraining order. That was a year and, what, four months ago. So," Shannon said, with a quick shift of gears, "what can I do for you?"

"You e-mailed me."

"I'm dying to find out how it went on your hot date with the famous author."

"What *is* your problem? Don't you understand the concept of a business engagement?" Once again Leslie had gone from totally cool to nearly losing it in about five seconds. Why did Shannon have this effect on her?

"Uh-oh . . ." Shannon lowered her voice: "Is he there now?"

Leslie slammed down the receiver. In fifteen seconds the phone rang. Leslie took very deep breaths while it rang a second, third, and fourth time, then she answered.

"I'm sorry," said Shannon. "Mars is in the sign of Bitch."

So what else is new?

"I really do want to know how it went. His book's OK—did you get my e-mail?"

"Yeah," Leslie said. "I stopped by the paper on my way home. Mr. McAuliffe gave me my very own personally autographed copy—which I think I left in the car. Should I bother?"

"Yeah," said Shannon. "I'm already halfway through it. I'd be finished already but Pix and I went tick collecting at Waskosim's Rock. Tell whoever's on the tick beat this year that we're looking at a bumper crop. Well, in my humble opinion Georgia Duvall—that's the protagonist—is really a George in drag, but the author couldn't figure out how to have a heroic *male* lawyer-sleuth stow away on a luxury yacht as a cocktail waitress."

"Where've you been for the last decade, Merrick?" Leslie demanded. "Hard-boiled female sleuths are very 'in'—de rigueur even." She called her interview notes back up on the computer screen.

"Benaron, you really do have an impressive vocabulary," Shannon said. "I wouldn't dare try to pronounce 'de whatever-it-is' out loud."

"What's the matter, did I say it wrong?"

"Hell no. That's exactly the way my favorite French teacher said it, the one I had the horrible crush on freshman year of high school."

Leslie relaxed. "Sometimes it does help to have a father who hobnobs with members of the Académie Française. Speaking of Dad, he's coming down this weekend. You interested in a free dinner at a chi-chi restaurant? No promises, of course—I don't know for sure that he'll offer, but from the message he left I guess things are tense at home. Domestic untranquillity always makes him generous abroad." *You do turn a nice phrase, Benaron,* she thought, *when you put your mind to it.*

Shannon chuckled. "I don't know what the weekend will bring," she said, "but do keep me in mind."

"Will do. Meanwhile—damn, I think my eggplant parmesan is incinerating in the oven. Gotta go—bye!"

Leslie dispatched the certified low-cal, low-fat dinner in less than half the time it took to heat it. The food sitting heavily in her stomach, she pondered, not for the first time, the best way to reach her father. The fastest way was to call home. To call home was to risk the statistically daunting possibility that her mother would answer the phone. To reduce this chance to zero she would have to call Dad's office and leave a message. When he was home, he generally checked his office messages two or three times a night.

Obviously this was the way to go. She put the aluminum foil dish aside and set the phone on her knees. She dialed. The voice-mail system picked up, featuring the suave, smoky voice of the indispensable Catherine. "Hi, Catherine," said Leslie. "Hi, Dad! Got your e-mail and your phone message. I've got time this weekend, it'll be great to see you. I'm working on a story about a guy who used to work for *The Asclepius Report*—Nick McAuliffe. Ring any bells? He knows your name, that's for sure. He wrote a best-selling novel, a thriller, *Devoted to Her Duty,* so he doesn't work for the medicos anymore. If I don't hear from you, I'll be at the airport at four p.m. Meanwhile—Catherine, give each of the cats a good scritch from me, and Dad, see you this weekend. Over and out!"

Slowly Leslie returned the receiver to its cradle. Her reflection gazed back from the glass of the slider: she looked like midnight and it was barely nine o'clock. Too late to run up to Cronig's for a pint of Ben & Jerry's; too early to go to bed. She could start working on the fire story. She could add a little to the tennis court story. It was still early enough to return phone calls, but she didn't want to talk to Quincy Hancock the Third.

She got up and headed for the kitchen, to pour herself a glass of wine and waste what remained of the evening watching TV.

CHAPTER EIGHT

Shannon pulled, pushed, and shook the sleep sofa back into its daytime position then piled the not so carefully folded sheets and comforters at one end. The room was beginning to look like her office again: computer on its desk just to the right of the picture window, crammed floor-to-ceiling bookshelves within easy reach of anyone sitting at the keyboard, purple and green plaid sofa under the window and worktable on the far side of that. She dragged the coffee table back into place. Almost back to normal—if one overlooked the heap of bed linens, and the baseball glove, bike helmet, and Boston Bruins sweatshirt on the worktable. Shannon overlooked it all. It was only till Saturday; she could overlook anything that long.

Her eyes cut to the left and stalled at the studio door. A door like every other door in the house: plain pine stained to look like oak, with a brass-colored knob. Unlike any other door in the house, it was locked. The key hung in the mud room on a key-shaped rack, along with the front-door key, the key to the unfinished walk-in basement, and a spare car key. The studio key was attached to a green plastic tag.

Alice came out of the guest room smoothing her dress with both hands. "Do I look OK?" she asked.

She was wearing a gray wool jumper over a light blue blouse, a black belt, black tights, and black low-heel pumps—no sneakers today, and no ponytail. Her light brown hair was brushed back and held in place with a gray headband that matched her dress, and she had even used a little eyeshadow, a lipstick only a shade darker than her lips. Shannon, in black denims, burgundy turtleneck, and gray herringbone jacket, felt slovenly. "You look like you're ready to interview for president of the bank," she said.

Alice glowed with pleasure. Very unusual for Alice.

Ten minutes later, after Shannon had coaxed Pixel out of the woods, tied her up, and told her that they really weren't going anywhere fun, she and Alice were on their way to their rendezvous with the chief of police.

Old County Road was not one of the Vineyard's more interesting routes, except when the leaves started turning in the fall and when the trees started to leaf out in the spring. What Shannon called the "feeling of green" had begun, though actual leaves were not in evidence. In any season Old County Road had the virtue of being the shortest distance between the Edgartown–West Tisbury Road, which ran straight east–west along the southern base of the island, and State Road, which came up from the island's southwestern-most point in Gay Head and meandered in a more or less northeasterly direction until it reached Vineyard Haven. Shannon and Alice rolled along in silence until the West Tisbury School slipped by on their left. Then Alice asked, "What do you think he'll ask?"

"How long you lived in the Butler house," Shannon replied. "When you left. Did you ever meet Nick McAuliffe. I hear he made a total fool of himself at the fire, by the way," she added. "Very bad first impression for the police chief, the fire chief, and a reporter from the *Martha's Vineyard Chronicle.*"

Alice glanced quickly over at Shannon. "This is going to be in the papers?"

"Yeah," said Shannon. "Unless the Steamship Authority cuts its fares in half, the fire is probably going to be the big story of the week." She stopped herself before she could go on:

If you want to talk to the paper, the reporter covering the story is a friend of mine. Today she was Alice's Advocate, not Leslie's Source.

"Oh, great," said Alice. "Lenny'll hear that I've been charged with burning down Uncle Zack's house, and he'll actually manage to *show up* at the hearing, and what judge is going to grant custody to someone who sets fire to houses?" She stared through the windshield, her hands clasped tight together and pressed against her lips.

"The police don't think the fire was set," Shannon said, hoping she was right. "That's what we're going to straighten out. And I bet we can keep your name out of the papers." *Did I really just say that?*

"I hope so," said Alice. Slowly her clenched hands returned to her lap and began to relax.

The Subaru was already rolling down the long hill into Vineyard Haven; Shannon turned left onto Main Street then took the right that led into the A&P parking lot. The parking lot was Vineyard Haven's closest thing to a town square, an asphalt "green" that sloped from Main Street—barely glimpsed between the backsides of its shops—down to the harbor. Three columns of parked cars sloped along with it, and Shannon counted herself lucky to find an empty slot in the first row. "Good omen," she said. Alice managed a small smile.

The Tisbury police station was new, and only a few diehard grumblers denied that it was an improvement on the old, a small, shabby shingled structure that still stood at the head of the parking lot. No one claimed it was a work of art: the graceless gray building looked like three cheap suburban town houses smooshed together. Shannon pointed to the big window on the right end of the second floor, above the oversized garage bay that housed one of the town ambulances. "That's the chief's office," she said, opening the door. The key buzzed in the ignition. "We're right on time."

"No. Wait." Alice was looking at the station's entrance, at

the man who stood lighting a cigarette as the door closed behind him. "It's him."

"Huh?" It took Shannon a moment. "Oh," she said, closing her door carefully, as if to avoid being heard. "Oh."

Nick McAuliffe, in the same trench coat and tweed walking cap he'd been wearing yesterday, pocketed his lighter and took a long drag off his cigarette. He consulted his watch, glanced right and left, then started straight toward them.When he reached the center lane of the parking lot, separated from them by ten feet and a compact red Dodge pickup, he hung a sharp left and headed down the row. *Maybe he's going over to the newspaper office?* Shannon wondered. Would Mr. Best-Seller recognize her from that one brief but close encounter at the *Chronicle* office? Probably not, but she wasn't taking any chances. She watched a young man and a young woman, both wearing daypacks, cross the open space and disappear past the A&P. An old golden retriever followed at a distance. It stopped by the benches outside the supermarket door to root around for dropped cookies and potato chips.

"There he is," said Alice, facing front. Looking like a Matchbox car, the red Mercedes convertible with the top down moved slowly up the middle lane of the parking lot, Nick McAuliffe at the wheel. It turned left and passed behind them. The two women watched it pause then make the right onto Water Street.

Shannon counted: "One one thousand, two one thousand, three one thousand . . ." Alice twisted in her seat to survey the parking lot's several entrances. "Ten one thousand," said Shannon. "All clear?"

"Yeah," said Alice.

"Ready?"

"Let's go."

They walked briskly, with feigned nonchalance, to the police station. Shannon held the door, then let it close behind them. She couldn't help peering over her shoulder and through the glass. No red Mercedes, no tweed-capped novelist. She told the officer at the desk that they had an appointment with the chief. He asked after Pixel, then told them to go on up.

Chief Francis was the perfect gentleman. He offered them coffee but recommended against drinking it; the bottled water in the corner dispenser was much safer, he said. He had a bowl of M&Ms on his desk. Alice wasn't sure it was all right to help herself, but when he nudged the bowl toward her, she took one. Then he asked her questions about how long she'd been in the Butler house, how she had come to live there, and what had happened since the house was sold last October. She got flustered once and apologized for being so bad with dates, but he didn't seem to mind. He even apologized for asking the question she and Shannon had been waiting for: "Just for the record, Ms. Chase—and please understand that I'm not asking this because I think you've broken any laws—would you tell me what you did last Sunday?"

With Shannon filling in the occasional time and detail, Alice recounted their pancake breakfast, their walk to Sepiessa Point, their afternoon hanging out at Shannon's house. The chief made a few notes but asked no follow-up questions. Shannon and even Alice relaxed.

Before they left his office, the police chief thanked Alice for coming down and assured both women that his men had turned up no evidence that the house fire was anything but accidental. "Between you and me," he said, "I don't expect them to. Arson is much more common on television than it is in real life. Which, come to think of it, shouldn't be too surprising, because it's difficult to make a thriller out of bad wiring."

"Unless it's your house," said Shannon.

"Very, very true, Ms. Merrick," the chief agreed.

Shannon suppressed a smile. Alice asked if there was a ladies' room on this floor. The chief escorted them to the door of his office and pointed down the hall. Alice struck off on her own. "FYI, Chief," said Shannon, "Alice and Mitch will be moving this Saturday, to Randall and Kate Hammond's."

The chief beamed. "Fine people," he said.

"Mitch was pretty impressed with Randy's computer setup. I think that's what clinched the deal. But—" She peered at the chief, one eye closed, the other wide open.

He peered back at her, both eyebrows raised. "Yes, Ms. Merrick?"

"Alice is a little uneasy. The Hammonds live in Oak Bluffs. Alice used to live in Oak Bluffs. Lenny Chase still lives in Oak Bluffs, and not far from the Hammonds either."

"The whereabouts of Ms. Chase and her son will be held in strict confidence," promised the chief. "I'll let Ms. Montrose and her crew decide who needs to know what."

"I do appreciate it," said Shannon, then paused. "One other thing," she added. "Wayne Swanson."

"For a pillar of the community, Ms. Merrick, you do know some unsavory characters."

"It's not me, Chief—it's my *friends*." Shannon grinned. *Me, a pillar of the community? Three generations of Merricks would split a gut at the very idea.* "It occurred to me that Mr. Swanson might be expected back any time now, since it's been about six months since—"

"Time does fly," said Chief Tay, shaking his head. "Just between us, if you will"—he glanced at her; she responded with a nod of her head—"the matter came up in a casual conversation yesterday morning with, hmm, a colleague of one of Mr. Swanson's former relatives?"

"Gerbil Turd," Shannon blurted, before she could stop herself.

The chief guffawed. Then he carefully composed his face. "You didn't hear that, did you?" he asked.

"Not a sound," said Shannon.

"The long and short is that Mr. Swanson is expected back any day."

"Thanks a lot, Chief," Shannon said. "You've been a great

help."

"A pleasure, as always. Speaking of which, the long-range weather forecast is for hot-fudge sundae weather toward the end of the week."

"I'll give you a call." She was still grinning as she stepped out into the hallway, and she heard Tay Francis chuckling as he closed the door behind her.

Burnt-toast smell enveloped Leslie at the door to the *Chronicle* office, and under it the faint scent of impending deadline. Fortunately, it being Tuesday, the deadline belonged to the features section: Chet and his reporters had another twenty-four hours before they parachuted into Hades with seven hours to find their way home. Of course Chet's pet—Steve DeKuyper, who always filed his stories early—was typing away, his shoulder hunched up to secure his phone receiver against his ear. The art director was sitting at the production manager's terminal, with Natalie the features editor standing behind her; Squirrel the Proofreader stood by the copy baskets, either asleep on his feet or unable to remember what he was going to do next. Chet's yuppie pickup truck, a gray behemoth with fog lights, roll bar, V-8 engine, and extended cab, was in the lot; he might be upstairs or he might be schmoozing Steamship Authority bureaucrats over breakfast at the Black Dog. Leslie turned her computer on and punched in the number sequence that retrieved her phone messages.

There weren't many, and none were from her father or Catherine; all but one had to do with Quincy Hancock III's tennis courts. She really did have to call him back, find out what was going on, but his stupid floodlights were nowhere as interesting as possible arson, a desperate single mother, and a famous novelist who used to flack for Big Health. Unfortunately, unless a big apple fell into her lap, this would be no more than spot news for this week; without a decent photograph, it might not even make the front page. Leslie dialed Chief Francis's private number at the police station; the department secretary picked up and said he was in a meeting. Fire chief Slater Robinson wasn't available either; it wasn't critical enough to warrant paging him through the county communications center, so she left a message on his voicemail. Leslie tried the Tisbury building inspector's office. Wonder of wonders, he picked up the phone himself. He confirmed that all permits were in order for the renovations at Nick McAuliffe's house; no inspections had been conducted because the work had just started, and if Ms. Benaron had any questions about the cause of the fire, she would have to speak to the fire chief and the police chief. She pulled her notebook out of her shoulder bag and extracted from it her list of questions:

CASH TRANSACTION—how? oversight?
WHERE IS ALICE??
Meg Hasbro, Burnham & W. Involvement???
JAY
"friends among the rats"?
fucked-up island wiring job—bldg. insp.? renovations?

She made a checkmark by the last entry on the list, then got up and went over to Alan Duarte's roost in Golden Gooseland. "Alan," Leslie whispered, "who do you know in the registry of deeds?"

He grinned at her. "Everybody," he whispered back, "starting with my Aunt Carla. What do you want?"

"A check on a property transfer from last October."

He pushed a memo pad at her. "Write it down. I'll take care of it."

She wrote: "Zack Butler to Nick McAuliffe—Tisbury— October. Price? Mortgage? Co-owners?"

"I'll buzz you," he promised.

In the middle of the office Laura the production manager was having an animated discussion with a stocky, dark-bearded guy in a red-and-black buffalo plaid jacket. From the

35mm camera slung over his right shoulder, Leslie inferred that he was a photographer. From Laura's harried expression, Leslie inferred that she needed relief. "What have you got?" Leslie asked.

A beat behind, Laura asked, "Have we got anything about a house fire for this week?"

"Yes!" Leslie almost shrieked. "You've got pictures of the fire? Sunday night, the Butler house, off Lambert's Cove Road?"

"Not the fire exactly," said the guy, whose melodic tenor clashed with his unlyrical lumberjack appearance. "I have the cops and the insurance people going through the ruins yesterday morning. They're pretty good shots."

"I want them," Leslie told Laura. She asked the photographer, "You got prints? Who are you? This may be the difference between a front-page story and a squib that gets buried on page eight!"

"Glad to be of service. I'm Chris Almeida. Regional high school class of '88. My parents live in Edgartown. I work for a paper you never heard of in western Pennsylvania. My dad always has the scanner on . . ." He shrugged.

"I love you!" said Leslie.

To celebrate, Leslie slung on her coat and headed up to Main Street. She didn't even tell her colleagues where she was going: she wanted a double dose of the Get a Life Café's pricey but excellent vanilla hazelnut coffee and she wanted it now.

Two grizzled carpenters sat smoking at a table outside the café. In Leslie's opinion it was far too chilly for coffee drinking al fresco, especially since one of the guys was only wearing a T-shirt. The other one eyed her with tentative interest. She ignored him.

Inside, she ordered a large coffee and a poppyseed bagel with cream cheese. Only after filling her cup and spritzing it with half-and-half did she notice that the woman sitting with her back to the window at the table just left of the front door was Shannon. For Main Street, Vineyard Haven, on a Tuesday morning, Shannon looked positively *neat.* Nowhere near as presentable, though, as her companion, who was wearing, believe it or not, a *dress.* A dress and *heels.* Well, well, well, thought Leslie; welcome to the secret life of Shannon the Recluse.

Leslie stopped at Shannon's table on the way out. This, she realized immediately, was a mistake: the other woman couldn't have been more than thirty (Shannon had been heard to swear that she never had and never would sleep with any woman more than five years her junior), and the space between them felt more like counseling than romance. The young woman was gazing awkwardly at her half-eaten square of coffee cake. *An AA newbie, or maybe the wife of one?* Shannon was friendly enough, but she didn't introduce her companion. "Back to tracking down the police chief, the fire chief, and the real estate agent for my fire story," said Leslie. "Looks like it'll be page one: a photographer just came in literally off the street, and it turned out he was up there yesterday shooting the cops sifting through the rubble. Can you believe it? Not only that, the pics are excellent."

"See?" Shannon raised her eyebrows. "The newspaper gods *are* looking after you."

"Don't I wish." Leslie rolled her eyes. "If they really liked me, Alice Chase would be waiting when I get back to the office."

"Hey, maybe she is," Shannon said.

It was not quite noon, and Shannon had the house to herself. She also had a new job to get into, so she'd lent Alice the car to get to a cleaning job and then pick Mitch up at the end of the school day. Now she felt trapped. If the car had been here, she would have taken Pixel for a walk in the state forest. Starting a new job was a bitch. It always took a couple of hours to study the computer files, read and reread the written specs, and begin to suss out what the client wanted. To make matters worse, this was a new client. It usually took two or three jobs before she could read a client's mind.

Procrastination said she needed coffee. She went to the kitchen to brew a fresh pot.

As the tantalizing scent started to waft through the house, she sat cross-legged on the sofa and flipped through several of the new client's recent publications: an annual report, an employee handbook, two promotional brochures, and a hefty training manual for new supervisors. Individually each one was OK, but as a group? You'd never know they were put out by the same company. So. Evidently she was supposed to come up with a design that was consistent with all of its mutually exclusive predecessors but looked "fresh." Everyone wanted "fresh," no one wanted "original." Not for the first time Shannon considered going back to slinging hash in summer, scalloping in winter, and giving up this nutty idea of a career in freelance graphic design and illustration.

She went to the kitchen, poured herself a mug of coffee, and returned to the sofa, grabbing a short stack of scrap paper en route. She laid the five publications side by side on the coffee table, considered them one at a time, then rearranged them so that the two brochures and the employee handbook were in the middle. Dollars to doughnuts they'd been designed by the same person. She hoped their designer hadn't been canned in disgrace. Could this person be reached? Why wasn't he or she doing *this* job? Probably because he or she had come in with a bid that was fifty percent higher than that of Pixel Productions.

She caught herself staring at the locked studio door, staring till her eyes began to water. Procrastination slipped a no. 2 pencil into her hand. Without thinking Shannon started sketching on the top sheet of scrap paper: a reasonable representation of the door, lit by early afternoon sun through the picture window behind her. Idly she sketched a question mark that filled two-thirds of the door. Hmm. She glanced at the door. She glanced back to the paper. She imprisoned the question mark behind bars. The question mark grew hands, which clasped the bars in poignant desperation.

Poignant, hell. Biggest cliché in the book: prisoner looks pathetic but is guilty as sin.

Shannon smashed the paper into a ball, tossed it over the coffee table, and confronted the next blank sheet. This time she started with the bars: horizontal at the top, horizontal at the bottom, six verticals from one side of the page to the other. *What's on the other side?* It took serious effort to bring it to mind: A six-over-six window on the short side and a long picture window on the other, light pouring in from the skylight overhead. Shelves, many shelves; shelves containing paper of all sizes and textures, paints, watercolors, pencils of many colors. Her own paintings hung on the walls, matted and framed: good paintings, technically proficient paintings, even salable paintings, and none of them less than six years old.

She sketched a paintbrush slithering up one of the bars, like a snake. She sketched another paintbrush slithering down, two bars over.

On the other side, Spanish moss hung so heavily that chunks of ceiling had collapsed from the weight, knocking easels sideways to the floor. Concealed beneath the moss was a faceless marauder who had come to steal the miserable paintings, to take them to a great convocation of Family Merrick, the dead as well as the living, who had gathered to rule on the question RESOLVED: That Shannon Merrick should be drawn and quartered, tarred and feathered, and burned at the stake for presuming to think she has any artistic aptitude whatsoever. . . .

"Giles, I'm going nuts." She had managed to pull the phone to her lap and dial Giles's number; Giles had actually answered the phone.

"I doubt *that,* girlfriend," he said. "What's up?"

"I'm sitting on the sofa. I'm supposed to be working. I'm drawing pictures of my studio door." *And hallucinating some kind of bayou*—"If the ceiling had fallen in, I'd know it, right?"

"Is there a draft coming from under the door?"

"Uh—no."

"Did you notice a suspicious hole in the roof the last time you were outside?"

She actually paused to think. "No."

"Then you're probably OK. So what do your pictures look like?"

"A jailhouse window."

"What media?"

Shannon barked out a sarcastic laugh. "Media? You're kidding, right?"

"No, dumkopf," Giles said patiently. "I'm asking what you're making the picture with."

"A number two pencil that needs sharpening. On a piece of beige scrap paper—" she turned the top sheet over "—a flier left over from a panel discussion I was on at the high school in January."

"Scrap paper? Why are you drawing on scrap paper? Get a sketch pad!"

Shannon stared uncomfortably at her lap. She wasn't going to admit that her sketch pads were behind the locked door and she didn't have nerve to bust them out.

After a very long silence, Giles said, "I get it. Listen, Shan: remember what I told you that insufferably hot morning last August when we were sitting on the porch at Alley's drinking Orangina?"

Shannon logged on to her mind, but the connection was slow: 14.4Kbps at most. "Refresh my memory," she said.

"We were talking about Step Three, 'Made a decision to turn our will and our lives over to the care of God *as we understood Her.*'"

She grinned in spite of herself: Giles used God language reluctantly, and only if he could change the pronouns. He liked making the old-timers sputter. "Now that you mention it, I think I do remember. You had the hots for a Brazilian guy who was biking to Gay Head with his girlfriend."

"We were talking about *painting*," he said sternly. "I said it wasn't about *making* yourself paint, it was about *letting* yourself paint. This is great, girlfriend. You're letting yourself sketch!"

"Yeah," Shannon muttered, "paintbrush snakes climbing up and down a jailhouse window. Very exciting."

"See where it goes, OK? Just keep doing it. The door is your kaleidoscope. Watch it, sketch it, see what happens."

"What happens when I start hearing voices? I think the Grand Inquisitor is walking up my front steps. Maybe I should run down to the office supply store—"

"No!" Giles roared.

In the aftermath of that explosion the house grew so silent that Shannon could hear the whirring of her computer's fan.

Giles giggled. "You still there?"

"Yeah." Shannon looked at the phone in her hand. "I think you blew out my eardrum."

"Doubt it, girlfriend. Tell you what: You sketch a little bit every day, on scrap paper, brown paper bags, pillowcases, shingles, whatever you want. Sketch for thirty days in a row, one day at a time, and I'll give you a special present."

"What kind of special present?" she asked suspiciously.

"Don't ask, don't tell," he reprimanded her. "On the twenty-ninth day you can ask what the present is, if you still want to know. All right?"

"All right," she said.

With a firm "Good!" he hung up the phone. Once upon a time she'd promised her first sponsor that she wouldn't drink for thirty days, one day at a time. That was, what? Nine years and fourteen days ago—but who was counting?

What the hell had Giles gotten her into?

CHAPTER NINE

Wednesday, deadline day: 8:25 a.m. Leslie Benaron stepped through the door, hoping for a half hour's uninterrupted work time before things got crazy. An irate voice had already taken over the newsroom, expounding to Diane on the conspiracy among the finance committees in the six island towns to conceal the details of the regional high school budget. Leslie thanked God that she'd managed to avoid the education beat the last time it was up for grabs. While she stood wondering whether she could sneak to her desk without getting derailed or shot at, Alan Duarte passed by on his way to the bathroom. He rolled his eyes, shrugged his shoulders, said, "Abandon hope, all ye who enter here," and thumped up the stairs.

A hush fell. Leslie made a break for her desk, only to find Chet sitting in her seat, unnoticed by Mr. Irate, waiting for her computer to boot. "I'm too old for this," he whispered, hand over his heart. "My father used to hold court in his office. He'd puff on his pipe and the right-wingers, the left-wingers, and the completely wingless would tell him their ideas in concise grammatical sentences. Not me, oh no. I park my truck, I'm in a good mood—despite the fact it's Wednesday and you and George haven't filed a single story yet—"

"Is this fair?" Leslie protested. "I told you yesterday afternoon you could read the tennis story, even though I was going to add to it, and I did those two shorts you wanted—"

Chet waved his hand. "Don't interrupt when I'm on a roll!

So what do I find on the doorstep but Calvin Chandler, who's waiting to chew me out for a letter in last week's paper. Why does he wait till Wednesday? Why does he blame me for a damn letter? Doesn't he know we print almost every letter we get?"

Leslie stood tapping her toe on the floor. "Chet, you should start smoking a pipe. Grow a beard. Wear tweed jackets with leather patches on the elbows. Make these crazy people come up to your office instead of letting them rant down here."

"You think that would work?"

"Of course it would work. Your father and his father are gazing down from the walls. Even Mr. Irate would mind his manners, right? Down here? Forget it. The newsroom is a chicken coop. Cheep cheep cheep! Squawk squawk squawk! Brings out the worst in everybody."

Chet peered at her hopefully. "You think so?"

"I think so. Now can I have my desk back? I've got work to do."

"Oh, yeah," said the editor in chief, getting to his feet. "Sorry about that. Call Quincy Hancock, will you? He's leaving whiny messages on my voice-mail. 'We've taken the lights *down,* we had no idea . . .' The hell he didn't. Please, Leslie, do me a big favor: call him up and let him whine at you."

"I'll do it, boss," she promised.

"Good girl. Laura knows to put it on page five with that hearing pic we held from last week."

"The Fitch sisters in triplicate glaring at Q.H. Three?"

"That one."

Leslie looked doubtful. "Will the Queen Mother approve?"

"She has already affixed the royal seal," Chet said cheerfully.

"Wise move," said Leslie. The *Chronicle*'s coverage so far had made Quincy Hancock III and his brother-in-law look like idle-rich airheads, which wasn't far from the truth. Poking a little pictorial fun at the Fitch sisters might keep Q.H. from writing another of his windy "I am a victim of great injustice" letters to the editor.

Chet's shadow wasn't going away. "So how about this fire story?"

"I'm working on it—" Leslie was stalling for time. She had calls to make. She had no idea where the damn fire story was going, or where she wanted it to go. Single mother struggles for housing? Best-selling author hits a shoal? If she couldn't find Alice, the whole story might cook down to a generic how-to: "Is Your Home Fire-Safe?" Leslie was beginning to feel nostalgic for the loathsome world of New York advertising, which, when she left it, had seemed like the lowest circle of hell.

"I'm putting it on page one. Guy came in yesterday with a good photo and Laur's done a high-contrasty print—looks good. Buzz me when you're ready, OK?"

"It's a deal," said Leslie. *Now go away.*

The boss went away.

Leslie extracted from her bag her twice-folded list, clipped it to her copyholder, and scowled.

"JAY." No way would Jay Segredo say anything useful in a five-minute phone interview. If she wanted to get something out of Jay, it would require a "deep background" conversation at some discreet location. Should she invite Jay over to meet her father this weekend? Her father would love Jay. On her list she scribbled: "Call J. Dinner?"

WHERE IS ALICE??

The sixty-four-thousand-dollar question. No Alice, no story. Without Alice this was just a house-burns-down story that accidentally wound up on the front page because a visiting photographer was listening to the scanner. Even *with* Alice there might be no story: What if Alice turned out to be a shrew widely suspected of driving her husband to drink and divorce court? But the right Alice, a long-suffering, modest, photogenic Alice . . .

So who might tell her where Alice was? No one at ISS,

that's for sure, especially not Jay or the Women's Resources staff, who were most likely to know. No police officer, no school official, no shrink. Not Shannon Merrick, not in a million years. *Dead ends, dead ends everywhere . . .*

So in one corner Leslie had Alice Chase, single mother struggling to raise her son. In the other corner was Nick McAuliffe, successful novelist. Trouble was, Nick wasn't a promising villain: he was too articulate, too charming, too accustomed to dealing with the press. True, he'd made an ass of himself at the fire, but Leslie couldn't count on him to do that again. Villain, villain, who's got the villain? Who really put Alice out on the street? Her ex was already history, and most people wouldn't think ill of Zack Butler for selling a house that wasn't earning him any money. Eviction proceedings could go on for months, especially where hardship was involved; no judge would have kicked Alice and her son out before the May custody hearing. Alice must have known as much; her caseworkers would have told her. So why did she decide to leave?

Those harassment rumors were looking more and more promising, but the harassment would have to have been major, *really* major, to make anyone jump ship in mid-April.

Leslie focused on her printed list: **"Meg Hasbro, Burnham & W. Involvement???"** Was Meg Hasbro the heavy she was looking for? *Glengarry Glen Ross* flashbacks dancing in her head, she pulled the local phone book out of her top left desk drawer and looked up Burnham and Wood, Real Estate. *Burnham and Wood? Maybe the script was* Macbeth, *with Meg Hasbro starring as Lady M.?* "Out, out, damned Alice"?

Meg Hasbro was slowly pacing a path in the office carpet, the carpet that looked like the spill of the *Exxon Valdez,* waiting for one client to show and another to call. The former wasn't due for another five minutes, but Meg suspected this guy might have a hard time finding his way here from the ferry dock—a journey of perhaps a hundred yards. The latter was

Douglas Trumbull. The message he'd left on her home machine had her counting commission dollars again: his daughter and one of his sons wanted to see the Makonikey house, could he make an appointment for late Friday afternoon or any time Saturday? She'd left a message with his personal secretary: yes! The extended weather forecast looked promising—maybe they could go for a sail?

She gazed out the window at the horseshoe-shaped parking area. A big red insulation truck pulled up and blocked her view; now her transparent reflection stared back at her from the glass. *Lips nuzzle at her neck as firm hands encircle her waist . . .*

She could almost see Douglas Trumbull's handsome face just behind her own.

The phone trilled. She spun and rushed toward it, catching it before the second ring started, primed for Douglas Trumbull's voice.

It wasn't. "This is Leslie Benaron, calling from the *M.V. Chronicle.* May I speak to Meg Hasbro please?"

"This is she," said Meg in her smoky voice, realizing that this was overkill at ten in the morning, especially when the caller was female. "Can I help you?"

"I'm doing a story on the fire last Sunday, at Zack Butler's old house?" the woman began.

That cretin, thought Meg. *Nick McAuliffe, I'll see you in hell.* "Fire?" she said.

"The house Nick McAuliffe bought last October. He says you handled the sale."

You FUCKER. "The property," Meg explained carefully, "was listed with Burnham and Wood. I showed it to Mr. McAuliffe."

"I understand. At the scene Mr. McAuliffe created quite a stir—he wanted the police to arrest someone named Alice Chase. Of course he was obviously distraught—" The voice on the line was a fast-flowing current, rising and falling with the words: a New York voice almost certainly, though not in a caricaturish way.

"I can imagine," said Meg, wishing she were in New York right this minute. "The man can go from half-asleep to full-blown tantrum in about sixty seconds." *Wait a minute, Meg old girl: you're talking to a reporter.* "That's off the record, of course," she said. *Not that I'd mind seeing the truth in print; just don't attach my name to it.*

"Not to worry. So he thought Alice Chase might have been responsible for the fire. The police haven't said for sure that it was arson . . ."

Meg's heart started to beat faster. *But it might have been? What do the police know? What about the neighbors? Has this reporter talked to them? Has she talked to Alice?* Meg fumbled around in her canvas carry-all for a cigarette. Too late she recalled that Andy Burnham, who had sworn to his wife he was quitting, had bummed her last one this morning. "Between you and me, Leslie—it was Leslie, wasn't it?—the wiring in the Butler house was probably done by a contemporary of Thomas Edison. The only room that was up to code was the kitchen. Mr. McAuliffe understood that when he made his offer."

"That seems to be the general consensus," the reporter conceded. Meg breathed a little easier. "My story this week is basically that there was a fire and the firemen put it out. But since the house was owned by Nick McAuliffe, whose first novel has been making such a splash—"

Meg had to interrupt: "Have you read it?"

"Uh, no."

"Do. Read it." Finally Meg's fingers found a crushed pack of Winstons halfway back in her top desk drawer. "Nick McAuliffe may have his faults, but *Devoted to Her Duty* is a very good book." She leaned back in her chair and exhaled a leisurely stream of smoke. Georgia Duvall would be pleased with Meg's magnanimity: Meg replayed in her mind the scene where Georgia told the law firm's senior partners that Damon Castelli would be an excellent choice to defend Senator

Walsh—*"but I, gentlemen, would be better."* As usual Georgia looked a lot like Meg as a young thirty-something.

"I intend to." The voice was smiling. "Alice Chase seems to have been a tenant in the house—"

"I bet Nick didn't say 'tenant,'" Meg said. "I bet he said 'squatter.'" She could almost feel the acid eating away at her tongue.

"Is that what she was, a squatter?" the reporter asked.

Meg dismissed the idea with a grand sweep of her arm. A curly stream of cigarette smoke followed her fingers, hung in the air, and drooped into nothingness. "Mr. McAuliffe"—she pronounced the name with exaggerated care—"doesn't understand the informality of leases and contracts on Martha's Vineyard."

"And Alice was—what? A tenant?"

"A naïve kid who came here just out of high school to wait tables and play on the beach. She fell for a handsome young man from an old island family who, surprise, surprise, turned out to be a garden-variety drunk. The Butlers took pity on her. No one was using the house; Alice and her son needed a place to live."

"So," said the reporter, "Mr. McAuliffe inherited Alice and son. What usually happens in a case like this, when someone sells a house that has tenants in it?"

Abstract procedures were easy: Meg relaxed a little. "Sometimes nothing changes. The buyers don't intend to move in immediately, so they renew the lease. If the rent income has to pay the mortgage, sometimes the rent goes up. If the rent goes up enough, sometimes the tenants decide to leave."

"But in Mr. McAuliffe's case—when I interviewed him yesterday, he said he wanted a place to get away and write. So a year-round tenant wouldn't be part of the game plan. Then what happens?"

So, did he put the make on you too? Meg wondered, and her snide subconscious couldn't resist adding: *And did you succumb?* Of course, for all Meg knew, Leslie Benaron might be an acne-scarred recent college graduate, or a gray-haired teacher supplementing her pension, but it was much more likely that Leslie Benaron's voice belonged to exactly the kind of woman Nick would be interested in: smart, cosmopolitan, sexy in a not-too-threatening way. Meg tapped her cigarette on the edge of her ashtray. "What usually happens," she said, "is that the new owner gives the old tenant written notice. Even if no written lease is in effect, the law requires notice of a month or a full rental period, whichever is longer. I advise new owners to give the old tenants as much time as they can: I don't need to tell you how difficult the housing situation is on Martha's Vineyard." *Meg Hasbro strikes a blow for the ethical reputation of Realtors everywhere.*

"Precisely," said the reporter. "Alice Chase's situation seems to have been especially—challenging."

Meg lit a second cigarette from the butt of its predecessor. "Mr. McAuliffe," she said, "was aware of that. Ms. Chase had a custody hearing scheduled for the middle of January, after which she expected to be able to move off-island with her son. I believe she has family in the New Bedford area. Mr. McAuliffe's notice gave her till the end of January. But the hearing was postponed till the middle of March. Alice's caseworker called Nick; Nick even had lunch with the family court judge. Then the March hearing was postponed till May."

"He said he was beginning to think this might go on forever," Leslie said.

"Exactly," said Meg. Leslie Benaron seemed to understand the situation: thank God for small favors. Meg had had her fill of trust-fund babies who thought that only the poor and downtrodden were subject to economic pressures.

"So why," Leslie asked, "did Alice move out last week?"

Meg's slumbering danger detector snapped to attention. "I wouldn't know," she said. *Aha—she hasn't talked to Alice. If she'd talked to Alice . . . She hasn't talked to Alice. Yet.*

A tall man in khakis and a dark green windbreaker was

standing outside the office door, studying first the real estate section of the *News Beacon* and then the name Burnham & Wood on the plate-glass window. If this wasn't her ten o'clock appointment, Meg's radar skills were slipping. Where was Abby anyway? Miss Third Runner-up was supposed to cover the office from nine to one on Wednesdays. With extravagant waves Meg encouraged the man to come in. He squinted at the door.

"According to Mr. McAuliffe," the reporter was saying, "you were the one who discovered that Alice was gone. Last Wednesday, I believe he said. She was there Monday morning, but she was gone by Wednesday. Is that right?"

If Meg ever saw Nick again, he was dead in the water. "Ms. Benaron, I'm very sorry," she said, hoping she sounded rushed but not too flustered, "but my ten o'clock appointment has just washed up on the porch, and I'm afraid he's going to wash out again if I don't throw him a lifeline." Meg stubbed out her cigarette. "I'm sorry I can't be of more help—" Another frantic wave, and the tall man reached for the door handle and raised both eyebrows. Meg noted how blond the eyebrows were, and even at apogee how far they remained from his receding hairline.

"I understand," the reporter said. "You've been very helpful. Listen, I'd like to ask you a few more questions when you've got a chance—"

"No problem at all. Give me a call." Mr.—Meg glanced down at her desk calendar—Larry Trevira was in the office and apologizing profusely for being late.

Phew! Leslie held the receiver at arm's length, surprised that cigarette smoke wasn't pouring from it. Meg Hasbro sounded like Lauren Bacall on the verge of a nervous breakdown. Was she hiding something? Had she helped drive a single mother and her kid out of their home with summer fast approaching? Leslie drummed her fingers on her desk. Maybe her story was really about the ethical standards of the Vineyard real estate industry. Wouldn't *that* give Chet a heart attack. How much did the *Chronicle* gross each year in real estate advertising? An army of Realtors storming Chet's office . . . And he thought Calvin Chandler was a headache?

Alan Duarte slipped a yellow sheet of paper under Leslie's left elbow. In neat block capitals was printed:

OCTOBER 9
TISBURY, OFF JOHN HOFT RD.
ZACHARY AND RUTH BUTLER TO DUVALL REALTY TRUST,
$190,000.
NO BANK.

Duvall Realty Trust? Leslie stared blankly at Alan. "This was the only transaction for Butler?"

"Sure," said patient Alan, pointing at the paper. "That's the house that burned down Sunday night."

Duvall Duvall Duvall . . . She followed the scent back to the Yankee Clipper. *Oy, what a dumkopf! Georgia Duvall is the heroine of Nick McAuliffe's novel.* "If there's no bank listed, does that mean it was a cash transaction?"

"I think so. There might be other reasons—I'm not a lawyer or a real estate agent, and I would commit hara-kiri before I played either one on TV."

"You're a better man than I, Gunga Din," said Leslie, wallowing in the pleasure of discovery. "I'd grab the part if they paid me enough." Alan returned to his desk; Leslie called up the file with her notes in it, saved it with a new name, and started typing:

Fire claimed a house off Lambert's Cove Road in Tisbury Sunday night, despite the valiant efforts of firefighters from Tisbury, Oak Bluffs, and West Tisbury. The house, a one-story wood structure built in the 1920s, was owned by Nick McAuliffe, whose first novel, *Devoted to Her Duty,* has been riding high on national best-seller lists since its release last fall. It was unoccupied at the time of the fire.

The flames were first spotted by neighbors, who called 911 shortly before 5 p.m. The Communications Center immediately relayed the alarm to the Tisbury fire and police departments. The West Tisbury fire department was called in at 5:20, Oak Bluffs at 5:24. . . .

Leslie punched in the police chief's private number. Chief Tay himself answered with a genial "What may I do for you, Ms. Benaron?"

"I'm finally getting around to the fire story, Chief, and I desperately need an official quote about the cause of the fire—"

"I am glad you asked that question, Ms. Benaron," said the chief. Leslie tucked the receiver between ear and shoulder and positioned both hands above the keyboard. "Several of my men, along with fire chief Slater Robinson and a representative from Vineyard Insurance, spent approximately four hours Monday sifting through the rubble—please do something about that phrase, Leslie, it's a terrible cliché."

"Don't worry, Chief. I'll fix it."

"They found no evidence of arson."

"What would be considered 'evidence of arson'?"

"Residue of gas or explosives, an empty box of matches, any sort of flammable material that would not ordinarily be found in a residential dwelling, that sort of thing. We didn't find anything along those lines."

"Do you have any opinion about the cause of the fire?"

The chief chuckled. "You'll have to get the official statement from Chief Robinson or the insurance lady—"

"Who was . . . ?"

"Melanie Bloch, Vineyard Insurance. Off the record? The house was being renovated. It was not a well-controlled situation."

"I understand," Leslie said. "Also off the record—Don

Everett next door said he went up there several times to help Alice with blown fuses, that sort of thing. The wiring was old."

"No surprises there," said the chief. "And Ms. Benaron?"

"Yes?"

"You won't say anything about those M&Ms, will you? It might give my wife the wrong idea."

"M&Ms?" Leslie asked, wide-eyed. "I don't remember a *thing* about any M&Ms."

"It's a pleasure doing business with you, Ms. Benaron, as usual," said the Tisbury police chief, audibly reassured.

Still smiling, Leslie called Chief Robinson and received complete corroboration of everything the police chief had said. For good measure, she dialed Melanie Bloch: "No evidence of arson, no evidence of negligence," said the insurance agent. "We are working with Mr. McAuliffe to facilitate the processing of his claim." Leslie studied the text on her screen and resumed typing. Paragraphs fell into place like scenery scrolling past a speeding car.

At the scene a distraught Mr. McAuliffe suggested that police question the house's most recent resident in connection with the fire. According to unconfirmed reports, this individual had been employed as a caretaker by the previous owners, Zachary and Ruth Butler. Her current whereabouts are unknown. The Butlers, both lifelong islanders, moved to Maine in 1994. They could not be reached by press time.

"Could not"? *You lazy schmuck, you call yourself a reporter? You don't even know what town they live in.* She went on to quote the fire chief, the police chief, and the insurance agent, none of whom gave any credence to the theory that the fire had been set.

Nick McAuliffe bought the house from the Butlers in

October 1997. According to the register of deeds, the owner of record is the Duvall Realty Trust. Georgia Duvall is the protagonist of Mr. McAuliffe's novel.

Leslie had a moment of vertigo as she realized just how little she knew about real estate. Why would one establish a trust to buy a property rather than buy it as an individual? Tax advantages? Meg Hasbro would probably blow her off if she called back this soon. Should she ask Chet? Cynthia Webster, who handled real estate advertising, might know. Cynthia, unfortunately, was not at her desk. *What's a reporter to do?* If all else failed, she could ask her father this weekend: he knew everything. After rereading her last sentence, she changed "protagonist" to "heroine."

On impulse, she logged on to the newspaper's ISP and headed for a nationwide online phone directory. Under First Name she typed **Zachary** and under Last Name **Butler.** She left Town/City blank and under State she typed **ME.** Then she clicked on Search, closed her eyes, and squeezed her mouse.

The Journalism Gods smiled: apparently there was only one Zachary Butler in the entire state of Maine, and the other name on the listing was Ruth. The address was in Steuben. Leslie jotted the phone number down on the inside cover of her notebook and dialed it. In Steuben, Maine, a phone rang and rang and rang. It did not surprise her that Zack and Ruth Butler did not have an answering machine. She returned to her screen:

At the scene a distraught Mr. McAuliffe suggested that police question the house's most recent resident in connection with the fire. According to unconfirmed reports, this individual had been employed as a caretaker by the previous owners, Zachary and Ruth Butler. Her current whereabouts are unknown. The Butlers, both lifelong islanders, moved to Maine in 1994. They could not be reached by press time.

She highlighted the last sentence in the paragraph and replaced it with

Attempts to reach them by phone at their home in Steuben before press time were unsuccessful.

Did "her current whereabouts are unknown" sound too shady, as if the unnamed tenant were a fugitive from justice? No, the real problem with the wording was that half the population of Martha's Vineyard probably *knew* Alice's whereabouts. Alice's whereabouts were unknown only to *her.* Leslie struck the sentence and then dialed Shannon Merrick's number. Shannon wasn't going to tell her anything; why did she bother? Maybe Chet wouldn't notice that she'd fudged Alice's whereabouts. While the phone rang, she took two very deep breaths.

Shannon was sitting cross-legged at one end of the sofa, staring at the studio door. A sketchpad rested in her lap. It wasn't a great sketchpad—the sheets were almost as flimsy as tracing paper—but it had been on the top shelf of her bedroom closet, and it was better than twenty-pound, eight-and-a-half-by-eleven-inch recycled fliers. Propped at the other end of the sofa was a sketch of the wall opposite, with an imposing portcullis replacing the problematic door. She put the finishing touches on its successor: a hedge of briars had overcome the pale yellow drywall, densely concealing both the door and the framed photographs on either side of it. Sleeping Beauty was lying in wait for her prince on the other side.

Shannon tore that sheet off the pad and laid it gently on the coffee table. She started the next drawing as she had started each of its predecessors: with an architecturally precise sketch of the door. She closed her eyes and squinted at the back of her eyelids; she opened them and stared into the empty space until they began to water. Her left hand smoothed the paper; her right started to move. Robinson Crusoe appeared on the left, long-haired and naked to the waist. His beard was impressive, but his face had no features. The figure on the right started off to be Ichabod Crane with a pumpkin head, but her fingers conjured instead the dipsy freckled face of Alfred E. Neuman, embedded in her subconscious from all the *Mad Magazines* she'd read as a kid. Between them grew a woman in elaborate court dress, vaguely Elizabethan. Her head sat upside down on her neck, with long dark hair spilling down the bodice of her gown.

Anne Boleyn? Weird. Very weird.

Bearing down hard on her soft pencil, she drew in the jailhouse bars. *Whatever lurks behind that door is going to damn well stay there.*

The phone, on the floor within reach of her left hand, started ringing.

It was Leslie. As per custom she began with "I hope I'm not getting you away from anything important."

"Nah," Shannon said. "I was just working. What's up?" *If it doesn't have to do with the fire, I'll—I'll—I'll open that door and walk right into the studio. No, wait: that sounds a little rash. I'll open that door and* look *into the studio.*

"I've got a couple of things," Leslie began. "What do you know about real estate trusts? Like what are the advantages to creating a trust as opposed to buying as an individual."

Uh-oh—maybe she isn't calling to wheedle an introduction to Alice? Shannon glanced uneasily toward the studio door. "Real estate? Trusts?" she inquired. "Me? The woman who managed to buy a house without meaning to, and without ever talking to a real estate agent?" She'd told Leslie that story, how fourteen years ago she had been renting the house from the Whartons; they'd decided to sell, but only if she wanted to buy; and in a burst of craziness she'd gone for it, scrounged a down payment and conned her lawyer ex-girlfriend into co-signing the mortgage application, which had then—to

Shannon's amazement—sailed uneventfully through the mysterious channels of a local bank. These days you probably couldn't buy a fully equipped SUV for that price.

"OK, OK," said Leslie. "Tell me about Georgia Duvall."

Nyah nyah, nyah nyah, I win, you lose. Shannon stuck her tongue out at the studio door. "What do you want to know about her for?" she demanded. "Read the book!"

"I'm going to, I promise. Meanwhile ... the house that burned down Sunday night is owned by the Duvall Realty Trust. McAuliffe says Georgia Duvall bought him the house. Does this just mean that the book bought him the house, or is there some particular significance to it?"

"How should I know? You're the one who went out drinking with the guy," Shannon teased, unable to restrain herself.

"I'm sure I can set you up if you think you're missing out on something," Leslie said sweetly. "Listen, I cross-my-heart-and-hope-to-die can't read the book before I have to file this story, so please, pretty please, tell me about Georgia Duvall."

Shannon settled back in her chair, gazing at the current wallpaper on her computer screen: a photograph of Pixel snoozing against the bottom step in the front yard. "Jeez, I don't know, Les," she said. "Georgia Duvall is your basic scrappy white working-class hero. Think Norma Rae, only she was born in Youngstown, Ohio, and went to parochial school, where the nuns thought she was the next Marie Curie. She works hard, gets good grades, blah blah blah, goes into law, not physics, makes law review, more blah blah blah—this is all backstory, you understand. I don't know—does that help? With Duvall Realty Trust, I mean. Maybe Georgia is based on the lost love of his life or something."

Leslie sighed heavily. "Makes as much sense as any theory I've come up with. Uh—one more thing, if you've got another minute?"

Here it comes. Shannon braced herself. "Shoot," she said.

"Remember yesterday I told you I was hearing rumors that

maybe Alice Chase had been harassed out of the Butler house? I just talked to the real estate agent. She dropped several borderline snotty remarks about McAuliffe—like maybe they had an affair and it ended badly? Then, when I asked why Alice moved out without warning, and only a month before her hearing, she pretty much blew me off with the my-client-just-walked-in gambit. Which isn't exactly *proof*," Leslie said, "but I'm not ready to dismiss those rumors."

Shannon felt the adrenaline coursing through her body, pursing her lips, tightening her jaw. *If this real estate agent was behind those phone calls, I'll fucking string the bitch up myself.* To counteract the angry surge, she visualized strolling down a quiet path through the woods, Pixel trotting just ahead.

"Besides," Leslie was saying, "why *would* someone in Alice's position move out in the middle of April?"

Because phone calls at all hours and tradesmen showing up unannounced were turning your son into the miserable, scared, rude acting-out kid that he was three years ago? Breathe, Shannon, breathe.

". . . a story that explores the specific impact of the housing situation on women with bad-news husbands, especially when there are kids involved—"

"You know who you should talk to?" Shannon interrupted. "Jay's sister Janice."

"Good idea," said Leslie. "Thanks. But I'd also need to tie it to this particular event—we're a *news*paper after all, right?"

Shannon finally took pity on her reporter buddy: "Which means you want to talk to Alice Chase."

"Yes."

"And you want me to set something up."

"Yes—no, not exactly—I mean," Leslie managed to pull herself together, "I don't want you to break any rules or anything. Just—put the word out. Leslie at the *Chronicle* wants to talk to Alice Chase. That's all. I won't bite. I'm on her side. Really."

After a long pause, Shannon said, "I think I could manage that." She was going to be in deep, deep doo-doo if—when—Leslie realized that she had been standing eighteen inches from Alice at the Get a Life Café yesterday morning. "I don't suppose you could manage to leave her name out of the story, could you?"

"I might be able to do that," Leslie said. "Thanks. Listen, you still interested in dinner on Saturday?"

"Sure," Shannon answered.

"Do you mind if I invite Jay?"

"He can't make it." Through the receiver she could hear someone in the *Chronicle* newsroom bellowing Leslie's name. "He's going to some conference off-island."

"Don't I wish I had his travel budget. Hold on a sec, will you?" The connection gave way to insipid pseudo-rock from the local radio station. It was a long thirty seconds before Leslie returned: "Listen, gotta go—the editor in chief is headed this way. Talk to you later."

Even before Leslie heard the click at the other end of the line, the Great Editorial Shadow fell across her keyboard. "So," Chet wanted to know, "how's my lead story look?"

"Sketchy," Leslie admitted. "I've got leads up the ying-yang, but none of them are going to pay out by 4 p.m. You want a list? Zack and Ruth Butler don't have an answering machine. Nick McAuliffe paid cash for the house."

"How much?" Chet asked.

"One ninety," Leslie replied.

"Not bad," Chet said. "What do we know about this guy?"

"Not much," Leslie conceded. "I interviewed him yesterday. He used to work for *The Asclepius Report,* a high-priced trade newsletter for, well, basically all the special interests that screwed Clinton's health-care reform plan."

"*Clinton* screwed Clinton's health-care reform plan. I'm not going to convince you of that, am I."

"Not in this lifetime," Leslie replied. "Yesterday he wasn't nearly as fired up to get Alice arrested as he was Sunday night. Off the record he even admitted that the fire might be a blessing in disguise."

"Must have had good insurance," Chet said.

"My, you're cynical this morning." Leslie made a face. "His real estate agent might have been playing the heavy, trying to push Alice out of the house. She got pretty flustered on the phone. I'll have to talk to her again—not that she's going to confess to any sleazy behavior, but maybe I'll get lucky and she'll let something slip."

Of course Chet wanted to know who the real estate agent was. When Leslie identified her, Chet almost sighed. "She's one handsome woman," he said. "Smart, too. Andy Burnham, on the other hand, doesn't have two brain cells to start a fire with."

"You're telling me he's off the hook?" Leslie asked. "So should I put in anything about McAuliffe's accusations?"

"Sure," Chet replied, scratching behind his ear. "At the scene Mr. McAuliffe urged the police to arrest, et cetera, et cetera. Reached on Wednesday after an exhaustive investigation of the site, Chief Taylor Francis said there was no evidence, blah blah blah. Slip something in there about McAuliffe being less vociferous when he'd calmed down."

"Do I have to use her name?"

Chet thought a moment. "No," he said. "That ex of hers is a loose cannon. She's got enough problems."

And off he went to pester Steve DeKuyper, probably about the latest county government fiasco.

Jay overshot the turnoff to his sister's house, and not because he didn't know the neighborhood; he'd grown up within literal shouting distance of the house where Janny and her kids now lived. He'd been preoccupied, and by the time he registered how close he was, headlights were closing in on his rear bumper so instead of slamming on the brakes, he accelerated and hung the next left.

Janny's one-car driveway was jammed with her old black Trooper and, behind it, Rainey's dark blue Saturn, so Jay squeezed off the road and parked as close as he could to the picket fence. The cape's windows glowed bright enough to reveal the newness of the shingles. Shadows moved on the other side of the curtains. He got out of the car, then retrieved Amy's present from the back seat. Amy had been obsessed with penguins since last summer; the parcel was wrapped in the emperor penguin wrapping paper he'd bought in Albany the previous November, hoping that Amy would still be into penguins when her next birthday rolled around.

The smell of roasting chicken greeted Jay as soon as he came through the door; under that was the fainter aroma of recently baked cake and the distinctive odor of broccoli. No newly minted teenager could possibly be into broccoli: Janny must still be on her anti-oxidant kick. Kevin, Amy's older brother, was leaning on the refrigerator. He straightened up, mimed a high five, and couldn't quite stifle his impulse to smile. Jay counted this as a small triumph: this past winter Kevin had been experimenting with an aloof persona whose only smile was close to a sneer. Jay returned the high five, also in mime, and raised his eyebrows: *What's happening?* Kevin raised a thumb.

Amy came barreling out of the living room wearing glittery black leggings and a slinky—and short—leopard dress with buttons from throat to hem. "Penguins!" she shouted. She snatched the package out of her uncle's hands and bore it over her head back into the room. Her path crossed her mother's; Janny seemed relaxed, happy. "I'm so glad you could make it," she said, giving him a quick hug and a kiss on the cheek.

"You think I'm brave enough to blow off Sheena here?"

Janice had her arm around her brother, guiding him toward the sofa. "Quite the outfit, isn't it. And speaking of which—what is *this?*" She tugged at the Free Radicals tie, which Jay had forgotten he was still wearing. "My brother, wearing a *tie?*"

"Unexpected appointment with the boss," he explained without explaining; invoking Wayne's name at Amy's birthday dinner would cast a darker pall than the appearance of Discord at the christening of Briar Rose. "Becca said I *might* get away with this shirt if I put on a jacket and tie. This was the only tie in the office." He glared at his running shoes and bright red socks. "As it happened, he caught sight of my socks and all was lost."

Janice shook her head. "You're hopeless. How many ties have I given you?"

"Many many." Jay couldn't help noticing Rainey Silvia standing awkwardly by the couch, wearing a simple green dress that followed the smooth curves of her figure and a bold silk scarf in black, orange, and red. His mother, watching them both from her favorite easy chair, was, predictably, decked in black from head to toe. It hadn't been three months since her husband died, but already Jay had forgotten what she looked like in anything other than black. Maria Segredo was traditional in many ways, but he'd never dreamed that she might turn into one of the stout old ladies in somber dresses who had regulated his youth, whether they were teaching Sunday school, baking cookies for the neighborhood, or serving up sopa at the annual Holy Ghost Feast. How old was she now? He subtracted in his head: going on sixty-seven. Kate Hammond had to be pretty close to that—and two weeks ago, she'd had to postpone an appointment because she was called on short notice to fly up to Boston to testify at a hearing on Beacon Hill.

Of course Kate Hammond and her husband probably earned more in an average year than his parents saw in a decade. That could make a difference.

He leaned down to kiss his mother on the cheek. She whispered, at a volume several decibels above *sotto voce,* "Doesn't Lorraine look nice? Tell her how nice she looks."

Figuring that Rainey, standing less than four feet away, must have heard the prompt, Jay smiled. "Mama still doesn't trust me to mind my own manners," he said. "You *are* looking great. That green is just right for you—and I bet my sister gave you that scarf."

"Jimmy!" To the younger women she said, "You see these gray hairs? I was gray long before my time because of this boy."

"You know that's not true, Mama," Janice said affectionately. "You hardly had a gray hair on your head before you were fifty."

"And you—" Maria Segredo pointed the maternal forefinger at her daughter "—you telling everyone in the room that I am no longer fifty!"

Janny laughed. "Mama! I'm thirty-nine, and Jay's almost forty-two." Jay dramatically hit his forehead with the back of his fist. "You better be over fifty or the ladies will talk."

Meanwhile Rainey was confessing to Jay that indeed the scarf came from his sister's collection, and did he think it was too loud? Red and orange together? "Too loud? Hell, no," Jay replied, pausing to study the effect of the vibrant scarf against the dark emerald dress. "Besides, what do I know? I just went to visit the boss wearing this brown jacket, this red plaid shirt, this pale lavender tie—and these bright red socks." He hiked his pant legs up high enough to reveal a glimpse.

Janice was spiriting her mother and her daughter off to the kitchen to tend to supper preparations, with Amy asking "When do I get to do presents?" as she went. "After supper," her mother answered firmly, "before cake and ice cream."

A wobbly silence settled into the room. Jay gazed at the merrily wrapped presents piled on the coffee table. "Looks like Amy's made out like a bandit once again," he said, at the moment that Rainey was saying, "The adults were having a glass of wine before dinner—can I pour you something?"

Jay spotted the two bottles and one empty glass on the chest under the window. "Sure, thanks, red if there's any left," he said, while Rainey began, "It's so hard to buy presents for girls her age . . ."

Dead silence. Embarrassed laughs. *High school couldn't have been this bad,* Jay thought. "Red," he said firmly. "Thanks." While she was getting it, he asked, "So where are the Katzenjammer twins? I don't guess you managed to ditch them at the Boys and Girls Club?" The "twins" were Jay's nephew Danny and Rainey's son Steve, best buddies since the first grade and now close to the end of the fourth.

Rainey laughed, more comfortably this time. "They got banished to Danny's room. They were racing those cars of theirs"—she handed Jay his wineglass then indicated the size of the cars with her hands—"*vroom, vroom, vroom,* and we couldn't hear to talk."

Jay gestured toward the seat on the sofa that Rainey had vacated when he entered the room. She sat. He sat. Long pause. "So," she said, "how was your day?"

"Not bad," he said. "I solved more problems than I created, and I didn't strangle my boss. That makes it a pretty good day."

Short pause. "Did—obviously you don't have to answer this question, but did any of the problems have to do with the fire last Sunday?"

Jay slumped into his seat. He hoped it looked like a conscious gesture, but the truth was that he was momentarily disoriented by the reminder of why he liked Rainey Silvia. Why was this so surprising? He'd liked her since he was a freshman in high school and she'd come to Janny's twelfth birthday party. The memory was still clear: he'd been tending the grill for the Indian summer cookout and watching helplessly as one young guest taunted another for her out-of-style shoes, and then Rainey Corbett, as she then was, had swooped in out of nowhere with "*Where* did you get those shoes? I saw them on the Academy Awards. They're *perfect.*"

Rainey had made it all up, so she confessed the next year, once she and Jay started "hanging out." But it had squelched the bully and saved the scapegoat, with a grace that Jay still recalled with admiration.

Now Jay forced his mind to focus on Rainey's question, and on exactly how much he could say. "I guess," he said, "you could say that some of them had to do with that."

"Is she OK?" Rainey asked quietly.

"I think she's going to be OK," Jay said. "She's got a court date for a custody hearing the third week of May, and if her ex blows this one off—I doubt the judge is going to give him another chance. We just found her a place to live until then, so we're hoping she's all set."

"Me too," she said. "I knew Lenny Chase in high school. For a while he was friends with one of my brothers." She shook her head. "The accident, losing John, having to pull myself together for Stevie—sometimes I can't imagine anything being worse than that." She leaned forward, retrieved her glass, and swallowed the rest of its contents. "Being married to Lenny Chase must have been worse than that."

He tried not to notice how much effort it took her to put the glass back down with a steady hand. "Yeah," he said thoughtfully. "Not worse, necessarily, but pretty bad."

"If she needs anything . . ."

"I'll pass that on," he said, so moved he had to concentrate hard to avoid tearing up. "Thank you."

A clatter of silverware announced that Amy had started setting the table at the other end of the room. "Amy!" Janny reprimanded from the kitchen.

Rainey smiled. "Should we go help the birthday girl?" she asked.

"Sounds like she needs it," said Jay, getting to his feet. He gave Rainey a hand up.

CHAPTER TEN

The air gateway to Martha's Vineyard then, as now, was the county-owned Martha's Vineyard Airport—the only county-owned airport in the state, local officials liked to say, as if this should be a source of pride. The airport terminal at the time, however, was more often a source of wisecracks, complaints, and, once in a while, genuine embarrassment. Built during World War II at the edge of the state forest, it had deteriorated over the years until it resembled a bus station in the run-down section of an economically depressed city. The wood veneer was chipped, the linoleum worn nearly through in several places; the lighting gave the healthiest complexion the look of a junkie extra in *Trainspotting,* and buckets had to be put out in the main waiting room whenever it rained hard.

After many years of official wrangling and bungling and kowtowing to the Federal Aviation Administration and the Massachusetts Aeronautics Commission, a new terminal was in the works. Local reactions to this political triumph were predictably mixed. Airline employees were elated, as were frequent flyers and small-plane pilots. Opponents of subdivisions, the ever-expanding tourist season, and the escalating year-round population took the new terminal as yet another harbinger of the island's doom; crummy facilities, they reasoned, would separate the dilettante visitors from those who thought Martha's Vineyard was worth suffering for, and hopefully discourage the former from trying to come back. Still others didn't take a stand pro or con. "You can't stop change," they said sagely, mourning the passing of an era while relishing the opportunities they would soon have to tell the latest wash-ashores about how things used to be.

Leslie arrived at the airport almost half an hour before her father's plane was scheduled to land. Wearing an outfit—a tailored, relatively new navy-blue wool pantsuit and matching pumps—that got her mistaken for an off-island lawyer at the Edgartown district court hearing from which she had just come, she was overdressed for Martha's Vineyard Airport, whose ambiance was better suited to someone who had spent the last three nights sleeping under a bridge. Nevertheless, Leslie sat up straight in her blue plastic bucket seat as she surveyed her surroundings. At the station nearest the door that allowed access to the tarmac, a USAir clerk glanced up at her computer monitor then down at her desk. The other stations were deserted. So were the rent-a-car counters. Leslie turned to look over her shoulder, down the dim, low-ceilinged corridor that led to the vending machines, the diner, and the office cubicles. No sign of life.

She had brought nothing to read. Like a fool she had lent Nick McAuliffe's novel, which she still hadn't started, to Natalie the features editor. The small pile of newspapers on a seat across the room offered a slim hope of respite from boredom. She retrieved today's *News Beacon* and the news section of yesterday's *Chronicle*. Her gaze swept the waiting room one more time, not wanting to be caught reading her own story in public.

The front-page photo really did look great. Police officers and insurance investigators picking through the rubble, dwarfed by spiky charred posts—it looked like a high-contrast manipulation but a closer look revealed that most of the starkness was in the scene, not the darkroom artistry (the *Chronicle* had pretty much given up on darkroom artistry, not to mention darkrooms, when scanning photographs became feasible). The story itself was unembellished but well enough done; it hinted at the larger issues but never strayed far from the facts of the fire. Would her father like it? Had Alice Chase seen it? Where was Alice? *Would Alice call?*

All yesterday afternoon and evening Leslie listened for the phone. It rang plenty of times: the League of Women Voters lady, a regular source in the Tisbury assessors' office, one marketing call from MCI, another marketing call for home delivery of the *New York Times,* Chet telling her that the planning board candidate she was supposed to interview at nine thirty tomorrow morning couldn't make it till eleven, and so on and on and on. All night she fantasized a timid female voice asking, "Is this Leslie Benaron?" and then introducing herself as Alice Chase.

It didn't happen. This morning she paused a dozen times at work to check the messages on her home answering machine. She even slipped out of the court hearing *(it was OK, Chet, really—the lawyers were conferring with the judge and I couldn't hear a word)* to collect the messages from both her home machine and her office voice-mail. Silence. Leslie was getting a little annoyed with Alice Chase: didn't she understand that this story was important? and that sympathetic coverage of her plight couldn't possibly hurt?

Fortunately, her worst nightmare had *not* come true: the *Newt Bacon* did not have an interview with Alice Chase splashed all over the front page. Au contraire: the rival paper's coverage was unimpressive. No photo, so the story was buried on page 2, where it looked like a press release.

"But it's absolutely essential that I be on that plane."

For a millisecond Leslie thought the words were in the newsprint before her, but no, they had been spoken out loud. A man at the airline counter was not happy. *Good luck,* she thought.

"I'm booked on the 6:14 from New York to Cleveland. If you can't get me on this plane, I won't make the connection."

Cleveland? Oh shit. Leslie cut a glance rightward. The

trench coat, the cap, the height, the voice: it could only add up to Nick McAuliffe, and indeed there he stood, gray garment bag slung over one shoulder, staging the airport version of his scene at the fire. Perhaps their pleasant tête-à-tête at the Yankee Clipper on Monday had been an aberration? Maybe he only made nicey-nice when he was trying to make a good impression? She had blown him off for their tentative Wednesday night dinner date with the feeblest of excuses; she absolutely did not want to run into him now. Could she rise and slip down the corridor to the ladies' room without anyone noticing? She stole a glance over her shoulder, as if anything more obvious might make a noise.

A woman stood in the corridor, not quite leaning against the wall. Her blond—or was it gray?—hair fell in soft curls around alert eyes and rose-pink lips that seemed pursed in secret amusement. Her blue-gray tweed coat was sleekly tailored but somewhat matronly: Leslie could hear her mother saying, *Take that thing off. It makes you look fifteen pounds heavier.* But the woman in the corridor was undeniably stylish.

Leslie sat very still, wishing she had worn a hat or some other form of disguise.

"I'm very sorry, sir," the clerk was saying. "I don't have you on the 4:25 to New York."

"How could I not be on the 4:25 to New York? I changed the reservation myself on Monday."

Studying her monitor screen, the clerk tapped away at her keyboard. "I have an N. B. McAuliffe booked on yesterday's 4:25. Is that you?"

"Yes—no, it's not me! I booked on *today's* 4:25."

"May I see your ticket, sir?" the clerk asked, all business, then, after a pause: "The ticket is made out to N. B. McAuliffe. That isn't you?"

"Of course it's me! What I'm trying to tell you is that I didn't book *yesterday's* 4:25, I booked *today's* 4:25."

"I have you on yesterday's flight." It looked as if the clerk meant to tough it out.

"Never mind," said the exasperated N. B. McAuliffe. "Just reissue the ticket for today's flight!"

"Today's 4:25 has been fully booked since yesterday morning," the clerk replied with no discernible sympathy. She did smile briefly at the elderly couple who were now waiting patiently behind her troublesome customer. "It's a very popular flight."

"God in heaven," swore Nick McAuliffe, "why does anyone come to this wretched island? Lewis Carroll's Wonderland has more internal logic."

Internal logic? thought Leslie. *I bet the phrase "internal logic" has never been uttered before in Martha's Vineyard Airport.* Was the best-selling author going to stage a meltdown right before her eyes?

"I couldn't tell you that, sir," the clerk said demurely. Leslie gave her an A for evasive action.

"All right, all right." Passenger McAuliffe seemed ready to throw in the towel. "Can you put me on the next plane to New York?"

There followed a long pause, during which Leslie heard the click of fingernails on keyboard. "Yes, sir, I can. Shall I make you a reservation?"

"Yes, yes, for God's sake, yes!"

More clicking. Mama Bear, Papa Bear, and two cubs ambled through the main door to the waiting room, with the taller cub hauling a huge suitcase. "There you are," said the clerk, as an unseen dot-matrix printer started to zip through line after line of type. "The 6:25 to New York. United Airlines has an 8:05 to Cleveland. Shall I book you on that flight, sir?"

"Yes, please!"

"There you are," said the clerk, who was beginning to sound like the generic female voice of countless voice-mail routing messages. "Your seat assignment for your flight to Cleveland is 24C. Breakfast is served on that flight. The Martha's Vineyard to New York flight is open seating; be here at least a half hour before flight time."

"That's great," said Nick McAuliffe. "Breakfast? Don't you mean supper?"

"No, sir," the clerk answered. "It's a breakfast flight. Sir? Your reservation is for tomorrow morning. The next New York flight leaves at 6:25 a.m."

Leslie was immediately overcome with a fit of giggles so powerful that, oblivious to the opinions of strangers, Nick McAuliffe, or the handsome woman in the hall, she bolted down the corridor toward the restrooms, inadvertently leaving her shoulder bag on the floor beside her seat.

Meg Hasbro felt the rush of the young woman's passage and drew farther back into the shadows. After a dignified interval, she followed, walking as quietly as she could in flats that resounded on the linoleum like her second-grade tap shoes. The ladies' room door was still hissing shut when she reached it, so she continued into the little diner-style restaurant and ordered coffee and a blueberry muffin.

She took her snack to the corner booth and slid in, her back to the door. Even if Nick McAuliffe came down to the restaurant looking for coffee or a cheeseburger, the odds were he wouldn't notice anyone else in the shop. He'd be too busy telling his troubles to the attractive dark-haired girl at the counter. Nick was a pro. Narcissus should be his middle name.

Leslie frowned at her reflection in the mirror, wondering where the green eyeshadow she so painstakingly applied this morning had disappeared to. Into her pores? her bloodstream? Should she do a little touch-up? She glanced down for her shoulder bag, panicked briefly when she realized it wasn't there, then reassured herself that it must be next to her chair in the waiting room. Makeup? What did she need with makeup? To meet her father? Even if she showed up with pallid cheeks and big bags under her eyes, he'd never notice. She didn't look anywhere near *that* bad.

Was it safe to go back to the waiting room? Had her father's plane touched down yet? All she could hear was a flushing toilet. She turned on the water in the sink and started washing her hands. A diminutive woman with tightly curled black-and-gray hair emerged from the nearest stall, stopped at the next sink without acknowledging Leslie's presence, passed her unmanicured hands under a trickle of water, and moved stiffly out of the restroom. *Like a wind-up toy with unjointed knees,* Leslie thought. *So where is Alice Chase and what did she think of the story?*

Meg used her knife to push the remains of her muffin into a little mound, then with thumb and forefinger she began to press them together—a habit that once drove her fastidious mother to squint-eyed distraction. *I drive Mother crazy, therefore I am.* Her mother might have been dead for nine years, but there was no statute of limitations on the mother-daughter relationship. Meg had long ago given up trying to break this particular habit. By the time the crumbs were kneaded into a semblance of their original dough, the four o'clock from New York was coming in for a landing. It touched down uneventfully, slowed, and rolled to a stop out on the tarmac. Meg took a deep breath and headed back to the waiting room.

The place had filled up: two of the USAir stations were now staffed, as were the rental-car kiosks. Leaning back against the counter talking to the clerk at Budget Rent-a-Car was Burger Boy, his suit jacket slung jauntily over one shoulder. All the other longtime real estate agents on the island despised Burger Boy because in the late 1970s he had wormed his way into the confidence of an Old Island Family, acquired from them just under a hundred acres of neglected West Tisbury scrub land, built two dozen faux-elegant houses (with association tennis, swimming pool, and the promise of a horse barn) at a time when anyone who was anyone lived in faux–Cape Cod, and sold them at the crest of the mid-1980s economic boom to arrivistes sans taste. High-commission, low-judgment clients were still eagerly treading the hydrangea-lined path to Burger Boy's fancy Vineyard Haven office. *Why Burger Boy?* his colleagues wondered. *Why did such stellar success come to this acne-scarred, unconnected klutz whose mouth spits forth words like automatic machine-gun bullets? Life really is unfair.*

Meg already knew that life was unfair: if life were fair, she would be a much-respected professor of English with a summer home on Martha's Vineyard, instead of an unappreciated seller of real estate to high achievers with delusions of class. Unlike some of her colleagues, however, she remained cordial to Burger Boy, even inviting him along to a few useful receptions whose hosts would not have included him on the guest list. In return he had invited her to co-broke on a few good listings over the years, from which her bank account and the IRS had benefited. She caught his eye and smiled; he smiled back and tipped an invisible hat.

Meg drifted toward the in-gate/out-gate, alert for a sign of Nick McAuliffe, who was nowhere to be seen. The forming but still ragged boarding queue stopped her not far from the airline counter, where the blue-clad young woman with the magnificent cascade of curly brown-black hair was talking to the clerk. Wonder of wonders, the topic was Nick McAuliffe.

"That man, the one who was in here before? Who's trying to get to Cleveland?" Unless Meg was much mistaken, Splendid Hair was from New York.

"I never forget a face," muttered the clerk. Meg stifled a laugh.

"Did he leave?"

"He went over to the other building to see if any of the guys were planning to fly up to Boston tonight. I told him they'll often take passengers for a fee. I also told him that one of the passengers on the 4:25 hasn't checked in yet. Dumb, huh."

Splendid Hair laughed, a full throaty laugh.

"You're not on the 4:25, are you?" asked the clerk.

"No, no," the woman replied. "My dad just landed—he came in on the four o'clock? It's just—I met that guy the other day. Interviewed him for the paper. I'm a reporter for the *Chronicle?*"

"Yeah?" said the clerk. "Don't quote me on that." She giggled, a little nervously.

"Don't worry, I'm off-duty."

It's Leslie Benaron, Meg realized. *Has to be.* Meg had visualized someone a little older, a little less, well, off-island.

"So who hasn't showed?" Leslie asked. "Anyone I know?"

The clerk evaded the query: "This guy *always* shows up at the last minute," she said, naming no names. Then she held up two fingers and spoke into her microphone. "Now arriving through gate 1"—*does anyone ever arrive through gate 2?* Meg wondered—"passengers on flight 148 from New York City. Flight 148 from New York City has arrived, ladies and gentlemen. Your luggage is being deplaned and will be brought to the front of the building. The baggage claim may be reached through the front door. Boarding call for flight 149, scheduled to depart for New York at 4:25. Flight 149 is on schedule."

Should I introduce myself? Since their phone conversation Wednesday, Meg had been nagged by the feeling that she hadn't made a very good impression on the reporter. After several moments of should-I-or-shouldn't-I, Meg took the plunge: "Excuse me, I couldn't help overhearing—you *must* be Leslie Benaron, right? I'm Meg Hasbro."

"Oh!" Leslie exclaimed. "I noticed you before—"

"I didn't want to meet up with Mr. Best-Seller any more than you did." Meg smiled.

Leslie pressed her fingers to her lips and grinned. "I almost lost it," she confided. "You're meeting someone?"

"A client," Meg replied. "Someone who's coming back for a second look at a very high-end property."

"Good luck," said Leslie.

At that moment Doug Trumbull came through the waiting room door, bypassing the congested in-gate/out-gate. He was chatting amiably with a curly-haired, somewhat rumpled fellow at least three inches shorter and apparently several years older than he was. Right behind them followed Artemis and Apollo, two fine blond specimens of affluent late-twentieth-century American youth. Both were carrying tennis racquets. A burgundy sports duffel hung from Apollo's left shoulder. *Bet it's monogrammed,* thought Meg. *In 24-karat gold.*

She caught Doug's eye and fluttered her fingers. He beamed at her. Meanwhile Leslie Benaron was throwing her arms around the short guy, who deftly managed to keep his laptop, folded newspaper, and overcoat out of range. *Her father,* Meg guessed, allowing as how his hair, with the addition of another X chromosome and a lot of luck, might have begotten hers. Doug was introducing her to his son and daughter, Apollo and Artemis—Jason and Jennifer?—and explaining that he'd reserved a rental car "so the kids can sample the fleshpots of Martha's Vineyard on their own." A witty retort was perched to fly from the tip of Meg's tongue when she spotted Nick McAuliffe coming through the door. He pushed his way through the noisy, swirling crowd with single-minded determination, heading, of course, for the ticket counter.

Meg looked toward the door: the coast was clear. "Shall we collect your bags?" she asked. Doug delegated Apollo to take care of the rental car, Artemis went with her brother, and Meg and Doug emerged into the milky late-afternoon light. "The sun hasn't been out for two consecutive hours since last weekend," Meg explained. "This is springtime on Martha's Vineyard. They don't turn the sun on till Memorial Day."

Leslie Benaron and her father were right behind them. Leslie leaned toward her: "That was close," she whispered. "Hope she can keep him busy at the desk."

"What's this?" asked Leslie's father.

"That man who just went barging through the waiting room? You know the story I told you about on the phone? That's the one. Nick McAuliffe. The one whose house burned down."

"Aha! Mr. *Asclepius Report!*"

"Mr. Board-Certified Putz," Leslie said.

"Don't let your mother hear you say that." David Benaron's eyes twinkled.

Father and daughter shared a conspiratorial grin before daughter introduced father to Meg, and Meg introduced Doug Trumbull to the Benarons—to Leslie, that is. Between New York and Martha's Vineyard, Doug Trumbull and David Benaron had become old friends. Not until Doug referred to David as "the only journalist in America who understands the politics of health care *and* gets the science right" did Meg realize that this was the same David Benaron who made frequent guest appearances on the more intelligent news shows. On TV he looked taller. Why was David Benaron's daughter working for the *Martha's Vineyard Chronicle* when she could surely get a job on the fast track? Surely Leslie was still too young to have been traded in for a new wife. Was she yet another celebrity offspring who had had a nervous breakdown and moved to Martha's Vineyard?

The baggage wagon, a flatbed trailer pulled by a glorified riding lawn mower, rattled to a halt on the far side of the chain-link fence. The driver dismounted and unlocked the gate, and about twenty passengers and their friends filed through.

Rapid movement in the periphery of Meg's vision made her glance up and over the fence. A dark blue compact car was racing along the access road; Meg caught her breath, fearing for a moment that it wouldn't make the tree-lined turn that circled around to the front of the terminal. But a minute later the little sedan appeared from behind the waiting taxis, rolling sedately into the only vacant slot in the fifteen-minute parking zone—the one marked handicapped only. A man with windblown dark hair, forty at most and boyishly energetic, emerged from the driver's side and immediately headed for the trunk. On the passenger's side a pretty brunette stepped out more slowly, using both hands to tame her straight but nicely shaped hair. She moved around the car and reached the man as he pulled out a black carry-on and a matching garment bag.

Her words were inaudible; his response was "Listen, I'm sorry, I'm *really* sorry—I don't usually drive like that, do I? But I can't miss that plane!"

The woman's arms were crossed over her belted beige jacket. To Meg the position said "stressed," not "furious." Gently the man rested his hands on her shoulders. She looked up. He said a few inaudible words. She nodded, turned, and walked briskly toward the terminal, dabbing surreptitiously at her eyes. He slammed the trunk shut and glanced at the fence. It wasn't Meg he was grinning at but Leslie Benaron, who had appeared silently a little off to Meg's right. "What is this?" he asked. "Preventive detention for journalists?"

"My father's here for the weekend, remember?" said Leslie. "You stood us up for dinner tomorrow night."

"Well, as you see," Jay replied with a look toward the door, "I really am going off-island. Catch ya later, Scoop." And he sprinted for the terminal with a bag in each hand.

Meg raised her eyebrows at Leslie. "Jay Segredo, director of Youth Services for ISS," Leslie answered. She was about to say something else, Meg was one hundred percent sure of it, but she stopped herself.

Meg said, "It seems that Mr. McAuliffe won't get to Cleveland tonight, hmm?"

"Oh?" Leslie looked at her, puzzled. "Oh. Oh!" Then Leslie burst out laughing, laughing so hard that she was literally holding her sides.

"Good heavens," said Meg. "Tell me."

"Alice Chase," Leslie managed to get out, through snorts

and a cough.

That wretched name again! Meg's heart began to pound.

"Jay's the director of *Youth Services*—he's the one who won't tell me where Alice Chase is hiding. Living. And he just kept Nick McAuliffe from getting on a *plane!*"

Disgusted as she was feeling about Nick McAuliffe, Alice Chase, and Martha's Vineyard in general, Meg had to admit that this was pretty funny.

CHAPTER ELEVEN

In retrospect, Meg admitted that she had not exercised the best judgment. It had not been a good idea to go to dinner with the Trumbulls, especially not at the country inn where they had reservations for the weekend. It would have been a better idea to excuse herself when "the kids," as Doug kept calling them, set off to check out the reggae band playing at the Atlantic Connection. They had finished dessert and had refills on decaf; they had made a date to go sailing tomorrow morning, weather and wind permitting. There was no good reason to stick around.

Meg had reached for the black morocco folder that contained the check. In retrospect, that had been a mistake. Yes, it was a business expense, and no, the tab, though well over two hundred dollars, was not unreasonable with a potentially one-point-nine-million-dollar sale hanging in the balance. But she should have *known* that he would have to pick it up, that his hand would settle over hers and linger there, that he would say, "Oh, you must stay for a nip of brandy in the library. Now that the kids have vanished, we have some time to talk."

Talk? About what? In retrospect, the obvious answer was "what next? " but at the time a nip of brandy in the inn's elegant Victorian library had seemed a harmless close to a most pleasant evening. In retrospect—well, without that last snifter, she would probably be waking up at home with one cat nestled against her back and the other curled up in the extra pillow. Instead she was watching the dawn light peer through the gap in the east-facing curtains of the inn's bridal suite, and Douglas Trumbull was still sleeping about three inches away. The bridal suite was not a suite at all, just a well-appointed room with full bath attached; no self-respecting country inn on Martha's Vineyard would do "bridal" the way it was done in, say, Las Vegas. Still, the four-poster bed was crowned with a lace-edged floral-patterned canopy, complimentary gold-wrapped chocolates rested on both pillows, and the brick fireplace came with a wrapped Dura-log to help create a romantic glow.

Well, what was done was done, and the only direction to go was forward. The sex, true enough, had been good, though not worth the loss of a five-figure commission if the client should be afflicted with postcoital guilt. The high point was when Doug had told her she could dispense with the diaphragm if she wanted—he had had a vasectomy the previous fall without Maryellen's knowledge because, as he put it, "She's so hot on the idea of having a baby that she might do something rash." Meg was deeply skeptical of any man who claimed to be infertile, whether for natural or surgical reasons, but she thought Doug Trumbull was telling the truth.

Still, she didn't tell him that she hadn't had to bother with diaphragms in almost two years.

Shannon was up and even dressed in time to make the 6:45 AA meeting at the hospital, but at 6:25 her resolve not to turn on the computer crumbled into dust and pretty soon she was reading all the posts from her MacGraphics list, her women artists list, her painters who aren't painting list, and her lesbians in recovery list. By the time she finished, the 6:45 meeting was long over. Too bad. She liked that meeting. Her sponsor was a regular, and most of the other regulars had been sober so long that nine years in the program made you a newcomer. It was too easy to get cocky at the meetings where half the members hadn't got their one-year coins yet, and several were still trying to string together thirty consecutive sober days.

Making a second pass down William Street five minutes before the ten o'clock step meeting was supposed to start, she remembered another reason for preferring the 6:45: it wasn't May yet but the sun was out (for the moment), the weekenders were here, and where the hell could you park your car in downtown Vineyard Haven? Pixel didn't care, of course; she had her head far enough out the window to feel the wind in her ears. The longer the ride went on, the better she liked it. It didn't bother her that the block of Center Street behind the town hall was torn up and unavailable for parking while the public works department looked for a leak in the water pipes.

The damn "season" was starting earlier and ending later every year. Shannon was not the only Vineyarder who suspected that some of the summer people never left at all; they'd moved here for good and registered their kids in the island school system, certain that the dearth of fleshly temptations would keep their darlings out of trouble. Hah. Any regular at any of the island's more than sixty weekly AA meetings could tell them that they were dreaming. The island was not kind to relocated suburban kids who expected to be entertained. Those who found a niche—theater, sports, academics, horses, it didn't matter what—usually did fine. Those who didn't hung out on Main Street or Circuit Ave., or at the Cumberland Farms convenience store, waiting for Fate to relieve their boredom.

Once more around the block and she'd be late. To any other kind of meeting you could blow in late and no one would think twice. At AA, however, if it happened often enough, someone might catch you afterward and say, "Late again?" in a tone that suggested it was time to discuss it with your sponsor. In AA it was worth cleaning up your act enough to be on time, if only so you wouldn't have to think about why you were late. She squeezed her Subaru as close as she dared to an unscratched silver gray minivan. Her front tires were solidly over the white line, but at least she wasn't blocking a fire hydrant or anyone's driveway. "Back soon," she told Pixel, and got out of the car. Giving her a put-upon look, the dog curled up on the passenger seat to wait.

Shannon stepped through the door to the parish hall just as the last kibitzers were taking their seats. It was a big meeting today: the second circle of chairs was filling up. As usual the mix ranged from the program's poster children to the bleary not-quite-sober guys who had probably been referred by the court. She knew nearly all of them by sight, and most of them by name. No one she was dying to see, however—until Giles K. caught her eye and beamed. She beamed back. He patted the empty chair at his side.

"Vacant at this late hour?" she whispered as she sat down. "You got cooties or what?" The leader of this morning's meeting was taking one last glance around the room.

An anxious redhead scurried to her seat in the outer circle. "Probably it's the demented artist look I've been cultivating, " said Giles. "Either that or the stench of turpentine. I wasn't drinking it, honest."

Shannon grinned. "Now that you mention it . . ."

The meeting was getting under way: "My name is Mark, I'm an alcoholic, and I'll be leading today's meeting." Mark was a lanky carpenter whose graying brown hair was losing ground to a furrowed forehead. He spoke mostly to the two blue books in his lap.

"Hi, Mark" rippled around the room.

"The Saturday ten o'clock meeting is a step meeting," Mark continued, "and today's meeting will focus on the First Step, *'We admitted we were powerless over alcohol—that our lives had become unmanageable.'*"

Shannon wished she'd made it to the 6:45 open discussion meeting at the hospital. She wasn't in a First Step mood.

Mark opened his copy of the "Big Book," the larger of the two books in his lap—*Alcoholics Anonymous,* one of AA's basic texts—and asked the silver-haired gentleman on his right to start reading from chapter 5, "How It Works." The man read the opening paragraphs and the Twelve Steps and then passed the book on. The voices reading were soft and loud, high and low, halting and fluent, but however they sounded, Shannon loved listening to them. They created a rich texture; they testified to diversity in an organization that rarely, in Shannon's experience, *talked* about diversity. They just did it.

Her attention, though, dropped in and out of the meeting like a blunt needle bouncing in and out of the worn grooves of an old LP. It dropped in for ". . . the alcoholic is an extreme example of self-will run riot, though he usually doesn't think so." She loved that phrase: "self-will run riot." It took her back to the women's community, where so many little individual wills ran riot that organizational dynamics looked a lot like a vigorous demolition derby. Like many another refugee from progressive politics, Shannon was awed by the Twelve Traditions. Most of the feminist groups she'd been involved with exploded or imploded before their second birthday. AA had been around since 1935—more than sixty fucking years, for God's sake! More than sixty fucking years run by *drunks.*

This was the miracle that had kept Shannon coming back to meetings in the earliest days of her sobriety, when the God language and the sexism and the homophobia so outraged her that she was ready to storm out of almost every meeting she attended. What kept her in her seat was partly her sponsor's glare and partly the knowledge that AA had been around since 1935. She wanted to know the secret, she wanted to be touched by the magic; she would keep coming back until she was satisfied. Nine years later she was still coming back. Going to meetings was simply part of life, like working and breathing and walking with Pixel.

A pale young man was reading with almost painful care:

"It is plain that a life which includes deep resentment leads only to futility and unhappiness." *Plain rhymes with Wayne,* Shannon thought, *and if Resentment wasn't Wayne's middle name, it ought to be. Gerb's too: Gerbil Resentment Turd.* Shannon visualized it inscribed in Old English script on his doctoral diploma.

Whoa there, Shannon. When she started sniping at others' faults, she was probably missing a big one of her own. But what? Her freelance business was growing, her health was fine, she was program chair for one of her regular meetings and treasurer for another. True, she had almost nothing to do with her family of origin, but her sponsor had assured her a dozen times that given the circumstances this made perfect sense.

One of the two older women in the meeting—older than Shannon, that meant—was reading the passage about fear: "This short word somehow touches about every aspect of our lives. It was an evil and corroding thread; the fabric of our existence was shot through with it. It set in motion trains of circumstances which brought us misfortune we felt we didn't deserve. But did not we, ourselves, set the ball rolling? . . ."

Can we guess who that's about? Hello, Jay! Did you know that the fabric of your existence is shot through with fear? You set the ball rolling, and if you don't watch it, it'll knock all your pins down.

Talk about late: a guy came through the door and stood, looking more confused with each passing moment. Chuck O., the meeting's current greeter, rose from his seat and went to welcome the stranger. They exchanged a few words, then Chuck escorted the newcomer to the seat next to his own.

Shannon knew this guy. She knew she knew this guy. Who the hell was he? Short dark hair, almost black. Eyes that didn't match the hair: hazel? The face looked too bare, like a field full of scrub brush one day and mown the next, but she was sure she'd seen him before. Her painterly mind lengthened his hair, made it darker. Gave him a mustache, a bushier mustache—a five o'clock shadow. More of a slouch.

She got it. She got it, but her mind had thrown up a firewall. The name stood at the gate, unable to get in. Then it slipped through her net, and all she could think of was racing from the room to raise the alarm. *Paul Revere's ride—one if by land, two if by sea. I've got to tell Jay, I've got to tell Janice, I've got to tell . . .*

"Giles?" she whispered, all but inaudible. "Giles? That guy who just came in?"

"What's the matter? Who is it?"

"Wayne. Wayne S.," she said.

Giles didn't get it.

"Jay's brother-in-law."

Jay's brother-in-law—ex-brother-in-law—the one who had probably taken a potshot at Jay's car on the Edgartown–West Tisbury Road last Columbus Day weekend. The one who had certainly showed up at Jay's house a few days later, firing an automatic pistol into the air. The one who'd been booked, arraigned, and sent off-island for psychiatric evaluation. Wayne Swanson. Wayne Swanson was here at the ten o'clock Saturday step meeting. Wayne Swanson was back on the island.

"I'm leaving," said Shannon.

"No," Giles said, "wait. Wait till the break."

Good advice. The break couldn't be more than a few minutes away. She could slip out then and no one would notice. Wayne Swanson wouldn't notice, on the off chance that Wayne Swanson knew she was the one who'd sheltered his wife and two of his three kids for the first couple of days after they walked out on his drunken, screaming, battering self.

But it wasn't her own safety she was afraid for, or even Janice's; it was Jay's. Shannon knew how the resentful alcoholic mind worked, how readily it dumped responsibility for all misfortune on someone else, anything to avoid "inquiring within." Wayne, unlike many drunks, did not blame everything on his spouse; in his view Janice was the innocent dupe of her brother. Jay was the true cause of Wayne's downfall. Wayne might have stopped drinking; he might even be honestly working the program. But it was most unlikely that he had already completed Step Four, "Made a searching and fearless moral inventory of ourselves," never mind the subsequent Step Eight, "Made a list of all persons we had harmed, and became willing to make amends to them all." When Wayne made amends to Jay, then, only then, would Shannon stop worrying about Jay's safety.

Maybe.

When the break came, she stood up and pulled her jacket on. Giles grabbed her arm. "Call me tonight," he said, and wouldn't let her go till she said yes, she would. She made a beeline for the bathrooms at the back of the parish hall, then swerved toward the door to the outside.

Soon she was rolling forward down William Street; she turned left, and continued up Church so slowly that a horn honked behind her. In the rearview mirror loomed a black Suburban, the kind of monster vehicle she loved to impede on its headlong rush to wherever. The driver was thirty-ish, blond, female, and talking on a cell phone—more good reasons to poke along at fifteen miles per hour. But the sight of the woman talking into her phone prompted her to settle on her own course of action: she would go home, try to track Jay down, and then pay a visit to Janice Segredo Swanson.

Pixel was not happy to find herself back at the house with no walk, but Ben and Mary Wharton were taking advantage of the sunshine to do some yard work. Without waiting for an invitation, Pix followed Shannon out the driver's side door—this was a big no-no—and hurtled through the post-and-rail fence. *"PIXEL!"* Shannon yelled.

The dog was already nuzzling at the big right pocket of Ben's cargo vest. Ben waved at her then produced a large biscuit from his left pocket. Pixel, obedience paragon that she was, immediately sat, big smile on her face, bushy white tail wagging vigorously across the grass. Shannon, one foot on the first step to her door, made a theatrical shrug. "How are you?" Mary called, leaning on her leaf rake.

"Can't complain," Shannon replied, her stock reply. "You?"

"Trying to hurry spring," Mary said. "The usual. Come to supper tonight. I'm roasting a chicken."

An evening with her neighbors, eating a good meal then watching TV or playing cards, was more tempting than dinner out with Leslie and her father. "Sounds good."

"Around six, six thirty."

"I'll be there," Shannon said. "Can I bring anything?"

"The dog," said Ben.

By the time Shannon closed the door behind her, Ben had interrupted his fence mending to throw a tennis ball for Pixel. Shannon hung her jacket on a peg in the mud room and passed into the kitchen, where she poured herself a cup of the morning's cooked-down coffee and dosed it with half-and-half. No one was home: probably one or both of the Hammonds had come by, picked up Alice and Mitch and a load of their belongings, and returned to Oak Bluffs. Sitting on the edge of her bed, Shannon held the phone and punched in Jay's private work number, the one that didn't go through the ISS switchboard. The outgoing message told her that Jay was off-island for the weekend but it didn't say where; it did give a local number to be called in case of emergency. Shannon wrote it on the inside back cover of her island phone book. The recording on Jay's home machine didn't even give his name, never mind his weekend itinerary.

Shannon still had the confidential Island Social Services phone list from the days when she was on the search committee for the Youth Services director. She ran her finger down the column of numbers till she came to the one mentioned on Jay's answering machine. It belonged to a colleague whom Jay habitually referred to as Gerbil Junior. Neither he nor Gerbil Senior needed to know she was trying to reach Jay. Why the hell had Jay left him on call anyway?

Instead she punched in the home number for Becca Herschel, office manager for Youth Services, de facto counselor, and all-round trustworthy person. Becca actually answered the phone. Of course she knew where Jay was: hadn't she made the plane, hotel, and car reservations her very own self? He was attending a conference on "Developing Leadership Potential in At-Risk Youth" at the Westin in Waltham, and he was coming back on the first plane Monday morning. "Anything I need to know?" she asked.

"Yeah," said Shannon. "Wayne Swanson's back on the island."

"Uh-oh" was Becca's response. "How'd you find that out?"

"I saw him about twenty minutes ago."

"Let me guess: he was hanging around Circuit Ave. waiting for the Ritz to open."

"Au contraire," Shannon replied. "He seems to have dried out." *Anonymity is the spiritual foundation of all our traditions . . .* She wouldn't blow the Twelfth Tradition by actually telling Becca where she'd seen Wayne; Becca could figure it out for herself.

"Ah-ha." Becca wasn't in the program, but she was surrounded by people who were; she understood the lingo and the allusions. "So what's with this? Don't they have to let someone here know he's loose?"

"Sure, they'll let his counselor know—but remember who his counselor is."

"Mister Twitchy Whiskers himself," said Becca. "You really think the Gerbil's slimy enough to sit on information like that and not tell *anybody*?"

"He's slimy enough," Shannon replied. "What I don't know is whether he's stupid enough to think he'll get away with it. Maybe he's talked to Janice. Maybe he's talked to Evalina—"

Becca snorted. "When cars fly," she said. "You think I should call her?"

"Let Janice do it," Shannon suggested. "You want to do

some Nancy Drew? See what's going on with the court. The probation officer has to know he's back; he has to be reporting to someone over there. Where he's living would be nice too. You probably won't be able to learn anything till Monday, though."

"Oh, I don't know about that." Becca chuckled. "I've got friends. Did you send the boss an e-mail?"

"Uh, no," Shannon replied, kicking herself. Of course Jay would be checking his e-mail while he was off-island; just because she refused to get a laptop didn't mean that no one else had one.

"I'll do it. You want to know if I find out anything?"

"Is the pope Catholic? You're good, Bec. Keep me posted."

After Becca hung up, Shannon got the number for the Westin Hotel, dialed it, got through to the front desk, and was put on hold. The canned message told her all about the 8 a.m. weather in the Boston area and all the ways that the Westin catered to business travelers, followed by a few bars of an upbeat string arrangement of—could it possibly be?—"The Times They Are a-Changin'." This was interrupted by a female voice assuring her that her call was important and would be answered by the next available operator. Halfway through the weather report reprise, a male voice asked how he could help her.

"I'm trying to reach a guest who's registered there," said Shannon. She gave Jay's name and spelled it out.

"I'm sorry, we have no one registered by that name. Could the room be in another name?"

Not if Becca made the reservations. She asked about "Developing Leadership Potential in At-Risk Youth."

Yes indeed, the conference was using most of the hotel's function rooms this weekend. Would the caller like to be put through to the conference's registration desk? The caller would, thank you very much.

The assistant who answered the phone didn't seem to recognize the name but offered to check the registration list, then through the phone Shannon heard "Jay Segredo? Of course!" and in a moment another voice came on the line, waxing enthusiastic about the *wonderful* panel that Mr. Segredo had moderated that morning—all the panelists were high school students from disadvantaged backgrounds, wasn't that just the most *original concept?* People were just *swarming* around him afterwards.

Shannon strongly implied that she was a professional colleague of Mr. Segredo's and it was extremely important that she speak with him. Was there a way to get him a message?

There was, but the woman explained that not all conference attendees were zealous about checking the message box. If she saw Mr. Segredo, though, she'd be sure to tell him he had a message.

Better than nothing, thought Shannon. Should she blurt out the news where anyone could read it or just tell Jay to call back? What if Jay called and she wasn't home? She settled on WAYNE'S HOME. CALL SHANNON OR JANICE.

The long narrow swath of Oak Bluffs that lay between upper Circuit Avenue and Dukes County Avenue was a vibrant tumble of small houses, backyard businesses, cars that ran but couldn't pass inspection, sandy soil tufted with grass, and kids of all sizes on trikes, bikes, and skateboards. On Dukes County Ave. pickup trucks and working vans bellied up to Tony's Market, purveyor of beer, wine, big sandwiches, lottery tickets, cigarettes, and a smattering of groceries.

In her pre-sobriety years, her catch-as-catch-can years of scalloping, house painting, and prep-cooking at long-vanished restaurants, Shannon had spent a fair amount of time inside, outside, and in the parking lot at Tony's. These days she grabbed her coffee at establishments in the island's dry towns and did what hanging out she had time for at Alley's General Store or the West Tisbury post office. As she drove slowly by before hanging the right that would take her to Janice's house, she stole a look at the loitering guys. Even the three she recognized looked seedy, not quite threatening but definitely alien. She hoped they wouldn't recognize her.

The house with the Swanson sign hanging over the gate in the picket fence was neater than either of its neighbors. The forsythia that flanked the front door was blooming generously; the lawn had already been mowed at least once this season, the grass trimmed on either side of the tidy bluestone walkway. From the front the cape-style home looked too small for a family of five—now four—but it concealed an addition that almost doubled the floor space.

Rainey Silvia answered her knock on the door. Hamburger smell hit her broadside, followed by the babble of boyish voices and the *zing! zing! zing!* of a computer shoot-'em-up game. Rainey was surprised—but not, Shannon thought, displeased—to see her. Shannon asked if Janice were here.

"Yes," said the slender brunette, "yes, of course. Janny?"

Janice appeared in the hallway, wiping her hands on a red-and-white-checked dish towel. She stopped dead at the sight of Shannon and had to force herself to keep her face working. Shannon managed a friendly smile. "May I come in?"

"Sure, of course." She managed a nervous laugh. "If you don't mind the grease. We're feeding Danny, Steve, and some of their friends."

"No problem," said Shannon, and followed Janice into the kitchen. A platter of hamburgers circled by toasted buns sat on the table, along with a big bowl of french fries and a smaller bowl of mini carrots, paper plates and cups, plastic knives and forks, ketchup, and two big bottles of soda. Generic album rock was playing on the radio.

"Help yourself to soda if you want," said Janice, pointing to the Coke and the root beer on the table.

Shannon poured root beer into a red plastic glass and watched the head froth just up to the rim. "Thanks," she said. She sipped; silence settled in.

"You want a burger?" asked Janice, with a lightness that

sounded forced.

"I'll pass," Shannon said, smiling. Given Janice's hasty exit from her house, and of course the reason for it, she took the other woman's uneasiness in stride. Even after her life settled down some, Janice had never called to apologize or even to explain. Guilt does turn to hostility, as Giles liked to say, or at least to considerable tension.

Patching up relations with Janice Swanson hadn't been high on Shannon's list either. In some ways she knew Janice's brother a lot better than Janice did; in Janice's presence, she had to watch her tongue and even her body language to avoid saying too much. That imposed its own tensions, its own resentments. Shannon had to admit that she was a willing accomplice in the distance that Janice imposed, and that the awkwardness was not all on the other side.

"What brings you to Oak Bluffs?" Janice was asking. A split second later five nine- or ten-year-old boys appeared in the doorway, wanting to know if lunch was ready. Janice pointed to the table.

Danny Swanson spotted Shannon over by the refrigerator. "Hiya!" he called. "Where have *you* been?"

She grinned at him. "Oh, around."

"Did you bring Pixel?"

"She's out in the car, sulking."

"Be right back," the boy promised, bolting out the door before his mother could remind him of either his lunch or his guests. Shannon watched out the window while Danny leaned over the driver's seat of the Subaru, where patient Pixel had turned into a wriggling bundle of furry anticipation. In seconds the other kids had deserted both lunch and the computer to go play with the dog. Pix, sprung from the car, was leaping into the air to snag high-bouncing tennis balls. She taught her new friends the play stance, somewhere between ballet's fourth position and the way the catcher stands behind home plate. First you did the stance, then you faked left, faked right, and dove for the ball. Steve Silvia caught on quickly, to Pixel's delight.

Janice and Rainey gazed at the table in dismay. "When did a kid ever turn down a cold hamburger?" Shannon said. Speaking rapidly to take advantage of the boys' absence, she added, "What I came over to tell you? Wayne's back on the island."

Janice froze. Obviously this was news to her. "Oh dear," said Rainey, moving closer to her friend.

"I tried to reach Jay—"

"He's in Boston," Janice said. "At a conference."

"I know. I couldn't get through to his hotel room"—jeez, what a smooth talker she was, fudging the truth without missing a beat—"so I left a message for him at the conference registration desk. I said Wayne was back and told him to call you or me."

"Thanks so much," said Janice.

Forgive me, Bill W. and Doctor Bob, for what I am about to do. The founders of Alcoholics Anonymous understood that in some cases it was better to break anonymity than to preserve it. The last line of the Serenity Prayer—*"and the wisdom to know the difference"*—flickered through Shannon's mind. "He was at the ten o'clock AA meeting in Vineyard Haven this morning. I saw him with my own eyes, but that's all I know. I talked to the office manager at Youth Services . . ."

"Becca?" Janice asked, with audible disdain. Janice had been known to make borderline snide remarks about Becca's nose ring, Becca's occasional forays into non-traditional hair color, Becca's choice of clothes. Belatedly it dawned on Shannon that Janice didn't like other women getting close to her brother. She picked at Becca, she'd cut Shannon off; she'd even drifted away from the Women's Resources women. Shannon filed the insight away for further consideration at a later date.

"Yeah. She's going to find out what she can find out and then let me know. If she can't reach me, she'll probably call you."

"Thank you so much," Janice said again, and Shannon, cynic though she was, knew she meant it. "I should probably call Evalina Montrose."

Shannon nodded. Rainey said, "I'll stay with her, I promise."

"Good plan," Shannon said. "You might want to let Kevin know." Kevin, at his own request, wasn't covered by last fall's restraining order; his father could contact him directly without breaking any laws. If Wayne was in reasonable possession of his faculties, he'd probably do exactly that. "Listen, Janice—he may be sober, he may have taken his own inventory and he may even be sincerely ready to make amends for everything he's done. That would be great, but at best it's probably premature. He may be a dry drunk. He might have gotten sober and played the game just so he could get loose again. He might not be sober at all. Speaking as an alcoholic, I can tell you that alcoholics are sneaky. He might still be dangerous, is what I'm trying to say."

"Don't worry," said Janice. "I'm not about to trust him."

"Call a few friends. Let them know he's back. Talk to Evalina. Write my phone number on the back of your hand." Shannon smiled. "You're going to be fine. You know the drill, Janice. If you feel a twinge, don't sit on it. Call somebody. I'm here, we're all here. And do me a big favor? If you hear from Jay, call me immediately."

"I'll do it. Really and truly, I'll do it."

Shannon believed her. Lesbians might not be worthy role models for children, but these straight girls sure as hell knew who'd watch their back in a crisis.

Rainey Silvia accompanied her to the door, ostensibly to call the kids in. To Shannon's surprise, the other woman followed her out into the yard, where Pixel was racing around with a tennis ball in her mouth, pursued by five boys. Pixel had mastered half the rules of fetch: she'd grab the ball, but she'd rarely give it back. "Time to eat, guys," Rainey said.

"Awwww . . ."

"Pix has to go home," Shannon added. She watched the children piling through the front door, Danny bringing up the rear. Pix dropped the ball at her feet and looked up hopefully, smile smile, wag wag.

Rainey made no move to go in. "I wondered," she started, "I wondered if it would be OK—I'm worried, about Janny?" She paused, looking back at the house.

"She's going to be OK," Shannon assured her. "Wayne's almost certainly going to be on his best behavior for the next few days. Besides, she's lucky, she's got friends like you keeping an eye out."

Rainey managed a brief smile. "Well, really, it's not just Janny, it's sort of about Jay too."

With considerable effort Shannon managed to *not* grab Rainey's arm and yell, "Oh my God, you and me both!"

"It's probably not a big deal," Rainey said, watching Pixel root around the rhododendrons, "but would it be OK if I called you at home?"

Shannon looked her in the eye. "Call me," she said. "Any time. You won't wake anyone up. I mean it. I'm in the book. Call me."

Rainey managed a little smile. "Thanks."

Shannon watched until the door closed behind her, then walked around her car to let Pixel in on the passenger's side. What did Rainey want to talk about? Shannon didn't know, but her hunch—her hope—was so strong her eyes watered and she wanted to shout out loud. No spy was ever more relieved to find support behind enemy lines.

The tumblers started to rattle—or whatever passed for tumblers in these key-card hotel locks. Adrenaline surged but didn't get far before Jay's mind overrode it. With an effort he remained where he was, sitting in bed, draped in a bathrobe, with conference papers spread out around him. The ice cubes had mostly melted in his otherwise empty glass; the Jim Beam bottle on the bureau was more than three-quarters full. So was its reflection in the mirror just behind it.

The vestigial hallway inside the door was full of shadows. It might be early afternoon outside the drawn curtains, but by the door it was late at night. A figure emerged from the gloom, like a pedestrian hurrying home through foggy London, just before the Ripper appears.

It was Adam—who else would it be? Sauntering in with the slightest smile on his lips, more at home in this room than Jay would ever be. A plain overcoat hung open over his bartender suit: pleated white shirt, navy blue vest, perfectly symmetrical black bow tie. He drew a paper bag from under his left arm and raised his dark eyebrows. Jay flicked his eyes toward the bureau, where Jim Beam stood. A bottle of Bushmills joined it.

"You didn't . . ."

"It's on your tab, choirboy," Adam assured him. "Employee discount."

Should he offer the visitor whiskey, or should he wait? Adam wouldn't pour unless he was standing behind a bar, or unless his companion was too drunk to hit the glass.

Adam shrugged his coat off and tossed it onto the extra bed. "Still sleeping under the window, huh?"

"Habit."

"Weren't you going to get a king this trip?"

"I completely forgot." The truth was that he'd lost his nerve when he booked the room. Bad enough he wasn't staying at the conference hotel—but asking for a room with a king-size bed? What if someone got suspicious? As soon as he'd hung up the phone, his jitters seemed like rank paranoia. Like anyone in the hotel office was going to notice? Or care if they did? Or immediately relay the information to someone at home?

Jay set his pile of file folders, loose papers, and two semi-scholarly journals on the table and rose from the suddenly puny double, leaving the robe behind. Adam might be a shade taller, a little broader in the shoulders, more muscular through chest and belly, but they were pretty much of a size.

Jay reached for Adam's tie. Adam's fingers grasped his wrists, firmly but without force. They slipped down his ribs, raising hairs as they went, and plunged under the elasticized waistband of Jay's shorts. Jay flushed. "I," murmured Adam, "have been thinking about that butt since I woke up this morning. Almost drove right off the turnpike on my way to work."

Jay's knees threatened to give out. He leaned against Adam's chest, catching a very faint whiff of leathery aftershave, the beginning of whiskers on a clean-shaven jaw, and a clear impression that Adam was horny as hell.

"Time to take your shorts off, mister," Adam said.

Sometime after that, it was Adam sitting up in the bed, pointing with one forefinger at the bottle of Bushmills. Jay went to the standard-issue hotel bureau. Bottle in one hand, two glasses in the other, he started to turn.

"Stand still!" Adam barked.

Jay gazed at the mirror, at Adam leaning forward from the headboard, eclipsed by his own left side. Tension sparked in the air between them. What did Adam see? Was he satisfied? What next?

"Bring it here," ordered Adam, and when Jay had obeyed, "Pour."

Jay poured generously into both glasses.

"Did I say to pour two?"

Confused, Jay said, "I thought—"

"Don't think!"

Adam sipped the whiskey, his eyes never leaving Jay's face.

"Pour that back." Adam pointed at the second glass. "No spills."

Jay's hand shook. The honey-colored liquid flicked one side of the glass then the other. He waited for it to still.

"Now!"

A trickle of liquid escaped down the neck of the bottle. Jay swallowed hard, staring at the glass rim till it blurred.

"You spilled."

"Sorry. I didn't mean . . ."

Pause. "How sorry are you?" The voice mocked and teased and terrified him. It dropped and chuckled: "Old Harry there doesn't look very sorry. Old Harry looks positively unrepentant." Adam savored another swallow.

Jay grabbed the glass from Adam's hand and drank. Liquid splashed on Adam's lap, dribbled over Jay's lower lip. Adam leaned down and squeezed Jay's right nipple. Jay gasped once, and again when the pressure vanished, leaving an excruciating memento of its presence. "Tell me what you want," said Adam patiently. "If you don't tell me, you won't get it."

What you did before . . .

Adam rose from the bed and started gathering his trousers and shirt from the nearest chair.

"No, don't leave."

"Tell me what you want," Adam repeated.

"What you did before," Jay whispered.

Then Jay was windsurfing, feeling the ocean through the board under his feet, the wind pulling against his arms, the torrent of air rushing past. Don't think: that was the secret. If you thought too much, you'd wipe out.

Showered and dressed, Jay glanced at his watch: 2:50. He could still make the 3:30 panel that he had circled in his conference program. The subject—whether Ritalin and comparable drugs were overprescribed for so-called problem kids—was a passionate interest of his, and a long-time Free Radical buddy was on the panel. So was the telegenic psychiatrist whom the Free Rads had dubbed "Dr. Ritalin" for his enthusiastic support of pharmacotherapy. Unfortunately, the moderator, an elder statesman in the field, was renowned for short-circuiting promising discussions with well-timed clichés. "There is no reason," he would say whenever one panelist was about to challenge another's sloppy thinking or unproven facts, "why we can't agree to disagree, is there?" He could deftly contain the "young hotheads" while congratulating the old rockheads for their statesmanship. Listening to the panel would probably be an exercise in frustration. Jay decided to skip it. He was having dinner with an assortment of Free Rads; one or more of them would be able to fill him in on what happened, and what would have happened if Mr. Moderation hadn't intervened. What to do in the three hours between now and then?

Sunlight was now streaming through the open curtains: a great afternoon for a walk in the woods, and Jay did know of several fine destinations within a fifteen- or twenty-minute drive. But though his current garb was casual by conference standards, Jay was not one to go hiking in new khakis, a suit jacket, or the half-size-too-small brown oxfords he had on his feet. Not to mention his Free Radicals tie. Jay glanced at it in the mirror. Was the knot off-center? He pulled it a bit right and prodded it a bit left.

He should check his e-mail, in case there had been any change in plans. He plugged his modem cable into the extra phone jack—for once he didn't have to rearrange the furniture or dislodge any dust to do it—and settled against the backboard of the carefully remade bed, flipped open his laptop, and logged on.

The small screen filled with a cascade of e-mail senders' names and subject lines. Jay skimmed through the latter, looking for references to the gang's dinner plans. Nothing—but in the left-hand column the name "Rebecca J. Herschel" caught his eye long enough to prompt a double-take. His office manager was "Becca," period; down in Youth Services, surnames existed only on desk plates and office doors. The message:

Hope you're reading this in the bar or the hot tub <g>.

Seriously, if she hasn't reached you already, Shannon needs to talk with you soonest. Have a ball, see you Monday.

XXOO <just kidding!>

Becca

It's about Alice Chase. Has to be. He'd actually managed to put that whole matter out of his mind since landing at Logan, despite having seen Scoop Benaron on the other side of the fence at Martha's Vineyard Airport. *Could she really have been charged with arson?* No: if the court hadn't moved by 4 p.m. yesterday, it wouldn't do anything till Monday morning, and besides, Chief Tay had all but said that the fire wasn't set. Maybe things hadn't gone well with the Hammonds. He sent off a "thanks, I'll take care of it " reply to Becca then gazed at the mirror. His right side gazed back; the left was cut off by the frame. The bottle of Bushmills was reflected, the Jim Beam was not.

His fingers moved the trackball to the Navigator icon and clicked. The browser loaded; he typed in the URL for a nationwide "white pages" directory.

```
NAME: Adam Kortmeyer
ADDRESS:
TOWN:
STATE: MA
```

The search took barely two seconds, and the results gave Jay a chill through his jaw and shoulders. There were only three listings: Kortmeyer, Adam D, in this very town, at a number whose exchange was the same as the hotel's; Kortmeyer, Adam D, in a suburb about twenty miles west and not far from the Mass. Pike; and Kortmeyer, Adam and Diane W, coincidentally in the very same suburb. *That must be fun for the post office,* Jay thought.

Except that the two listings had the same phone number.

CHAPTER TWELVE

Whispering the number to himself over and over, Jay logged off, laid his laptop aside, and reached for the phone. He pressed the digits into the keyboard. On the other end the ring was cut off by "Hello?" It was a child, probably a boy, who couldn't have been more than six years old. "I'm sorry," said Jay, "this must be the wrong number." He hung up and dialed again.

This time there were two rings before a woman answered. "Hello?"

"Hi, sorry to bother you again," Jay said. "I must have the wrong number. Is this . . ." and he pronounced the digits slowly, one by one.

"Yes, it is," said the pleasant voice. "May I help you?"

"I'm trying to reach Adam Kortmeyer."

"This is the right number," the woman said in a pleasant voice that betrayed not the slightest sign of annoyance, "but he's at work. Would you like to leave a message?"

"No, thanks," Jay replied. "I've got his work number. I'll try him there."

Jay stared at his reflection in the mirror. He hardly recognized himself: so neatly dressed, hair neatly combed and parted, about to head off to yet another conference where total strangers kept gushing about how *creative* he was. If people thought *he* was creative, the whole society was in worse trouble than he thought. *Could Adam really be married, with children?*

He'd better call Shannon. Shannon wouldn't be trying to reach him if it wasn't important.

When her answering machine picked up—"This is the number for Pixel Productions, Shannon Merrick, proprietor. We're sorry . . ."—he was disappointed. Dutifully he started to leave a message: "Hey, Shan, Becca said—"

Shannon picked up: "Hey, man, I'm here, I'm just working, if you can call it that. Becca got you, huh?"

"I got her e-mail. What's the word?"

"Are you sitting down?"

"Yeah," Jay replied, "staring at myself in the mirror of your garden-variety hotel room, sitting on the garden-variety floral print of your typical hotel bedspread."

"The word is that Wayne's back on the island. I thought you'd want to know."

Jay's heart started pumping ice water. "Who said?"

"I saw him with my own eyes," said Shannon. "At a ten o'clock meeting of the anonymous fellowship."

"Damn," he said. His blood started to thaw, but not fast enough. *What was Wild Man Wayne up to? What was he planning? How much did he know?*

"Don't panic, kiddo," said Shannon. "I went over to Janice's and told her. She's doing all right. Rainey's with her. She's going to call Evalina. I asked Becca to see what she could find out, hope that's OK. Who he's reporting to at the courthouse. Has to be somebody, don't you think?"

Shannon was way ahead of him, but he wasn't going to tell her that. "Good plan," he said. "What's your take—how did he seem to you?"

"I didn't stick around long enough to do a full assessment," Shannon said. Jay could see the sly grin on her face. "He was at a meeting. That's a good sign, as signs go."

"I'll call Janny," he decided.

"Good," Shannon replied. "She'll be glad to hear from you."

"Should I come home early, do you think?" he asked, not enthusiastic about the prospect.

"Nah," she said. "You want this drunk's take on that drunk?

Jay had a hard time with recovering alcoholics who referred to themselves as drunks. Like Shannon and Wayne seriously had something in common? He would trust Shannon with his life; he wouldn't trust Wayne with enough change to buy a pack of gum. "Sure."

"He wants his family back. He thinks that's the payoff for getting sober and playing by the rules. So he's going to play by the rules. He's going to obey the restraining order to the very letter."

"Meaning," Jay mused out loud, "he's going to contact Kevin first."

"I wouldn't be surprised," she said.

After a long pause, Jay asked, "Alice and Mitch get moved OK?"

"They're in the process," Shannon replied. "Kate and/or Randy must have come by while I was running around. There's another carload left, though. I'm expecting them to walk through the door any minute."

"Tell them I'll call as soon as I get back Monday morning, and if they need to talk to anyone before then—"

"They can call Gerbil Junior?" Shannon asked mischievously. "His number's on your office answering machine."

"Damn, I almost forgot . . ." Jay shook his head. "It was a last resort. Every trustworthy backup was either off-island or dying with the flu or organizing a fiftieth anniversary party for the in-laws."

"Becca and the Women's Resources gang can probably handle any problems till you get back," she said.

"I'm sure of it—listen, I gotta go," he said, having abruptly decided that he really did want to catch part of the Ritalin panel; all of a sudden he was in the mood to flap the unflappable moderator with irrefutable facts and unanswerable questions. "My conference is calling, you know how it is. ISS pays my way; I better do some work."

"What dedication, what integrity!" Was Shannon being sarcastic? He couldn't tell. "I left a message for you at the conference registration desk. You can chuck it. Keep me posted."

"I will," Jay promised.

As soon as he hung up, his mind went into overdrive. *The shoe's dropped—Wayne's back.* He squeezed his laptop into his already overstuffed attaché, scooped change, car keys, and key card off the bureau, then took one last look around. *And did Wayne step off the boat this morning, just in time to stroll up the street to an AA meeting? Not likely, which makes it most likely that the Gerb was stonewalling on Wednesday—which is to say "lying through his perfectly aligned and polished teeth": either Wayne was already back and he knew where, or Wayne was due any minute and he knew when. What a weasel, what a ferret, what a rat. "I know something you don't know, nyah nyah, nyah nyah."*

And Wayne had gotten sober, Jay thought, heading out the door. No, strike that: Wayne had showed up at an AA meeting that Shannon happened to be at. This was a serious piece of luck. Christ, where was Jerry Turner's mind? Why hadn't the probation officer called Janny? Jay would never leave people in the dark like that. Was it fine with them that Wayne might show up unannounced at Janice's front door? No wonder these "Megan's Laws" were so popular—the good ol' boys calling the shots were so clueless about when to notify and when to shut up, they needed a rule to tell them how and when to do the right thing.

On the whole, though, Shannon's theory made sense: Wayne wanted to prove that he'd gotten his act together, therefore he was going to follow the rules. *At least as long as he thinks it'll get him what he wants.* Meaning he would not contact Janny directly. Meaning he would probably try to contact Kevin. *Five gets you twenty he'll be in the high school parking lot at two o'clock Monday afternoon.*

Jay reached his rental car, a metallic gray Honda Accord, without any physical memory of making his way down the corridor and two flights of stairs, across the motel lobby, through the revolving doors, and into the parking lot. He'd even forgotten to notice if Adam was behind the bar. He unlocked the door and slid into the driver's seat. According to his watch, the panel had barely started. Not bad: the fireworks rarely started until the prepared presentations were over, and often not until the Q&A. He could check his messages, maybe grab a Coke . . .

I left a message for you at the conference registration desk.

How? Shannon must have talked to Becca—Becca who assumed he was staying at the conference hotel, because that was where she'd booked him a room. So Shannon had to know that he *wasn't* staying at the conference hotel. *Shit.* He better cook up a plausible explanation, just in case she asked. Not that Shannon would ask: Shannon would look at him as if she already knew. *Shit. Shit shit shit.*

The car bolted backward. Fortunately there was nothing behind him. Damn automatic transmissions anyway.

Shannon printed out the dummy pages she'd been working on. Even after several years of designing on-screen, she still liked to see the hardcopy. This job had tables and charts out the wazoo, and the client wanted some of them to incorporate cutesy graphics that Shannon hoped to talk her out of. Maybe that was why the old designer had quit? *So, question: Why isn't Jay registered at the conference hotel? Answer: Because he's not staying at the conference hotel. Why isn't he staying at the conference hotel? . . .*

Shannon made a mental note to bring the Tenth Step up with her sponsor: *"Continued to take personal inventory and when we were wrong promptly admitted it."* She was trying to run someone else's life again. Jay might be having an off-island affair—hell, he might be supplementing his ISS salary by turning tricks on weekends—but she couldn't control his behavior, even if she thought he was headed for a fall. Which she did, and he knew it, because she'd told him so. It was her right to issue warnings; it was his right to ignore them. It was his right to understand how sneaking around ruined other people's lives while being totally clueless about how it might be threatening his. She didn't need her sponsor to tell her that it was long past time to detach from Jay's private life. What she did need her sponsor to tell her was why she couldn't manage to do it.

It wasn't her sponsor's number that she dialed, though; it was Leslie Benaron's. She carried the phone away from her little office area and plunked herself down on the sofa. Leslie answered on the fourth ring. "Hey, girlfriend, what's up?" Shannon asked. *I should really stop calling her "girlfriend," too, since I know it pisses her off.*

Leslie didn't growl about it this time, though. "Well, my dad's here, and while we've been running around doing errands, he's been telling me how smart I was to not go home for Pesach. I guess it was the scene to end all scenes."

"Next year in the loony bin," Shannon said.

Leslie laughed. "So are we still on for dinner?"

"That's what I was calling about. I have to beg off. I've got too much work."

"What is this working on Saturday? You want to borrow my copy of *Women Who Do Too Much*?"

"I work on Saturday because I goof off Monday through Friday," said Shannon. "No, really: I'm finally into this huge complicated job, I know what I'm doing, and I'm afraid that if I drop it for a couple of hours, I'll forget."

"I've had stories like that," Leslie said. "Your loss. Dad was going to take us to the Lambert's Cove Inn. Now he's just going to take me to the Lambert's Cove Inn."

"Have an extra dessert for me," said Shannon. "But don't tell me what I missed. Enjoy your dinner and think of me eating cold chicken vegetable soup out of a can."

"You could still change your mind—"

"Lead me not into temptation." Shannon grinned at the phone. "Nice front-page pic, by the way. Who's Chris Almeida?"

"A news photographer from around Pittsburgh somewhere who's here, believe it or not, visiting his parents in Edgartown. The man literally walked in right off the street with these pictures. Lucky for me—otherwise the story would probably have ended up as filler somewhere back in the classifieds."

"I thought it was pretty good," Shannon assured her. "Covered all the bases—"

"Oh sure," Leslie said. "All the bases except Alice Chase. Without Alice it's a zero story. I've been sitting here staring at the phone ever since the paper came out. Every time it rings, I hope it's Alice. Every time I pick it up, it's Quincy Hancock the Third."

Shannon caught the edginess in Leslie's voice. Was Leslie smoking again? Or was it just that her father was here for the weekend? "I'm sure she'll call," Shannon said. *And you'll meet at some cozy, out-of-the-way spot, and it'll dawn on you that, hey, you've seen this woman before, and then you'll remember where, and—and I'm ragging on Jay for riding toward a cliff with blinders on?* Shannon hadn't exactly encouraged Alice to contact the *Chronicle,* either before or after the story came out: "Wait till you get settled at the Hammonds'," she'd said. And when she checked her motives, a little bird kept chirping that this was not *entirely* about Alice's best interests—that it was partly about saving herself from the Wrath of Leslie. "Meanwhile," she said, to assuage her uneasiness, "guess who's back on the rock?"

Leslie thought, then "Hah! Wild Man Wayne?"

"Got it in one," said Shannon. "I can't go into details, but I saw him with my own eyes. Took me a minute to recognize him, though: he's cleaned up quite a bit."

"Like he's probably not going to be disturbing the peace

anytime soon?" Leslie sounded a little disappointed.

"Don't bet against it," Shannon advised. "Wayne Swanson needs a lot more than a shampoo and a shave. We're talking termites in the foundation here."

"Speaking of Wayne, guess what happened at the airport yesterday?" In an instant Leslie had shifted from gloomy to downright gleeful. "While I was picking up my dad?"

"Damned if I know," said Shannon.

"Nick McAuliffe showed up. It was a riot. He thought he had a reservation on the 4:25 to Boston, but it turned out he was accidentally booked on *yesterday's* 4:25. Talk about a kvetch. He hung around and around hoping that the only no-show passenger on the 4:25 wouldn't show up, but he did at the absolute last minute. And here's the best part: guess who bumped the best-selling author off the plane."

Shannon knew only one person who was flying to Boston yesterday, so it was his name that came out of her mouth: "Jay Segredo?"

"His very self. And," Leslie went on, so obviously gloating that Shannon was tempted to hang up while she was ahead, "you missed the most touching parting scene in the parking lot. If that wasn't his girlfriend who was seeing him off, I'll take my L-U-V antenna in for repair."

That's not his girlfriend, that's his cover. But Shannon couldn't think of a snappy comeback that could be said out loud. And she wasn't about to ask Leslie for a play-by-play either.

"If Jay is gay, then so's—so's my mother," Leslie said triumphantly.

"Oh?" said Shannon. "And how long have you known about this?"

"Oh, come on," Leslie said, exasperated. "Jay isn't gay. You think everyone you like is gay, whether they think so or not. Get over it."

Leslie still thought the only gay people on Martha's Vineyard were the ones who wore pink triangle T-shirts in public—all three of them. Shannon hung up the phone.

Damn Leslie and her damned daddy-supported life. Shannon sat on the sofa and fumed. In the back of her mind she knew she was fuming because she'd acted like a jerk on the phone, then compounded her error by hanging up. Knowing why didn't help: she was still pissed off. *Year-round house on the water, no rent; must be nice.* It was nearly impossible to work for either island newspaper unless you were being supported by a trust fund or a high-earning spouse. She knew this for a fact because about six years ago she'd interviewed for a job at the *Chronicle* designing and typesetting ads. Laura the production manager had been wowed by her résumé, her clips, her self-taught but intimate knowledge of Quark XPress. For her part Shannon had been wowed—"flabbergasted" was a better word—both by the salary offered and by the fact the hours were just below the *Chronicle*'s threshold for full-time work. In other words: no benefits, and less annual leave than she could provide for herself. She knew for a fact that Laura had gone to bat for her, tried to get Chet and Arabella to up the salary. Laura had struck out. No surprise there: what did Old Money Arabella or Chet Son of Old Money know about making a living on Martha's Vineyard? Not a goddamn thing.

Pixel padded over to the door and made a little "RrrFF?" The dog always knew when Shannon's thoughts were turning daggerish, and with an instinct for avoiding trouble that any Twelve-Stepper would envy, she'd immediately move out of range. Shannon got up and headed for the door. "Sorry about the bad karma, Pixie-Pixo. Why don't you go out and see if you can find some of the good stuff."

She watched Pixel thump-ka-thump down the stairs and meander over to the scraggly woods that bordered the lawn.

Satisfied that Pixel wasn't about to race off in search of the Impossible Squirrel, Shannon closed the front door. She paused in the kitchen to taste the leftover morning coffee, poured it into a mug, and stuck it in the microwave. Waiting for it to heat, she wandered into the living room. Her gaze turned to her computer, to the sofa, to the telephone on the coffee table, to the studio door. If she squinted she could almost see the iron portcullis of her most recent sketch, framed by an archway of granite stones.

The microwave beeped; she retrieved her coffee and took it to the sofa. She dialed Giles's number. His machine picked up; she left a message: "I've been working very, very hard: I went to visit Janice, I reached Jay at the conference, I printed out a dummy of that new job. The good news is that I didn't tell Leslie Benaron to get over her delusions of heterosexuality; the bad news is that I hung up on her. Call me when you get a chance. I'm having supper with the neighbors, but I'll probably be home early and up late."

All the while she was staring at the studio door. After she hung up, she grabbed her crummy sketchpad. The portcullis, the granite stones took shape in no. 2 pencil. It was too faint: color, she needed color. She dragged herself up from the couch and picked dark blue, red, and emerald green pencils out of the Antique Power Show mug that stood at the ready beside the computer monitor. She sketched a hydrangea to the left of the portcullis and gave it three big blue flower balls. Satisfied, she did the same on the right. Then she scribbled a little green grass around the base of the two shrubs.

This was too feeble, too desperately, hopelessly feeble to be borne. Pencils could never do the thing justice. Shannon swatted the sketchpad aside and stood up. She walked to The Door. *Bzzzzzzz! Zzzap!* No fucking way was she gonna get suckered through that door, even if her oils and acrylics were on the other side of it. On the other side of that door, her paintings were hanging on the wall, waiting to laugh at her, waiting to mock her, waiting to snicker that she was a hack with no talent and less guts.

She started tracing the portcullis with her right forefinger, and abruptly inspiration came slithering up through the floor. To the mud room she went, opened the door to the basement, groaned at the junk cluttering every step all the way down to the concrete floor, and quickly closed the door. Instead she went around outside, interrupting Pixel's snooze at the bottom of the steps, and entered the basement through the slider. Paint. She had paint left over from almost every home improvement project she'd attempted since she'd bought the house, paint in large cans, paint in small cans, paint probably all dried up and cracked like the Sahara in summer. There had to be something down here she could use.

While Pixel rooted in the dark, cobwebby corners of usually forbidden territory, Shannon pried the cans open one by one with a screwdriver. Fifteen minutes later she was lugging the best ones upstairs, two at a time: the milk chocolate brown she'd used for the outside trim four years ago; a rich rose that had proved too dark for the bathroom but that, liberally mixed with a creamy white, had worked very well for her bedroom; a small can of black that had never been opened; another small can, this one of blue enamel that she'd used for the trim and the coat rack in the mud room; the remains of a large can of egg-yolk yellow—she had no idea where she'd used that, but she'd evidently used a lot of it. She carried up the turpentine, she carried up a dark gray dropcloth, she carried up the old coffee can full of brushes, she carried up the stepladder that Ben Wharton had given her for a housewarming present—"so you won't break your neck on mine," he'd said.

She spread the dropcloth on the floor before the studio door, then arranged the paint cans on its outer perimeter. What to mix the paint in? Cereal bowls? Mugs? She found a generous stash of jumbo paper cups in the cupboard above the fridge and, tucked back on a shelf in the cleaning closet, two battered old thrift-shop pots that she'd forgotten she had. After mixing three shades of gray, she went to work: turning The Door into a portcullis. Then she created an arch of stones, squares alternating with oblongs, with a keystone on top; the first few stones were meticulously rendered, then they got a little more irregular and a good deal less detailed as they went up the door and came down the other side.

Pixel sat down in the middle of the room and launched into an indignant "rrrr-RRR!" Shannon let her out, then she mixed up some credible green and started painting hydrangeas. The hydrangeas, she decided, looked much too tacky; she turned them into rhododendrons.

The phone rang. Dimly registering that it was nearly dark outside, Shannon answered it. It was Mary Wharton: "Pixel's here, where are you?"

It was six forty-five. Shannon apologized profusely and said she'd be over as soon as she got the paint off her fingers, not to mention her face, and changed her clothes.

When she went to services as a kid, Leslie used to thank God regularly that she had inherited her looks from her mother and everything else from her father. Even in his impeccably tailored dark gray suit, David Benaron looked, well, underdressed, and the serene dignity of the Lambert's Cove Inn dining room only made matters worse. Leslie's mother would have been straightening her husband's tie by now, or pointing out that the sleeves of his jacket were a quarter inch too short. Now Leslie thanked God that she wasn't the kind of person who was impelled to do such things in public.

David exchanged a few words in German with the innkeeper, Louisa, who was playing maître d' tonight in a stunning floor-length blue velvet dress with a touch of antique lace at wrists and throat. Louisa, half Swedish by birth, spoke five languages fluently; David, from his years as a foreign correspondent, could get along well in three and fake it in three more. Leslie could order food and ask directions in Paris and Rome.

"You must not let these people lure you into an argument," Louisa was saying, the tips of her fingers pressed together and pointing at David. It took Leslie a moment to realize that Louisa was speaking English. "They are a waste of your time.

You are doing the right thing for the working people, and this makes them angry."

"I agree one hundred percent," David said. "You cannot know how much I appreciate your support."

Evidently a momentous controversy was going on, probably in the *New Republic* or the *Washington Post* or some other prestigious publication that Leslie read far less frequently than she should, that concerned her father. Of course she'd missed it completely. She, Leslie Benaron, high school salutatorian, voted Most Likely to Succeed (Female), and Barnard graduate magna cum laude, was slowly getting sucked into the pernicious assumption that if it didn't happen on Martha's Vineyard, who the hell cared?

Louisa escorted them to a table in a secluded corner and laid a menu on each of the two plates. "The rack of lamb is spectacular tonight," she confided. "The cioppino also. And do save room for the crème brulée. Enjoy your dinner," she said graciously, and went off to greet the next arrivals. Her blond French braid looked spectacular against that deep blue velvet. *Thou shalt not covet thy maître d's hair.*

"Now *that,*" said David Benaron, journalist and world traveler, "is a woman."

"What does that mean?" Leslie asked crossly. "What am I, iceberg lettuce?"

"Now, now," said David. "I didn't come here to have dinner with your mother."

Leslie wanted to flounce out of the room, but she wasn't dressed for it. Just before the angry flush reached her cheeks, their waiter brought David's red wine to the table. He uncorked the bottle and poured for David, who had to taste and nod before he would pour for Leslie. *What are we supposed to do if we don't like it, send it back to the liquor store?*

Leslie sipped her wine and took a deep breath. "So which Philistines are at your throat now?"

"Your friends from the *Asclepius Report,*" David said,

obviously delighted to be asked. "I've been invited to testify at a Senate hearing—hah! The Asclepians are furious. Their Republican friends have said some very, very mean things about your poor father." He leaned close to her and stage-whispered, "Not only do they accuse me of being a *liberal journalist,* they say I support *socialized medicine!*"

Leslie couldn't help laughing. Then she stage-whispered back: "You love every minute of it."

"You are absolutely right," he said, catching the eye of their waiter, who was standing at a discreet distance from their table. "I would like to tell them, 'Of course I support socialized medicine, and so would you if you didn't have such a cushy-cushy benefits package, courtesy of the U.S. taxpayer.'"

"And why," Leslie asked, acutely aware that their waiter was standing by to take their order, "don't you tell them that?"

"Because," David said, including the young waiter this time, "it would lead my friends in the media into too much temptation. You see the banner headlines?" He punctuated each word by stabbing the air with a piece of french bread: "'Eminent Journalist Endorses Red Medicine.' My AMA friends would stop inviting me to their parties. I would have to accept a university appointment and become a very serious Marxist economist to whom nobody listens."

Leslie couldn't help noticing that a smile was slipping across the waiter's professional face. She ordered the cioppino and her father the rack of lamb, both to be prefaced with a salad of island greens, a selection of baked cheeses, and another basket of bread. "Now," said David once the waiter had disappeared, "about this story you're working on." Leslie hadn't launched into her explanation about Alice Chase, the fire, and Nick McAuliffe till she turned down the long driveway to the inn, which meant that she was barely halfway through.

"It's not really a big deal," Leslie said. *It's not going to get me invited to testify before Congress.*

"Who knows? So what does the story look like now?"

"What it doesn't look like is arson," said Leslie.

"And this disappoints you," her father prompted.

Leslie shrugged. "So a house burned down: the wiring was substandard, what else is new? Arson would at least make it interesting. A personal vendetta, or someone's out to swindle the insurance company, or someone's out to make it *look* like someone's out to swindle the insurance company."

"What did I tell you?" David did his wise-old-owl imitation. "You're bored with small-town life, small-town news. You're ready for some excitement—"

"Oh yeah, gang wars, hostile takeovers, White House sex scandals—" Leslie stopped dead. Louisa was escorting across the dining room the woman who had sold the burned-down house to its current owner of record. Accompanying her was a tanned, silver-haired gentleman of perhaps sixty who fairly oozed health, affluence, intelligence, humor . . . Leslie, who had never been accused of liking older men, seriously considered cutting in.

"That's Doug Trumbull," her father said. "You met him at the airport; he was on my plane from New York. An MD who has made it impressively big in pharmaceuticals, but he is not a friend of the Asclepians, not for one minute. 'The Thatcher-Friedmans,' he calls them."

"That's Meg Hasbro with him," said Leslie, refusing to be one-upped. "The real estate agent who brokered the sale of the house. Some people think she helped harass Alice into moving."

"Perhaps she had an affair with your famous novelist," David mused. "Women often do foolish things for the men they love."

With great care Leslie guided her wineglass back to the pristine white tablecloth before its contents sloshed all over her lap. "Dad!" was all she could say.

David shrugged philosophically. "Doug is here to see a property on Makonikey," he said. "He loves it. His wife—his second wife—hates it. He didn't bring her this trip."

"Aha," said Leslie. "So he's wining and dining his real estate agent?"

"It would seem so."

"Who might just crawl into bed with the client in order to seal the deal?" Leslie rolled her eyes. "Come *on.*"

"No, no, no!" said David Benaron, as if *tsk-tsk-tsk*ing a pupil who was uncharacteristically slow on the uptake. "Nothing so crass as that. Making a deal is like dancing. Some deals are stately, stylized—like minuets. Some are like tangos—now this way! now that way! The unready dancer could get whiplash." His beaming face indicated that he was most pleased with the image. Leslie, however, couldn't guess where her father was going. "Like an interview," he said, apparently sensing her confusion. "You know this: an interview is a dance. Question, answer, forward, backward, sidestep, catch me if you can! The adrenaline builds, ebbs, flows, maybe *over*flows—it feels like passion, maybe it *is* passion. And then: voilà!" After a pause to savor the moment, David added, "Not often, of course, and thank God for that! Washington is torrid enough as it is. But sometimes."

Leslie went from bewildered to embarrassed in zero point five seconds. Thank God Shannon had cancelled. Shannon already thought she'd jumped into bed with Nick McAuliffe, and now her own father was squirting kerosene on Shannon's suspicions. "You don't really think . . ." Leslie began.

Her father pointed a knife in her direction. "Have some of this bread. It's excellent."

After that they talked like professional colleagues about the worsening housing situation on Martha's Vineyard, how employers were already complaining about labor shortages for the coming summer, and about some work that David was arranging to have done on their house before the family descended in June.

Louisa stopped by their table as they were savoring their coffee. "You were absolutely on target, as usual," David said.

"The lamb was outstanding, and the crème brulée may have been the best I've ever tasted."

"I will tell the chef," Louisa promised. "Very carefully, of course: one must be careful with these chefs, or they will demand more money." When she smiled, the hint of dimples appeared in her cheeks.

"Tell me," said David, lowering his voice, "if you will, who is that handsome woman dining with my friend Doug Trumbull." Leslie bit her lip: Her father knew damn well who "that handsome woman" was. Could he be *flirting* with Louisa?

"You know Mr. Trumbull, do you? Such an intelligent man. He is here to see a house on Makonikey. The house is haunted, I am told, but I hope he will buy it. That is his real estate broker, Meg Hasbro. She is much better suited to him than his wife. Oh, his wife! She is no older than your daughter"—Louisa beamed in Leslie's direction—"and such a, what is the word? Kvetch. She is a kvetch. Complain, complain, nag, nag. Last weekend she came with him. This weekend—no. He brought his children instead. To see the house."

"Ah," said David Benaron. "Some women are not meant to live on Martha's Vineyard." He mimicked a nouveau-riche country club matron: "'The only caviar to be found is outrageously overpriced, and the quality is well below mediocre.'"

"That is very true," Louisa said.

Leslie noticed that her father's country club matron sounded a lot like her mother.

"I do not believe that Mrs. Trumbull has a taste for caviar," Louisa confided. "She would be impressed by instant onion dip. I think he will buy the house," she added. "He would not be the first person to have a wife in New York and a lady on Martha's Vineyard!"

* * *

Alice sat knitting at one end of the sofa; at the other, Kate was engrossed in the *Utne Reader.* Alice enjoyed the fire burning merrily in the fireplace, though when Kate had asked, "How about a fire?" her reaction had been "I'm not cold at all." Kate's husband—he told her to call him Randy, but he was so dignified, like a minister almost, that she couldn't call him anything but "Mr. Hammond"—and Mitch had gone off to the movies in Vineyard Haven, and with every tick of the clock on the mantel the moment of their return was growing closer. Alice had a question to ask Kate: *"Do you think I should call the newspaper?"*

Alice's ex-mother-in-law, Bobbie Chase, was always saying that "a decent person's name only appears in the newspaper three times: when he's born, when he's married, and when he dies." To learn who had fallen from decency, she turned to the court reports first thing every week, the *Chronicle* on Thursday, the *News Beacon* on Friday, and clucked over every name she recognized. "Justin Carver," she'd say, "a chip off the old block," or "Scott McGarrett—wondered when they'd catch up with him," or "That Lizzie Smith has been riding for a fall since grade school." How did she feel seeing her son's name in the court news for drunk driving, violating restraining order, failure to appear in court? Now her brother Zack's name was in the news too, right there on the front page. Mama Chase's left eye must be twitching away, the way it did whenever she was upset.

Alice missed helping Mama Chase serve holiday dinners from her big old country kitchen; it was like helping her own gramma when she was a girl, then her mother when she got a little older. But she also had many vivid memories of Lenny in that same kitchen, straddling one of the dark green straight-back chairs and ranting on and on to his mother about how this boss had canned him because he showed up to work ten minutes late or that store manager had refused his check because the last one bounced. His mother would nod sympathetically, refill his mug with fresh coffee, and tell him to stay for lunch or supper. Not that Alice expected her to ask him right out if he got fired because he showed up ten minutes late or because he showed up *drunk* and ten minutes late. When Uncle Zack let Alice move into his house, quite a few eyebrows had hit the ceiling: Zack Butler couldn't have made his displeasure with his younger sister's son much clearer if he'd taken out a full-page ad in the *Chronicle.*

Alice took a deep breath and let her knitting lie still in her lap. "Kate? Do you think I should call the newspaper?"

"Call the newspaper?" Kate looked in her direction. "Oh. I see." The confusion passed from her face. "Do you want to call the newspaper?"

"Yeah," said Alice. "Well, sort of. It sounded like maybe they might want to talk to me. Probably they don't know where I am."

"They probably don't," Kate agreed. "Where is that newspaper anyway?" Her eyes skimmed the coffee table, the end table, the raised hearth in front of the fireplace. She twisted and looked over her shoulder. "Ah," she said, and got up to retrieve the paper from the dining room table, where her husband had been consulting the movie ads. Standing behind the sofa, she read: "'At the scene a distraught Mr. McAuliffe suggested that police question the house's most recent resident in connection with the fire. According to unconfirmed reports, this individual had been employed as a caretaker by the previous owners, Zachary and Ruth Butler. Her current whereabouts are unknown.'"

"They didn't put my name in," Alice pointed out. "He must have used my name."

"'Distraught,'" repeated Kate. "That means he was overemotional. It sounds as though he was telling the policemen how to do their job, and policemen *never* like that." Kate smiled, tapping the photograph with her forefinger. "This Leslie Benaron is a very good writer. She implies that

Mr. McAuliffe made a fool of himself without actually coming out and saying so. I wish she were covering Oak Bluffs, instead of that fellow who seems to think that none of our selectmen ever tell a lie."

"So I should maybe call her?"

"I believe," Kate said, smoothing the paper against her lap, "that she would do a good job communicating your story to the newspaper's readers. She doesn't seem overly impressed by Mr. Nick McAuliffe. He may be a best-selling novelist, but he pushed you out of your home, and then he seems to have accused you of having something to do with the fire. That's not the way the island does things."

Alice recalled the night she locked herself in the bedroom and called 911 because Lenny was pounding on the door and screaming, "Let me in, dammit! You're my wife, bitch, you can't lock me out." The night it took that pork-bellied cop half an hour to show up, and then he just had a little chat with Lenny in the front hall and went away. Never bothered to talk to her. *That's the way the island does things too.* "It might make it easier for Lenny to find me," she said. "Our hearing isn't till May nineteenth."

"You can talk off the record if you want," said Kate. "In any case there's no reason for the reporter to tell where you live."

Alice made her decision. "I'll call them on Monday," she said.

"Monday?" Kate asked. "Why wait till Monday? Call her at home!" Kate laughed and went off to the kitchen, where the island phone directory was on top of a stack on the shelf just under the wall phone.

In the dark Leslie picked her way down the hill to her front door. How much of that wine had she drunk anyway? She hadn't felt the least bit woozy till she stepped out of the car, then it was *My God, I drove all the way down Lambert's Cove Road? I can barely walk!*

Other than stubbing her toe on the edge of the patio, she made it to the door without incident. Inside the dark apartment, the first thing she noticed was the flashing light on the answering machine and, just beside it, the red number 2. She hit Play then set about turning on some lights. "Saturday, eight thirty-two p.m.," said the machine's syrupy voice, but there was no message. That was weird. Usually the syrupy voice didn't kick in unless a caller had left a message. "Saturday, nine eighteen p.m.: Hello, Ms. Benaron? This is Alice Chase . . ."

Leslie shrieked while the tape continued to play, then she remembered that her father was upstairs. "Damn," she said, loudly, but not as loud. "Damn, oh damn, oh damn." Alice Chase had called. Alice Chase had called twice: she was completely one hundred percent sure that the hang-up was Alice. It was now nine twenty-six p.m. Leslie had missed Alice by eight glorious minutes. She hit the repeat button.

"Saturday, nine eighteen p.m.: Hello, Ms. Benaron? This is Alice Chase. I used to live in the house you wrote about, the one that burned down last Sunday? I thought maybe you might want to talk to me? I'm sorry"—here Alice had a brief, inaudible conversation with someone else in the room, probably with her hand over the mouthpiece—"I can't leave my number. If it's OK I'll call you in the morning. Before nine, is that OK? Thank you. Bye."

Alice was still awake wherever she was, and Leslie didn't know how to reach her. "Fuck," she said. "Fuck fuck fuck." That settled it. First thing Monday morning she was going to call the phone company and sign up for Caller ID.

At nine thirty Shannon held her front door open till Pixel trotted up the steps and into the mud room. It had been a very pleasant evening for both: Mary had stuffed the roast chicken, so supper felt like Thanksgiving in April, and Pixel got a bigger than usual share of the leftovers. The dog's attention was still focused on the foil-wrapped parcels that Shannon carried: one contained a drumstick and some dark meat, the other covered a cereal bowl with a generous scoop of stuffing. "Forget it," said Shannon, setting the food on the gray utility shelf while she took off her jacket. After the dishes were done, Mary had worked at her sewing machine in one corner of the living room while Shannon managed to hold her own against Ben in a game of cribbage. "Holding her own" meant not getting shellacked; she'd actually been within sixteen points of finishing when Ben pegged out. Balancing the chicken containers on her palm and giving the dog a "No Begging!" glare, she opened the door into the living room.

The arch and portcullis on the wall opposite took her completely by surprise. It wasn't that she'd forgotten painting them—even in her heaviest drinking days she'd never progressed to the blackout stage. But in the shadowy light cast by her desk lamp at this end of the room and the bureau lamp she'd accidentally left on down the hall in her bedroom, the portcullis looked massive, heavy, *real.* So did the stones: a master mason had set those stones, she knew it.

She was less impressed by the rhododendrons, especially after she pushed the knob for the overhead light. They improved after she dimmed the light a bit, but not much. The real problem, of course, was all the dead space on either side of the door. She squinted: briars started growing up from the bushes. *Yes!* She started a fresh pot of coffee, changed her clothes, then surveyed the mess she had left when she rushed off to dinner. At least she'd remembered to stick the used brushes in turpentine.

She started painting big stone blocks to the left of the door, quickly obliterating the rhododendron. Up, up went the wall, row upon row of gritty gray stones, almost all the way to the ceiling. The lower rows extended to the edge of the wall where it turned the corner and became the hallway. When the coffee smell insisted, she stepped down off the ladder and headed for the kitchen. En route she noticed that her answering machine had logged in a new call—while she was at the

Whartons', or had she really been so absorbed in her work that she'd missed the spine-tingling blat of the phone? Doubtful, very doubtful. She hit the Play button and went to pour herself some coffee.

It was Giles: "Hey, girlfriend, sorry I missed you. I'm at the restaurant, it's busy but I'll probably get out by midnight. I'll call you from home. Can't *wait* to hear all about it—if you go to bed early, turn your ringer off!"

"Honey," she told the answering machine, "you don't know the half of it." She set her mug down on the edge of the computer table and picked up the phone. After Giles's outgoing message played all the way through, she said, "You can't wait? You're damn right you can't wait. You've got to see what's happening here. It's a trip and a half—get your butt over here and *you* tell *me* what's happening. Like, tell me I haven't gone completely round the bend! If I've fallen into a deep sleep, it's 'cause I've pricked my finger on a spindle but I'm really OK, you just have to give me a magic kiss. Ta-ta, Prince Charming!"

Bam, bam, bam! By the third *bam* Shannon registered that someone was knocking at the front door. At this fucking hour? It must be past midnight. *Oh God, Mary's sick, or Ben . . . ?* Pixel, though, wasn't alarmed: she roused herself from the sofa, where she wasn't supposed to be snoozing, and stretched herself deliberately from her pink-tinged black nose to the tips of her hind toes. She looked up at Shannon, waving her tail back and forth. Shannon was sitting on the fifth step of the step ladder, and she wasn't coming down till she finished the third of her pale wild roses in the upper reaches of the briar hedge. "Come in!" she bellowed.

Pixel was waiting at the inner door when Giles came through it. "Heavens, girl, you gave me such a scare! From your message I was afraid you were having a slip—"

"A slip?" Shannon cried. "Me? After slogging through nine bloody years—"

"Oh. My. God. Oh my God. Jesus H. Christ, what have you done? This is wonderful, this is great, this is worth getting a speeding ticket on the Edgartown–West Tisbury Road for!"

"You didn't!"

"I did," said Giles. "No, I lie—I almost did. An Edgartown cop chased me for doing sixty-five past the airport—"

"You weren't!"

"More like seventy, but I pulled over like a good boy, I said, 'Officer, officer, I'm an anonymous alcoholic and I'm rushing to the home of a friend who I'm afraid is about to drink again, and I may already be too late.'"

Shannon banged her forehead with her fist and started laughing.

"The officer's brother is a recovering alcoholic, AA saved his brother's life, his brother sponsors an Alateen group in Plymouth—he let me go! He said no ticket, be careful, get there safely! Shannon girlfriend, what have you done? This is wonderful, this is brilliant, I wish we could go out for a drink!"

"Coffee's in the kitchen," she said. "It's reasonably fresh."

CHAPTER THIRTEEN

The bedside clock woke Leslie at the preposterous hour of 6:30 on a Sunday morning; a notoriously sound sleeper, she had set the alarm in case Alice Chase chose to call back early. The phone still hadn't rung. At 6:55 her father knocked at her front door to invite her to join him for a walk down to the lake. She begged off: she was expecting a phone call. David Benaron's eyebrows went up: *At seven o'clock on a Sunday morning?* Alice had called while they were at dinner, she said. She hadn't left a number. She was going to call back. David headed off down the path. At 7:03, Leslie was sitting at the computer gazing at the A-list, the Alice list, and willing the phone to ring.

CASH TRANSACTION—how? oversight?
WHERE IS ALICE??
Meg Hasbro, Burnham & W. Involvement???
JAY
"friends among the rats"?
fucked-up island wiring job—bldg. insp.? renovations?

Now that she'd met Meg Hasbro, Leslie didn't want her to be a heavy. In the light of a new day, she also had to admit that her father had a point: smart women often did really dumb things for the guys they got involved with—she had to remember to remind him that smart guys occasionally did likewise—and Leslie couldn't dismiss the possibility, based on her own interaction with Nick McAuliffe and her sighting of Meg in the after-hours company of another client, that Meg had had an affair with Mr. Best-Seller.

Could Alice Chase really have "friends among the rats" who might have set the fire to get revenge on her behalf? Outside of mob movies and mystery novels, or when a lot of money was involved, did this ever happen? Not often, and certainly not on Martha's Vineyard. Petty vandalism, sure, graffiti on the wall or a cherry bomb in the mailbox, but not arson. If Alice knew any rats, they were most likely of the four-legged variety, the kind that gnawed through insulation and allowed wire to contact wire and start electrical fires. Face it: Chet and all the authorities were right, the fire had been caused by old or incompetent wiring, there was no criminal activity involved.

Her big story was looking more and more like another big nothing. But miracles did happen, and maybe Alice would turn out to be photogenic, drop-dead articulate, and possessed of previously hidden knowledge that would transmute all these humdrum facts into gold. If reality stomped on her miracle, she could still score a few points with Natalie by recycling her Nick interview into an author profile—providing Nick hadn't recognized her at the airport, and had forgiven her for blowing him off at the last minute on Wednesday.

The rest of the Nick angle was, in a word, dry. How did one go about buying a property with cash, and what were the advantages of forming a trust to do it? Why had he *really* bought that particular house? It was modest, it needed work; it was one step up from a dump. With the proceeds of his best-selling first novel, its movie rights, and the contract for his next novel, not to mention a prior job with the *Asclepius Report* that presumably had paid well, he surely could have done better than Zack Butler's old house, even given the ridiculously inflated prices of island real estate. Maybe she could pry a little more out of Nick.

No matter what she learned from him, or her, or the bank, she would have to go back to Meg Hasbro. Underneath the first item on her list Leslie typed:

Why that house? Meg??

As she looked up from her terminal, David Benaron emerged from the woods and headed, once again, toward her front door. *If he stops by, fine. If he doesn't, I'll go back to work.* Quincy Hancock III and the Case of the Forbidden Floodlights were beginning to look like a welcome diversion from Alice, Nick, and the Case of the Dump That Burned Down. Knuckles rapped firmly on the door.

"So how about brunch at the Dog? I'm meeting Spence there at 9:30."

Spence was Spencer Wyman, a veteran journalist and long-time friend of the family who had recently semi-retired to the Vineyard. The Dog was the Black Dog, the waterfront restaurant that had spawned a garishly successful T-shirt business. Islanders liked to sneer at the place and its wealthy owners, but plenty of them wore Black Dog T-shirts in public, gave Black Dog gifts to friends and relatives, and ate at the restaurant whenever someone else was paying the bill. Leslie's own T-shirt, in tasteful light blue, had been hibernating at the bottom of a summer-clothing box ever since Shannon laughed at her for wearing it to an art opening. "To maintain your credibility as an island journalist," she said, "you cannot go out in public wearing a Black Dog T-shirt that is less than ten years old. Put it away. Bring it out in ten years."

"Brunch?" repeated Leslie. "I'd love to go, but Alice still hasn't called."

"So bring your cell phone."

Leslie didn't have a cell phone.

"You don't have Caller ID either."

"No."

David Benaron, who hadn't had a budget or an expense voucher questioned in at least thirty years, shook his head. "Your newspaper should give you these things."

"The *Martha's Vineyard Chronic Tightwad*?" Leslie snorted. "You aren't serious. I have to swear an oath in blood before I can take the crummy laptop off the premises for twenty-four hours."

"Far be it from me to distract you from your duty," said David. "I plan to leave at—" he checked his watch "—nine fifteen. You have forty-five minutes. I'll give you a buzz before I leave."

"Sure, fine," Leslie replied. "If she calls before then, I'll come."

"Good. Your uncle Spence would love to see you."

"I'd love to see him, too, but I'm sure he'll understand." She smiled weakly.

"You are absolutely right: he doesn't have a cell phone either." David shook his head. "He writes his columns on a manual typewriter, then retypes them on his computer so he can file them by e-mail. Meshugge. I'll call you before I leave." Her father headed up toward the front door.

A cell phone might be useful, Leslie thought. Maybe her father would spring for one? It took her a moment to realize that her not-quite-obsolete plug-in phone was ringing.

Shannon woke up feeling shittier than she had on any morning since her drinking days, but she was alert enough to realize that this was a different kind of shitty. It had an explanation, and the explanation was not that she'd gone to bed shitfaced. The explanation was that she'd gone to bed at four fifteen in the fucking a.m. and it was now five minutes to seven. Why was she awake? Because her fucking dog was licking her face and snuffling at her neck, then sitting back and making little "rrff-rrffs" that signaled a desire to go out. "Arrrghhh," she said, tossing back the covers, swinging her legs over the side of the bed, and standing up. She yanked her ancient red chamois cloth bathrobe off its hook and pulled it on over her navy blue pajamas. She stared down at Pixel, who never needed coffee to wake up, who could bounce through the day on an hour of sleep and catch a few naps here and there. Pixel gazed up at her: smile smile. "Arrrghhh!" said Shannon again. "Wanna go out?" Smile smile, wag wag!

Coffee, thought Shannon. *Coffee.*

When she got to the living room, she seriously feared that she had the DTs. Having been a relatively high-bottom drunk, she had never sunk to the point of hallucinating pink elephants, purple dogs, or straight men with good manners. What the hell was Giles Kelleher doing in her living room at seven oh five on a Sunday morning? Giles was painting her wall. Why was Giles painting her wall? Why was there a gray dropcloth on the floor, a stepladder in the corner, and cans of paint all over the damn place? *Christ, was I drunk last night . . .*

Memory kicked in: Last night she'd been going at that wall like Michelangelo at the Sistine Chapel ceiling. Giles had shown up at god-knows-what hour—late, very late. He'd egged her on while she painted wild roses in the briar patch. They'd talked, and talked, and talked. About art, and sobriety, and the concept of "turning it over," which Giles had been trying for some time to persuade her was common to both art and sobriety. Shannon was on the brink of believing him. Finally, fighting to keep her own eyes open, she'd told him he couldn't possibly drive home without getting a ticket for driving under the influence of sleep. "The guest room's empty, the sheets are clean," she said. "What do you want to sleep in?"

"A coffin," he said, and toddled off to bed. He might be fifteen years younger than she, or close to it, but he looked as awful as she felt. She took some satisfaction in that.

Now he was fully dressed and disgustingly chipper. He put the finishing touch on whatever he was doing and stood up. "Promise you won't be mad?" he said, blocking her view of the wall.

"Mad? Why would I be mad?"

"I painted on your wall."

Shannon burst out laughing. "Look what *I* did on my wall. Why would I be mad at *you*?"

A set of pruning shears now hovered on each side of the briar-swathed portcullis. They made her think of iron butterflies. With a broad wave of one arm Giles offered her the wall: "Your weapons, milady." He made a sweeping bow that would have won him a part in *The Three Musketeers*.

The shears were sharpened to a keen edge. She stared at the tangle of briars. "Oh," she said. "Oh." She gazed at the door, blocked by a portcullis, and the wall, nearly obliterated by brambles. She could almost imagine taking shears in hand and cutting her way through to the studio. *I'm not up to this,* she thought. *But maybe . . . ?*

"Let's go out for breakfast," she said. "I think the earth is wobbling, and I want to get out of the house."

"You buying?"

"I'm buying."

"Deal. Put some clothes on while I polish up these swords."

A few minutes later they were rolling down Old County Road in Shannon's Subaru, singing "We're Off to See the Wizard" and exceeding the speed limit by a modest ten miles per hour. The clouds were breaking up enough to let the sun through; Shannon squinted so obviously that Giles flipped the sun visor down. Pixel, riding happily in the back seat, leaned out the window and let the wind dry her nose.

Several weeks remained before Memorial Day, so parking was easy on the dead-end block outside the Black Dog Tavern and no one was waiting to be seated. The old ceiling beams looked down on a dining room that was only half full, and Leslie had at least a nodding acquaintance with most of the people she saw. Spence Wyman, a tall, discreetly bearded WASP who probably looked more presentable in his pajamas than her father did in a Brooks Brothers suit, was holding down a table at one end of the enclosed porch, which boasted a glorious up-close view of Vineyard Haven harbor. This morning the sun danced on the wavelets, the 104-foot schooner Shenandoah pulled eagerly at her mooring, and two lesser craft were being rigged for a day sail on the sound. What trendy restaurant in Manhattan could do better?

"My daughter," David confided as he took his seat on the well-varnished bench, "almost didn't make it. She was waiting for a call from a source. She's like you—" he wagged a finger at his old friend "—she doesn't hold with cell phones. Wonder of wonders, the source called in time, and here she is."

That handed Spence a perfect opportunity to ask about the story she was working on. It still hadn't occurred to Leslie that this brunch date, this entire weekend, was a setup. Her mother had been meddling in Leslie's life since before Leslie entered kindergarten, her efforts usually clumsy and obvious because they were based on what a generic daughter was supposed to want. Her father, however, meddled the way he wrote his stories, with insight, attention to detail, and a clear-eyed assessment of possible consequences; his meddlings were rare, but they usually had far-reaching effects. Clueless to a fault, Leslie launched into the tale of Alice, Nick, and the Dump That Burned Down. With all its sidebars and footnotes this version was much more interesting than what had appeared in the previous Thursday's paper, or what would appear in next Thursday's paper: it incorporated the neighbors' observations, the best-selling novelist's on-site tantrum, the fall of Jay's predecessor at Youth Services, and the Tisbury police chief's passion for peanut M&Ms. Leslie waxed eloquent. When she finished, she could barely wait for her one o'clock interview with Alice. Maybe she really should write a book.

Her narrative was interrupted—or, more accurately, flustered—by the appearance of Shannon Merrick on the Black Dog porch, accompanied by A Man.

Of course The Man was queer. He walked queer, he gestured queer; the way he followed the hostess with Shannon trailing behind was definitely queer. Leslie was sure she had met this guy, but she couldn't come up with a name. He was barely three inches taller than Shannon (who was two inches shorter than Leslie) and probably weighed twenty pounds less; his shaggily bohemian hair was an enviable reddish brown. Of course he and Shannon did what everyone did upon entering the Black Dog: survey the dining room to see who else was there. And of course Shannon noticed that Leslie and her father were sitting at the far end of the porch. Still, Shannon didn't have to grin broadly in their direction, kiss the tips of all her fingers, and blow them a big kiss in full view of everybody.

Nor did her father have to kiss the palm of his hand, aim it in the direction of Shannon and her friend, and blow it back.

The hostess paused at a vacant table for four. Giles quickly slid onto the bench with his back to Leslie and her father. Shannon raised an eyebrow as she sat down facing him. "Yes?"

"Not the Woody Allen type—the other one," Giles whispered. "The one who looks like Gregory Peck with a beard."

"I'm not sure who he is, probably—"

"If I were a sugar-daddy queen, he's exactly the type I'd go for."

Shannon snorted. "I should go down there and be polite," she said. "Want me to get a phone number?"

"I said *if,* girlfriend. I keep my prospects and my fantasies *straight,*" he said, his rare dimples appearing with the attempt to suppress a grin. "Like supper at my mom's. The broccoli goes over *here* and the mashed potatoes go over *there.*"

"Ah," said Shannon. "So that's the secret. I used to take the vegetable, the potato, and the burger and mash 'em all up together. Then drown 'em in ketchup. It made my mother sick."

"And that's why you did it."

"Damn right."

"Traditional family values," they said in unison, and slapped high fives across the table. Their waitron appeared to fill their coffee mugs.

"If it looks like they're about to leave, I'll go and say hi," Shannon decided. "Woody Allen over there is Leslie's father. Did I tell you I blew Leslie off for dinner last night? Not without advance notice: I'm not *that* rude. It's just that supper with the Whartons seemed more, well, relaxing. Leslie wanted to invite Jay. I had to tell her he was off-island. If he'd been around, I might have gone. And speaking of which—I need to talk to you in a program way, OK? But if it's too personal, feel free to say no."

Giles covered his eyes with his left hand and reached out with his left, imitating a fortune-teller in the Circus Mélodramatique. "Wait," he said. "Don't tell me. It's about—it's about—the Hanged Man. The Man on a Hook?"

"OK, so I'm obvious," Shannon said. Their waitron was standing by; Shannon asked Giles if he was ready to order. He nodded; she caught the young woman's eye. Breakfast burrito for her, an omelette with sausage, swiss, and green peppers for him; at the last minute they splurged on an order of deluxe homefries to share. Giles moaned about the cholesterol, the fat. Shannon told him to shut up and get used to it; now that he'd rounded thirty, he'd be forty soon enough, even if he didn't believe it, and when he got that far he really wouldn't care. Then she recounted her adventures since leaving the 10 a.m. AA meeting the day before, her visit with Janice Swanson—omitting her brief conversation à deux with Rainey Silvia—and her successful attempt to locate the conference Jay was attending.

"But," she said, "he wasn't at the hotel Becca booked him at."

Giles was not surprised by this. He was surprised that Shannon was surprised. "And when was the last time you had to reach the man at one of his conferences?" he asked pointedly.

Very pointedly. Shannon rested her temples in the palms of her hands. "You're telling me I've been missing something," she said.

"You've been missing something," he confirmed.

Leslie was floundering. Uncle Spence had just told her that a college buddy and longtime colleague of his was in New York screening prospects for two reporter jobs, one in Seattle, the other in Florida. Both papers in question were widely seen as promising rungs on the ladder to fame and fortune, or at least what passed for it among aspiring journalists. "Oh, I could never work for a *daily*," she said. "The stress would push me right over the edge."

"You think so?" Her father was looking at her, his infernal eyebrows raised almost to his hairline. He speared a forkful of pancake and jabbed it at her. "You're getting bored, I know this. Listen, daughter. This island is a wonderful place to get away from excitement. It is not an exciting place. By itself this is not a bad thing, but Leslie, Leslie—journalists *thrive* on excitement. *You* thrive on excitement. This house fire is trying to tell you something: listen!"

"Oh, come on, Dad," she said. "Get real. I'm not a *real* journalist. I ran away to Martha's Vineyard because I couldn't hack Madison Avenue anymore. Working for the *Chronicle* was an *accident.* I'm an *accidental* journalist." But part of her mind was flying overhead, looking down, and thinking that in the larger scheme of things Martha's Vineyard was not only small but small-minded. "So," she went on, gazing out the window, "I've won a few awards writing for the *Martha's Vineyard Chronicle.* Big inky deal. I know what you *real* journalists think of weekly newspapers." She drew a finger across her throat while rasping dangerously. "You wouldn't be caught dead working for one."

Her father and Spence Wyman looked at each other. *Well, duh,* thought Leslie. *How much more obvious could they make it that they have been discussing this very issue? So who had taken which side?* This she probably didn't want to know. It was Uncle Spence who spoke first, acknowledging that, true, most old-timers didn't hold weeklies in high esteem, but they also hated to admit that, say, ex-cops and ex-teachers could make top-notch reporters, even if they hadn't dropped out of high school during the Great Depression to run copy at some big-city daily. "You've got what it takes," he said firmly.

Instinctively she glanced to her father for confirmation.

"What *is* so fascinating at the other end of the porch?" Giles finally demanded. "I'm dying to twist in my seat and look, but that's much too rude."

"Huh?" Shannon started. "Nothing."

"Must be something. You're practically ignoring the homefries." He scooped one up to make his point.

"OK, so I'm dying to know what the journalists are talking about. Whatever it is, all three of them are engrossed."

"One: Where is Alice Chase. Two: Who was Deep Throat. Three: Why did the prez give Monica a Black Dog T-shirt?"

"Damned if I know," said Shannon. "That's an impeachable offense, if you ask me."

"You still interested in her?" Giles asked, pushing the homefries in Shannon's direction.

"In *Monica*? Gag me with a cigar."

Giles rolled his eyes. "I was referring to the female at the journalists' table."

"Me, interested in Leslie Benaron?" Shannon had to fight hard to maintain control of her cool. "Sure, she's the number one informant for my graduate seminar in human sexual confusion."

"You don't say! I signed up for that course. Why don't I ever see you at lectures?"

Shannon smiled. Their waitron was heading in their direction, stopping at each table to refill coffee mugs. Shannon kept an eye on the young woman's progress; she was ready for the check.

* * *

Jay packed belts, underwear, shaving kit, and the running shoes that he hadn't put on once back into his suitcase, wondering for the thousandth time why he bothered to unpack at these weekend conferences. It wasn't as if a hotel room became home when you stuffed your belongings into the drawers. Why not just sit the suitcase on the bureau and live out of that?

Because Mama wouldn't approve, that's why. Six months after he'd received his MSW and moved into the top-floor apartment of a Worcester triple-decker, his parents had paid him a visit on one of their rare excursions off-island. The kids skateboarding on the street spoke more Spanish than English, and most of the neighborhood faces were darker than his own, which prompted his mother to ask, as they made their way up the stairs, whether he was sure he was safe here. But what sent her to the barricades was the half-unpacked boxes: books in the living room, clothes in the bedroom, and, worst of all, pans and dishes in the kitchen. "Jimmy!" she cried, shocked. "How long have you been here and you're still living out of cardboard boxes? How do you eat? You need someone to take care of you!"

And with the purpose and steady chatter of a brook running downhill, she had set up his living room and rearranged his kitchen, while Jay and his father talked basketball and town politics in the living room. Only their plans to head into Boston for an early dinner and the Celtics game distracted her from the cartons of books, and thank God for that, because Jay wasn't a hundred percent sure exactly what books he'd brought with him from the group house that had been his home through graduate school. It was an excellent bet that some of them were not for his mama's eyes.

Now his modest dwelling not far from the West Tisbury

post office—a guest house, in planning-board vernacular—was appointed to make any mother happy, though his mother rarely visited; once the emphysema started slowing his father down, she had stayed closer and closer to home, and holidays and other family occasions were celebrated at Janice's house. "Why must you live so far away, Jimmy?" she would ask. No use wasting his breath to explain that he was barely seven miles away. On Martha's Vineyard distance was rarely a matter of miles. Not only did Jay live in West Tisbury, he lived in a subdivision that hadn't existed when he was born, and Maria Segredo didn't recognize any of the names on the mailboxes at the end of the subdivision road. Going from her house to his was like crossing a DMZ.

The first chasm had opened when Jay made his first trip home from college, no longer answering to "Jimmy"—now he insisted on "Jay"—and dropping names of authors and politicians his parents had never heard of. The ideas he brought home were also new, and so was his zeal in defending them: if his father brought up a story from the TV news or a radio talk show, something about the crime rate or the divorce rate or teenage pregnancy, Jay had to refute the statistics, demolish the arguments, and disparage the reporters who were too lazy or corrupt to do the same. It took several years for Jay to realize that he was the main reason his father didn't want to talk about "issues," and by then the door between them was pretty much closed. They stuck to safer topics. Even Janny got uneasy if he inadvertently called attention to his off-island life.

The silence went both ways. Among off-island friends, he rarely mentioned going hunting with his father. In some quarters he couldn't even admit he was from Martha's Vineyard: some colleagues would cozy up to him while others backed off suspiciously, all of them assuming that his family was wealthy and well-connected, that he was on a first-name basis with James Taylor and Walter Cronkite and the Kennedys (along the way he stopped trying to explain just how hard it was to get from the Vineyard to Hyannis if you didn't have a boat). He'd gotten used to keeping each of his lives in its own box. No big deal there: most people had their own sets of boxes, and they all took it for granted that you didn't raise this subject with that person, or introduce that person to this one.

This afternoon, as soon as he could slip away, Jay planned to head west on Route 9 to hang out with some of his old Worcester buddies. Most of them had been clients of the agencies he worked for, or the fathers and uncles of those clients. Few of them would be caught dead at a conference like this, hobnobbing with PhDs, social workers, and government officials, though these experts talked incessantly about "reaching" them, the ones with credibility and influence in their own neighborhoods but no name recognition on Beacon Hill. Jay moved with apparent ease from one world to the other, knowing almost instinctively what could be said and what must be held back, able to read from the faces of his companions when he had gone too far, or when he was on the verge. After the conference, it would be a relief to sit around drinking, smoking, and talking with Nate and his friends, and then after a few hours of sitting around drinking, smoking, and talking, it would be a relief to fly home to the Vineyard, where no one would understand a word if he tried to explain how he'd spent the weekend.

In the mirror Jay watched his hand hesitate over the bottles, the Bushmills and the Jim Beam. Should he leave them with his tip or should he pack them up? His mother never touched anything stronger than wine, and that only on special occasions; his father had been a beer man to the core. Oh, why not? He'd be drinking Bud and maybe smoking a little weed tonight, but the whiskey would be a treat once he got home. Even Janice and Rainey might enjoy a little nip.

Besides, he'd paid for them.

Managing a garment bag over one shoulder and both flight

bag and attaché in one hand, fumbling in his pocket to make sure that his key card was still there, Jay didn't notice the man leaning against the wall a few feet from his door, not until a voice said, "Not so fast, boyo," and a hand was pushing him back into his vacated room. *"Hold-up?"* crossed his mind before he recognized Adam—*what was Adam doing here at ten a.m.? He got off at midnight and wasn't due back until four in the afternoon*—and his next thought was that Adam had come for a quickie, or for the leftover booze.

Adam's strong hands forced him up against the narrow wall between the bathroom and the closet. "You know what you've done?" Adam breathed into his face. Jay inhaled aftershave and a faint minty trace of toothpaste. He didn't have a clue what he'd done. "You've broken the rules."

Jay stared at him.

"You and I exist in this room. This room, or some other room that looks exactly like it. Nowhere else."

The phone call. He knows I called his house. How the fuck could he know I called his house?

"Forget that, boyo, and I might start forgetting it too."

Adam's face was barely an inch away from his, close enough to kiss. Adam's words were pounding at the door, but Jay's mind was having trouble making them out. Jay's mind was still stuck on the phone call. *He knows I know he's married.* How could Adam's wife have known who he was?

"Extension one-six-eight—mean anything to you?"

It did, but Jay couldn't get any words out to acknowledge it.

"One-six-eight," Adam repeated. "What's that?"

"My office extension," Jay managed to whisper.

"You made quite a splash last October, didn't you." The fingers of Adam's right hand slipped under Jay's jacket and across his chest. Jay's nipple was already at attention. "Someone took a shot at your car. Caused a little accident, but you walked away. Lucky man, aren't you." Fingers pinched flesh with a force that made Jay gasp. They didn't let go. "It happens in the best of families. So I hear. Even on Martha's Vineyard. Nice place, I hear. Wouldn't know. Never been there. Maybe I should come for a visit."

Was Adam planning to kill him? No, Jay's left brain reassured him; that was crazy, that kind of stuff only happened in horror movies and mystery novels. *Just like the maniac brother-in-law who tried to pick you off in your car. Never happens in real life?*

Adam's left hand drew a piece of pink paper from his trouser pocket. "Shannon Merrick—she a friend of yours?" His voice put a suggestive underscore on "friend."

He knows I called Shannon. How could he know? Does he know her number? Does he know where she lives? Does he know who she is? Adam had to be smelling his fear by now.

"Do I make myself clear?" Adam asked with the hint of a genial smile. "Outside that door I don't exist. That's the rule. Break the rule and I'm going to break it too. Understand?"

Jay couldn't speak.

The vise grip on his nipple tightened. "Understand?"

"Yeah," he managed. "I get it."

"Good," said Adam with a big smile of approval. "Don't forget. See ya later."

And he was gone, the door closed behind him.

A bad thriller movie, a really bad thriller movie. Is this what a psychotic break feels like? Post-traumatic stress syndrome? A nightmare? Did I wake up this morning?

"See ya later"? Does that mean it's OK to call next time I come to town?

The blood rushing back into his left nipple created a physical pain so sharp that for a moment he felt dizzy. When his vision cleared, he made his way to the bed and lay down. He closed his eyes. *"You've broken the rules."* Opened them again, and gazed at the ceiling. This one was colorless acoustic tile overrun with cracks, like dried puddles during a summer drought. Were the cracks really there, or was he hallucinating? He managed to pick out the almost imperceptible edges of the tiles, which reassured him that both his vision and his brain were functioning normally. He squinted: the cracks started to wriggle. He opened his eyes wide: they stopped. *Almost* normally.

He sat up, swung his feet over the side of the bed, and reached for the phone. His hand stopped in mid-reach; he stared at the unremarkable black telephone, identical to a million other black telephones. It had betrayed him. He didn't know how, but somehow it had. He wasn't going to trust it again.

CHAPTER FOURTEEN

Leslie slammed on her brakes just past the new Oak Bluffs School: that *had* to be the turnoff she was looking for. Was it her fault it looked like a driveway? Sure enough, the bluestone track led past two modest ranch-style houses to a small, unruly meadow, beyond which stood her objective. Kate Hammond had said the house looked like "a random tumble of old gray blocks." She was exactly right.

Its angularity was much softened, however, by generous plantings of rhododendron, lilac, azalea, and shrubs that Leslie couldn't identify. Nothing was blooming yet, of course, but if spring ever showed up in earnest the place might be less drab. She drove slowly into the cul-de-sac, listening to the gravel crunch under her tires, and pulled up behind the late-model dark blue Volvo wagon and the immaculate tan four-wheel-drive Toyota Tacoma pickup beside it.

The main entrance had to be through the side door, the one with the black mountain bike propped up against the outside wall, not the one out front with the flared brickwork steps. After checking her shoulder bag for notebook, pens, and the mini tape recorder that she didn't expect to use but wanted to have on hand, Leslie stepped out of the car and headed for the door. Before she got there, a handsome woman with dark gray hair loosely caught up in a twist opened it for her. "You must be from the *Chronicle*," she said. "Leslie, wasn't it?"

Leslie nodded.

"Good for you. We've had people drive back and forth for

half an hour without finding the road."

"It does look like someone's driveway," said Leslie.

"Doesn't it? I'm Kate Hammond. You *must* be David Benaron's daughter. We've seen him on the news shows a hundred times—you have the same eyes and eyebrows." Kate's fingers traced her own eyebrows.

"I confess," said Leslie with a smile. "The same David Benaron who had chocolate and walnut pancakes at the Black Dog this morning—but please *don't* tell my mother about that."

"My lips are sealed. Come in, come in."

Kate Hammond had to be one of those upper-crust country WASPs who swarmed all over the Vineyard: who else could look so well-dressed in jeans, a pastel blue turtleneck, and an autumn-colored sweater jacket? Not to mention those cameo earrings that had to be a family heirloom. She ushered Leslie through a cluttered but clean mud room where waders and overalls hung from pegs, as well as an assortment of coats and jackets, none of them frayed or patched or even noticeably faded. Among the duck boots and shoes on the floor were several toolboxes, at least two full of trowels, shovels, and hand-held spades and one stocked with tools of the handyman's trade: hammer, T-square, screwdrivers, wirecutter, wrenches, a coil of thin wire.

Country Living, thought Leslie as she stepped into the airy living/dining room. Dark beams crossed high above the floor, and afternoon sun glowed through the skylights and the huge south-facing picture window. What her mother would call a "conversation nook"—though as practiced by Judy Benaron, "conversation" came closer to what gladiators practiced in the arena than to what less contentious individuals practiced in overstuffed chairs—was organized around the fireplace on the left: comfy sofa, two easy chairs, all in matching dark purple and blue. Leslie was especially taken with the balcony high up to the left, a dark Tudor-style railing against white faux-stucco walls. You could play Juliet from that balcony.

"Alice will be right out—she just got back from work, she had to change, you know." Kate smiled. "May I get you something? Coffee? Tea? Fizzy water?"

"Coffee would be great," said Leslie.

Kate waved toward the fireplace. "Have a seat," she urged. "Do you often work on weekends?"

"Weekend? What's a weekend?" Leslie laughed. Settling into the sofa, she watched Kate moving about the kitchen. She couldn't help glancing at the several framed family photographs on the table behind the sofa. Evidently both Kate and her husband had been married before. One large picture showed Kate being simultaneously bussed on each cheek by two nearly identical young men; the greenery and candles on the mantel behind them suggested Christmas. In another photo a handsome gray-haired, gray-bearded man had his arm draped around the shoulder of a striking young woman who was nearly as tall as he was. Each held a tennis racquet in their free hand. Leslie noted with a bit of a jolt that Randall Hammond was black.

Kate set a tray down on the coffee table: three mugs of black coffee, silver creamer and its companion sugar bowl, three silver spoons, and several packets of artificial sweetener. She smiled at the photograph. "That's Randy and his oldest, Denise," she said with a proud smile. "You don't want to play tennis against either one of them. Denise used to play professionally. Now she's a college coach in North Carolina."

A woman paused warily in the doorway to the right of the fireplace. Leslie took in the new arrival's green corduroy jumper, the orange and yellow blouse that was too vibrant for her pale, serious face, the straight shoulder-length brown hair held back with a green ribbon. Nick McAuliffe's assessment—"a mousy little thing"—wasn't far off the mark.

The Get a Life Café last Tuesday morning.

It was one thing to know for almost certain that Shannon knew where Alice was, and to understand—sort of—that this information had to be kept confidential. It was something completely *else* for Leslie to realize that she had been standing twelve inches from Alice that morning and Shannon hadn't said *a goddamn fucking thing.*

Kate rubbed her hands on her jeans. "Alice, this is Leslie Benaron, from the *M.V. Chronicle.* Leslie, this is Alice Chase."

"I'm glad to meet you," Leslie said smoothly, as if she weren't sorely tempted to excuse herself, drive to West Tisbury, and strangle Shannon with her bare hands. "I'm so glad you called."

"Glad to meet you," Alice said, brushing an invisible lock of hair off her forehead. She sat at the edge of one easy chair, leaving Kate in the middle. Alice glanced at Kate, whose hand was poised over one of the coffee mugs. Kate looked at Alice and nodded slightly. "I can only talk to you," said Alice, carefully, almost apologetically "if it's OK some things don't go in the paper. My ex-husband can't know where we are."

"I understand. That's fine." Leslie leaned forward; Kate's fingers grasped the handle, lifted the mug, and passed it to Leslie.

Alice spoke clearly if sometimes barely audibly. Here and there she apologized for not knowing the exact date, the exact time that something had happened. Leslie would reassure her, and she would go on. She didn't dwell on the horrors and terrors of her marriage to Lenny Chase, but she conveyed them eloquently nonetheless. Leslie's hand raced forward and back across her notebook while Leslie's attention was focused on Alice, Alice's eyes, Alice's mouth, Alice's hands as they twisted and untwisted a blue paper napkin.

Alice described how she and her son had come to live in the Butlers' house, and how grateful she was to Uncle Zack for breaking family ranks and extending her a hand. "We lived there almost two and a half years," Alice said. "I paid the utilities. I kept the garden going, not as big as Aunt Ruth's garden, but I had peas and beans and lots of tomatoes. Strawberries too. Mitch loves strawberries."

"Where do you work?" Leslie asked.

"I clean houses," Alice said, glancing at Kate. "I've got a friend who has a business. I work for her. It's pretty good money except in winter. I do some sewing too. My mother taught us all to sew when we were little."

"So you were able to make ends meet," Leslie said.

"Pretty much," Alice replied. "Here you can't ever stop worrying about money. It's not like we were rich when I was growing up, but it wasn't this hard."

"Where did you grow up?" Leslie asked.

Alice told her about growing up in the New Bedford area, where her mother and sisters still lived—her only brother was in San Diego—and where she desperately wanted to return.

"So," Leslie asked, "did your uncle Zack tell you when he sold the house?"

"Yeah," Alice replied. "He said we could stay there till spring. He and the new owner had a gentleman's agreement, he said. That was OK. We were supposed to go back to court at the end of January, to get the custody agreement changed? The old one says Mitch and I can't move off-island without Lenny's permission. He doesn't want to see Mitch, but he doesn't want to give permission either."

"And then?"

"Lenny didn't show at the hearing. His lawyer said he was working off-island and it would be a hardship for him to come back in the middle of the week. The hearing was rescheduled for the beginning of March. Same thing happened. People see him on Circuit Ave., in the bars, of course, big surprise. Like he's not off-island at all, or not as much as his lawyer says. The real estate agent started bringing people by—"

"You mean Meg Hasbro, from Burnham and Wood?" Leslie asked, her neck prickling.

"Yeah. She brought the architect over, the plumber, the electrician, you name it. That was OK, I could understand, the whole hearing thing had gone on so long, but they left a mess every time they came. Then the phone calls started. In the middle of the night, five thirty in the morning—most of the time the person would hang up. Sometimes there'd be a voice, whispering, telling me I didn't belong there, that my son was—was . . ."

"Was what?" Leslie nudged.

"A *juvenile delinquent,*" Alice said. "Or a *retard.*"

Leslie looked concerned and a little disgusted. "Can you tell me anything about the voice? Could you tell if it was a man or a woman?"

"Not really," Alice replied, shaking her head. "It's hard to tell when people whisper. Miss Benaron—"

"Leslie. Please."

"Leslie, sorry. Mitch has had such an awful life." Alice was trying hard not to cry. "He's not a bad kid, he's really not a bad kid. What happened was, we had a room in a nice house up-island, but Mitch was taking money from the lady's purse, change off her husband's dresser, that kind of thing. Finally they asked us to leave. I was so angry at Mitch. I said, 'Why did you do this?' And you know what he said? He said, 'I wanted us to have some money in case we had to run away.'"

Kate was standing behind the sofa, holding a box of Kleenex. Leslie half rose, took the box, and handed a white tissue to Alice.

"How will I ever make it up to him?" Alice asked, biting her lip as tears flowed down her cheeks.

"You are making it up to him," Kate said firmly. "You're fighting to make a better life for him and you both. You'll see: the custody order will be changed, and you'll be able to leave the island as soon as school's out."

Leslie left the house feeling depressed. Not that it had been a bad interview, not at all; it had been a very good interview, and she'd certainly be able to use some of it in the paper. But any fool could see that although Alice had had a terrible time, Alice's problem was going to solve itself in the very near future, and even if Meg Hasbro had been making those phone calls, Leslie's prospects for proving it without risking a libel suit were dimmer than dim. With no wrongs to expose or right, her big story was about as consequential as *Fitch v. Floodlights*. In the listless murk that would never congeal into an award-winning story, only one little stone remained sharp and bright—and infuriating: *Shannon had known where Alice was.*

Shannon lay back against the sofa's armrest, the latest issue of the *Chronicle* propped against her upraised thighs. Her attention, though, had migrated from the newspaper to The Wall. The Wall made her smile. Even she had to admit that The Wall wasn't half bad, especially considering that she'd done it with an odd assortment of leftover house paints and brushes. What would the local art scene make of it? It sure wasn't your typical Vineyard landscape. The local shrinks would have a field day.

To hell with art scenes, and shrinks as well. Maybe she should hang out her own shingle, or place an ad in the *Chronicle*: BUILD YOUR DREAM HOUSE WITH CREATIVE BLOCKS. CALL WALLFLOWER CONSTRUCTION.

Shannon started laughing, hard enough that her belly pushed the newspaper up and down against her legs. Pixel, who had been stretched out full-length along the front of the sofa, raised her head, saw no cause for alarm, and went back to sleep with a put-upon sigh. Shannon contemplated the pruning shears. What would the shrinks say about pruning shears?

Giles would have an answer. Maybe she should call Giles? The phone was on the far edge of the coffee table, sitting on top of Georgia O'Keeffe. She reached for it, almost rolling off the couch in the process. The *Chronicle* cascaded onto Pixel, who got up in disgust and relocated to the mud room door. Belatedly Shannon remembered that the restaurant was now open on Sunday nights; Giles would be at work. If he weren't, he'd probably just remind her that pruning shears weren't Freudian symbols, they were *tools*. She dialed Leslie's number instead.

* * *

The afternoon was aging rapidly and Leslie was still in a dither: her mind was a roiling lake in which wavelets from her interview with Alice Chase splashed against her extreme annoyance with Shannon Merrick, and all of it was being sucked downward by the whirlpool started at brunch by her father and Uncle Spence. On top of that, she couldn't reach anyone in the court system till the new work week started around eight thirty the next morning, and she couldn't bring herself to bother her contacts at either Women's Resources or the county housing authority on a Sunday afternoon, especially since it was the first sunny weekend afternoon in at least a month. Forced inactivity gave her the jitters. Dad and Spence were crazy: how could she possibly cut it on a daily newspaper if she didn't have the chutzpah to bother people at home, and if she didn't have a reliable source to call when the courthouse was closed? Worst of all, she couldn't come up with the angle that would make House Burns Down an important story. Couldn't they see that she was just a semi-pro in a holding tank of rank amateurs? Sure, she was good at talking her way into places, but what if she actually got hired? What happened when she washed out?

Just before she went up to have supper with her dad, the phone rang: Prudy from the zoning board was calling to relay the "reliable rumor" that Quincy Hancock III and his brother-in-law had summoned their contractor and the offending floodlights and unpermitted wall were due to be removed in the morning, starting around ten o'clock. This confirmed the impression Leslie had received from Mr. Hancock the previous week: he was looking for a graceful way to back down. "Yeah? We could send a photographer . . ." she thought out loud. "Exactly how reliable is this rumor?"

"About as reliable as tomorrow's weather forecast," Prudy said.

"Which is . . .?"

"Ninety percent chance of showers before noon, 25 percent chance of clearing before Memorial Day."

Leslie groaned and giggled at the same time; the combination caused an uncomfortable hollowness in her chest. "Thanks, Pru," she said. "I'll check with the contractor first thing in the morning."

"You're more than welcome." The other woman laughed. "I'm just returning the favor. The *Chronicle*'s coverage of the whole issue has been much more sensible than the *Newt Bacon*'s—do they think anyone doesn't *know* that Q.H. has been chums with their senior editor since they were classmates at Deerfield? I mean, Chet Roth is Cassandra St. Christopher Fitch's *nephew,* for Christ's sake, but that didn't stop him from running that photo of the Three Weird Sisters, did it? What a hoot. It's now taped to the inside of my cubicle door, where the public can't see it. Whose idea was that?"

"Chet picked it, but if he didn't run it by the Queen Mother first, I'd be very surprised."

Prudy guffawed into the phone. "You and the rest of the island. Well, have fun with your bone. I can't *wait* to hear what those boys have come up with—"

"Free tennis lessons for at-risk youth?" Leslie was getting horribly cynical in her old age.

The other woman sputtered in delight. "Benaron, you're on a roll," she said. "I don't believe for a minute that Q.H. is clever enough to come up with anything like that, but it would probably placate the Fitches if he did."

After she hung up, Leslie walked around the house and up to the front door, obsessing about stories that fizzled and stories that were trivial to start with. Who the hell cared about *Fitch v. Floodlights* and that stupid tennis court? Her father, undaunted, was full of ideas of what she should do when she went to New York for her interview with the recruiter. Along with a delicious, vaguely Tex-Mex chicken casserole, he served up a half dozen phone numbers of colleagues and family friends she should contact while in the big city. During the visit, she mentally vowed and unvowed at least four times to make airline reservations before she went to bed. "Your friend," said her father, "the one who waved to us at the Black Dog this morning?" He mimed blowing a kiss off the tips of his fingers. "Shannon, that's her name. How is she doing?"

"Shannon," Leslie said, "is the worst underachiever I've ever met, and on Martha's Vineyard that's saying something."

David shook his head, smiling in his most avuncular manner. "Leslie, Leslie," he said, "sometimes you do remind me of your mother."

Talk about getting hit with a bucket of ice water. "OK, OK," Leslie relented, "it's not as bad as all that. She has a freelance graphic design and pre-press business. She meddles in Island Social Services. If she walked in right this minute, I might—I might—" *throw the casserole in her face? How very mature of you, Leslie* "—cause a scene. She really could have given me a clue," she insisted stubbornly.

"Clue? Clue about what?" asked her sensible father.

"About Alice Chase! I spend the whole week looking for Alice Chase, I'm going crazy trying to find Alice Chase. This afternoon I finally interview Alice Chase, and you know what? Alice and her son were staying at Shannon's house for *ten lousy days.* Not only that—I ran into Shannon at a coffee shop on Main Street on, what was it, Tuesday? Wednesday? Tuesday. Shannon was eating bagels with this other woman. We said hi, we chatted, I went back to work. It was Alice Chase! Right under my nose!"

"I see," said David, bending down to retrieve his napkin from the floor. "And your friend was unreasonable because she didn't tell you that Alice Chase was right under your nose?"

Leslie loved watching her father demolish the feeble premises, misplaced moral indignation, and logical fallacies of his opponents on *Meet the Press* or *Firing Line*. She hated it when he trained his rational mind and his fierce grasp of the

English language on her. A half hour after she returned to her apartment, she was still pacing the hall between her office and her bedroom, talking back to her dad, trying to persuade him that Shannon really had done her wrong. But she couldn't even persuade herself. It was all she could do to keep herself from running out the door, driving into town, buying a pint of ice cream, and eating it all in the car. Instead she splashed some dry sherry into a wineglass and dropped into her living room sofa. *New York,* she told herself. *I'll make reservations before I go to bed.*

Why should she think twice about leaving Martha's Vineyard? The Vineyard was an opaque web that only revealed itself to her when it wanted her to do something. The rest of the time everyone else was laughing at jokes she didn't get; everyone else knew who was related to whom, who'd been implicated in this or that boondoggle and whose involvement had gone undetected, what ancient feud was fueling this or that political dispute. Shannon seemed to know all this stuff by osmosis; Leslie could dig and dig and dig and still not get it all. It wasn't fair. It just wasn't fair.

When the phone rang, Leslie was drowsing off under the influence of her second sherry. She snapped awake at once, but all through the conversation she had the feeling that her mind was huffing and puffing to catch up with her mouth.

"Hey, Scoop," said Shannon Merrick. "What's up?"

Leslie sat up as straight as the sofa and the sherry would allow. What's up? What's *up*? "What's up is that I talked to Alice Chase this afternoon."

"Yeah? How'd it go?"

How'd it go? How'd it *go*? "How it *went* was that it turns out Alice and her son were staying with you all this time." Leslie hoped that abrupt silence would get her point across.

There was a pause on the other end of the line. "And?"

Evidently her pause had failed. "And *you* didn't say a word."

Another pause, followed by a controlled explosion: "What do you *expect* me to do? Nick McAuliffe's howling for her blood, she's got an ex who put her in the hospital at least once, and I'm going to tell the newspapers where she's living? I don't *think* so."

"I'm not *the newspapers!*" Leslie knew she was whining. "You know I'm not going to put it in the paper if it's going to hurt somebody!"

"Listen, Leslie, you know this: your priorities as a journalist and my priorities when I'm doing shelter work are not exactly the same. If I'm acting as an ordinary person, and if it's my own safety that's at stake, I trust you, one hundred percent. But we're not talking about *my* safety—"

"It's because I went out for a drink with Nick, isn't it? You think I'm sleeping with him." *J'accuse.*

Shannon took a deep breath. "Leslie, it's not because you went out for a drink with the guy. And I don't care if you're sleeping with him . . ."

The hell you don't.

"There are certain guidelines to follow when you're dealing with cases like this—battered women, child custody cases, that kind of—"

"Oh fuck the guidelines! It's so much bureaucratic crap. You know and I know that I'd never spill that stuff in the paper—I'd never even tell Chet about it."

"It's not 'so much bureaucratic crap.' Listen, when I was fifteen I was in exactly the same position. For one solid week I was living in the office of the parish priest. If he'd told his secretary, or his mother, or the head of the damn altar guild, and they'd let it slip to someone else, I could have been beaten up or maybe *locked* up. You're damn right I take it seriously, and it's not because I learned it in a training session either."

Shannon was angry and Leslie knew it: time to pull back. "All right, all right," she said, her voice higher than usual because her throat was so tight. "Forget I brought it up."

"That's cool," said Shannon. "Forget I called."

CHAPTER FIFTEEN

Flying to Martha's Vineyard was always strange. After a mad dash to Boston's Logan Airport, you dropped off your rent-a-car and took the rental company's shuttle around to the Cape Air terminal, rushed through the waiting room and out to the tarmac, tossed your check-through to the baggage handler, climbed on the plane, taxied to the runway, waited for clearance, and finally took off. This process, which might easily take two hours if you were coming from the central part of the state, culminated in a flight that lasted all of thirty-three minutes before the eighteen-seater touched down at Martha's Vineyard Airport. It was an expensive thirty-three minutes, so Jay generally took the bus unless Island Social Services was picking up the tab.

Gazing out the dirty windows of the airline's reception area at Logan, Jay was glad that he hadn't gone home early. The Ritalin panel had turned out to be a high point of the conference. The skeptics had showed up in force, and the ones who rose to speak had been so well informed, so articulate, and so adept at sidestepping the moderator's traps that Jay actually dared believe that his profession wasn't flushing itself down the toilet.

And hanging out with the old gang had been better than an all-expenses-paid vacation. Everyone on the Vineyard, starting with Mama and Janny, thought it a minor miracle that he had survived all those mean city streets. No one believed him when he told them that most city neighborhoods worked a lot like the island he'd grown up on. Most of the people, especially the women—especially the older women—realized that looking out for each other was a survival skill, possibly the most important one of all where no one had enough money to buy an individual solution. Jay had walked down very few city streets that demanded the same hair-trigger wariness as the waxed linoleum hallways of Island Social Services.

True, Nate ol' buddy had taken time out to rag him about his love life: "There's something going on with you, man, I can tell. I've got radar!"

"You better tell me about it, man," Jay had bantered back, "because this is the first clue I've had about it."

Nate's left eyebrow had almost reached the top of his closely cropped head. "Aww, c'mon, man," he'd started, before something in Jay's face told him to back off. "Sometimes we are the last to know," he conceded. He didn't push; he never did, though he'd been seeing through Jay's fronts since he was fifteen and Jay was a wet-behind-the-ears MSW of twenty-five. Even then he'd been wise enough to let Jay figure things out for himself—wiser, in other words, than most helping professionals. So Jay hadn't mentioned Nate's live-out boyfriend, who probably knew he was sleeping over, and Nate hadn't asked Jay if he'd come out to his family yet.

Once the little plane was airborne, Jay peered out the window. A few harbinger raindrops were making their way across the glass from upper left to lower right. Despite the clouds, the Boston metropolitan area was visible below; it spread for miles and miles, square city blocks giving way to houses that looped around sinuous suburban roads, and to sizable splotches of green: golf courses, parks, town forests . . . The deciduous trees were just starting to leaf out, the grass on the many baseball diamonds glowed deep emerald green, the most vivid color in the landscape. Miniature cars zoomed along curving roads, eventually reaching the asphalt pipelines that conveyed them into Boston at ever sludgier speeds. All those wheeled carapaces rushing into the urban maw made him melancholy. Inside each shell was one—maybe more, but probably one—U.S. citizen with delusions of individual autonomy, rushing off like a lemming to a job he or she lived mainly to take vacations and retire from.

You and I exist in this room. This room, or some other room that looks exactly like it.

Maybe Adam was driving one of those anonymous cars. No, probably not: Adam worked late, he rarely got to work before two in the afternoon. He probably wasn't even awake. Did he sleep through his wife's preparations to get their kid off to school? Did they have more than one kid?

Commuting was insane. Many years ago, fresh out of grad school, given a choice between a ten-mile commute and living in a neighborhood his new colleagues considered "bad," Jay had without hesitation chosen the dicey neighborhood. Within a week it looked a lot less dicey. For sure it was suspicious of outsiders, including most white people and most people in uniform; too many young men had nothing better to do than hang all day outside the fried chicken joint on one corner or the taco stand just opposite. But he sat on the front steps of the three-decker whose top floor was his new home, exchanging first curious glances and eventually smiles with the old ladies pulling their carts home from the grocery store. Eventually Amélia across the street asked if he'd help her bring the bags in; her son wasn't home from work yet. A few days later Henry, the son, asked if he played basketball. Jay raised one thumb and was invited to a pickup game at the elementary school playground. The playground was padlocked in those days, so they all climbed over the high wire fence. "So how come it's locked?" he had asked.

Henry had shrugged. "Crime," he said. Then he made a wicked face and mimed shooting up. "Drugs."

"*Estúpidos,*" Jay had muttered. He looked at Henry, he

looked at the other guys. "I could try . . ." he said.

"You try," they said. They knew he worked for the city.

And he'd talked the school principal into leaving the playground open till dark, though the principal only gave in after the local precinct agreed to station a cop on the block after school let out. Pretty soon the girls were coming down to watch the boys play, often accompanied by their mothers or younger siblings; by spring, tournaments were being organized, block against block. Jay had been flying by the seat of his pants, but after a year or so he had a reputation with the local civic, political, and law-enforcement authorities for "turning neighborhoods around." The whole experience told him that he was in the right profession, though it didn't give him much respect for his senior colleagues.

Cape Cod curled out to his left, protecting Massachusetts Bay from the rough Atlantic. Just ahead was Vineyard Sound, sneeze and you'd miss it, the marine boundary that the island-bound tended to believe was wider and less permeable than it really was. It took thirty-three minutes to fly from Boston to Martha's Vineyard; it took forty-five minutes to cross Vineyard Sound by ferry. In both cases the distance wasn't fully expressed by minutes or miles; you had to factor in the cost and, even more important, the hassle factor. When you were pressed for time or pressed for money, the mainland might as well have been Tierra del Fuego.

The pilot announced over his intercom that they were beginning their descent to Martha's Vineyard Airport. "Yahoo!" said a guy at the back of the plane.

Crap, thought Jay. *Crap. Most of us crawl around under our own little carapaces, and no one ever bothers to knock on the top. No one cares what's going on inside. Go through the motions, meet your obligations: that's all that really matters.*

The plane bounced once then rushed headlong into a smooth landing. A familiar sensation rose from Jay's belly, up his backbone, through his bloodstream to his heart, through his nerves to his brain: *Home; home at last.*

* * *

Another Monday morning at the *Martha's Vineyard Chronicle,* a Monday morning like every other, and yet this one was different. It wasn't the staff: the staff hadn't changed much since Leslie's first day on the job. The same conversations had probably been playing the first day she set foot in the office: Diane was explaining to a confused walk-in the difference between a display ad and a classified. Natalie was informing a blustery elementary school teacher that her press release had not gotten into last week's paper because it had come in forty-eight hours after deadline. Cynthia in ad sales, audibly exasperated, was telling Squirrel the Proofreader that real estate advertisers were allowed to describe a house as "fully applianced" because prospective home buyers couldn't care less about Strunk and White.

Today, however, Leslie was vibrating so much faster than everyone else in the newsroom that they all looked pale and wavery. The phones were ringing on a distant planet. The conversations had nothing to do with her. She was supposed to be calling the guy in New York. When she saw her father off at the airport this morning, making the call had seemed like no big deal. Now it was right up there with crossing the Atlantic in a kayak. If she'd been smart, she would have called from the airport. *Right, at seven fifteen in the a.m. How to make a good first impression.*

Leslie made phone calls to everyone other than the man in New York. She talked with Nick's editor, Nick's agent, and even a friend of Nick's in Cleveland who might have been the inspiration for Georgia Duvall. All of them were quotable; none of them were pithy. What the hell: *Chronicle* profiles weren't about psychological or literary analysis. She would write a cordial, informative profile, and for the next week or two people would come up to tell her what an *interesting* article it was, how well-written, how insightful; how they'd bought *Devoted to Her Duty* on her recommendation and were glad that she'd brought it to their attention . . .

Crap. Crap, crap, crap. Who the fuck cared?

"I can't believe it's over," Abby Wood was saying. She crossed her right leg over her left and studied it with furrowed brow: evidently her last wax job had not been up to snuff.

Her father was pouring himself a second mug of coffee from the Mr. Coffee in Burnham and Wood's reception area. "I bet a bright girl like you can find something else to do on Sunday nights. Meg, would you recognize a tick bite if you saw one?"

"Dad, it was a great show," Abby whined. "You'd know if you ever *watched* it."

"As opposed to what?" Meg muttered. *Close your eyes and you'd swear that Abby Wood was fifteen years old.* "The kiss of the vampire spider woman?"

"I'm sure it was," said Andy Burnham, doting father.

"Oh, what do you know." Abby pivoted on her desk chair, eyes still fixed on her right calf. "You should have watched it while you had the chance. Now it's gone for good, and your totally boring baseball and *golf* games will go on forever and ever."

Meg Hasbro sneaked a glance over the top of her monitor. Andy was sipping coffee, browsing the magazines spread across the window seat, and devoting maybe five percent of his attention to his daughter's distress. He didn't seem especially concerned about his possible tick bite either. No doubt Samuel Beckett had been subjected to conversations like this, day in, day out, and then in retaliation he had written *Happy Days,* which forced theatergoers to pay handsomely for the experience that Meg got for free: listening to insipid people emoting about the nothings that loomed large in their little lives.

What would Beckett have made of her colleagues? After five minutes of Abby and Andy, he probably would have

bought a one-way ticket back to Ireland. If Meg had anything
on the ball, she'd be waiting to hear from her agent right this
minute: "This is brilliant! You're America's late-twentieth-
century answer to Pirandello! Did you really write this in a
real estate office? It's the existentialist answer to *Glengarry
Glen Ross*. The marketing people will love it!"

So far this morning, Meg's greatest accomplishment was
not shouting "Shut up!" at her colleagues.

The effort cost her, though: she was so fixated on her
computer screen that she didn't notice Doug Trumbull
knocking at the door, so it was Andy Burnham who welcomed
him into the office. Meg's heart leaped and thudded. She
poised the four fingers of each hand along the edge of her
desk, as if she were about to launch into Tchaikovsky's First
Piano Concerto, and took two deep breaths. Then she rose
graciously to welcome her client. Doug looked quite
distinguished, albeit a little damp, in his yellow Gore-tex rain
slicker, which hung open over a navy blue V-neck sweater.
"We're on the way to the airport," he said, a delightfully
discreet smile on his lips, "but I wanted to get these back to
you."

He handed her a neatly folded brown paper bag. She took
it with a slightly conspiratorial smile, noting out of the corner
of her eye that Abby Wood was paying rapt attention to the
transaction. Of course it was the keys to the Makonikey
house—and something else: a book? Abby was doubtless
fantasizing something more exciting: a black lace negligée left
in the gentleman's room? *Eat your heart out, Miss Third
Runner-up.*

Doug dropped into the chair beside her desk. Even Andy
was paying attention now: he raised his coffee mug and
mimed *Would he like some?* Meg shook her head, still
smiling. Doug bent his head close. "My kids love the place,"
he said. "So do I, but . . ."

But your wife hates it? Meg listened with an expression
that said *We both know that if you buy this house, my income*

goes up by tens of thousands of dollars; if you don't, I need to sell half a dozen overpriced termite-infested shacks in order to pay the mortgage. But of course I want only what's best for you.

"So do I, but I've got to do some razzle-dazzle with my accountants. They'll come along eventually, but they'll make me jump through a few hoops first. You know these bean counters," he said, shaking his head. "Do me a favor? Feel the sellers out. See if they might entertain an offer of one-point-six."

What half-decent real estate agent could survive without an intuitive grasp of Method Acting? "I'll see what I can do," said Meg, her tone suggesting that the assignment would surely daunt a lesser agent but that she had the extraordinary eloquence, tact, and patience to pull it off. "They just might go for it." Since both she and the Switzlers would be close to ecstatic with one-point-two million *if* the deal actually made it through closing, she might, just might, be able to coax them into one-point-six. If she thought for an instant that four hundred thousand dollars would make a difference to Doug Trumbull, or even to Doug Trumbull's accountants, she could almost certainly talk the sellers down to one-point-two. "Where can I reach you tomorrow morning?"

"E-mail is best," he said. "You *are* online, aren't you?"

"But of course," Meg said, a bit smugly: hadn't she been the one who sold Andy on the idea of signing up with a local Internet service provider? If only she could persuade him that the World Wide Web was the coming thing in real estate marketing.

"Let me . . ." Doug Trumbull stood behind her and manipulated both her keyboard and her mouse over her shoulder, loading Eudora, opening her address book, and adding his own e-mail address to it. Abby's eyes were bugging out, and Andy was trying to act as if this sort of thing happened every day at Burnham and Wood Realty, Inc.

After Doug left for the airport, Meg's stock was so high

with her boss that she probably could have weaseled out of office duty for the rest of the calendar year. Instead she played Ms. No Big Deal and picked up the phone. While making arrangements to show a property listed with another agency, she watched Abby rearrange her desk: swapping the vase of jonquils with the mug of ballpoint pens, moving the phone half an inch closer to the wall, selecting three pens from the mug and placing them in the top drawer. Perhaps Abby had taken up feng shui.

Abby pulled a folder from the stack of plastic trays and laid it down on her desktop. "So, how serious is your friend about Switzler?" she asked, addressing the open folder.

"Ohhh," said Meg, recognizing the opening of a familiar gambit, "I think he's fairly serious."

Abby forged ahead: "Well, as long as you don't have a P and S—my Lowensteins *think* they want up-island, but Makonikey might be just what the doctor ordered—"

"Not this doctor," Meg said. It really wasn't fair to match wits with Abby, not unless she left thirty-five IQ points and half her vocabulary at home, so she explained: "Douglas Trumbull, the gentleman who wants Switzler, is an MD—he's made it very big in pharmaceuticals, but he tells me he still maintains a small general practice."

"Whatever." Abby poked the folder with her forefinger. "The Lowensteins are very fine people. They don't sound like they're from New York at all."

"I'm sure they'd love Switzler." Meg extracted the house keys from the brown paper bag and dangled them at eye level. "Want to show it to them?"

Andy Burnham cleared his throat and set aside the real estate classifieds from Friday's *News Beacon*. "Honey, let's wait until Dr. Trumbull makes a decision. We don't want the Lowensteins falling for a house that's almost under agreement, do we?"

Oh Abby, poor Abby, Dad's hung you in the closet and I'm trying so hard not to gloat. Doug Trumbull was going to buy the house; Meg knew it in her bones. And she was going to see him again, and again—

The phone rang. Abby grabbed it on the first ring. Her lips tightened as she glanced at Meg: "For you," she said.

Doug's plane's been delayed—he wants me to come down to the airport for a quick coffee . . . No such luck: it was that big-haired reporter from the *Chronicle,* and she wanted to talk about yesterday's news. She was fishing for dirt on Nick McAuliffe, specifically corroboration of certain rumors that he'd either done or caused to have done some sleazy stuff to get Alice Chase out of the Butler house. It would have been pleasant to see mud dripping off Mr. Nick's face, but mud had a way of splattering everyone in the vicinity, and at this point—with a one-point-six-million deal in the works, not to mention . . . —she wasn't interested in promoting a mud fight. "You'll have to talk to Mr. McAuliffe" was her mantra. Nick wasn't going to say anything that could implicate her; presumably his rage had worn off by now, so he probably wasn't going to say anything at all. If he was smart, he'd settle back and let Martha's Vineyard adopt him as its newest literary luminary.

Astonishingly enough the reporter—who, Meg knew for a fact, currently lived in a waterfront house owned by her parents and appraised at more than nine hundred thousand dollars—wanted to know what the Martha's Vineyard real estate industry was doing about affordable housing. Did Meg laugh in the woman's face? Meg did not. Meg graciously referred her to a colleague in Edgartown who was active on the issue and would be a far more reliable source of information than she, a self-supporting single homeowner with scant time for volunteer activity. When the only open line rang, she seized the opportunity to end the conversation: "Sorry, I've got to get that. If I can be of further assistance, *please* feel free to call, anytime."

Triumphantly she hung up and glanced around the office. Andy had retreated to his private office; Abby was chatting earnestly on the phone while critically studying her nails and trimming them with quick swipes of an emery board. Meg answered the incoming call and transferred it back to Andy. Life was looking up.

Leslie was fuming. Leslie wanted a smoke. Hell, Leslie wanted to claim business in Oak Bluffs, hit the liquor store for a bottle of wine, and then chug it in the car. Meg Hasbro wasn't talking. If Leslie were her father, she could have manipulated Meg into confessing despite her determination to do otherwise—but Leslie was unworthy. She hadn't managed to get anyone to confirm Nick Damn McAuliffe's insinuations that Meg had helped push Alice out of the Butler house. Worse, she hadn't even got around to hinting to Meg that "people were saying" that Meg had helped push Alice out of the Butler house. What Leslie wanted was proof, or at least strong circumstantial evidence, that Nick Damn had done something shady: bought his house with laundered drug money, hired goons to scare Alice out, or at least plagiarized his novel. What she had was nothing nothing nothing.

Damn Shannon anyway. If it hadn't been for Shannon's scruples, Leslie could have had the Alice interview for *last* week's paper, when people were still interested in the fire. Seattle and Florida were looking better and better. She really did have to call that interviewer. Imagine working for a paper where interesting stories came along more than once every six months! What if the interviewer blew her off?

Her intercom buzzed. Hardly anyone used the intercom: she glanced around the office to see who might be beeping her as a joke, to tell her to stop staring into space and do some damn work for a change. No obvious suspects: Alan Duarte was the only one with a phone pressed to his ear, and he was obviously engrossed in a real conversation. She picked up the receiver. "Leslie," said Arabella Roth's crisp voice, "when you have a moment, would you please come see me in my office?"

Oh God, I've done something horrible, I'm about to get

fired, Nick knows I've been checking up on him and he's complained—No sooner had this thought surfaced than she almost laughed out loud: it was that ridiculous. "Sure," she told the *Chronicle*'s formidable publisher. "Be right up."

Again she surveyed the office, to see who was paying attention, then she headed for the back of the building as if her objective was the lavatory under the stairs. No one looked up; no one noticed the notebook and pen in her right hand. Arabella Roth met frequently with the business staff, but she rarely conferred with reporters: she left the editorial side of operations to her son, and when she wanted to monitor the progress of a news story, she invariably did it in Chet's office, and with Chet present. Chet wasn't even in the building; what could Arabella want with her? *Oh God. She knows I'm thinking about leaving.* Leslie felt her heart speed up; her ankle started to turn on the stair, and she instinctively grabbed the banister. *How could she know?* Leslie hadn't even managed to call the guy in New York; Arabella couldn't possibly know what Leslie was planning to do. *If I get out of this alive, I'll call him. The minute I get back to my desk.*

The publisher's office resembled a den in an elegant Victorian house, dark-paneled, well-upholstered, and conducive to *sotto voce* conversation, except for the wall-size window on Vineyard Haven harbor. That window was impossible to ignore: it filled the room with light, color, and motion. Characteristically, the *Chronicle* publisher worked with her back to the view, and she held court not from behind her writing desk but from a leather armchair at the round conference table. No computers were in sight, nor evidence of any other late-twentieth-century digital technology, but cyberware sales representatives assumed at their peril that Arabella Roth was out of touch. As she liked to tell new hires, and to remind the veterans, when she started working at the paper, the man who would eventually become her father-in-law, then both editor and publisher, had insisted that she learn how everything worked. This was good practice, in her view, whether the technology was Linotype or a network of Macintosh computers.

Portraits of Arabella's father-in-law and his father—Chet's grandfather and great-grandfather—looked down upon Leslie as she knocked at the open door. Arabella, at her desk, peered over the top of her glasses. "Ah, Leslie," she said, pushing her chair back and rising to her feet. "Thank you for coming up. I know you're busy; I won't keep you long." She gestured to a straight-backed chair at the conference table and took up her customary station in the burgundy leather armchair. "About Mr. Hancock's notorious tennis courts—Mr. Hancock and Mr. Holt's notorious tennis courts," she corrected herself. A smile lifted the corners of her eyelids and even touched her lips.

"At times," said the *Chronicle*'s publisher, "the story looks less like a news story and more like a sandbox spat between supposedly mature adults, doesn't it?" She raised both shapely gray eyebrows. "It *is* a sandbox spat between supposedly mature adults. The maturity is an illusion. You know, of course, that Cassie Fitch is my eldest sister?" She smiled. "Of course you do. Cassie is bright, she is generous, and she is stubborn to a fault. Sometime," she mused out loud, "I must tell you the story about Cassie and Quirky Hancock—as Quincy Hancock the Second was known in the long-ago days of our youth. Our Mr. Hancock's father. *Not* the brightest bulb on the family tree, I'll tell you. . . . In any case, it seems that Mr. Hancock and Mr. Holt have realized that they were out on a limb without a net, if I might mangle a metaphor in order to make an allusion to tennis."

Thank you, Prudy, Leslie thought.

"They have agreed to remove the lights, dismantle the great wall, and make the equipment shed look less commercial. They have also, to make the neighbors happy, agreed to make the courts available during the day to the up-island schools for occasional tournaments and clinics."

Leslie barely suppressed a disgusted laugh. "Does Q.H.—uh, Mr. Hancock have an interest in working with young people?"

Arabella Roth glanced down at the table, but not soon enough to conceal a gleeful smile. "Mr. Hancock has never displayed such an interest," she said. "Until now, Mr. Hancock has regarded young people primarily as a drain on the public coffers. It has been his self-appointed civic responsibility to monitor the school budget and take both the town finance committee and the regional school district to task whenever they decline to follow his advice."

Leslie had waded through many letters to the editor penned by Quincy Hancock III. "How could I forget?" she murmured politely.

The publisher continued: "My sister Cassie, in particular, has long taken an active, and generous, interest in young people's activities. She is also a very astute chess player." Arabella glanced at Leslie, the smile in her eyes just touching her lips. "Do you play chess?"

Leslie shook her head. "No, sorry," she said.

"A good chess player is a formidable adversary!" Arabella chuckled, mostly to herself. "I cannot tell you the mind of Sister Cassie—she might tell you directly, if she respects your game well enough, and she has enjoyed the *Chronicle*'s coverage of the story—"

"Even the photograph?" Leslie asked. *Open mouth, insert foot: Leslie, that was really dumb.*

"She was, off the record, rather amused by the photograph. Our two sisters, however, think it was most unflattering." Clearly Arabella Roth was amused herself, both by the photograph and by the family's reaction to it. "Sukey in particular—that's Sarah, the next eldest—she has let me know in no uncertain terms that my son is indulging in 'yellow journalism,' as she calls it, and that my late husband would be ashamed of what the *Martha's Vineyard Chronicle* has become, and of me for not arresting its slide into mediocrity." She glanced at her late husband's portrait on the wall, next to those of his immediate forebears. "He looks so somber, doesn't he, hanging up there? I can tell you, he would have taken one look and roared, 'Great shot! Run it!'"

The intercom buzzed on the desk. With a glance at her watch, Arabella Roth got up to answer it. Diane's voice on the speakerphone announced that the hospital's development director was here for his ten-thirty appointment, should she send him up? "I'll come down, Diane, thank you."

"He's rather a pompous young man," she explained to Leslie. "He'll be flattered no end if I escort him up the stairs. What was I saying, before I started rambling?"

"About chess players," Leslie prompted.

"Ah, yes. Chess players. Sister Cassie is, without a doubt, interested in fostering the well-being of young people, but she is, equally without a doubt, an adept chess player. In other words," she said, gesturing toward the office door and then following Leslie through it, "she may well be making the opening move in a Free Tennis Gambit—"

"Trying to catch Mr. Hancock off-guard?" Leslie guessed.

"Exactly!" Arabella led the way down the stairs. "Mr. Hancock is something of a traditionalist when it comes to women. Women and children are so linked together in his limited imagination that he is likely to take at face value the Fitch sisters' sudden interest in fostering tennis among up-island young people."

"Not much of a chess player," Leslie observed.

"If he knows how to set up the pieces, I'd be very surprised. Thank you for coming up," said the publisher as they separated at the entrance to the newsroom, she to greet the hospital official, Leslie to figure out her next move.

Procrastination had been Shannon's close friend and devoted companion for so long that Shannon knew Procrastination's every curve, twist, and sneer. Procrastination was the one who sat her down and told her frankly that her work on behalf of battered women and abused children was far more important than any painting she could ever do. When Shannon balked at starting a new design job, Procrastination pointed out that long hours at the computer strained the eyes and ruined the posture, and suggested that a walk in the woods was in order. When gentler tactics failed, Procrastination invited Shannon to sit down for a game of Tetris: "What's to lose? It has a beginning and an end, and more to the point, you're good at it."

Over the years, Shannon and Procrastination had bickered, dickered, and generally worked it out. Procrastination understood that Shannon had to make a living. Shannon understood that Procrastination had her own agenda. Their tussles had evolved a predictable choreography: Shannon always knew what Procrastination would offer, and what she would do or say in response, and, most of the time, how Procrastination would respond to her response. Until this morning. Procrastination was still snoozing on the sofa. Pixel was lying sphinx-fashion in the hall, chin resting on front paws, plaintive eyes reminding her that drizzle was forecast for this afternoon and now was a good time to go to the beach. And Shannon, forty-five minutes past her self-imposed deadline, was painting a window in the door behind the portcullis. Of course this was a total waste of time, but so what if she got a little behind on her work? It was nothing that a few all-nighters couldn't fix; she was still pretty good at all-nighters.

It was odd to be painting with the room behind her full of light. It was even odder to be painting sober. In the old days, whatever job she held at the time, the pressure would start imperceptibly and then build all afternoon, till it felt like it was dragging her somewhere she desperately didn't want to go, to the edge of a cliff, the door of a furnace. Once home, she'd toss back a few beers with her then girlfriend, a writer whose latest novel in progress was languishing in a file drawer with its predecessors, then the two of them would kill a bottle of rotgut red with supper. If the phone didn't ring, if no one stopped by, if there was nothing good on TV or at the nearby movie theater, she would go, beer can or wine glass in hand, to her "studio"—the uninsulated spare bedroom at the back of the house that they couldn't rent out because in winter ice formed on the inside of the windows. And there, if she'd drunk enough to suppress the terror but not enough to make her sleepy or sick, she would paint. After midnight the windows held the world at bay, but she kept catching wavery glimpses of herself in the glass: she was sharing the room with a feral window woman who might spring for her throat at any moment.

During her first years on Martha's Vineyard, the only brushes she touched were for interior and exterior house painting, and the paint was mixed not on a palette but in gallon cans and plastic buckets. She no longer drank in order to paint; she drank because all the guys she worked with drank, and the people she hung out with drank, and who didn't drink? There were a few—well, quite a few—who drank too much and got maudlin or surly or foolish, but Shannon wasn't one of them, thank God. Growing up had taught her more than any human being needed to know about alcoholics, and she had no desire to become one.

Hah. All the gods, fates, and her family members must have been looking down laughing their heads off. Well, probably not her family: the dead ones weren't in any place they could look down from, and the so-called survivors were too far gone to know what they were seeing. How many drunks had the distinction of bottoming out while helping conduct a training for Women's Resource Center volunteers? A guest speaker was addressing the connection between alcohol and domestic violence. Shannon, having heard it all before, was doodling on the checklist the speaker had passed out: "Do You or Someone You Love Have a Problem with Alcohol?" No, she'd never been arrested (except for blocking the door to a porn shop); no, she'd never been stopped for DWI; no, she didn't get into fights (at least, not since she'd left home); no, she'd never been fired from a job (the ones she'd quit in a huff didn't count)—but some of the questions, about relationship problems, avoidance behavior, and general health (for years she'd been making jokes about buying Tums by the case), made her a little uneasy. *OK,* she thought, *I'll show them. I won't drink for a week.*

She couldn't get through a single day. After three days of trying, she knew she had a problem. After three more days, she confided in her friend Chris, another Women's Resources volunteer, who she knew was in AA. Chris took her to her first meeting. The first time she said, "My name is Shannon and I belong here," she knew it was true.

Life was strange. Just over nine years later here she was, in broad daylight, painting while not intoxicated. Sure, it was just her living-room wall, but still she was painting, and in her own not so humble opinion, the wall wasn't half bad.

The phone rang. She squinted at her new window: she couldn't see through it, it was too opaque.

The phone rang again, and then again. She stepped back off her stepstool, laid the brush beside several others on the real estate section of last week's *Chronicle,* and went to answer it.

"I know you're probably busy—tell me if this isn't a good time?"

Shannon wasn't even sure who it was, so she said, "Don't worry, it's fine," and the woman kept talking.

"You said it was OK . . . I've been meaning . . . I don't even know where to start. I must sound like a complete idiot. Out with it—I met Jay at the airport this morning . . ."

Rainey Silvia. Shannon breathed a sigh of relief. Then Shannon's worry motor kicked into overdrive. "Yeah, he stayed an extra night in the big city, didn't he." *But not in the hotel that his office manager booked him at.* Thinking about Jay gave her a headache.

"Yeah, he went back to Worcester; it sounds like he had a good time with his friends. But, Shannon, the conversation we had this morning—I picked him up at the airport, you know his car was in the shop, it just hasn't been right since . . ."

So Rainey didn't like to say it out loud either. "Since the accident?" Shannon offered.

"Yes. Since the—accident. We had breakfast at the restaurant—Listen, I'm having a hard time talking on the phone. Could we meet at Mocha Mott's or something?"

Shannon began to relax. "I hear you," she said. "I've been cooped up working all morning. My dog is guilt-tripping me big-time. What say we meet at Lambert's Cove and go for a walk on the beach?"

"Good idea," said Rainey. "I can be there in—what time is it now?—fifteen minutes. Make it twenty. Twenty minutes."

"See you there," Shannon said. Her gut was rumbling, as if she'd sent three cups of high-test coffee into a stomach that had been running on junk for the last twenty-four hours. Something was seriously screwed up, and a cheery little bird was chirping that it was about to get worse.

Shannon hadn't been waiting two minutes when Rainey's dark blue Saturn pulled into the parking lot. Pixel, who had been rooting around in last fall's oak and maple leaves, went trotting over to greet the new arrival, tail waving happily. Shannon rolled her eyes: why did her reasonably intelligent dog not realize that getting in the way of oncoming cars, even slow-moving oncoming cars, could be hazardous to her well-being and her owner's mental health? When the car stopped, the dog was in place by the driver's door, eager to jump up and look in the window. "Pixel!" Shannon yelled.

Rainey climbed out smiling, and gave the dog's ears a vigorous scratching. "I don't mind," she said. "I love dogs."

Rainey looked trim and well organized in blue jeans, a dark floral-pattern blouse, and a gray tweed blazer. Shannon, dressed in a variation of the same outfit, felt like a Ford dually at a Volkswagen convention. It didn't help that the knees of her jeans were going white with wear, or that they were liberally flecked with paint she'd hardly noticed when she left the house. "Pixel likes you too," she said, coiling a braided leather leash in her hand. She carried it in case they encountered timid people, or hostile dogs, and in case Pixel had one of her bouts of selective deafness and decided not to come when called—by which time, of course, it was too late for the leash.

They headed down the sandy woodland path to the beach. Rainey gazed into the woods, apparently tongue-tied, and Shannon groped for a leading question that didn't give too much away. Only Pixel was wholeheartedly enjoying the expedition: she trotted along, tail held high, sniffing for new adventures. At last Rainey said, "It's so peaceful here. I don't know why I don't come more often. It's not like it's that far."

"Dogs are good that way," Shannon said. "I'd probably be chained to the computer all day if it wasn't for Pixel. This is a good place for dogs—except in the summer. It's way too crowded, and I'm too cheap to spring for a permit."

The path became more and more sand, less and less dirt. Just before it sloped upward, beach walkers often parked their footwear along the long slat-rail fence. Pixel paused to check out the only ones in evidence, man-size running shoes with athletic socks stuffed in. Keeping their shoes on, the women half scrambled, half sprinted through the deep sand then paused at the crest of the dune. Lambert's Cove spread out before them, a rippling expanse of blue-gray-green held in the wide-spread arms of the gently curving beach. On the horizon to the right was the green mainland coast; straight ahead and a little closer was Naushon, one of the small islands that rode like an outrigger along the Vineyard's north shore. As they watched, a ferryboat appeared from behind the bluffs far to their right, gliding toward Woods Hole.

Pixel was already wading in the shallows. "Which way?" Rainey asked. The town beach stretched about six hundred yards to the right, but during the off-season, from Columbus Day to Memorial Day, few summer residents laid claim to their private beaches, and year-rounders walked pretty much wherever they wanted. Shannon glanced right and then left. A few hundred feet to the left, someone was walking toward them—probably the owner of those mammoth running shoes. "Right," Shannon decided, and they struck off to the right. "So," she said, resisting a strong impulse to clap her hands over her ears, "how did Jay seem when you saw him this morning?"

"Wired," said Rainey.

"Wired?" echoed Shannon. "Wired" was a swarm of fireflies; Jay was more like a laser beam: he could focus on a person or a problem with an intensity that was scary. The only time she'd seen him wired was in the days immediately following "the accident." "Wired how?"

"Like we were playing charades, and he was acting out the name of a movie, and I just wasn't getting it." Rainey watched Pixel trotting along just above the waves, leaving perfect pawprints in the wet sand. "Sounds like he had a great time at the conference."

"He told me he was dreading it, he doesn't know why he bothers with these things, so many of his colleagues are neanderthals he wonders why he doesn't get a real estate license like everybody else."

Rainey laughed. "You know how he is. He takes it so personally."

In thoughtful silence they picked their way over a spill of rocks. Shannon watched Pixel sniffing her way along the base of the bluffs to their right. A hand-painted sign read PLEASE KEEP OFF BLUFFS. It had been years since Shannon saw anyone scrambling up the steep slopes, using clumps of grass for foot- and handholds, but each time she walked this way, the bluffs seemed to have lost a few more inches to the wind, the rain, the sea. Stunted scrub pines slid slowly toward the beach; the brave zigzag staircases buckled in places and had to be shored up with wooden blocks or rebuilt altogether. This morning great vertical gouges in the dirt suggested that three or four amphibious monsters had tried to claw their way up to the summer houses of Makonikey Head.

"Does he talk to you?" Rainey asked finally.

Shannon's laugh sounded bitter even to her own ears. "Talk, like *talk*?" she said. "We used to talk a lot, but since the accident? The word 'stonewall' comes to mind." And speaking of stonewalling—how much was *she* willing to say? How much was ethically OK to say? In six and a half months she had discussed it only with Giles. She hadn't even brought it up with her sponsor, though it had been nagging an ever-larger hole in her conscience in recent weeks. If Jay had been drinking himself toward disaster, it would have been an easy call. Since alcohol wasn't involved, it was hard. "Accident, right," she said.

"Janny thinks Jay and I should get married," Rainey said. "So does Mama Segredo."

Shannon couldn't help it: she stopped in her tracks and stared at her companion.

"I'm sorry, that sort of came out of the blue, but—well, I guess I figured you knew that already."

Shannon grinned, a big irrepressible one-hundred-percent from-the-heart grin. "Well, yeah," she admitted, "but it's a long way from knowing it to hearing someone else say it out loud. Janice and I have had our—differences."

"I guessed." Rainey resumed walking. "It wasn't a big deal at first. It was sort of a joke. But after Jay got—shot at, and after Wayne—well, Janny sort of lost her sense of humor about the whole thing. At Thanksgiving, at Christmas, at Ernie's funeral, even at Amy's birthday supper last week—it's like she's on a mission. It's getting pretty awkward, but what can I do? Steve and Danny are best friends, and we're all practically family."

Shannon thought of the photo on Jay's desk, the one of Rainey decked out for cross-country skiing: whose idea had that been? And what part was Jay playing in all this plotting? He sure hadn't told her, but she didn't dare ask Rainey either. The gods smiled: she didn't have to.

"Jay and I rolled our eyes a lot. I mean, it's been like high school all over again. Back then we dated some—dating wasn't that big a deal, mostly it meant we sat next to each other when our crowd went to the movies, but Janny was always saying 'You should marry Jimmy'—the family called him Jimmy then—'and then we can be sisters for real.'" Rainey took a deep breath. "I thought we were reading it the same way, then this morning—"

Way ahead of them Pixel had started up one of the long staircases. "Pixel!" Shannon roared. The dog paused, looked in her direction, then scampered up to the first landing. She sat then stretched out in sphinx position, paws hanging over the edge. "Damn dog," Shannon muttered.

"Should we—?"

"She'll come when she feels like it," Shannon said, keeping one eye on Pixel. "So what happened this morning?"

They walked a dozen long steps in cadence, then Rainey said, "Well, he asked if I had time for breakfast, and I said sure—it was still too early to pick his car up from the mechanic's—and he's telling me about sitting up half the night with his friends, and do I ever miss having someone around to talk to like that? I said something dumb, like 'who has the energy to stay up all night anymore?' Then the food came, I guess, and he was saying how much he appreciated my picking him up, it was a drag coming into the airport with no one there to meet him. I said it was no trouble, Janny was making sure Steve got off to school, I didn't have to worry about that. So he asked about Steve, was he doing OK, did he miss having a dad—I mean, none of this is weird by itself, but it was almost like a job interview, you know what I mean?"

"Yeah," said Shannon. "It sounds pretty, well, formal." A movement up ahead caught her eye: Pixel was on her feet again, gazing down at the beach.

"Well, next thing he was asking if I ever thought about getting married again." Rainey forced a little laugh.

Pixel was racing up the next flight of stairs. "Shit," Shannon muttered. Part of her wanted to start bellowing at the dog, so that this conversation would never reach the point-of-no-return that it was fast approaching. "Sorry," she said.

Rainey watched the big gray dog disappear over the top of the bluff. "Smart dog. I sort of wanted to do the same thing. At the same time I wanted to shake him and say, 'Exactly what are you getting at?'"

They had finally reached the foot of the stairs. Shannon gazed at Rainey. "Why didn't you?"

Rainey gazed back. "Because I didn't want to know."

Shannon wrapped her hand around the top of the first post; her eyes followed the wooden handrail as it snaked its way up toward the sky. *Damn dog. Damn Jay.* "And that, in a nutshell," she said, "is why Jay and I haven't had a real conversation in the last six months. Listen, do you mind hiking up the stairs? I better find Pixel before she starts looking for buried treasure in someone's flowerbeds." As they climbed, she went on: "Ask about the accident, ask about Wayne shooting up his front yard"—*ask why he wasn't staying at the conference hotel*—"and he takes evasive action. Laughs it off, changes the subject—"

"Says, 'Don't worry so much,'" Rainey said.

"Yep. So we just talk about the weather, or somebody else's troubles. Don't ask, don't tell," she muttered bitterly.

"Jay is—I mean, I've thought since high school—maybe I was wrong? Janny would never say anything, but I just assumed—"

"Yes," said Shannon.

Rainey stopped. "Good," she said, and sagged back against the railing. "I mean, maybe 'good' isn't the best word, but I was beginning to think I'd fallen through the looking-glass."

Shannon climbed the few steps to the last landing and sat down. She studied the water: no boats in sight from one side to the other, but a few sparkling patches signaled that here and there the sun was managing to break through the clouds. No walkers on the beach either; just a few gulls on the lichen-coated boulders far below. "Silence does that to people," she said. "It's crazy-making."

Rainey sat down next to her. "So what should I do?" she asked.

"Damned if I know," Shannon answered. "I can't even figure out what I should do. Probably we should go find my stupid dog."

From the top of the stairs a short path through huckleberry bushes and other scrub growth opened into a vibrant green, impeccably manicured lawn, above which brooded a massive summer house. In contemporary showplace style, a mahogany deck jutted out over the stone terrace at the edge of the grass, obscuring the curtained ground-floor windows beneath. On the second floor nearly three-quarters of the north-facing wall was glass.

"Nice view," said Rainey, at the same time Shannon was saying, "I'd hate to have their heating bills." They laughed. Shannon led the way around to the left, confident that the owners were nowhere to be found but ready with an excuse in case they encountered a caretaker or a neighbor. There were no cars in the driveway, either behind the house or at the guesthouse near the apple orchard off to the right, and the only tire tracks were pocked with last night's rain: the coast was clear. Shannon bellowed, "Pixel! Come *here*!"

The dog appeared almost immediately through the forsythia hedge to the left of the driveway, big wolfish smile on her face, followed by a black Lab with a red collar. She stopped when she hit the forcefield of her human's displeasure, still smiling, tail waving more tentatively.

"Pixel," Shannon warned.

Pixel sat down. The Lab, barely past puppyhood and Labbishly certain of a friendly reception, came wriggling over to greet the strangers. Shannon reached into her pocket and produced two biscuits. The Lab quickly dispatched one and waited hopefully for the other. Shannon watched Pixel. Pixel watched Shannon. Shannon beckoned Pixel with one hand. Pixel came and sat up straight, tail vigorously sweeping the dirt of the driveway. Shannon held the biscuit just above the dog's nose; the dog stretched up and took it gently from her fingers.

"You see," said Shannon to Rainey, "why Pixelina here is spoiled rotten. She knows when I'm ready to kill her, and she won't come within grabbing distance till she figures it's safe. If I try to grab her, she backs off. She's even been known to bolt completely and come back when she feels like it." Ceremoniously she snapped the leash onto Pixel's collar.

Accompanied by both dogs, they completed their circuit of the house. Shannon glanced up the steps to the deck, then looked at Rainey, who was looking out to sea. "Want to play Peeping Thomasina?" she asked.

Rainey grinned. "Sure."

The curtains were pulled almost all the way back, affording a generous view of the expansive living/dining room and; through an open door and a large pass-through, the yellow-tiled restaurant-size kitchen behind it. "Who do you think lives here?" Rainey asked. "Martha Stewart?"

"Actually I think it's the Switzlers—remember from, what, three, four years ago? Their daughter died here." Shannon gestured vaguely toward Vineyard Sound. "It was in the papers. She had a big fight with her parents and went off in a huff. She tripped on the stairs, fell and broke her neck."

"Yuck." Rainey grimaced. "And we have to go back that way?"

"Supposedly it was the middle of the night, and supposedly it was pouring down rain, and supposedly she was four sheets to the wind. Some people think it was suicide, but you'd have to be pretty ripped to think you could kill yourself jumping off Makonikey Head. Anyway, they put the house on the market after that and it still hasn't sold. It's supposed to be haunted. That's her, see?" She pointed slantwise toward the window, toward a large portrait hanging above a waist-high bookcase: it was a girl of twelve or thirteen with glorious black hair cascading over the shoulders of a lace-trimmed burgundy velvet dress.

"No wonder they want to sell the place," Rainey said.

You never know when it's going to be too late, Shannon thought. "Don't ask, don't tell" was digging a hole in the pit of her stomach. "Listen," she said, turning away from the window. "There's another piece to the story."

She didn't have to explain what story she meant. Rainey crossed the deck and sat on the edge, feet resting on the top step. She patted the place beside her. For a minute or two they sat looking over the water to Cape Cod and the Elizabeth Islands. Shannon's fingers scratched Pixel's ruff, partly in affection, partly in a search for ticks. "You know Wayne's back," she said.

"Yeah. I was at—"

Janice's house when you came by Saturday. "Of course," said Shannon. "My mind must be going." *Saturday. Damn, that was only two days ago.* "Last fall—"

"The accident," Rainey said.

"One thing that never came out in the papers was—"

"Where Jay was coming from at that hour."

Shannon glanced sharply at Rainey. "You already know this story?"

"Sorry." Rainey smiled, her gaze moving from her knees to the lawn to the bushes, to the top of the staircase where the Switzlers' daughter had run that night. "It jumped off the page at me, that's all. Finally I asked him, sort of joking, 'So why were you driving home at eleven o'clock p.m.?' We'd all been at Janny's for a Columbus Day cookout, but that broke up by seven. Janny and the kids and I were going to watch a video; Jay said he had too much work to do, so he was going home. He dropped Mama Segredo off on the way."

"What did he say when you asked him?"

"That I knew he couldn't talk about his casework."

Shannon shook her head, grinning in spite of herself. "Cagey, cagey, cagey," she said. "That's probably what he said to the police—except he probably didn't have to, because the cops probably assumed it already."

"He wasn't out on a crisis call."

"No." Shannon took a deep breath. This was worse than breaking into a house: everything in her being was conspiring to clamp her mouth shut. *Almost everything.* "He was—in a relationship, at the time. The guy lived—lives—in Edgartown, off the West Tisbury Road, back behind the car place. So," she said, "the thing is, if it was Wayne out there with the shotgun—"

Rainey snorted. "Like there's another suspect?" She paused, then her hand flew to her mouth. "If it was Wayne, then how did he *know* . . . ?"

"If it was Wayne," Shannon repeated slowly, "how did he know."

CHAPTER SIXTEEN

"Oh man, what a shock: it's raining." Kevin Swanson and his buddy Bobby Francis, known to his friends as "Weed"—the nickname suited his lanky build, but it also prompted an endless succession of jokes, since his father was the Tisbury chief of police—both laughed as they headed for Weed's car in the student parking lot outside the Martha's Vineyard Regional High School. It was a misty rain, not a real drizzle; the asphalt was barely speckled, and Kevin didn't bother to put on his cap, which protruded from one of his back pockets. Weed was giving him a ride to Vineyard Haven, where both had after-school jobs, Weed at the A&P and Kevin at the Texaco station. Kevin couldn't wait to get wheels of his own. He almost had enough saved for a down payment on something decent, and his uncle Jay said he'd front him the insurance money if he needed it. By the end of the school year Kevin would be mobile. Not one day too soon.

Weed was recounting a funny incident from lunch when the slow-moving white van caught Kevin's eye. He didn't need the red and black lettering on the side to tell him who it was. His jaw clenched; his heart stopped short then started pumping overtime. Weed immediately picked up on it: "What's up—" he began, as his eyes cut over to the left. He read the name: he got it. "Shit," he said.

"Stick around," Kevin said under his breath.

"I'm here, man," said Weed.

The van cut them off as they stepped off the curb and into the access road that circled the parking lot. Kevin noted the current inspection sticker on the right side of the windshield: that was new. His father got out and came around the front of the van. For sure he looked better than he had in the fall: his dark hair was trimmed, the biker mustache was gone, he'd dropped a little weight. He wiped both hands on his jeans and extended one to his son. His son made no move to take it. He did manage a polite nod and a mumbled "Hey, how's it going."

"Hey yourself," said Wayne. "How are things? I thought maybe you'd want a ride—"

"Weed's giving me a lift into town," Kevin said. "I've got to be at work by two thirty." In truth Jorge left at three, and Kevin wasn't expected till ten of.

Wayne glanced at Kevin's companion with no sign of recognition. This didn't surprise Kevin: his father rarely went to basketball games, so he didn't know that Weed had been the team's high scorer for two years running, and he certainly didn't know that Kevin and Weed had been chosen co-captains for their upcoming senior season. "Yeah?" said Wayne. "Where you working?"

"Texaco."

"What about working for me this summer? It's good money. Better than being a gas jockey."

Sure, if you have any customers left, Kevin thought. When Mom told them all that their dad was back on the island, she'd said that he'd stopped drinking. Cool. Maybe now he'd keep his word, and stop ragging on everyone who contradicted him. Kevin would believe it when he saw it. "I'll think about it," he said, neutrally. "Thanks." Involuntarily he glanced toward the right, where Weed's old red Oldsmobile was waiting. Wouldn't it be cool if you could whistle to a car and have it come to you like a dog? "Listen, this isn't a good time to talk," Kevin said.

"Aww, c'mon," said Wayne, with a pointed look at Weed.

"I'll give you a ride to town. We can talk on the way."

"Weed's giving me a ride," Kevin said firmly, though his gut was starting to churn, like before a big game. "How about this weekend? Want to go fishing? The blues have been running at Wasque—"

Wayne looked over his son's shoulder, at the bland brick and glass wall of the high school. "Guess you're doing fine without your old dad, huh," he said.

"It's been six months, Dad," Kevin pointed out, keeping his voice calm almost to the end of the sentence; "Dad" came out slightly more sarcastic than he wanted it to. "Life goes on, you know?"

"Guess your uncle Jay's moved right in and taken my place. Right? Just like he's been itching to for years."

Kevin fought the urge to haul back and punch his father in the jaw. "Uncle Jay's helped out a lot," he said carefully. "But it's not like he's the only one."

Wayne was muttering under his breath, in a fluttery pseudo-feminine voice: "Jay this, Jay that, Jay says, Jay wouldn't . . ." He fixed his son with a challenging glare. "I could tell you things about your uncle Jay."

It was out of Kevin's mouth before he could stop it: "I could tell him things about you." It came out straight and chest-height, right into the forward's hands. *Wham.* He jumps, he shoots . . . Beside him he felt Weed Francis rock slightly forward on his feet.

Silence. Wayne's eyes narrowed; his face was turning red. Kevin recognized the warning signs. Had his father really stopped drinking? He stood his ground, waiting.

"Is that right?" Wayne asked. "And what would that be?"

The words kept coming: "Like what were you doing the night someone shot at his car?" Kevin watched the color keep rising in his father's face. How red could a face get anyway? No one moved.

Then Weed grabbed Kevin's left elbow and said close to his ear, "C'mon, man, this isn't a good scene. Let's go."

Kevin let Weed guide him toward the car, suddenly aware that the parking lot had emptied while they stood talking, and that several kids were hanging back, near the wall behind them or the front of the school's new performing arts center, just off to the left. The freeze frame had started to thaw: kids were moving warily, one eye on the angry man, keeping their voices low. Not until Kevin slammed the car door shut was he sure that his father wasn't going to come after them. "Outta here," he said.

Weed peeled out of the parking lot, his gaze shifting from sideview mirror to rearview and back again. Once they were safely out on the Edgartown–Vineyard Haven Road, he wiped his forehead with the back of his hand. "Shit, man, I cannot *believe* you said that," he said.

"Shit, man, neither can I." Kevin turned in his seat and watched out the back window as they passed the blinker light and rolled past the golf driving range. No sign of the white van.

Weed watched in the rearview mirror until after the downgrade and curve in the road made watching useless. "Just between us," he said, "do you think he did it?"

"Who else? Some Serbian terrorist?" Kevin replied, watching the car's basketball hood ornament as it led the way to Vineyard Haven. He had been pissed at his father for a very long time, but he choked on the thought that his father might have tried to kill a man. Even if he hadn't *meant* to kill anyone—what if the bullet had gone through the side window? What if it had smashed the windshield? What if Uncle Jay had swerved into an oncoming car? Part of him ached to tell Weed about his rifle being fired—his uncle was the only one who knew—but despite that "just between us," it mattered that Weed's dad was the police chief. Not that he didn't trust Weed to keep it quiet—he'd trust Weed with his own life—but it was wrong to put his best friend in that position, no matter how much he hated being the only one who knew. OK, so his uncle knew, but it didn't take a shrink to see that he didn't want to talk about it.

"So," he said, "you think Coach is really gonna let Jeff pitch on Thursday?"

Wayne Swanson almost punched the fender with his tightly clenched fist. He wanted to yell at the stupid kids cowering by the brick wall. *HALT,* he remembered. *Don't get too Hungry, Angry, Lonely, or Tired.* His counselor at the rehab told him that. Sometimes they said it at AA meetings. He should go to a meeting. Last Thursday's *Chronicle* was on the passenger seat, folded open to the schedules for AA and other Twelve-Step groups.

He climbed into the van and slammed the door shut. The kids were skulking away. What a sorry lot. Green hair, ratty hair, or no hair at all; earrings in their noses and ears and God knew where else; baggy pants riding low enough to expose the cracks in their sorry butts . . . Either they looked like faggots or they looked like gangsta rap drug dealer wannabes. No, scratch that: the faggots and the drug dealers dressed better than these kids. These kids looked like they got their clothes at the dump.

Kevin looked pretty good, though. Kevin was all right. Give him time: he'd come around. Maybe Wayne had rushed things a little bit. Probably Jay had been working on him, and his mother too: Janice couldn't stand up to her brother if her life depended on it.

No AA meetings till 7 p.m.—and one of them was at the jail. That made him chuckle. Maybe he'd go to that one, show them he really had turned things around. Meanwhile, meanwhile . . .

Island Social Services was just up the road. He'd go over there and see if Jerry was in. *Sorry to bug ya during the day, Jerry, but I need a meeting and there isn't one till seven o'clock. Gotta minute?* He knew his man: that would impress the hell out of Dr. Jerome Turner.

The section of the parking lot near the Family Services

entrance was crowded. Wayne pulled into the space closest to the walkway, ignoring the blue handicapped-only sign. He opened the van door and found himself staring at Jay's green Volvo wagon. Looked like Mister Jay hadn't cleaned up his act any: empty coffee cups and mashed-up potato chip bags on the floor in front, mail—most of it junk and catalogues, mixed with a few envelopes—spilling off the seat; newspapers, a couple of notebooks, and books on the back seat, along with another coffee cup and a Snickers wrapper; a suit bag hanging from the handle above the window; in the luggage area in back, a carry-on bag and some sports stuff—baseball gloves, a basketball, a soccer ball, a rolled-up volleyball net. What if he had a triple-X-rated video in there or—even better—some kiddie porn magazines? Wayne grinned to himself: he felt better already. *Mister Jay might be too smart to be driving around with real sleaze in his car, but he isn't as smart as he thinks. Or as smart as his sister thinks. Not even God is that smart.*

Wayne himself was no dummy. The restraining order said he wasn't supposed to go within a hundred feet of Jay's house or Jay's office. Didn't say anything about Jay's car, did it? But no way was he going to push his luck by opening the car door. It wasn't like he had to get within a hundred feet of Mister Jay to make his life a little more interesting.

A blond woman and a dark-haired kid were waiting in the reception area of the Family Services office, and an old guy. The kid was bouncing up and down on his chair, the woman looked strung out, the guy was reading a magazine and pretending that he had nothing to do with the other two. When Wayne walked in, the sourpuss receptionist looked up suspiciously then smiled when she recognized him. "Mr. Swanson, how are you?" she asked. "Do you have an appointment?"

He drew close to her desk. "Sorry, no appointment. Listen," he said confidentially, "I was having a sort of, sort of *crisis,* and there aren't any meetings till tonight. I was in the area and I wondered if maybe Dr. Turner—"

The receptionist beamed. "I'm almost sure he could," she said. "There's someone with him now, but I think—Why don't you have a seat, and I'll let him know you're here."

"Sure," said Wayne. He took a seat in between the woman and kid and the old guy. Anne-Marie Kincaid: he read the name off the nameplate on her desk. He smiled at Anne-Marie. She had to be at least forty, but she was still pretty good-looking. Probably worked out, or played tennis, or jogged, or something. Anne-Marie smiled at him. She picked up her phone, waited, said a few words. She caught Wayne's eye and nodded. He smiled back. It was a long way from a come-on, but it was definitely friendly.

"He'll be about twenty minutes," she said. "Can you wait?"

In the old days he would have taken big offense—*keep me waiting, will you? I'll show you*—and stormed out. Now he could see that wasn't the smart thing to do, especially when he didn't have to be anywhere anytime soon. "Sure," he said. "No prob."

Anne-Marie Kincaid cut her eyes toward the woman and child. "They're waiting to see one of Dr. Turner's associates." She raised her eyebrows toward the older man. "He just wants to check on a prescription. He won't take long."

"Sure, thanks." Wayne smiled all the way back to his seat and picked a copy of *Personal Computing* off the table to his right. He didn't know shit about computers. Maybe something would rub off. Was Anne-Marie Kincaid married? He watched her surreptitiously over the top of the magazine: sure enough, she had a diamond ring and a gold band on her left ring finger. Pretty puny diamond, he thought.

Did Janice have a boyfriend? The question came buzzing out of nowhere and bit him like a mosquito. First he slapped at it, then he scratched it, then it made him chuckle to himself. *That's a laugh. She'll never find a guy who measures up to her dear brother.* He shook his head. *Little does she know. Wait till she finds out!*

He heard voices down the hall; he pretended to read his magazine. He didn't understand the article; hell, he didn't even understand the ads. His kids understood a helluva lot more about computers than he ever would. Jerry emerged into the reception area, one reassuring hand on the shoulder of a guy who looked vaguely familiar. The guy seemed upset. Wayne stared at his magazine. "Thanks, Doctor," said the guy. "Thank you so much."

"Mr. Swanson?" said Dr. Turner. "Good to see you. I'll be with you in a few minutes. Mr. Lawrence?"

The older man set his newspaper aside and got up. They disappeared down the corridor talking about Mr. Lawrence's wife, who'd recently had surgery for—Wayne didn't get that part. Probably some female thing.

A moment later a chunky brunette blew through the door, clutching a briefcase in one hand and a wide-brimmed green hat in the other. "I am *so sorry*," she said to the blond woman. "I got stuck in traffic, if you can believe it. Some moving van was taking up one whole lane and it was taking *hours* for everyone to crawl by. No police officer in sight, needless to say. And how are *you*, Eric?"

"OK, I guess," Eric mumbled, looking at his knees.

The whirlwind disappeared into the office directly behind the receptionist's desk, followed by her charges, leaving the waiting room empty. Wayne glanced at Anne-Marie Kincaid, who was looking not too intently at her computer terminal. "Pretty busy place," he said.

"You think this is busy?" she said darkly. "Wait till September. People manage to hold it together all summer—they're too busy to crack up—then round about Labor Day it all falls apart." The phone rang; a moment later, she was typing into her computer and checking her Rolodex at the same time. Wayne went back to his magazine. It sounded as if Anne-Marie was going to be tied up for a while—the phone rang again. Wayne gave up on *Personal Computing* and picked up *Psychology Today*. He hadn't even got to the table of contents before Dr. Turner reappeared, showing Mr. Lawrence out. The man's eyes were red. *Not me, Sherlock,* Wayne thought. *What kind of man starts bawling in a shrink's office?*

A few minutes later he was settled back in Jerry's desk-side chair, launching into his story: "Well, I was probably pushing things some . . ."

Had Wayne nailed it or what? Dr. Turner was just *so* pleased that Wayne had figured this out on his own, that he'd come here instead of hitting the bars, and that he was planning to go to a meeting tonight. "Let Kevin call the shots, why don't you," he suggested, pointing out that it was Kevin who'd suggested going fishing this weekend. "Does he have his own phone?"

"Yeah," said Wayne.

"Well, see, you can call him without crossing the line with your ex-wife."

"Ex-wife" made Wayne's fists clench. Fortunately his hands were out of the good doctor's sight. He half listened as Jerry laid out a possible way to talk to Kevin, nodding as if he were taking it all to heart. "So what's the chance I'll be able to see my other kids anytime soon?" he asked.

Ol' buddy Jerry turned into *Doctor* Turner. He swiveled his big chair in Wayne's direction and looked Wayne in the eyes. "Well, as you know, the custody agreement leaves that to the discretion of your ex-wife—"

Wayne cracked his knuckles. "Not till hell freezes over, you're telling me. Even if Janice decides it's OK for a father to see his own kids, her *brother*—"

"Hell does not have to freeze over, Mr. Swanson. You are free at any time to petition the court for a change in the custody agreement. The court does not want to keep you away from your children. It wants what is best for them. The custody agreement was based on—certain conditions. What you want to do is show the court that those conditions no longer apply. You are well on the way. You're sober, you're in

AA, you're about to establish responsible contact with your oldest son. That is exactly what the court wants to hear."

"Yeah," said Wayne. "I get it. The judge is going to listen to the kids' father before he listens to their *uncle,* right?"

Jerry smiled; *Doctor* Turner had receded into the background again. "That is entirely possible," he said, "especially if you can communicate to the judge that Mr. Segredo's resistance may have more to do with his animosity toward you than with the best interest of your children."

Wayne nodded. He glanced at Jerry; what he saw there said *Go ahead.* "Yeah, well, I know Mister Jay walks on water, or so my wife seems to think, but we've never been what you'd call best buddies." He grinned. "But I can't help thinking, you know, that where I grew up, no way would a guy like him be allowed to work with young people. No *way.* Not that I'm against it, you understand—it's just a sign, you know, how much things change. Get with the program, Mister Wayne!" he admonished himself.

Wayne knew without looking that he had the one hundred percent undivided attention of Dr. Jerome Turner. "Everybody says he does a good job, and don't get me wrong: I may not like the guy—that's no secret—but if he's doing a good job, hey, that's fine by me. But you know how it is: something bad happens, something really bad, like that priest in Brockton, and everybody's saying, 'We had no idea, he always helped old ladies across the street'—that kind of thing."

A smile played around Doctor Jerry's lips. "Exactly what are you telling me, Mr. Swanson?"

"I'm telling you, *Doctor* Turner," Wayne said, a responding smile toying with his voice, "that my *ex*-brother-in-law is a homosexual."

The director of Family Services leaned back in his chair, pressing the tips of his fingers together. "And how do you know this, Mr. Swanson? Did he bring his—" the professional talker seemed to be having a hard time finding a word "—*friends* home for Christmas with the family?"

The idea was just too wild: Wayne guffawed. "No way, José. The family doesn't have a clue. Not that he ever brought any *girl*friends home either, you understand. The man is very discreet." He saw what Jerry was getting at: prove it. How much could he say without saying too much?

"So," said Dr. Turner. "How do you know?"

"Sorry, I have to keep that confidential," Wayne said. "I hope you won't take offense. I can't be snitching on my—sources."

"I understand completely," Dr. Turner assured him. "Just as long as you understand that I can't—act—without evidence. Real evidence. Hearsay isn't enough."

Wayne smiled. "I think I can help," he said.

"I hope you can," said the director of Family Services. "I sincerely hope you can." He rose from his chair; Wayne followed his lead. As they walked down the short hall to the waiting room, Jerry was saying, "I can't tell you how pleased I am that things are working out so well for you. By all means, call me after the meeting tonight. You have my home number? Of course you do. I want to hear how it goes."

Wayne practically danced down the stairs leading out of the building.

So much for the therapeutic benefits of a weekend getaway: since getting home this morning—that was a joke, since he hadn't been home yet—Jay had already done two days' worth of work, and his looming three o'clock appointment did not promise any chance to relax. The Women's Resource Center had been hit with two crises since Friday, both involving children. The messier of the two cases had just left his office: a fifth-grader who had confided to her math teacher that her stepfather played "tongue-kiss" games with her. The girl wouldn't say anything in front of her distraught mother, so, in response to a discreet buzz on the intercom, Becca Herschel had saved the interview by coaxing the woman from Jay's office to her own, there to be treated with coffee, Kleenex, and maybe Becca's secret stash of Reese's Peanut Butter Cups.

Jay returned the three phone calls that had come in while he was talking with the girl: "Yes, I'll be there," "How about ten fifteen on Thursday?" and "You've worked a miracle: the wobble is gone" took care of them all, one, two, three, and in less than five minutes. Very satisfying, and very unlike his newest case: The marriage was already headed for divorce court, and if incest was involved . . . ? It was almost dead certain that when New Year's rolled around, the family's file would still be near the front of his "current" drawer, and a lot thicker than it was now.

The family hadn't been on the island very long: the school records made it less than three years. Jay would have bet a month's salary that they'd been in trouble before they moved to Martha's Vineyard, that this was yet another couple who thought that the island paradise was going to save them from themselves. Everyone said that the island was a good place to raise kids, but most of them had no idea why. It really didn't have to do with the "quaintness," the dearth of fleshly temptations, or the thin band of water that separated it from the mainland. What made the Vineyard—or had made it—a good place to raise kids was the web of family and friends that took some of the insane pressures of parenting off the parents. Here vestiges of the extended family still existed, embedded in echoes of real community. It was a long way from perfect, but it was better than a subdivision of nuclear households, each holed up in its own little box and remote from the "neighbors," who might be as few as twenty-five feet away.

But not even the most persuasive orator would ever convince, say, Alice Chase that this was a good place to raise kids. Jay reflected, not for the first time, on the similarity between Alice's situation and that of his sister Janny. Both had grown up in tight-knit families. Neither one had been to college. Both got trapped in miserable marriages to abusive, alcoholic men. Janny had three kids; Alice had one, about the same age as Janny's youngest. But Janny had a home and

Alice didn't; Janny was doing fine and Alice wasn't. As far as Jay could tell, the biggest difference between the two was that Janny's family was here and Alice's was across the water.

Come to think of it, Lenny Chase's family was here, and even he was doing pretty well, considering he was a ne'er-do-well drunk who couldn't hold a job for three consecutive weeks.

Jay's eyes surveyed the office and came to rest on the big family photo on top of the bookcase. It had been taken the previous year, when members of the clan came from all over New England, and even farther away, for Maria and Ernie's Labor Day cookout. With Pop gone, would the cookout even take place? Of course it would: Janny and the aunts and female cousins would see to it. There was Kevin towering over his mother; Amy was nearly as tall as Janny, but Danny still looked like a little kid. He and Steve Silvia both held baseball gloves—they'd probably been yanked away from a pickup game in the back yard. Rainey was grinning up at Kevin as if asking "How's the air up there?"

Of all the people in the picture, only Rainey and Steve Silvia didn't belong by blood to some branch of the Segredo clan. But they were family, no question about that: Rainey was the sister Janny had always wanted, and now Steve and Dan were pretty much inseparable. Danny had asked him at the kids' trout derby in early April, "If you married Steve's mom, would that make Steve and me brothers?" Steve was standing by waiting for the answer; Jay wondered which one had put the other up to asking the question. He thought it through, wishing he'd paid more attention to those infernal kinship questions on the standardized tests of his youth: "If I married Steve's mom," he said, "then I would be Steve's stepfather, and Steve's mom would be your aunt. I think that would make you first cousins."

"See? We wouldn't be brothers unless your mom married my dad," Dan had said, giving Jay an immediate case of the creeps. Shortly thereafter Steve hooked the sea robin that won him the derby's second prize in his age group. The topic hadn't surfaced since.

No wonder everyone wanted them to get married—and, Jay thought stubbornly, why not? What was the big deal really? The kids would be happy, Janny would be ecstatic, Mama would love presiding at the wedding, and all the relatives would be—relieved.

But that morning at breakfast in the airport diner, Rainey had thwarted his every attempt to broach the subject. No matter what opening he offered, she checked him. It couldn't have been accidental. Finally he asked if she thought she'd marry again; "if the right man came along," she replied, all too seriously, then she smiled rather slyly and said, "I think I'd live with any guy at least three years before I married him."

Jay wasn't about to press on under those conditions, not without getting a reading from someone else. And who exactly would "someone else" be? His sister? Out. Becca? No way. Shannon? Hah. You didn't need a weatherman to know what Shannon would say; you just needed a three-mile head start before she blew up.

Jay stood up, stretched, and picked the picture off the top shelf. He gazed into it; he dusted the frame with his shirttail. Who had taken the picture? Mattie, probably, the avid amateur photographer—but no, there she was on the porch, holding someone else's toddler on her hip.

Shannon. He had invited her to the cookout; she had done so much for Janice's family, and Jay was embarrassed by Janny's coldness to her. Janny had managed a semblance of cordiality at the celebration, or so he remembered. Probably there had been undercurrents he had missed. But Shannon had certainly taken the picture.

Carefully Jay replaced the photograph. The one next to it was much older: Nate and the original Worcester gang, on a basketball court, of course. The first time they'd applied for a grant—probably for playground equipment, Jay couldn't remember—they'd had to come up with a name. "Our Gang,"

Jay had suggested facetiously, thinking of the Little Rascals. Nate had shaken his head in mock exasperation: "Gang? Don't crack me up. That'll flip those old white foundation dudes right over the wall. We're a *youth corps*." Five minutes later the group had its name: B Court Youth Corps. The social services and funding types all thought that B Court was an address in the projects. It stood for Basketball Court, of course. Those who knew liked to snicker at those who didn't.

I've got radar, man. Nate better not really have radar. If Nate had a clue that he was thinking about getting married, Nate would say, "Really?" and walk away shaking his head. *You do what you have to do, Nate,* Jay thought.

Not a minute too soon Becca buzzed him to announce his three o'clock appointment and the mind movie dissolved into another crisis.

At 3:55, Jay stuck his head into Becca's office. "I'm wasted, I'm gone, I'm history," he said. "Have a good night. See you in the a.m."

"Bright and early," said Becca. "How's R.G. doing?" R.G. was his three o'clock, a high school freshman.

"Not bad, under the circumstances," Jay replied. "I told him it sucks, no two ways about it, being underage and smarter than your parents. He liked that."

"Were you smarter than your parents?" she asked.

Jay pushed the door open and leaned against the jamb. "Good question. When I was a high school freshman —absolutely. Now? I don't know. I would have made a hash of their life. They would have made a hash of mine. What can I say?"

With both hands Becca slid her glasses down to the tip of her nose. She gazed at Jay over the top of the frames. In a Sigmund Freud accent she said, "A very vise answer, Herr Segredosky. Go home. Watch stupid television. Order yourself a pizza. Go to bed early."

Jay resisted the temptation to say *You're so smart, why*

aren't you married? Becca thought she wanted to get married. Becca's subconscious was evidently resisting the idea. Becca was a bit too zaftig to attract most men's immediate attention. Besides, she was too astute, witty, and competent to be wasting her time on straight guys. Becca and Shannon really would make a good match. How to get Shannon over her odd ideas about dating younger women? "Yes, ma'am," said Jay. "Thanks for everything. You're the best."

"I know," she said smugly, then she smiled a big smile. "Speaking of making hash, did you hear the one about the congressman's son?" She pushed the *Cape Cod Times* toward him.

Below the fold on the left side of the front page was a color photograph of two EMTs assisting a woman in a blue dress. Behind them was a dark sedan with a bashed-in front end. Jay didn't like looking at bashed-in cars.

"Imagine," said Becca, her voice oozing pseudo-censoriousness. "Right here on Martha's Vineyard. Nice legs, don't you think?"

The woman in the blue dress was the son of a conservative congressman from upstate New York.

Jay's car was halfway down the parking lot, so he cut across the wet lawn rather than follow the concrete path. *Things could be worse,* he told himself. *Things could be much, much worse.* Approaching the car, he suddenly recalled that he'd locked the doors because his luggage was inside—he hadn't locked his keys in, had he? A quick search found them in the left pocket of his jacket: four keys on a key ring from his bank, house key, car key, keys to his office and the building's outside door. In Worcester he'd had two keys for his apartment, two for the outside door, one for his mailbox, one for his Kryptonite bicycle lock, one for the car, about six for work, and one whose purpose he'd forgotten that he didn't dare throw away. More island people locked than used to, and you even heard car alarms going off on Circuit Ave., but you could still leave your wallet on the seat of your car and it would still be there untouched when you remembered it three hours later. Jay sprinted up the grassy rise to his car, thinking that despite all its sad stories, Martha's Vineyard was a great place to be from, and not a bad place to live. *Not, however, the best place for a man to be driving around in a dress.*

"Tsk-tsk, Mr. Segredo," said a baritone voice off to his left. "Did you miss the last department heads' meeting, or were you not paying attention when we were enjoined not to walk on the lawn? I don't recall that any exceptions were made."

And Island Social Services, thought Jay, *is not a bad place to work, but conditions would improve dramatically if Jerome Turner, EdD, MPH, LICSW, took early retirement.* The Gerbil was turning the key in the door of his immaculate white BMW. "Hey there, Jerry," Jay said brightly. "Nice day to be leaving early, isn't it." At the last department heads' meeting, Dr. Turner himself had urged his professional colleagues to set a good example for clerical and administrative staff by arriving promptly in the morning and remaining at their posts until at least five o'clock.

The Gerbil's whiskers twitched. "I might say the same for you, Mr. Segredo."

"You might, Dr. Turner, but you won't, because you recall that I accrued sixteen hours' comp time at the Developing Leadership Potential in At-Risk Youth conference this weekend." Jay's genial smile added *And we all know it wasn't me who logged the most days at off-island conferences last year, don't we?* The Gerbil's eyes narrowed somewhat: he seemed to have gotten the message. "All the same," said Jay magnanimously, "you're right: I should not be walking on the lawn. By the way—while I was off-island, I heard that Wayne Swanson was back. So you don't have to worry about letting me know, or letting my sister know, or letting Women's Resources know. We know already."

Jay knew immediately that he had gone too far: his boss's professional smiley face froze for an instant then started to morph into a very hostile glower. Not only that, the Gerb might easily infer from Jay's words that Women's Resources had leaked him the information. Big mistake. Relations between Women's Resources and the Family Services director were perpetually tense. No need to exacerbate them further. Hyperalert to the Gerbil's vibes, Jay waited, poised on the balls of his feet.

"As it happens," said Dr. Turner, speaking with the deliberation that signified barely controlled rage, "I just saw Mr. Swanson. He is doing very, very well. I don't believe his ex-wife has anything to fear."

That's good to hear. Jay might have said it aloud, but his synapses were firing *Danger danger danger!* A deer saved its life by standing still and lost it by moving.

"However, Mr. Swanson had some interesting things to say about you, Mr. Segredo. I certainly hope they aren't true." With a triumphant smirk Jerome Turner slid into his car and inserted his key in the ignition. The engine rumbled to life.

Jay forced his mind to direct his hand to put the key into the lock, turn it, open the door, get into the car. Insert key in ignition. Open window. Turn key. Shift into reverse, look over shoulder; bring clutch up to friction point. As the car began to roll backward, Jay couldn't remember where he was going. Home, that was it. Home.

CHAPTER SEVENTEEN

Mr. Swanson had some interesting things to say about you.

Jay waited for two minivans and a UPS truck to go by then pulled out into the Edgartown–Vineyard Haven Road. *I could say a few interesting things about Mr. Swanson,* he thought. *Mr. Swanson, sober or not, is not the world's most credible witness.*

But Wayne knew something. On the deep shit scale this was roughly equivalent to Slobodan Milosevic getting the bomb. And now Jerry Turner had it too.

Without signaling Jay hauled the steering wheel hard left and his wagon crossed the bow of an oncoming blue Toyota pickup, close enough that the pickup's driver leaned on her horn to blow off the adrenaline rush.

Sorry.

Jay accelerated down Barnes Road, speedometer heading upward past 30, 35, 40, 50 . . . 65 as he sped by the deer weighing station. The speed limit on Barnes Road is 45, as fast as it legally gets on Martha's Vineyard. Barnes Road is one of the long straightaways where islanders keep in practice for highway driving off-island.

What did Wayne know? Wayne couldn't *know* anything. But Wayne didn't *have* to know anything—any ignoramus could start a rumor. If it made a good story and involved a reasonably public figure, it would travel at the speed of light from Oak Bluffs to Gay Head, to Chappaquiddick, to Vineyard

Haven—to Jack Purcell, executive director of Island Social Services; to all Jay's clients, and the parents of his clients. To Janny and the kids. All of whom would abruptly realize that not only was Jay Segredo not married, he had never been accused of breaking up someone else's marriage. QED: The rumor must be true.

Mama wouldn't hear the rumor. However, when she went over to the parish hall for bingo tomorrow night, one of the other ladies—maybe with honorable intentions, but then again, maybe not—would come up to her and embrace her and say, "Don't cry, Maria, don't cry; Our Lady will give you strength . . ." Then when Mama fainted dead away, someone would bring smelling salts and someone else would explain, for the benefit of those still out of the loop.

Jay's hands clenched on the wheel. At 72 miles per hour, give or take, the uneven pressure jerked the car to the right. Jay regained control on the wide grassy shoulder and brought the car to a halt. Nothing was approaching in the rearview mirror. The dark-haired kid in the white Honda Civic coming from the other direction didn't even glance his way. No cops in sight. *Why didn't I aim at that tree?*

He crossed his arms against the steering wheel. His predecessor had effectively ended his island career in a speeding motor vehicle: after the state police officer pulled him over on the Beach Road, he flunked the Breathalyzer test and whatever test it was that said that forty-eight-year-old social services administrators were not supposed to be careening around the island in the company of intoxicated high school girls. Leslie Benaron had scored a major coup with that one: she'd been methodically building a case that the man's sterling reputation had a flimsy foundation, while the *Chronicle* fought off backstage machinations and letters bearing thinly veiled libel threats—one of them from Dr. Jerome Turner, EdD, MPH, LICSW, backing his subordinate to the hilt—when that arrest on the Beach Road sank the opposition without a gurgle. What *had* become of the unfortunate Mr. Randolph? Had he sobered up? Had he survived the spectacular nosedive of his brilliant career? Maybe he had run his car into a tree.

What if he ran *his* car into a tree? Leslie could write the story: all she'd have to do was recycle the one she'd written after the shooting last fall. All those nice testimonials would make a great obit, and Jack and the others would be spared the challenge of saying something complimentary after the fact. Sooner or later Leslie would get to talk to Wayne, whose little doggy brain probably figured that if he knocked Jay out of the game, Janny would take him back. Till death do them part, take two.

Over my dead body.

The thought startled him. He laughed, a brief, hard laugh that hurt his throat. Here he was, half contemplating a short fast run at a stand of oaks, just up the road from the deer weighing station. Dead deer at the weighing station, dead deer getting weighed, dead men getting laid till death do them part, laid end to end . . . *Over my dead body.* He laughed. It didn't hurt this time: he stepped out of his own way and the laughter poured out. He laughed till he literally cried, and when he moved an arm to brush the tears away, the horn honked. His head snapped back. He looked warily up and down the road. Nothing was coming.

He drove home at a more moderate speed, slowing down to the rarely observed legal limit to pass the Martha's Vineyard Airport while the taxi van behind him bleated its displeasure. The rest of the way home, he tried not to think. Instead he noted the model of every vehicle that passed in the opposite direction, and counted license plates from outside the New England states—three before he got to the triangle near Parsonage Pond, only one between there and the turnoff for the subdivision he lived in. But underneath these mantras his mind was working: what does Wayne know and how does he know it, what will he say and who might listen to him, what tune will he play and who might come out of the woodwork to dance?

It took mere seconds to come up with the two-night stand who would blab to a sympathetic ear for the price of a drink, and the summer-long affair who would overcome his scruples if flattered subtly enough (providing he could be located), and one more who could go either way—but would probably remain silent, because he valued his rep as a ladies' man. The only one who would absolutely say nothing under any circumstances was Giles Kelleher. *Let that be a lesson to you,* he thought to himself, unable to remember if the phrase came from the Bible or if someone he'd known—who? when?—had simply said it a lot. *What was the damn lesson anyway? Chickens come home to roost, lightning never strikes twice, criminals return to the scene of the crime? Oho, now I've got it: You can't go home again.*

His house seemed blessedly familiar when he pulled into the driveway. Who knew what disaster was on his answering machine or waiting to be downloaded into his computer— he'd find out soon enough—but the little clearing was quiet, and a long way from Island Social Services. Suit bag slung over his left shoulder, attaché and carry-on clasped together in his right hand, Jay hurried up the steps to the deck, then peered through the slider before he opened it. His living room was as he had left it: Friday morning's coffee mug and cereal bowl on the coffee table, stack of books and magazines on the floor where he'd put them so he could spread his papers on the table. He slid the door open. Should he start locking now that Wayne was back? Nah: petty property damage wasn't Wayne's style. Wayne was more into bodily harm.

Mindful of the laptop it contained, he disengaged the attaché from his fist, set it down on the coffee table, and carried the rest of his baggage down the hall to his bedroom. As always when he came home from a business trip, his bedroom reminded him of the hotel he'd just stayed at. This was no big surprise, since most of the furnishings, from the double bed to the bureaus, the bedside table to the oak framed mirror to the armchair in the corner, had come from an island hotel that a few years back had sold off three floors of furniture so it could redecorate. The generic seascape prints looked as if they'd come from the same sale, but no, they'd been hanging in the exact same places when he moved in. Jay dumped his junk on the bed and retraced his steps, looking for a beer.

Harpoon bottle in hand, he dropped into the brown recliner, the only truly comfortable seat in the house. It had been his father's favorite TV-watching and newspaper-reading chair. After his father went into the nursing home, his mother had urged Jay to take it. "How could I sit in your father's chair?" she had asked. He had had no answer to that. Now it was his own favorite chair, the one with the magazines piled next to it, the one with the phone and the TV and stereo remotes within easy reach.

The answering machine had twenty-three new messages on it. Twenty-three voices locked in a black plastic rectangular box. Amazing. Sometimes living in the late twentieth century was like being transported to Oz. Who was in the box? Shannon, probably, and Becca and Janice: everyone who had tried to reach him after Wayne was sighted back on the Vineyard. Jerry Turner? The Gerb wouldn't have been trying to alert him to Wayne's return, but maybe he was goading him with thinly disguised threats. *Mr. Swanson had some interesting things to say about you.* Maybe Gerb had said something indiscreet on the tape, and Jay would have the pleasure of playing it, at an opportune moment, for Jack Purcell or the board of directors or someone from the paper. *In your dreams, Jay my man.*

What could Wayne possibly know, as in "know for sure"? One by one, Jay tried to hypothesize a link between Wayne and each of the most likely suspects. Anything was possible, of course—after you lived on the Vineyard a few years, unless you were a complete hermit, you probably knew somebody who knew somebody who knew somebody and were somehow connected to just about everyone else on the island—but even his wildest, most paranoid fantasy couldn't connect any of them to Wayne. Giles was the only one who even knew he had a sister whose last name was Swanson. Besides, Wayne had been back less than a week: how much snooping could he have done in five or six days?

Unless he *had* known something last October. Wayne had been seen in Giles's neighborhood early last fall; Shannon had tried to make a big deal of that, and Jay had laughed, told her she was getting paranoid—Wayne was a plumber, wasn't he? Giles's neighbors needed plumbing like everyone else. *Danger danger danger!* Every time Jay's thoughts crept toward that maelstrom, his mind pulled them back, reeling with vertigo. This time he edged, very cautiously, a little closer. Wayne—if it was Wayne? Of course it was Wayne—had stationed himself just *east* of where Barnes Road ran into the Edgartown–West Tisbury Road. Jay's regular route between home and work, which he might travel two, three, four times on any given day, passed just *west* of that intersection. Why hadn't Wayne staked out a blind on that side? True, sniping at the beginning or end of the workday—even a habitually long workday—was likely to attract more attention than sniping in the middle of the night, but it was impossible to avoid the hypothesis that Wayne had known Jay would be traveling the entire length of the Edgartown–West Tisbury Road on that particular night, which meant he might have known that Jay was spending occasional evenings in Edgartown—or maybe had followed him to Giles's house from the family cookout.

But—but—but . . . Wayne was no model of self-restraint under the best of circumstances. When Wayne showed up at Jay's house the following Sunday, he had been drunk, he had been furious, he had been firing a loaded pistol in the air. If Wayne had had wind of anything that might destroy Jay, wouldn't he have been screaming it at the top of his lungs? Wouldn't he have dropped a hint or two to good Dr. Turner long before this? And if he had, wouldn't Dr. Turner, who could not keep a poker face for two consecutive hours, never mind six consecutive months, have let something slip?

The obvious solution hit Jay with his mouth full of beer. For an instant it paralyzed his mind and his muscles, then he carefully let the liquid slide down his throat. Adam. Adam knew about the shooting; maybe Adam knew about Wayne. Maybe Adam had intercepted Shannon's message, or even listened in on their phone call. Maybe Adam had contacted Wayne. *Break the rule and I'm going to break it too.*

But he hadn't broken the rule, not since Adam read him the riot act yesterday morning. Could Adam have launched a pre-emptive strike, to make sure he didn't do anything foolish? But he hadn't said . . . That wouldn't have been . . . Adam wouldn't have done . . .

Jay had no idea what Adam would have done, or what Adam was capable of doing. Adam was the night food and beverage manager in an upscale business hotel off Route 128, Adam had a taste for adventure—other than that, Jay didn't know shit about Adam. Adam had a life beyond the hotel: Adam was married, with child, or children. Adam might be all talk—or he might be like Wayne, a guy who'd stake out a place in the woods, who'd wait for hours stretched on the ground, rifle braced against his shoulder, until a certain car entered his sights.

If Adam were that kind of guy, Jay thought, *he wouldn't hit the tire if he was aiming at something else.* He drained the rest of his Harpoon in two long swallows. The beer pinned him in his chair like the force of a plane racing forward.

Adam, he decided after weighing what he did know about the man, would not have tipped Wayne off without first telling Jay he was going to do it. Adam would want to make him sweat. In which case there would be a message on his machine. Jay lifted the answering machine into his lap. Twenty-three messages—was one of them from Adam D. Kortmeyer? Did he really want to know?

He set the machine aside, got up, and went in search of another beer. Without thinking, he detoured down the hall to his bedroom; there he unzipped his carry-on and lifted out the bottle of Jim Beam, the bottle of Bushmills. Back in the kitchen he picked a beer from the fridge and a juice glass from the cupboard. Leaving the Bushmills on the counter, he carried the whiskey, the beer, and the glass back to his chair.

With the help of Jim Beam, he started listening to messages. Shannon, Becca, Janny—all taken care of: delete, delete, delete. Two minor work-related calls—skip, skip; he'd get back to them later. One of the guys he sometimes played pickup basketball with, calling on Saturday afternoon to see if he wanted to play—delete. A college classmate in Baltimore who was coming to the Cape over Memorial Day weekend, any chance of getting together?—skip. It was like playing Russian roulette. Are any of the messages loaded? Adam had his number, Adam might be in there, Adam might have talked to Wayne . . .

After message number 16, he splashed a little more whiskey into the juice glass. Maybe he didn't want to know. Maybe he should delete the rest of the messages without listening to them. Maybe it didn't matter if he knew or not: did you want to know before you left the house that a barely licensed teenager in his daddy's monster pickup was going to run you down in the crosswalk at Five Corners? But what if someone really needed to talk to him?

Jay kept listening, pausing longer and longer between each message, his heart beating harder as the counter approached 23. Number 22 was his nephew Kevin, calling from the pay phone at the gas station. In the background a male voice called out to someone some distance away, "Hey, where you been? I heard you were gone." Underinflated tires squealed off the tarmac and onto the Beach Road. Kevin said, "Listen, I'm at work and I can't talk, but maybe we can talk later? Are you back? Mom's picking me up at eight. Don't say anything to her, OK? See ya."

Jay checked his watch: quarter to six. "Don't say anything to her"? Don't say what? Don't say you called? *Wayne; it has to be about Wayne.* Hadn't he bet that Wayne would show up at the high school Monday around dismissal time? Wasn't it still Monday? Why did so many of his hunches have to be right? What if Adam was behind door number 23?

He tossed back the last swallow of whiskey. Feeling a little light in the head and uneasy in the stomach, he took the Jim Beam and the juice glass to the kitchen. The glass went into the sink, Mr. Beam and Mr. Bushmills into the booze cabinet. Should he call Kevin at the gas station? Should he stop by, maybe offer Kevin a ride home? What if Wayne were hanging around, waiting for a chance to talk with his son, waiting for a glimpse of Janice? Jay had downed at least two stiff shots of Jim Beam in the last forty-five minutes, on top of three or four beers. He could probably get to Vineyard Haven in one piece, but he'd smell like a lounge lizard when he got there.

He thought of his unfortunate predecessor; he thought of Jerry Turner sitting in his office, rubbing his hands together, licking his whiskers or whatever it was that grew out of his gerbil face. This was not a good time to get stopped for DWI. He dumped the water out of the tea kettle, refilled it with fresh, and put it on to boil. He retrieved Friday's mug from the sink, rinsed it, and set it beside the stove. Cone, filter, a heaping scoop of ground high-test. The phone rang. For a moment he didn't know where the sound was coming from.

Adam?

Kevin?

Wayne?

It stopped before he got to it; the answering machine didn't kick in. Wrong number, or some damn telemarketer: this was their prime feeding time. He dropped back into the chair, studied the Harpoon bottle, and took a swig.

It was getting dark. Actual sunset might be almost an hour off, but the oaks were so dense on the west side of his house that dusk came early. Answering machine in his lap, red 23 beaming up at him, he watched his still reflection in the slider. *People who live in glass houses,* he thought. *I might as well live in a glass house. What people don't realize about glass houses is that once the sun goes down, all you can see is your own self, and it's very dim and wavery.*

Martha's Vineyard isn't an island. It isn't about water: Martha's Vineyard is made of glass.

Jay looked at the beer bottle. He must have had more than he thought. Coffee: he'd been making coffee. He made his way back to the kitchen, carrying the bottle in one hand. The water in the kettle was half boiled away. He poured the filter full and let it drip. *I should eat something.* The freezer contained four trays of ice cubes, half a bag of frozen corn, half a bag of frozen peas, and a stack of frozen pizzas. That was a no-brainer: he picked the top pizza, double cheese, double everything, and too big to fit in his half-pint microwave. He turned on the oven with one hand while pouring more hot water into the coffee filter. Open pizza box, remove plastic wrap, deposit on cookie sheet . . .

Jimmy, it's your own fault you have a tummy ache, look how you eat . . .

Yeah, Mama, I know, I know: I can't take care of myself, I should get married.

He snagged another beer from the fridge and carried it in one hand, black coffee in the other, to the living room. He watched his reflection in the slider: sipping the coffee and grimacing at the blackness of it, twisting the cap off the beer bottle and washing the coffee down with a mouthful of beer. He looked surprisingly good for a guy who was strapped to a log and drifting head-first toward a buzz saw. Normal, even. A guy who made most of his lay-ups, though he was on the downhill side of forty and not especially tall, and nearly all of his free throws, because he wasn't rattled by anything.

"My buddy here," Nate had once explained to a skeptical newcomer to the neighborhood courts, "my buddy here isn't a hair over five-nine—"

"Five-ten," Jay had protested. "My license says so."

"My buddy," said Nate, "doesn't know how easy it is to get a license that lies, but trust me, on the court he's six-foot-two. No one with a brain fouls him when he's shooting because at the line he's Laser Man. Bomb goes off on the bench, he still makes both shots."

Laser Man. Once upon a time Laser Man could penetrate the most persistent defense, extricate himself from any problem, help other people extricate themselves from their problems. But right now Laser Man can't focus for shit. Laser Man can't make a decent cup of coffee, Laser Man is too lazy to go get more sugar, Laser Man doesn't dare listen to message 23 on the answering machine. There's an answer out there and Laser Man doesn't know where to look.

In those pulp novels that had circulated in junior high and high school—old and yellowed by then, probably swiped from forgotten boxes in people's basements—this was where the hero's best friend since grade school took pills, or slit his wrists, or shot himself, or, in the rare optimistic ending, bought a one-way plane ticket to Paris, determined to live with "his own kind." After sweeping out of the church with his childhood sweetheart on his arm, the hero might spare a thought for the tragic fate of his friend, who would have been his best man if he hadn't—if he hadn't . . .

Get a grip, Laser Man. The fifties were nearly over before you were born. It's the nineties now.

Yeah—you tell my mother that. You tell this whole fucking island that.

The scent of about-to-scorch tomato sauce and mozzarella reached his chair. But the pizza was fine; he liked his crust crispy. He stirred a scant spoonful of sugar into his coffee and stuck the mug in the microwave to zap while he slipped the pizza onto a dinner plate and ripped a generous handful of paper towels from the roll mounted under the cupboard. At the last minute he grabbed another beer from the refrigerator. *Last one,* he told himself. *What's pizza without beer?*

Nate's right: I should move back to Worcester.

Eating pizza and drinking beer was far more challenging than most people realized. As he pulled his cooling fourth slice from the plate, he pondered the splotch of sauce on the coffee table. Slowly from the splotch emerged a hypothesis about the viscosity of cheese at declining temperatures. Maybe he should do an experiment? He had the vague idea that he'd had this thought before. Maybe he'd already done the experiment?

The phone rang. Automatically he reached for it, hesitating a moment when he recognized Shannon's number in the Caller ID window.

"Yo, Shannon," he said.

She laughed. "I can always tell when you've been hanging out with the homeboys," she said, and rushed on without giving him a chance to respond. This was probably good, because if he said one more word, her AA antennae would pick up that he'd had several too many in too short a time. "I'm glad I caught you," she was saying. "This could be important."

Oh, brother.

"Nah, it's not all that bad, unless you like flying blind."

He hadn't even realized that he'd said it aloud.

"You still there?"

"Yeah," he said. "Don't mind me—I'm finishing off my last slice of Mama Celeste pizza."

"It is always," she said, "good to know that there is someone on this nauseatingly self-consciously health-conscious island who eats more junk than I do. Pix and I had popcorn for supper—her favorite, with cardboard parmesan and Red Hot sauce. I held out for the barbecue, but I lost."

Shannon was nuts. Jay loved her to pieces, even though he knew he was a terrible disappointment to her. Like now. If Shannon knew he was floating down the millrace strapped to a log—hell, if she knew he didn't dare listen to the twenty-third message on his answering machine—she would give up in disgust.

"OK," she was saying, "here's the deal. Giles called me fifteen minutes ago. Wayne's hanging around the nabe again. Well, he's not sure it's Wayne because he didn't go up and knock on the window, but it's definitely Wayne's van. Same MO as last fall: he drove around slowly like he was looking for a particular house, then he pulled into a driveway where he had a clear view of Giles's front door and his parking space."

"You don't think he's working?"

"Jay my man, you are slipping." Shannon was grinning into the phone. "It was six thirty p.m. This is Martha's Vineyard. A plumber working at that hour would get excommunicated."

Jay didn't quite understand what Shannon was saying, but he guessed she would explain soon enough. He took a long sip of coffee. The coffee was still hot. The beer was still cold.

She did: "My man, the neighbors aren't home, and Wayne isn't their plumber."

All of a sudden the fog between Jay's ears vanished. Sunlight blazed on the soggy synapses of his brain. "Wait," he said. "Hold on a minute. Are you saying this is the first time Wayne's been seen over there since—since he got sent off?"

"That's what I'm saying. That's exactly—"

"This is good," said Jay. "This is great. This is the best thing I've heard all day."

"Jay, are you all right?"

"No, yes, sure I'm all right—" *liar, liar, pants on fire* "—you don't understand what's going on—" *But I do, not all of it maybe, but I get this much: Adam didn't talk, and Wayne doesn't know anything—maybe he suspects, but he can't prove anything, he's still looking for proof* . . .

"I don't understand?" Shannon demanded. She wasn't kidding anymore. Talk about lasers: her voice was a heat-seeking missile programmed to search, find, and take no prisoners. "I understand fucking more than I want to understand. Listen, Jay: you get in your car and you get your butt over here. Now. If you aren't here in fifteen minutes, I'm on my way over." She paused and then added, not into the phone, "Yeah, don't worry, Pixo, you can come too."

Drive? Jay wasn't driving anywhere: he might not be three sheets to the wind yet, but the ropes were looking pretty loose. "Shan, I shouldn't—" he said.

"Get your butt over here!" Shannon roared into the phone. Then she hung up.

So who's surprised? Procrastination's passed out in the cellar, I'm going great guns on this job, I'm cruising, the dog's asleep, the phone isn't ringing—and I have to fuck it up by making a fucking phone call.

But Shannon wasn't really angry, she wasn't even surprised. She was scared. She'd been fearing this since Jay went to ground after the "accident." She'd been dreading it since she saw Wayne at the Saturday morning meeting, and it sure hadn't helped that Jay wasn't where he was supposed to be when she tried to tell him what she'd seen. Did she have any right, any right whatsoever, to be doing what she was doing, to be thinking of doing what she was about to do? On one hand, all she was doing was telling him to get a grip, make some choices, stop hiding behind his family's inability to deal—or his assumption that his family wouldn't be able to deal. On the other hand, what did she know about families? She'd never had to risk her family's good opinion because she'd never had it, and it wasn't worth much anyway. *Would* Jay's family shut him out? What would happen to him if they did?

Well, maybe she could relate to what he was up against. As she celebrated her first AA anniversary, she had been acutely aware that she'd never come out in a meeting. She rarely spoke at meetings, period, because by the time she ran each comment, each story, through her Internal Censor to make sure it didn't contain any incriminating pronouns or other details, the discussion had moved on. She ranted at her sponsor about homophobia and sexism and those smug old-timers who assumed everyone was straight, and finally her sponsor held up four fingers—for Step 4, "Made a searching and fearless moral inventory of ourselves"—and asked quietly, "What's stopping you?"

Whereupon Shannon understood that the problem wasn't sexism or homophobia or smugness: these had never stopped her before, had they? The problem was her own fear. Her first-year coin was still such a wonder that she kept reaching into her pocket to touch it, rub it, press it into her palm. What if she came out and they barred the door against her? Some of them might be sexist and homophobic and smug, but all of them collectively were saving her life. What if she couldn't come back?

When she finally mustered the courage to say "the L-word" in a meeting, the ceiling didn't fall in. One of the old guys had come up later to tell her that his daughter was gay. One woman squeezed her hand, and several people told her to "keep coming back." True, in the following weeks a few others edged away, or narrowed their eyes at her, or even muttered about "making a big issue of it." She got used to it. She acted as if she didn't see the hard eyes, didn't hear the snippy remarks. *Live and let live,* she told herself; *they may be endangering their own sobriety, but I won't let them mess with mine.* So as it turned out she could both come out and stay sober. The only thing she couldn't do was paint, and now, gazing at the strange mural she had painted on her living room wall, she let herself believe that eventually she was going to get that back too. *You can have it all,* she thought stubbornly, *all the gods willing and if you wait long enough.* But what was true for her wasn't necessarily true for Jay.

How many times in the last six months had she discussed this with her sponsor? Chris was enigmatic; Chris never stopped smiling with her eyes. "Turn it over," she said. "Check your motives. When in doubt, don't. Share your experience, strength, and hope."

"That makes it a draw," Shannon wailed. "Two yes, two no. What do I do?"

"Wait till they all give the same answer," said Chris, and that was as close to advice as Chris ever got.

So Shannon had waited, and prayed, and talked to Giles, and thought, and made snide remarks to Jay, and waited some more. This weekend she'd hit the slots: all four questions turned up GO! And still she feared she was making a horrible mistake.

Recovery meant never knowing for sure you were right, never entirely trusting your motives, but knowing you had to act anyway.

Well, she was acting, and it made her sick to her stomach. But when she heard Jay pull into her driveway and cut his engine, calm spread all the way down to her fingernails and the tips of her toes. Pixel was already standing at the mud room door, with a big smile and a wagging tail.

As soon as Jay came through the door, she knew he was a basket case. He spent ten full seconds talking to Pixel, when he usually just rubbed her head and moved on; he didn't make a snide remark about the popcorn smell that had to have hit him as soon as he walked in. He even kissed Shannon on the cheek. She said, "Jesus Christ, I think I just had a slip. What were you doing behind the wheel of a motor vehicle?"

"You said—" he started to protest, then he sucked in his breath and said, "Jesus, Mary, and *Joseph.* Where did that jungle come from?"

He was the second human being, other than herself, to see The Wall, and the first—Giles—had had pretty much the same reaction. She turned around slowly and gazed at her work. She'd grown so used to it that she could barely remember what the plain old wall had looked like. "Is that a polite way of saying I should hire a new decorator?" she asked, a little concerned.

"Hell no. Maybe I should hire him—her?—to redo my office?"

He crossed the room to study it up close. Pixel sat then stretched out sphinx-like near the coffee table: she hadn't given up hope of further attention, and maybe cookies, from the visitor. Shannon rubbed her temples with both hands: Jay had probably leaped to the conclusion that Giles had painted her wall. "Her," she said. "You can't afford me."

"Well, hot damn," he said, with that cute old Jay grin—something she hadn't seen since October. "You painted that? You're painting again? Since when?"

"Since the day before yesterday. If you call that painting—the materials mostly came from Shirley's Hardware."

"So what?" he asked. "This is great!" He was so transparently happy for her that she thought her heart was going to melt, or break, whichever came first. "So why did you decide to paint the wall?"

"It's a long story." She managed a feeble excuse for a smile. "Some other time. I didn't call you up to talk about painting."

Jay groaned. "Mind if I make some coffee? Do you have decaf?"

"I'm way ahead of you," she said. "I'll get the coffee. You sit." She pointed to the sofa. Pixel flopped onto her side with a deep sigh. "You think about a good place to start, because if I have to ask the questions, it might get ugly."

She moved around the kitchen, knowing that he was watching her. "I ran into Gerbil Turd in the parking lot this afternoon," said Jay. "My friend the Gerb, last heard reminding everyone on staff that the workday ran until five o'clock, was exiting the office at approximately four p.m. 'Mr. Swanson,' he tells me, "had some interesting things to say about you.' When last heard from, Mister—make that Doctor—Turd was telling me that Mr. Swanson's whereabouts were none of my business, and none of my sister's business. Now all of a sudden he's volunteering confidential information."

Shannon paused in the doorway, a purple carton of half-

and-half in one hand. "The same Mr. Swanson who was seen several times in—a certain Edgartown neighborhood early last October, and who turned up in the very same neighborhood earlier this evening? What do you take in your coffee these days?"

"Two Tylenol?" he said hopefully.

"Not unless you want my standard lecture on the effects of excessive alcohol consumption on the brain, the stomach, and the liver, along with the hazards of mixing your poisons." She fixed him with a stern teacherly eye.

"A little of that," he said, pointing at the carton she was holding. "I think the Gerb doesn't know shit. I think he's on a fishing expedition. I think Wayne's looking for evidence. He doesn't know shit either."

Shannon set two steaming mugs on the coffee table, pulled up the easy chair, and dropped into it. She sipped her coffee, gazing at Jay through the steam, a lazy smile on her face. *Higher Power, for what I am about to do I promise to make amends eventually—if it turns out to be necessary.* "So," she said. "Where exactly *were* you staying this weekend?"

Jay's coffee splashed over his hand and onto the table. "Jesus fucking Christ—"

Shannon ignored him. "Becca made you reservations at the conference hotel," she continued evenly, "but that's not where you were registered." Implying that she knew where he *was* registered: she didn't, but she didn't mind if he thought otherwise.

"That's not a crime," Jay said, sucking his finger. Fear and defiance were fighting for control of his face. It was not a pretty sight.

"No," said Shannon, "it's not. The first hundred times it's probably not even a problem. Then something happens at home and someone needs to reach you—" She watched his face: fear seemed to be winning, or maybe it was common sense? Maybe he'd managed to get this far on his own? She leaned forward and set her mug down. "The point *is,*" she said, "that Wayne *knows*. He can't prove it, and he's not going to prove it by staking out Giles Kelleher's house, but he *knows*."

Jay snorted. "How could he possibly know?" he said, a hopeful glimmer flickering in his eyes. "He can't prove anything."

Shannon was ruthless. "How doesn't matter," she replied, "and it doesn't *matter* that he can't prove anything. What *matters* is that he's right."

Jay was staring at her computer, which was as far as he could look in the opposite direction without twisting in his seat. The room was so quiet that Shannon heard the fan cooling the hard drive. From where she sat she couldn't see the screen saver cycling through "The Life of Pixel," but light from the changing images flickered in the window behind Jay's head.

"It also matters that he seems to have told Jerry Turner—"

"We don't know that," he said, still studying the computer.

Jay, Jay, Jay, don't go stupid on me, please don't go stupid on me. "Humor me, then," she said lightly. "Say that Gerbil knows what Wayne knows. You think he's going to sit around waiting for Wayne to rustle up some evidence? Jerry Turner may be a Class A prick, but he's a *smart* Class A prick. He knows the ropes and he's got sources; he's not going to depend on Weak-Link Wayne." Shannon took a deep breath. "Back to not being registered at the conference hotel," she said. "How long is it going to take him to find something out?"

Jay studied his fingernails. "Not long," he said. He looked directly at her. "Not long at all."

Shannon the hard-boiled interrogator was so startled and so relieved that her eyes filled up.

"Don't go mushy on me now, Merrick," he said. "What am I going to do?"

Do I lay down the law or let him figure it out for himself? Shannon listened to the room. Pixel breathed softly, her furry side rising and falling. She heard the silence too: she half raised her head, looked at Shannon, and fell back to sleep. The computer hummed and so did the refrigerator, in different keys, oblivious to each other.

"I forgot to call Kevin," Jay said, glancing at his watch. "He left a message—I think Wayne might have . . ."

Shannon looked around for the phone: where had she left it? Her eye followed the cord, then she pointed to the floor at the end of the couch nearest the computer. "Be my guest."

Jay dialed and waited. After a few moments, he looked up and whispered, "Answering machine. OK if I leave your number?"

"Sure," Shannon mouthed back.

Thirty seconds after he hung up, the phone rang. He looked at her. She nodded. He picked up the receiver. "Hey, man," he joshed, "you been screening your calls. Too many girls on your trail?"

Shannon went to the kitchen and poked around looking for something to eat—not that two people who had had pizza and popcorn for supper, respectively, ought to be snacking at this hour, but these conversations were easier when your fingers had something to fidget with. When you didn't smoke and you didn't drink and your stomach couldn't deal with any more coffee, eating was the obvious alternative.

Shannon's cupboards were—well, not quite bare, but the prospects for preparing any reasonably healthy food were not good. The sound of doors opening and closing roused Pixel, who came padding into the kitchen, tail waving, hopeful grin on her face. "Sit," said Shannon, and tossed her a biscuit. *If only we were so easily satisfied.*

Discreetly she surveyed the living room. Jay had pushed his shoes off and was sitting cross-legged in one corner of the couch: this might take a while. She turned on the oven, shook the last of the tortilla chips into the little cast-iron skillet, doused them with salsa, covered it all with thin slices of cheddar, and stuck it in a medium oven. The nachos were ready when Jay hung up the phone and replaced it on the floor.

Shannon set the hot pan on top of last week's *Chronicle,* with a roll of paper towels alongside.

"You're going to make some beer-swilling football fan a great wife someday," said Jay, extricating a nacho from the pile and deftly twisting it so the melted cheese didn't fall on his lap.

They hadn't bantered like that since Wayne screwed everything up last fall. Was Jay really back, or was he subconsciously trying to make her forget what they were talking about? "If I had a rolling pin in my hand," she said, "I'd hit you with it."

He gave her the cute-little-boy look again. "I know. Thanks for the nachos. Wayne was waiting in the parking lot when Kev got out of school."

"And . . . ?"

"Kev thinks maybe he blew it," Jay said. "Like maybe he wasn't giving his dad enough of a chance. Wayne offered to give him a ride to work—he's still pumping gas at Five Corners—and Kevin said no thanks, he was already getting a ride with Weed Francis. Who was there at the time. Wayne started in on the old line, only the old line has mutated, I guess: it's not 'your mother's trying to turn you kids against me,' now it's 'guess you don't need your old dad anymore, now that your uncle's moved in.'"

"That's mature," Shannon muttered. "Well, six months' sobriety—if he's got that much—is six months' sobriety, it's not a personality transplant."

"Kevin called me from the gas station," Jay said, addressing the fingers of his left hand, which were splayed out on the sofa arm. "He was worried. He thought I ought to know . . ."

Just when I thought we were getting somewhere, Shannon thought, bracing herself. *No way is this rock going to roll back down the hill.* "He thought you ought to know?" she prompted.

Jay gazed at the nachos as if they were on the top of a very high shelf. "Wayne said, quote, 'I could tell you things about your uncle Jay.'"

Shannon held her breath.

"Kev says he's sorry, he lost his cool. He said, quote, 'I could tell him things about you.' So Wayne said, yeah, and what would that be? And Kevin said, 'What you were doing the night someone shot at his car.' Then Wayne started to lose it but Weed said, 'Let's get the fuck out of here,' and they left."

Talk about ice water pumping through your arteries: Shannon couldn't feel the tips of her fingers. When she looked at them her knuckles were white from clenching her chair. She forced them to relax and then deliberately moved her hands to her lap and made them rest quietly, left hand cradled in the palm of the right. "I think," she said, "that you had better explain."

"Yeah." Jay let out a long, long breath. "OK." Breathe in, breathe out. "Last fall, after the accident—"

"After you got shot at," Shannon interrupted sharply.

"Yeah." He managed to meet her eyes. "You're right. After I got shot at. That Wednesday morning, early, I went looking in the woods. All I found was a couple of butts. Marlboros."

"That the police didn't find."

"Wayne smokes Marlboros." Jay shrugged. "The police never went hunting with my father. Besides, it rained hard that Tuesday. They probably left the serious search till it cleared up." He gave her a look that seemed to apologize for what he'd found, for what he was about to say. "How to say this? Kevin called that night, Wednesday, very late. Before my dad died, he gave Kev his classic old Winchester .30-30—he knew there wasn't much point giving it to me. Kev keeps it in a locked cabinet, and the ammunition in a separate place, also locked." Jay half smiled to himself. "He cleans it every weekend, whether he uses it or not. He's a regular at the Rod & Gun Club, especially during vacations." The smile disappeared. "He called to say that the gun had been fired since the last time he cleaned it. He asked if he should tell anyone."

He paused. The pause spread into the room, hovering almost tangibly over the coffee table. "And you said?"

"I remember exactly what I said. I said, 'Keep it to yourself for now. Can you do that?' And he said, 'I can do that.'"

"You know, buddy," said Shannon, "for such a smart guy you are without a doubt the stupidest dumb fuck I have ever met." But her words weren't angry; she wasn't angry. Exasperated to the point of kicking furniture and hurling a cast-iron pan across the room, sure, but not angry. "What a tangled web we weave when first we practice to protect ourselves. Shit."

"You think I *liked* putting my own nephew in that position?" Jay protested, leaning forward. Then he fell back into the sofa and glanced at the computer. "I didn't have a whole lot of options."

"Like calling the police was out of the question?" Shannon asked sarcastically.

"Jesus, Shannon." He got up. For a moment she wondered if he was going to walk out but no, he headed for The Wall. She twisted in her chair and watched over her left shoulder as he studied the tangled brambles, traced them with one thumb. She pulled her knees up and draped her legs over the chair arm. "So," he said, "what's behind the thorny hedge?"

"Sleeping Beauty," she said, trying to sound casual. "What did you think?"

He stood before the portcullis and even tried to peer through the small window painted in the gate behind it. His hand reached for the door handle. Touched it.

"You don't want to do that," said Shannon.

He turned, surprised at the warning tone that suffused her voice. "It's locked."

"Damn right it's locked," she said, fighting the impulse to throw her body between him and the door. "No one goes in there."

"What's on the other side?"

"Never mind." Resolutely she straightened up in her chair, the soles of her walking shoes flat on the floor; she was willing him to return to the couch before she stood up and did something rash. She heard him hesitating. She felt him gazing at her through the back of her chair. The floor creaked behind her; she let herself breathe.

He stopped behind the chair. "I should have called the police," he said. "Sticking a fifteen-, sixteen-year-old kid with a secret like that is some kind of child abuse. And protecting *Wayne,* the jerk who made my sister's life hell for so many years—Wayne, the guy who was shooting live ammunition in my front yard and swearing he was going to get me? I mean, who should have been sent off-island for psychiatric evaluation?"

Shannon's lips curved into a brief, bitter smile.

"I sat through that entire pre-trial conference—Evalina Montrose from Women's Resources was the only woman in the room, and the guys, Jerry Turner, the probation officer, the deputy sheriff, Wayne, Wayne's lawyer, Janny's lawyer, were telling each other that of course *Mr. Swanson* was distraught because his marriage had broken up, and of course he's an alcoholic who needs *help.* It was like I was watching myself sit there: like, when is this Segredo fellow going to mention that he's got enough evidence to get *poor Mr. Swanson* indicted for attempted homicide? Segredo wimped out. Evalina came up to me later. 'You were awfully quiet in that conference this morning,' she says. 'Nothing to say, I guess,' I tell her."

What comes next? Shannon thought frantically. *I've forgotten my damn lines.* But words started coming out of her mouth, and to her immense relief they made sense: "Jay, can I point something out to you?" they said. "Sorry if it sounds too obvious, but, hey, you can take their ammo away. Wayne and the Gerb can wave their guns all over the place, they can aim right at you and pull the trigger, but if they don't have any bullets—"

Jay started talking like a wind-up doll: "I can't do that to—"

Shannon scrambled around till she was kneeling on the seat of her chair, her eyes almost level with his. "Jay, it's going to happen whether you can or can't. The only question is, do you tell your sister and your nephew and your mother or do they find out from the grapevine, or the newspapers, or from goddamn Wayne. Do the kids hear about it on the playground or do they hear about it from you. And do *not,* do not fucking tell me that they'd all be better off if you ran your car into a tree. This is not a pulp novel from the fifties. Sure, it might get rough, but you've survived rough, right?" He looked a little shell-shocked, so she poked him in the chest. "Right?"

"R-right," he said. "Christ." The silence lasted an eternity or two, then he walked, a little unsteadily, back to the sofa and sat. "So now what?"

Shannon the Organizer hit the ground running. "I'm going to the top," she said. "Jack Purcell may spend most of his time sucking up to foundations and state officials, but what you're doing makes his job a lot easier. He likes you, and he had a pretty rocky time before you arrived. And my good friend Cassie Fitch is the chair of the ISS board, and her baby sister is still the publisher of the *Martha's Vineyard Chronicle . . .*"

Jay shook his head. "You'd do it too."

"I would do it? I'm going to do it. Tomorrow. Meanwhile, your mission—should you decide to accept it—" She grinned at him, daring him to even consider otherwise. "Your mission is your family."

Jay startled like a jacklighted deer.

"Jay, I'm about to say what you'd say if you were counseling you, so don't get mad, OK? Jay, read my lips: they aren't going to be very surprised. If anyone drops dead of a heart attack, it's not going to be because you're gay, it's going to be because you said it out loud. OK? Rainey knows, by the way. Maybe you could sic her on Janice." She practically bounced in her chair. "I'll work out the details. Meanwhile, you're in no condition to drive, so you're spending the night. The guest room's made up, towels in the top drawer."

"I can't do that," Jay began, unconvincingly.

"Of course you can," she assured him. "If Wayne cruises by tonight and sees your car, it'll do wonders for your reputation."

CHAPTER EIGHTEEN

The sound of the chain saw, as familiar a sign of island spring as the thrumming of the pinkletinks and the flowering of the shad bush, calls her to the narrow strip of crabgrassy lawn that separates her house from the Whartons'. Ben Wharton is cutting the top off the post-and-rail fence, severing each post just above the middle rail. He notices her watching him and grins. "Pixel's not getting any younger," he says.

The dream dissipated into the buzzing of her alarm clock, but the lingering image made her scramble to her knees, pull the curtains, and peer down at the lot line. Ben was nowhere to be seen; the fence was intact. Astonishingly, bright sunlight shone on the early leaves, and on the Whartons' roof. More astonishing, the chain saw was still buzzing. It seemed to be in the living room. At last her brain kicked in: it wasn't a chain saw at all; it was a vacuum cleaner.

After a moment's fantasy of small appliances run amok—speaking of which, didn't the air smell a lot like coffee?—it came to her that Jay Segredo had spent the night. A refreshing thing about gay guys was that they usually didn't believe that running a vacuum cleaner diminished their libido. Jay must be running the vacuum. Had they made such a mess? Other than spilled nachos, which Pixel would have taken care of? Where was Pix anyway? Shannon usually woke up to cool canine nose in her face, not to weird dreams. Pix was not a big fan of the vacuum cleaner. Jay must have let her out.

Shannon hoped it wasn't pieces of his psyche that Jay was vacuuming out there. Her bedroom door was half open; her inner wimp wanted to sneak it shut and pretend to be asleep till Jay had to leave for work. *That's very mature, Merrick,* she told herself. *You deliver an extended lecture on consequences and the futility of trying to avoid them, then you want to hide out in your bedroom?*

Jesus, morning-afters were hard. Mornings after you'd gone on a bender, mornings after fights, mornings after dates that got hotter than expected—mornings after truths got spoken, and especially when they also got heard. You couldn't go back to silence, and you couldn't pretend nothing had happened: there was nowhere to go but forward. Plenty of relationships didn't survive the first excruciating steps.

If Jay was vacuuming, then he was still here. *Duh.* All at once she was so determined to make contact that she padded into the living room still wearing the extra-large Wintertide Coffeehouse T-shirt she'd slept in.

The sound of the vacuum continued, but Jay was nowhere to be seen. A little befuddled, she made her way to the kitchen. Sure enough, there was fresh coffee in the machine, and a spoon and a nearly empty mug close by. She picked a clean mug from the cupboard, filled it with coffee, splashed it with half-and-half and a little sugar, stirred it with the used spoon, and set out to solve The Mystery of the Phantom Vacuum.

In the kitchen doorway she stopped. She blinked. She stared. She blinked again. From this angle it was easy to see: a gap had opened in the wall of briars and brambles. *The door was open.* Jay was vacuuming the studio. Somehow he had gotten into the studio. She was furious, she was flabbergasted, she felt a little dizzy. Fearing that the open door might suck her in, she stepped carefully forward, right foot, left foot, right, left. Finally she was peering through the portcullis. Jay had taken the carpet attachment off and was directing the long silver tube up one corner, along the ceiling, around the six-over-six window at the far end of the room. Shannon's right fingers curled around the mug handle; her left hand braced against the door jamb. "What the fuck do you think you're doing?" she asked.

No answer. Of course there was no answer: *You know I can't hear you when the vacuum's running.* She probably didn't want to say "what the fuck" this early in the morning anyway. She watched as Jay set the tube down—without turning it off—and opened the window, then she risked a quick pan of the room. The floor was not caked with rat dung. The paintings were not draped with Spanish moss. The two easels had not crumbled to the floor; in fact, they were both neatly covered with pastel-blue bedsheets. How long since she'd been in here anyway? Four years? Five? Abruptly she recalled with startling clarity the hovering image she had been trying and trying to convey to her canvas, a little girl sitting at the end of a pier studying her toes as they dangled over the water. After weeks of pencil sketches, ink drawings, pastels and even watercolors, she was no closer to her mind's image than she had been at the beginning. It all looked as if she'd been channeling Norman Rockwell.

Shannon's eyes darted to the tall black metal wastebasket. It was probably still packed to the rim with her mashed-up failures. That saccharine little girl was probably still under the bedsheet, dangling her perfect little toes over perfect blue water.

But the paintings hanging on the wall, they weren't half bad. The nearest was also the oldest: an unframed canvas, two by three feet, of five crusty fishermen grouped around the door of a Menemsha fishing shack. They all wore classic foul-weather gear, yellow sou'westers, drab rubber boots. You had to look closely to realize that they were too young to be crusty, and that one of the five was a woman: herself. These were the guys she'd hung out with in her scalloping days. They had worked out of Edgartown, not Menemsha, but when she'd broached the idea of a painting, they'd insisted on being portrayed as a crew of old-timers, though none of them had reached thirty at the time and only two of them had grown up on Martha's Vineyard.

One of the two natives—Derek, the rumpled gray-eyed blond with his left foot resting on a lobster trap—never did reach thirty. He was HIV positive when they posed for the painting, though Shannon was the only one who knew it. When the first lesions appeared, he moved with no warning to New York, where he knew he'd be better off than he was at home. That was in the mid-eighties, when Vineyard Sound was presumed to be protecting the island population from the epidemic that was gathering force in the rest of the country. *Vineyard Sound as saltwater condom,* she thought—except that in those days and for several years following even the brave didn't talk publicly about condoms, or sex, or homosexuality. If all your information came from the public statements of counselors and school officials, you would have concluded that AIDS could only be acquired through tainted transfusions and dirty needles.

Shannon had kept up with Derek till he died, making regular trips to New York, a city she hated, to visit him. No one else on the island even knew he was sick, including his immediate family and his more distant relatives, whose Vineyard roots reached back before the Revolutionary War. No, that wasn't quite true: John had known, John the hearty, dark-bearded fellow in the center of the painting, his left arm draped over Shannon's shoulders. Derek had taken John, his best friend in the group, into his confidence. John had freaked out and cut him off.

Derek's illness and self-imposed exile had kicked Shannon's butt: to relieve the grief and anger, she'd started volunteering for Women's Resources, eventually becoming part of the small group that had spearheaded the island's first child abuse prevention project. That and Derek's death had helped her get, and stay, sober. *So far—one day at a time.*

Jay was looking at her—waiting for her to say something? She looked at him: what was she supposed to say? Her screen had gone blank. "You can come in, you know," he said.

She shook her head.

"My inner Prince Charming made me do it," he continued, watching her carefully. "I picked the lock with my jackknife. Then it all"—with a wave of his free arm he offered her the room—"it all looked so *abandoned* that I had to get—"

Shannon giggled. She laughed; she laughed so hard her stomach hurt and her knees wobbled. Finally she sat down on the floor in the open doorway, trying to take deep, steady breaths. She lay back, knees bent, feet on the floor, hands on her belly, trying to breathe. It occurred to her that wearing only an extra-large T-shirt this posture might be borderline indecent, so she sat up again. Jay was standing in front of her, extending his hand. She took it, and he pulled her to her feet. "Oh, Christ," she said. "That was brilliant. That has to be what this wall's about. I've been waiting for Prince Charming, and he finally showed up."

Prince Charming made a pretty impressive courtly bow for a guy dressed in jeans and a plaid buttondown shirt. "I was afraid you'd be ripped," he said. "Really ripped."

"I was," said Shannon. "About five minutes ago."

"These are all yours?" He gestured toward the paintings.

"Yeah."

"But they're *good*."

"Jay, my man," she said, "if they were bad, I wouldn't give a flying fuck. I'd be in here every stupid morning turning out ditzy little watercolor flowers and pastel sailboats in the mist and making so much stupid money . . ." The words balled up in her throat, making her eyes water. "Don't mind me," she said hoarsely, "I'm just losing it a little."

"That's OK." He put his arm around her shoulders; she put hers around his waist. He pointed at the fishermen. "I *love* that one. It cracks me up. That's you, isn't it, second from the right?"

"Yeah, that's me." She was about to tell him who the others were, and who they were to her, but he wasn't through.

"Next to you has to be John Timofey," he said. "I remember that old sumbitch when he still had his beard. And the last one on the left—that's Derek Thompson, isn't it? You knew him?"

"Yeah," she started, then gagged: the words had risen to the top of her throat and jammed themselves between her tonsils.

"He was a year ahead of me in school. He was in West Tiz, I was in OB, but we both played Little League. In about eighth grade he won some national award for being a math genius. Then he went off to private school. It was AIDS, wasn't it?"

"Of course," Shannon said. The words were spilling into her mouth, spreading bitterness on her tongue.

"No one said anything. Mama sent me the obituary from the *Chronicle.* 'Derek Thompson died suddenly in New York City. He was 28.'"

"Died suddenly in New York City, died suddenly in San Francisco—there was a lot of that going around at the time," Shannon said. "You would not believe how much I hated this smug little island then. I hated it so much that I started volunteering again, which I'd sworn I'd never ever do in a million years. I was just thinking, if it wasn't for Derek, I wouldn't have marched myself down to Women's Resources, and probably I never would have met you."

"Meaning you would have had a lot fewer headaches."

She considered poking him in the side but both her hands were otherwise occupied. "Jerk," she muttered.

Jay raised an invisible glass to the painting. "I owe ya one, buddy," he said.

Shannon tightened her arm around his waist. "I was hoping you weren't thinking of slashing my tires or anything," she said.

"Jerk." He laughed. "Though you could have told me way back when what I was getting myself into."

"I tried," she said. "Honest to god, I tried, and tried—"

"Don't I know it," he said. "Now."

* * *

Driving home, showering, donning fresh clothes, heading to the Island Social Services complex by way of Vineyard Haven, Jay felt encased in a cylinder like the ones the banks used in their drive-up windows. He could see through the tough plastic shell, but what he saw was dingy and distant; what he heard was muffled, as if someone's hands were covering his ears. Several people waved at him on the road; he recognized them but didn't wave back. He wasn't ready to deal with the rest of the world. There were five new messages on his answering machine; he didn't listen to any of them. He wasn't feeling hostile; hell no, he was almost giddy. He felt weirdly reborn as he drove down the Edgartown–Vineyard Haven Road, running out onto the court ready for a new game—but his teammates hadn't arrived yet, and the metal bleachers on either side were vacant, and his opponents were off in some locker room somewhere, plotting strategy. The giddiness was giving way to vertigo, and the sensation of slipping, slipping . . .

He pulled into a parking place in the ISS lot and cut his engine. Becca's old blue Tercel wagon was already in its usual place, about as far from the stairs as you could get: Becca was trying to make herself walk more. Once out of his car he scanned the parking lot: no sign of the Gerbil's snazzmobile. *Of course not—it's only 8:45.* Inside the building, he started up the stairs toward Women's Resources, then pivoted on the fifth step and jogged back down: Becca first. Becca was on his team; she deserved to be first. There was also the small but ever more troubling question about how he was going to tell Evalina Montrose that last fall he had concealed evidence that might have gotten Wayne indicted for attempted homicide.

Youth Services still smelled faintly of whatever piney ammonia product the cleaning service used on the floors at night, the music coming through the half-open door to Becca's office was heavy on the bass and a little too loud, and there was a bakery box of fresh doughnuts on the coffee cart. Jay lifted the cover: only one cinnamon-dusted creme-filled left. They were Becca's favorite as well as his. He glanced guiltily at her door then reached for the doughnut and a paper napkin to put it on.

"I left that one for you," she said, suddenly standing in the abruptly open doorway. "I ate mine on the way over."

He made a sign of the cross with the doughnut. "Bless you, bless you. Any sign of Heather or Jackie?"

Becca stood at attention and recited: "Jackie: address breakfast group at up-island senior center. Heather: at OB School for conference re Kid Skinhead."

Kid Skinhead, a fifth-grader, had been caught spray-painting swastikas and iron crosses in the boys' bathroom at the school. His father had been apprehended at a similar age doing pretty much the same thing, only his target was the Sacred Heart parish hall on Wing Road. "Another poster child for the bad-seed theory," Jay said, taking a big bite of his doughnut. "Becca, we have to talk."

She looked puzzled, even a little concerned. "Sure thing," she said. "I'm not going anywhere. Your place or mine?"

"Yours. If you'll turn that boombox down." He poured his mug half full of coffee, hesitated, then filled it to within two centimeters of the brim.

"For you I'll even turn it *off*." She led the way into her domain.

"Nah, down is fine," he said, following. "I can handle anything if it's not too loud."

"Must be a generational thing," she mused.

"I cannot *wait* to dance at your thirtieth birthday party."

She dismissed this with an airy wave. "If you're not confined to a walker by then."

"O-ho!" He grinned. "It's not that far off. You forget: I have a copy of your personnel file in my office."

Becca sat down at her desk and gestured toward the chair that didn't have the stack of magazines on it. Jay pushed the door shut with his foot.

OK, deep breath. No small talk. No asking what those magazines are doing there or where the dracaena went or how long the Georgia O'Keeffe poster has been hanging crooked. "Bec, the shit is heading toward the fan," he said, "and I think you ought to know before it gets there."

Becca was all business. Except she was peering at him over the top of her glasses in a way that made him think she was taking the information right out of his mind.

"As you know," he began, "Wayne Swanson is back on the island . . ." How tempting to go on and on about Wayne, bad Wayne, Wayne whom his sister married in a momentary lapse from her usual good sense—"smart women, foolish choices," chapter 1—but he resisted. Wayne, he explained, had stopped by the regional at the end of the school day yesterday, hoping to run into Kevin. At this he had succeeded, but he had not found the filial reconciliation he had obviously sought—*with his usual obtuseness*—and afterward had come over for a conference with his good buddy the Gerbil. In the Gerbil's cage, Wayne had evidently spilled some beans . . .

Becca listened without watching the clock. Jay had no doubt she'd make an excellent therapist if she ever made up her mind to go back to school.

Jay took a deep breath. He had taken so many deep breaths lately it was a wonder his lungs hadn't burst. "The upshot," he said, "the upshot is that I'm gay, and the Gerbil is about one step away from figuring it out." He stopped breathing and willed her to say something.

Becca rolled her eyes. "Like," she said, exaggerating her blaséness, "I am so surprised."

She was, he guessed, saying that she already knew. "It's that obvious?" he wondered out loud.

"No, Bossman," she replied. "You are what my mother would call the very soul of discretion. Whatever that means.

But I've been sitting at this desk longer than you've been sitting at that one—" She waved toward his office.

Becca had come to work at Island Social Services during the reign of the now infamous Terrence Randolph, also known as Mr. Tarantula. Before he completed his second month on the job, Mr. Tarantula's first office manager, an ISS veteran, had elected early retirement, and Becca was promoted out of Infants & Toddlers to replace her. When Jay moved in, he'd been skeptical about Becca: she reminded him too much of the earnest but soft suburban high school girls who came into the big city to tutor kids variously described as "deprived," "disadvantaged," "at-risk," and "challenged." That impression hadn't lasted long. The retro bobbysoxer persona— slightly mitigated by the multiple earrings and the penchant for bright jazzy clothes—was deceiving. Becca was way overqualified to be the Youth Services office manager. She should get off the rock, complete the six semesters she needed for a college degree, get a *real* job—but Jay didn't want her to leave, because she was the best support staff person Jay had ever worked with.

"And," she continued, raising both eyebrows, "whatever you think, I was not born yesterday."

"OK, OK—the day before yesterday."

"You know about black holes?"

"Black holes?"

"Black holes are cool," she said. "I saw a program about them the other night on the Discovery Channel. It's not just that there's no *there* there, it's how the scientists figure out where they are. You can't see them, right? Even with super-high-power telescopes? They figure out where they are because of what isn't there."

He thought he was beginning to get it. "Like I'm not married, or engaged, or shacked up with some babe," he said.

She gave him the "you really aren't this dense" double eye roll. "Like you have never once in my hearing alluded to, mentioned, or trashed one single ex. That's unnatural. You also get fewer personal phone calls than anyone I have ever worked for. This wouldn't be weird if you were, say, ugly, or antisocial, or a born-again—"

"You're saying I'm cute, friendly, and obviously lapsed?" He looked at her hopefully.

She scowled; her eyebrows almost hit the ceiling. "But you aren't," she continued. "Even Mr. Tarantula got lots of personal phone calls, and he was a Grade-A creep."

Jay heard something—what? almost coy in Becca's voice. "He wasn't ugly," he began, then stopped. Becca was sitting back in her chair, fingering the long spiral gold dangler hanging from her left ear: the very picture of a woman deeply and confidently pleased with herself. A possibility occurred to him. He walked around it, studied the angles; it checked out. *God DAMN.* He slapped his hand on the desk. The only missing link in the saga of Mr. Tarantula's Precipitous Departure was how the *Martha's Vineyard Chronicle* had gotten wind of the irregularities that had escaped the search committee and the upper echelons of Island Social Services. Everyone assumed that Leslie Benaron had gone fishing and lucked out. Jay never quite believed it. The territory was too big, and other targets more promising; Leslie never would have gotten some of those people to bite if she hadn't had good bait. A phone call from Becca to Leslie? Or Becca to Shannon, Shannon to Leslie? That would have done it. Motive. Opportunity. "You're saying I'm more discreet than Mr. Tarantula," he said, vaguely flattered.

"Oh, no contest," she said. "However—"

Uh-oh.

"There is," she continued delicately, "some cause for concern. We're talking about the man upstairs now, OK?"

"OK, I'm ready," said Jay. "Out with it."

She held up both hands. Today's nail polish was a downright conservative pale mauve. "I wear my fingers to the bone setting up your trips, then half the time you don't even stay in the hotels I book for you. I should be insulted. This past weekend—forget about this weekend. I tell Shannon Merrick where you're staying, she calls the desk, they've never heard of you. What gives?"

Jay must have looked stricken, because Becca told him, "Don't worry, I'm not insulted—my *mother* would be insulted, but not me. OK? But some of the credit card statements come back with refunds on them—because you're such a dork that you actually cancel the rooms you don't stay in, and the planes you don't take. You probably put the ones you do use on your personal card. Am I right?"

She was right. Jesus. Honest to God, he hadn't considered that for one minute. "But . . ." he started. But he couldn't think of what to say.

"Listen, don't feel bad: it's a genetic thing. New Englanders are frugal, and Vineyarders are frugal squared. In Westchester County we call it 'cheap.'" She was smiling at him. "I'm only telling you because there is a paper trail. The girls in Accounting don't care about refunds—they *love* refunds. For all they know, you didn't go to those conferences after all. Doctor Turner, on the other hand—he's got your monthly itineraries and your weekly reports, and if he decides to check one against the other, well . . . You and I both know how anal the man is, and if he thinks it'll get him your head on a platter . . ."

Jay let his head fall against his cupped hand. "I'm an idiot. More to the point, I'm up to my armpits in something that makes mud look, well, *sweet.*"

"Bossman, you are not thinking straight." She giggled. "Excuse my French. It's virtual *merde,* boss. It isn't really there."

He splayed the fingers of his hand and peered at her through them. "Huh?"

"How to put it? OK. If, after an investigation taking many months and costing millions of dollars, some crusading DA announces that the pope is Catholic, is that going to make the front page? Of course it is. The headline is going to say DA

FIRED FOR INCOMPETENCE."

* * *

As she dialed Giles's number, Shannon kept eyeing the open door to her studio. For years the wall had been moribund. Now flickers of light kept catching her attention. She half expected something from another dimension to stick its head into the living room.

Her eye kept recoiling at the thin edge of the door: it was still late twentieth century light oak veneer. An impressive steel portcullis couldn't have an oak veneer edge; she would repair it at the earliest opportunity—which wouldn't, unless she was drastically misreading the current situation, come till the end of the week at least.

Giles picked up the phone. His "hello" was obscenely chipper. "What's up, girlfriend?" he wanted to know.

"Boyfriend," said Shannon, "you are not going to believe it. First things first: any sign of the white van?"

Giles reported that it had cruised the rutted roads of his neighborhood this morning, slowly but without stopping. "The only vehicle in my driveway was my itsy bitsy pickup," he said, "but don't you dare tell any of my admirers. I have a reputation to protect! So tell me, tell me *everything*."

"Not—quite—yet," she said. "Something's going to happen, I can tell you that. I can't say what yet, but something's happening."

After half a moment's silence she heard a sharp exhale of breath. "Are you trying to say," he asked carefully, "do you mean to say that I might get to hang *The Hanged Man* after all?"

"I am saying," Shannon said, fighting giddiness, "that something is definitely going to happen. Oh, and by the way, the door is open."

"The door is open?"

"The door—the gate—to my studio is open."

What came through the line sounded like a dozen fire engines screaming toward a burning house.

Giles placated for the moment, Shannon paced the hallway, pondering her next move. She dropped into her desk chair to download e-mail. Nothing interesting. She started a game of Tetris, but her heart wasn't in it; she exited before her tally reached 5,000. *Get moving.* She rose, plucked the phone off the coffee table, and sat down on the sofa. She punched in the ISS number and asked for Jack Purcell's extension. "I don't think he's in," said the agency receptionist. "Let's see what happens."

What happened was that Joan, Purcell's scarily efficient administrative assistant, picked up the phone and said, "I'm sorry, Mr. Purcell is out of the office today. May I help you?"

Oh wonderful, he's in Boston, he's in Washington, he's in Timbuktu. Shannon identified herself, hoping that her credit with Joan was still good. Joan was pushing sixty if not a little past it, an English immigrant whose accent hadn't slipped a millimeter in the thirty-some years she'd been in the States. She played vigorous tennis several days a week and, according to the ISS grapevine—which was to say Becca Herschel in Youth Services—had recently taken up aikido. You didn't get to Jack Purcell without going through Joan, and if you wasted Jack's time, Joan never forgot it.

Shannon's credit had been golden not too long ago. Jack had been an ex officio member of the search committee that brought Jay Segredo back to the Vineyard. Not that the other members had seen much of him: he had given a brief pep talk at the first meeting, spoken privately with each of the top four candidates when they came for their interviews, received the committee's final recommendation, and formally announced the appointment. But Shannon knew for a fact that he had recognized her efforts both on the committee and behind the scenes; at the Christmas party year before last, he had introduced her to his wife as "the one who solved our Youth

Services problem." Here's hoping her halo wasn't one of those things like unused sick leave that expired at the end of the calendar year.

She was in luck. "Shannon," said Joan, "I am so sorry; I didn't recognize your voice. Mr. Purcell is in an all-day meeting—I *am* sorry, it's very hush-hush, but it does involve some top state officials and foundation people. This is important, is it? It must be, or you wouldn't have called."

"It's important," Shannon said grimly.

"I expect he'll be checking in at the midday break. Shall I give him a message?"

Shannon smiled. "If you would, I'd be so grateful. Ask him to call me at home, would you? Tell him—tell him it's about a personnel matter he needs to know about, and if it isn't dealt with soon, the papers may get hold of it." She could almost see Joan's perfect eyebrows rising a subtle but significant centimeter. *Don't ask, don't tell,* she thought. Joan would never, ever ask. Joan would, however, let her boss know that something was up.

"I'll tell him at the first possible opportunity."

"Bless you," said Shannon.

After hanging up she walked, phone still in hand, to the window, looking for a sign of Pixel: there was no dog rooting in last year's fallen leaves, no dog sprawled in the splash of sunlight on the side lawn. Trailing the phone cord, she crossed the living room and passed into the kitchen. No dog out that window either, even though Ben Wharton was out in the driveway, changing the oil in Mary's car. Shannon set the phone down and went through the mud room and out the front door. Still no dog. *Just what I need: I'm trying to avert a catastrophe and Pixel's gone AWOL.*

She clattered down the steps and hailed Ben from the post-and-rail fence. "Hey, Ben, you seen my buddy? About yea high, looks like a wolf advertising toothpaste?"

"Yep." His eyes cut toward his front door. "Mary's baking a cake for one of the grandkids' birthday party. Your dog's in there helping. Going anywhere?"

"Not yet. I was just getting antsy."

Ben aimed a long look in her direction. One eye squinted, the other was open wide. One hand beckoned her over. She slipped between the rails, wondering what the hell this was about. "Mary has this idea," he began. "Don't you get mad; you know how she is, wants to know what's going on every minute of the day and night . . ."

Shannon was confused. "Me, mad? No way."

Ben glanced up, as if to make sure that his wife wasn't watching. Unless Mary were baking her cake in the master bedroom or its adjoining bathroom, there wasn't much chance that she was keeping an eye on him. Shannon suspected he was putting her on. "Mary saw—" he lowered his voice "—she says she saw a *gentleman* leaving your house before eight o'clock this morning."

Conspiratorially Shannon lowered her voice. "That was no gentleman," she said. "That was my buddy Jay. He came over last night to discuss a *problem* he's having, and he was so skunked when he got here I wouldn't let him leave."

"See, I told her there was a good explanation," Ben said. "So, you thinking about buying a truck?"

Shannon's first response was mild panic: Ben had changed her oil not two weeks ago; was this his way of telling her that her trusty Subaru was terminally ill? "Truck? No, I wasn't thinking—should I be?"

"Nah," said Ben. "Your wagon's good for another fifty thousand miles. Could use a new muffler, though. Mary saw that little Mitsubishi out here *yesterday* morning and wondered if you were thinking of buying it. I said nah, you'd tell me before you did any such thing."

Shannon almost snorted out loud. "You bet I would. That was another friend of mine. An artist."

"Oh?" Ben raised both eyebrows. "He show up drunk too?"

"No, that one doesn't drink. We were—working on a

project. It got late. You've got to come see it. I've been painting a mural on one of the walls." *Maybe if Ben and Mary see The Wall, they'll believe all the rest of it?*

"You say when," said Ben. "Want me to have Mary send the dog home?"

"Nah," said Shannon. "She can hang out here, if you guys don't mind."

"You know it's OK with us, anytime." He grinned at her, a decidedly sly grin. "How's your oil?"

She thought she was going to crack up, but she managed to match him grin for grin. "Pretty good, probably, since you changed it two weeks ago," she said.

"You don't say. Don't worry about anything," he said. "The dog's fine."

Longtime Vineyard people tended to have strong opinions about Cassandra St. Christopher Fitch, and they tended to have few reservations about expressing them behind her back. The Fitches belonged to West Chop, a headland jutting into Vineyard Sound, which had long been home to one of the most exclusive communities of summer WASPs—people neither bound nor protected by year-round reticence. The family had money, money so old that no one remembered where it came from, and if they didn't seek the spotlight, they didn't exactly run from it either. In other words, they were fair game. "She looks like the next strong wind would blow her to Boston" was one of the kinder ones, along with "remind me not to go to *her* hairdresser." More typical was "The good Lord in his wisdom didn't let her have children—can you imagine having her for a mother?"

When Shannon first met Miss Cassandra St. Christopher Fitch, she saw her through unflattering lenses. One had been ground by the class- and ethnicity-conscious progressive community she had abandoned for Martha's Vineyard. The other was the creation of her family, whose good opinion she had long ago stopped seeking but whose self-conscious

Irishness she seemed to have absorbed in the most embarrassing ways. Now she would happily have traded either of her real-life grandmothers for Cassie Fitch, and she was ever so pleased that Cassie Fitch seemed to view her as a de facto niece. They never talked politics, and Shannon would have died before she asked, "Just why *didn't* you ever get married?" but each understood that the other was on a similar wavelength. After Cassie Fitch picked up the phone, the first words out of her mouth were "I am so glad you called. May I impose on you for a favor? I have a lunch engagement in Edgartown, and I seem to have a flat tire."

Cassandra St. Christopher Fitch was like a tornado: she caught you up in her reality and set you down when she was done. Maybe Cassie liked Shannon because Shannon was usually free to drop everything on a moment's notice and come to tea, help mulch the garden—or drive to Edgartown.

The gods were not only smiling, they were sniggering up their sleeves: Cassie's lunch engagement was at the Harbor View Hotel with ISS executive director Jack Purcell. Shannon blessed her flexible schedule and headed for Vineyard Haven. Windswept West Chop, so desolate and deserted during the winter, was bright with the young green of forsythia leaves and the vibrant yellow of daffodils. There were few people about; when Shannon drove up to the sprawling, multi-gabled and generously porched family "cottage," Cassie was commanding the attention of a landscaper Shannon had worked for briefly many years ago. Shannon headed off to the garage and changed the flat. She was heaving the old tire into the back of her Subaru when Cassie, still deep in discussion with the landscaper—*when did he get so gray, and so paunchy?*—came around the corner of the house.

"What a dear girl you are," said Cassie. "You *will* still drive me to Edgartown, won't you?"

"But of course," Shannon said.

* * *

Shannon told Cassie the story, most of it, between Vineyard Haven and Edgartown—"What a tangled web we weave," Cassie murmured, watching long Sengekontacket Pond pass on the right.

"And it usually starts with one innocuous thread," Shannon said, checking her rearview mirror. A sporty red Camaro that had seen better days was obviously thinking of passing. Shannon slowed down a bit to spite him.

"One never knows, of course," Cassie said, "but I believe this—situation can be managed. Between you, me, and the fish in the sea, Dr. Turner offered to resign after the unfortunate Mr. Randolph met his Waterloo on the Beach Road. Jack declined, of course, but I believe he's been kicking himself ever since."

This was encouraging news, and Shannon used it for a lodestar during her nervous-making audience with Jack Purcell. Like any capable politician, Purcell could turn opaque on a moment's notice. In the hushed hotel lobby he greeted her genially, without missing a beat, though he couldn't have been expecting her in her scruffies to walk through the carved double doors with Cassandra St. Christopher Fitch—*unless he'd already spoken with Joan, who, come to think of it, must have known that he was lunching with the chairman of the board of trustees.* "You must join us for lunch," he said, though he certainly hoped she would do no such thing. She didn't: she pleaded another engagement, then belatedly realized that Cassie would need a ride home. The business-suited, carefully coifed men and women passing through the lobby made her uneasy. *If we get out of this alive, Jay Segredo, you owe me a big one.*

At Cassie's suggestion, they retired to a table in a secluded corner of the restaurant, and Shannon launched into the tale that she had told on the road to Edgartown. Though she monitored Jack Purcell for his reaction, she couldn't get a clear reading; at some points she couldn't get any reading at all. *Jesus fucking shit,* she was ready to yell, sturm und drang and pounding the table, *he's one of the best guys you've got and you're thinking of throwing him to the wolves?* For once the impersonality of the suits, the inaudibility of the voices worked in her favor: self-righteous explosions, often explainable but rarely wise, were almost unthinkable here. *Keep cool, Shannon. Back to basics: You guys are on the same side. One, Jay's doing a good job. Two, the Gerbil has made mistakes. Three, we don't want to read all about it in Thursday's paper.*

A waiter came by, filled their water glasses, and asked if they were ready to order. "A few more minutes, if you please," said Cassie with a smile that asked for his forbearance. After he left, she plucked a roll from the linen-lined basket, broke it open on her plate, and commenced to butter it. Unconsciously both Shannon Merrick and Jack Purcell followed her lead.

"Fortunately," said the executive director, "we don't have organized right-wingers to worry about."

True: on Martha's Vineyard, the overtly right wing, religious and otherwise, was strictly lunatic fringe. Shannon worried much more about the moderates whose hearts and minds were more or less in the right place but who seemed collectively ill at ease with public gayness of any kind. It was OK to *be* gay, it was OK for others to *know* you were gay; what wasn't OK was for them to know that you knew that they knew . . . And god forbid you should ever bring it up in conversation. Not surprisingly, gay teachers, gay parents, any gay person with any connection to young people stayed pretty much in the closet. Shannon still didn't really know what to make of it, never mind what to do about it. Like anyone else who'd been around for a while, she had learned to walk warily while letting the subject lurk in the deep background.

"Feel free to tell me it's none of my business," said Jack

Purcell, who seemed to have forgotten the hunk of French bread in his right hand, "but—are you aware of anything that might, shall we say, blow up in our faces?"

Meaning what, exactly? Semi-anonymous sexual encounters with consenting semi-strangers in hotel rooms paid for by Island Social Services? But this wasn't the right time to strike a blow for clarity—*and when exactly was the right time to strike a blow for clarity?*—and besides, Shannon knew without asking that Jack Purcell meant sex with anyone under the age of consent. Mr. Tarantula's gadding about with teenage girls was considered reprehensible, though quite a few adult men—those without teenage daughters—responded with more hearty har-har than censure. Had he been caught with a teenage *boy*—had two or three teenage *boys* come forward to say he'd copped a feel, or more? There would have been no discreet disengagement, no polite out-of-court settlement. Tarantula would have done time—if he'd managed to get off the island alive. Had Jay done anything that might blow up in their faces? "No," said Shannon, meeting Purcell's uneasy gaze with a steady, confident one of her own. *And if I'm lying, Jay, my man, you are dead dead dead.*

When she left the hotel, her mission was to have Jay Segredo in Jack Purcell's office at four o'clock sharp. Between now and then she had four hours—well, maybe three and a half—to get some work done.

Or she would have had three and a half hours if her car hadn't, apparently of its own volition, taken a hard right on the narrow road that led into Giles Kelleher's hidden-away neighborhood, and if Giles hadn't been home, heating up some cassoulet that he'd spirited away from the restaurant on Sunday night. She did remember to call Becca and give her a progress report. Before the food was gone, she had told Giles everything and then some, and the four o'clock meeting was barely an hour away.

CHAPTER NINETEEN

The sunlight streaming in through the dirty front windows didn't cheer Leslie up. It was Tuesday morning, she was stuck here pretty much till the paper went to bed late tomorrow afternoon, and her stories for this week sucked. True, Natalie was raving about the early draft of the Nick McAuliffe profile. Leslie had stayed up till three a.m. finishing *Devoted to Her Duty*. She had to admit it was pretty good, that even her father, who relished a good thriller, would like it—if he deigned to read anything written by a former flack for Big Medicine. Leslie had already cast herself as Georgia Duvall in the movie version. Crashing a politicians' stag party disguised as a cocktail waitress *(sure, if I lost fifteen pounds)*, stowing away on a Lake Michigan speedboat then swimming to safety when she found out what she needed to know *(I should get to the health club more often and start swimming laps)*, demolishing the prosecutor's arguments with a bravura courtroom performance *(yeah, right, when I can't manage to get useful information out of a routine interview)* . . .

Maybe she should go to law school. She was thirty-four—for three more months—was that too old to get into law school?

She still hadn't called the interviewer in New York. The deadline she set for herself kept receding: after lunch, before she went home, first thing in the morning . . . At present it stood at "when the paper goes to bed."

Yet again she'd been saved by a photographer: the Alice story dominated page three because the pics were outstanding: Alice reading to Mitch in the Hammonds' living room, Alice helping Kate in the kitchen, Randy out in the garden showing Mitch how to work the Rototiller. It was nearly done, lacking only a few quotes from social service types, but Leslie hadn't been able to motivate herself to make that last round of phone calls because no matter what she did, the story was going to be a pale shadow of what it might have been.

Leslie took a deep breath, dialed Island Social Services, and asked for Jay's extension. Becca Herschel picked up. "Sorry, Les," she said, apparently through a piece of bubblegum, "you're outta luck. Jay was called out on an emergency and God knows when he'll be back."

"So what else is new? Tell him I called," she said. "Ask him to call me? Tell him I'm on deadline. Not that he'll care. It's about the Alice Chase story. Tell him that. It might make a difference." *You wish.*

Shannon would know how to reach Jay wherever he was, Leslie thought, and even if she didn't, she could probably fill in some policy-and-procedure details. No answer at Shannon's house. Leslie gave up.

OK, so she could finish up the stupid tennis court story. She already had the mealy-mouthed excuses of Quincy Hancock III, delivered in his ludicrous New England imitation of a *Brideshead Revisited* accent, so she called Cassandra St. Christopher Fitch. The phone rang, and rang, and rang. Ten roads diverged in a yellow wood and they all led to brick walls.

Get a grip, Leslie. Get—a—grip.

The office phone rang. She reached for it, hoping it might be Jay, returning her call already. Alan Duarte beat her to it. "Hey, Steve," he hollered, "it's your lucky day. It's *People Magazine* and they want your accident pix. Should I have them call your agent? Who is your agent anyway? You got one yet?"

From the corner Steve DeKuyper yelled, "Will you lay off? Shut the fuck up!" *Touchy this morning, aren't we?* Leslie thought. Steve snatched up the receiver and started talking way below Leslie's threshold of hearing. Leslie, however, was curious. She mouthed toward Alan: *Really?*

"You don't know?" Alan stage-whispered back. He beckoned her over.

Sunday afternoon, it seemed, when all sane people were playing golf, or raking leaves, or tilling the garden, or at least swinging in the hammock enjoying the rare weekend sunshine, Steve had been holed up here in the newsroom, studying a leaked Steamship Authority report on internal operations. A call had come in on the police scanner: accident on the North Road in Chilmark, just past the West Tisbury town line. A minute or two later a voice from the Communications Center called for EMT response. None of this was any big deal: once or twice a week half a dozen EMTs could be counted on to converge like so many hungry crows on fender-benders where no one needed medical attention. But Steve was ready for a break, and it was a fine afternoon for a drive up-island. He was out the door, according to Alan, thinking he might go for a walk at Waskosim's Rock, a large tract of conservation land near the reported accident site, when he thought to come back for the trusty old Canon single-lens reflex that was usually in the production manager's drawer.

The accident was serious enough to send both drivers and one of the passengers to the hospital. And get this: one of the drivers was the son of a right-to-life congressman from upstate New York. And get this, even better: the congressman's son, who sustained only minor injuries, was wearing a dress. "A nice dress, so I hear," said Alan. "Navy blue, not risqué at all."

And Steve had it all on film. The contact sheets looked excellent.

Where was Leslie at the time of the accident? Interviewing

Alice Chase in Oak Bluffs. An interview that could have taken place a week earlier if not for Shannon fucking Merrick's fucking scruples. Why wasn't Nick McAuliffe a congressman's son? Why wasn't Alice Chase the president's illegitimate daughter?

"I told him to hold out for the *National Enquirer,*" Alan was saying. "They could pay off their mortgage if they gave the *Enquirer* an exclusive, but no, Steve's such a straight arrow—he's dealing with *People.*"

Leslie managed to keep the lid on till she was out of the office and into her car, till she'd maneuvered into Beach Road, through Five Corners, and into the line of traffic heading out of town on State Road. Then she started: "Shit. Fucking shit. Fucking shit shit shit." And continued in that mode all the way to her house.

Driving the twisty part of Barnes Road north of the blinker light, Jay felt more than a little giddy. *I should be terrified,* he thought. *By tomorrow I could be out of a job and my mother might be in the hospital with a nervous breakdown, or in jail for disturbing the peace.* But whatever might happen tomorrow, things were moving *now,* and strangely enough that was less scary than hunkering down in the bunker trying not to obsess about the tons of earth that could collapse any moment and crush you. So far at least things were going OK. Becca was cool, Shannon was out pulling strings on his behalf, and he was en route to meet his sister for lunch in the hospital cafeteria. Janny had sounded frazzled when he reached her at work. She was worried about Kevin. Wayne had been trying to reach him, she was sure of it; maybe they had talked, she couldn't tell, but whatever it was, Kevin was alternately surly and snappish and wouldn't tell her what was bugging him. So Jay had suggested lunch; that had been his reason for calling in the first place, and unwittingly she had given him a perfect opening. It had to be a good omen.

Pulling into the parking lot nearest the hospital's main

entrance, he was sure he could ease his sister's anxiety. He could explain what was bugging Kevin, and with any luck it would put his own news in some kind of perspective. He crossed the access road, heading for the old, less-used entrance. Should he just have told Kevin on the phone last night? Maybe the kid had gotten it double-barrel from his dad this morning. *Not smart, Jay,* he thought. *Not smart at all.* Walking down the dim corridor toward the cafeteria, he stopped so abruptly his crepe soles squeaked on the linoleum: *Jesus Christ, I'm about to come out to my sister.* But he didn't look back. If he did, the double glass doors would suck him right back out into the parking lot and that would be it.

For several years now the Martha's Vineyard Hospital cafeteria had been one of the few places on the island where you could count on getting a decent, reasonably cheap meal. In the early days of her separation from Wayne, when Janny worked in Admissions, she would call Jay whenever she felt shaky and they'd talk it out over lunch. Though she'd been working in the school superintendent's office for well over a year now, this was still their default rendezvous: roughly halfway between her workplace and his and easily accessible except in high summer, when the risings of the nearby Beach Road drawbridge brought through traffic to a standstill several times a day.

His sister was over in the darkest corner of the room, nursing a cup of tea. He refused to let this bother him, because Janice from childhood had taken pleasure in arriving early and tapping her fingers till everyone else showed up. She came over to join him in line. "I only have an hour," she said. "It's really busy today."

While I, thought Jay, *am taking it easy. All I have to do is stalemate my boss and turn my life inside out.* He glanced significantly at his watch, knowing that she'd notice and know exactly what he meant.

She did. "I know, I know," she said, managing a small laugh. "I just thought you'd be early for once."

"Someday," he said, pointing through the glass case at the jag, a savory Portuguese rice with linguiça and kidney beans, "I am going to surprise you." To go with it he choose chicken breast smothered in onions. Janice, of course, chose lite: chicken noodle soup, a crusty whole-wheat roll that she wouldn't eat, and the salad bar.

He watched as she picked a plate off the top of the stack and used the tongs to fill it with green stuff. Even from the back she looked rigid. Tense, or just determined? He guessed the former. She had to be feeling the pressure: Wayne was back on the island, and Wayne, it was no secret, wanted to talk her into a reconciliation, even though the marriage was—Jay hoped—history, gonzo, kaput.

He'd never tell his sister this, but he feared that she might eventually give in. He knew the danger signs, and Janny was showing several of them: she was trying to go it alone, having dropped out of the support group she'd been in and drifted away from Al-Anon, and she was showing no interest in expanding her social circle, never mind dating again. Though she frequently expressed gratitude to the Women's Resources staff, her interest in volunteering hadn't survived the four-session training course. His questions had been met with a vague but implacable "I just don't have the time." He knew it had more to do with her uneasiness around even the mildest forms of feminism, not to mention the fact that not all of the volunteers were straight, but he wasn't going to push.

Jay tasted his rice: it was a little spicier than usual, pleasantly so. He forked up a generous mouthful. "So," he said, "you're worried about Kevin."

Janice pushed some salad around on her plate, caught a lettuce leaf flecked with carrot, then laid her fork down. "Yes," she admitted. "He's not talking, and I *know* he's stressed—his phone must have rung half a dozen times last night, and that only happens during finals or when a practice has been changed."

Jay raised his hand. "If it helps any, one of 'em was me. He left me a message; I called him back."

Janny fixed her eyes on his. "He called you?" Meaning *Out with it. Now.*

"Wayne showed up at the high school yesterday, at dismissal time."

Janice slammed the table with her right hand. Her soup sloshed in its bowl but didn't spill. "He didn't say anything to me."

"Maybe he thought you'd be upset," Jay said mildly. "Kev was with Weed; Weed was giving him a ride to town. Wayne wanted to talk. Offered to drive him to work. Kevin said no. They had words."

"What kind of words?"

"Words," Jay said. Ever since her kids were old enough to hang out with their uncle, Janice had assumed that she was entitled to know whatever they said when she wasn't present. Jay was a strict constructionist about confidentiality, with kin as well as clients. Brother and sister had fought this one to an impasse. Jay smiled half apologetically, to avoid another skirmish on the issue. "Kev suggested getting together over the weekend, going fishing or maybe shooting baskets at the school."

"Why didn't he tell me? He should have told me."

"The court—"

"Damn the court! Kevin's a *child*—"

Child? Sure—a child who used to watch his father hitting his mother, who called his uncle up long-distance pleading for help; a teenager who knows enough to suspect that his father took a shot at my car. "He's got a hunting license, and a learner's permit," Jay said. "This summer he'll be driving himself to work, probably in some rent-a-wreck that looks like it couldn't get to Gay Head and back. Kevin's at the age where he's going to try dealing with things on his own. Listen, Janny: you've raised a kid who's smart enough—"

She had actually started eating her soup. Suddenly she was all smiles. "That's what Rainey said. We talked on the phone this morning. She met you at the airport yesterday morning, didn't she? She didn't say a thing about that."

The chicken in his mouth turned dry as a communion wafer. *Rainey was doing you a favor,* Jay thought. If only he could go back to the point where he was getting off the plane and just erase the tape. He had to talk to Rainey. Soon. "What's there to say?" he said lightly. "The airport is the airport; it wasn't raining, so nothing leaked. Paul's finally fixed that wobble, I think."

"I don't see why you don't get a new car," she said. "How can you drive around in a car that somebody *shot* at?"

"You wait," he said. "Someday I'll show up in a big black Suburban, tinted windows, A/C, five miles to the gallon. It won't even fit into your driveway." Getting no uptake for that, he returned to the subject of breakfast: "We had breakfast at the Nunne-pog. The omelettes are still perfect rectangles, and the cheese is about the color of those carrots." *And I lost my head, but Rainey managed to block every pass I tried to make . . .*

"Jay," said Janny, shaking her head like an exasperated schoolteacher, "why do you keep treating her like just a second kid sister?"

Jay flashed his most boyish of grins. "What's wrong with kid sisters? They're nice to have around."

"Do I have to put it up in neon?" Janice zeroed in. "She was crazy about you in high school. Sure, a lot's happened since then, but why not? You're perfect for each other."

"So," Jay said, unable to believe, first, that his voice was so steady, and second, that he still had enough appetite to be working on his chicken, "she's said something to you?"

"No, Jay," she said, as if humoring a dimwit, "she hasn't said anything. She doesn't have to say anything. We've been best friends since fourth grade."

"Well, you might want to take it up with her, Janny," he said, sucking the last of his Coke up through a straw, "because I have reason to believe that she's not all that interested in, as they say, changing the nature of our relationship."

Janice's gaze turned from condescending to determined. She started to protest; Jay held up his hand. "And neither am I," he said. "Sure, I've thought about it. I've been tempted—it would solve a few problems, wouldn't it? Sure it would. Or it would have: at this point it's probably too late." His sister had clapped both hands over her ears and scrunched up her eyes; he pretended not to notice. "Listen, Janny, I'm sorry to spring this on you, but things are spinning way out of control, thanks in large part to that ex-husband of yours. To make a long story short, I'm gay, I've known it since I was twelve years old, and my only real reason to get married is to hide that from the world—and, I hate to say it, from myself. I've made some really stupid—"

Janice was stamping her feet on the floor, hissing, "Shut up, shut up, shut up!"

Jay kicked her under the table and hissed back: "Janny, cool it. We're in the *hospital cafeteria*."

"What's the matter with you?" she demanded. "You think I don't know who put that idea into your head? Your *dear* Shannon Merrick, that's who. Her and her radical feminist propaganda—"

Jay couldn't help it: he burst out laughing. "*Shannon*?" he managed, half choking on the name. "Did you hear what I just said? I've known I was gay since I was *twelve*. Shannon and I didn't even live on the same *planet* then."

"You sick, selfish . . ." Janice rose to her feet. Her wrath was not magnificent; it was ridiculous, like a monumentally bad amateur theatrical. "Do me a favor. You may be bound and determined to tell it to the world, but spare a thought for my kids, OK? Leave them out of it. And have you bothered to think about what this will do to Mama? Of course not, not you. Every hard-luck case in the world comes before your *family*."

He stared at her, speechless. This was so untrue, so unfair, *so* off the wall. She wasn't looking at him either: *she knows she's throwing rocks, and she doesn't want to know if any of them hit the target.* Taking a long breath, he reminded himself that he was not ten, she was not eight, and he didn't have to accept her terms of engagement. "Don't look now, Janice," he said quietly, "but if Kevin doesn't already know, he has an idea. Wayne has been dropping hints—"

"Shut up," she said. "It has nothing to do with Wayne. I don't want to hear another word." And she exited the cafeteria most haughtily, drawing, as far as Jay could tell, very little attention from the rest of the lunch crowd. One of the servers, though, raised her eyebrows and then rolled her eyes in apparent sympathy. Family spat, lovers' quarrel, whatever it was: the woman took it in stride and seemed to be advising Jay to do likewise.

Becca didn't think it was the least bit odd when Kevin Swanson sauntered in, dropped a stack of textbooks on her desk, placed both hands on top of the stack, and leaned forward, peering at the bar fridge in the corner. "Got any root beer?" he asked.

She thought. "I don't—" She opened the fridge. "No. The machine at the top of the stairs was working last I looked."

His right hand plunged into his pocket and fumbled around. "Got any quarters?" The dollar-bill slot in that machine was notoriously fickle.

She took four from her top drawer and gave them to him. "Wait," she said, trying to separate change from paper clips from push pins from loose clumps of staples. She picked out a second dollar, mostly in dimes and nickels. "Get me a Diet Coke?"

"Sure." He beamed at her. Kevin's features resembled his father's, but the disposition they expressed was so different from Wayne's that she rarely noticed the similarity. "You should ask for a bigger allowance. Is the unk due back anytime soon?"

"He's got a four o'clock, an extremely important four

o'clock," Becca replied. "Like if he doesn't show, I'm calling the state cops." Kevin started to pivot on one foot; Becca pointed at his books. He grinned a "thought you'd never see them" grin that reminded her of Jay and scooped them off the desk before he left.

It was 2:16. The office had been nearly deserted most of the day; thanks to the phone, however, she had not been bored. At 11:48 Janice Swanson had called and asked, exasperated, if her brother was in: "He's *supposed* to be meeting me for lunch."

Becca knew that. She also knew that the date was for 11:45. "He's on his way," she said soothingly, thinking, *Hey, sister, an hour from now you might be wishing he never got there.* A far snarkier thought than she'd ever speak out loud, but Janice Swanson did not bring out the best in Becca Herschel. Janice was forever calling her Becky, and for variation Rebecca, Roberta, and even Ruth. She didn't like the way Becca dressed, the way she talked, or the diamond stud that twinkled in her nose—not that she ever said anything out loud, of course; she had a small arsenal of disapproving looks that she used liberally in lieu of words. Like Becca was the secretary she suspected her husband of having an affair with, even though Jay was her *brother,* not her husband. *You don't have to worry about me, ma'am,* thought Becca. *Or about him.*

Shannon called at 12:30, give or take; Becca was zapping her chicken pot pie when the phone rang and didn't notice the time, because the clock on the microwave was set to a time zone on Tatooine and no one could figure out how to change it. "Yo, Becca," she said. "Jay in?"

"Jay's out. So to speak." Becca giggled; she couldn't help it. "Sorry. I don't know for sure but he's outer than he was earlier."

Shannon groaned. "Do not, repeat do *not,* get me started. You talked?"

"Like I'm supposed to be surprised? We might have a problem, though." She told Shannon about the expense account records, and gloomily guessed that Dr. Jerome Turner was even now hiding behind his own locked door, blowing off clients and underlings in order to check itineraries against receipts, or lack of same.

"That's exactly his speed," Shannon admitted. "Well, we may be able to head him off at the pass."

"Yeah?" Becca asked. "What's the plan, Kemosabe?"

"Don't think I've been idle," Shannon assured her. "I've just been hobnobbing with the rich and famous, or at least the affluent and influential, specifically Jack Purcell and Cassandra St. Christopher Fitch—"

Becca managed to plant a big smacking kiss on her fingertips without losing control of the phone.

"The short version is that we've got a meeting with Purcell at four o'clock. Purcell's OK—I think—but he's definitely nervous. Fitch is on our side, and she says 'Jack' doesn't much care for our Gerbil friend, so who knows. Your mission is to get the word to Jay well in advance of the deadline. When he gets back to the office, don't let him leave. Screen all calls. Route emergencies to Women's Resources. Where'd you say he was again?"

"I didn't," Becca said. "OK, so I shouldn't tell you this . . ."

"Behhhhh-cca . . ."

"He's having lunch with Janice. Janice called to tell me he was three minutes late." All at once Becca realized that Janice also treated Shannon like the secretary her husband was having an affair with. *How could I have missed it? Is there a pattern here or what?* Except that Janice didn't dare get Shannon's name wrong. And if Janice thought Shannon was trying to hook Jay, Janice was one dumb chicky.

"Jesus," muttered Shannon. "Has he got an exit strategy?"

"She only gets an hour for lunch," Becca pointed out. "Seven or eight minutes to get to the hospital, seven or eight minutes to get back—that gives them forty-five minutes to eat. Or talk. Whatever."

"Cool," said Shannon. "They're probably rushing Janice to the ER this minute."

* * *

Forty-five minutes later, at slightly before 1:30, Jay called from home. Lunch with Janice had been a complete disaster. Becca wasn't surprised. Briskly she informed him about the four o'clock meeting. "I'll be there," he said.

"No plaid shirts," she warned. "Dress *conservative*. Dress worse than conservative. Dress as though you're on a speaking tour for the Traditional Values Coalition. No hair spray, no *scent*. On second thought, get here early. Bring three choices of tie, two pairs of socks, and if you show up in those filthy Nikes, I'm sending you home."

Kevin was in Jay's office, supposedly doing his trig homework and apparently oblivious to the fact that, because each of the office's five lines had a button on her own phone, Becca knew that he had spent quite a lot of time on Jay's private line. With any luck he was just cheating on his homework, not trying to reach his mother.

Shannon blew in at a few minutes past three. Since Shannon was almost certainly going to attend The Meeting, Becca checked her over: the brown corduroy pants, burgundy turtleneck, and V-neck Fair Isle sweater vest were informal but presentable. Dr. Jerome Turner wouldn't tolerate such casual dress in his office, but then again, the meeting wasn't in his office, Shannon wasn't applying for a job, and Dr. Turd couldn't stand her anyway. "Do you mind if I use the phone?" Shannon asked. "Pixel's at the neighbors', and I said I'd be home two hours ago."

"Be my guest," Becca said, gesturing in the general direction of Heather and Jackie's office. "They're out. Kevin's in the boss's office, talking up a storm." She looked pointedly at the lit button on the bottom of her phone.

"What does he know, do you know?"

Becca shrugged. "The boss's lunch with Sister," she confided, "did not go well."

"Uh-oh," said Shannon, raising her eyes very briefly to the ceiling. "Are we surprised?"

"We are not," they replied in unison.

Bless the Whartons: not only were they taking care of Pixel, they were broadening her cultural horizons. Ben had taken her on his rounds, to the gas station (where she picked up a free biscuit), the auto parts store, the post office, Ace Hardware, and the drive-up window at the bank (another biscuit)—Shannon could just see her riding in the bed of Ben's pickup, forepaws on the edge, thick fur rippling in the wind—then she had accompanied Mary and her daughter Sally on a walk to Sepiessa Point. Shannon hung up the phone and stood gazing at it for a minute. Surely there was someone else she should be calling? Women's Resources? No, she decided; not yet. Purcell didn't need to get the impression that his entire agency already knew what was happening. Jay was generally liked and respected within Island Social Services, but Jerome Turner—hard as it was to believe—had his allies as well; otherwise he would have been defenestrated without a parachute after the Tarantula Affair. Shannon's gut told her that Jack Purcell would do the right thing if it didn't cost too much. This was no time to get heavy-handed.

She knocked lightly on Jay's nearly closed office door. Kevin called out, "Yo?"

"It's me," she said, slipping through the opening. "Mind if I hang out in here till The Man arrives?" Not that she couldn't have waited in Jackie and Heather's empty office, but this one was so much more familiar.

"Be my guest," Kevin said. He waved toward the conference chairs. "Need any counseling or anything? Crack? Ritalin?" He opened Jay's top drawer. "Sorry, spoke too soon. All he's got is Life Savers."

Shannon chuckled. "Wiseass." She dropped into the chair, pushed the magazines around a bit, and finally selected the most recent issue of *Time*. As usual, she started from the back, from the arts and sciences and health coverage. The last thing she wanted to read about was Congress, the stock market, the president, and the rest of the depressing dreck in the opening pages.

After a while she realized that Kevin was watching her. When he realized that she realized that he was watching her, he glanced quickly toward the right, where the Robert Kennedy poster issued its challenge: "Come, my friends, / 'Tis not too late to seek a newer world. . . ." His eyes continued around the small office, passing at least a foot over Shannon's head. His left hand rolled a ballpoint pen up and down Jay's desktop. "You mind if I ask you something?"

Ready, get set . . . Shannon felt her heart speed up, cueing her brain to send adrenaline into her arteries. "Shoot," she said.

"My dad's saying my uncle's gay," Kevin said, looking Robert Kennedy in the eye. "Dad hates Uncle Jay's guts. He'd say anything to make him look bad. So is it true?"

Shannon remembered Kevin looking at the framed Lesbian Herstory Archives poster in her bedroom—this was before his mother asked that it be hidden away where "the children" couldn't see it—and asking, *So. Does that mean you're a lesbian?* She had been thrown way off balance by a teenage boy asking one of the Vineyard's unaskable questions, and without a sneer in his voice. But she had recovered pretty damn quick if she did say so herself, and answered, *Not necessarily, but in a word: Yes.* But this time it wasn't about her. "I guess," she said carefully, "that's something you'll have to ask him."

Kevin took a deep breath. "I guess that means he is, huh."

She looked at him. He was looking right at her. "You figure?"

"If he wasn't, you'd have just said no."

It knocked the words right out of her. She stared at him blankly then she started to grin like a fool. She took aim with an invisible basketball and sent it toward an invisible hoop.

"Round the rim and in," she said.

* * *

When Jay walked in, Kevin was telling Shannon about how his mother was trying to fix her brother up with her best friend, and about how his mother didn't get that it was making both of them feel weird.

"You think?" Shannon asked.

"I *know*," said Kevin.

Silence fell so fast and hard when Jay came through the door that he looked from one to the other and said, "It's the tie, right? Becca made me wear this tie."

The tie was blue, diagonally striped with thin red lines. "You applying for a job, boy?" Shannon asked. "Didn't anyone tell you we don't dress like that on Martha's Vineyard? We recognize a man's worth no matter what he's got on."

"Yeah, right," said Jay. "Who fed you that junk, the Chamber of Commerce?"

"You kidding? They *dress* at the Chamber of Commerce." Shannon studied him critically. "You'd fit right in. They'd even hire you at the bank."

Jay shot Kevin an invisible pass. Kevin caught it. "What's up, man?" Jay said.

Shannon slipped out, regretting she couldn't warn Jay that she'd just, pretty much, outed him to his nephew, and went over to Becca's office. Becca was on the phone wheedling General Supply into upgrading the #10 envelopes it ordered by the truckload: not only did the flaps stick without being licked, the paper was so thin you could read the contents through it. Shannon pulled up a chair. When Becca got off the phone, she *tsk-tsk-tsk*ed and shook her head. "I cannot tell you," she said, "how relieved the boss was to know that you were here. He was *frantic*. 'I tried three times to reach her at home, she wasn't there, do you have any idea, she *said* blah

blah blah.'"

"Where's he think I'm going to be?" Shannon grumbled, secretly pleased. "Cruising the Steamship dock?"

Becca raised her eloquent eyebrows.

Shannon shook her head. "Not my style. Besides, the only reason I, the notoriously out lezzzbian, have any credibility with all these movers and shakers is that I'm *single*. I don't *flaunt it*. I don't *parade down Main Street holding hands with other women*. No, I parade down Main Street with my dog—my *female* dog, I must confess, but she is duly licensed and leashed and up-to-date on all her shots—and that doesn't get anyone upset. Becca, do you think I need Prozac?"

Becca giggled. "I think you need a Reese's Peanut Butter Cup," she said, bending down to reach the refrigerator. "Which I just happen to have . . ." She passed one over to Shannon and kept the other for herself.

Shannon twirled her chilled cup slowly at eye level, holding it carefully by the crinkly brown paper. She took one careful nibble, getting mostly chocolate and only the barest hint of peanut butter. Becca was cutting hers in quarters with a table knife. Shannon stared.

Becca didn't notice. "Mr. Jay was also trying, without success, to reach his erstwhile girlfriend—"

"Rainey?"

"Yeah."

Shannon glanced at the clock on the wall. "Rainey's working nights this month, but she says she's always awake when her kid gets home from school." She reached for the phone book, then looked at the phone. "May I?"

"Be my guest."

The answering machine picked up, and after it ran through its very brief outgoing message, Shannon started: "Rainey? It's Shannon Merrick—" What should she say? What if Rainey's son, Steve, or Rainey's dear friend Janice was there when she played back her messages? "I've got an update, uh, on what we discussed yesterday? Give me a call when you get a chance—I'm at, uh, ISS right now, but—"

Rainey picked up the phone. "Don't hang up, I'm here," she said. "What's going on? I've got two messages from Jay, one from Kevin of all people, and one from Janny, who sounds—"

The phone started ringing. Rainey asked if she had to answer it, Shannon realized that she was tying up the only receiver in Becca's office, and Becca was out the door faster than Shannon thought she could move, mouthing, "I got it."

"It's OK," said Shannon.

"Janny sounded frantic, *really* frantic. She's not home, I was just about to call her at work, I'm afraid Wayne—"

Wayne. What a concept, thought Shannon. "It's not Wayne," she said. "It's Jay."

A sharp intake of breath. "Oh my God."

"No, no," Shannon said. "I'm sorry, I didn't mean—Jay's fine. He's—"

"Whew. I thought—I was afraid—I don't know what I thought . . ."

Maybe that Jay had run himself into a tree? Girl, we've been having the same nightmare. "Jay's in his office even as we speak," Shannon reassured her, "with—a client." *Just don't ask me who's counseling whom.*

"Whew," Rainey said again. "Whew."

"However. There is a 'however.'" After yesterday, Shannon wasn't worried about Rainey, so she forged ahead. "Jay just came out to Janice. Janice was, in a word, freaked."

"But how could she possibly—I mean, if I—I mean, she's his *sister.* She can't really be all that surprised—do you think?"

Denial is not just a river in Egypt, Shannon thought, but didn't say, because you had to have been there, done that at least a hundred times before it stopped sounding flip. "You ever hear the phrase 'the elephant in the living room'?"

"Yeah," Rainey replied immediately, then "Oh, *yeah.* It comes up all the time. Everyone knows that something's wrong with Dad, but no one wants to think about the fact that he goes through a bottle of gin in two days."

Becca slid back into her chair. She caught Shannon's eye, raised her eyebrows and pursed her lips: *Wait till you hear this!*

"You got it," Shannon said, thinking that she really liked this woman and sincerely regretted having dismissed her as another dupe of the patriarchy. "In brief, the deal is that Jay's boss, who is not a nice man, has sort of forced the issue, and we've got a four o'clock appointment with the ISS executive director and the chairman of the board. They already know, and I *think* it's gonna go OK, but it may get a bit tense. So if you could—"

"Take care of Janny?"

"—it would be a big help," Shannon finished.

"I'll do it."

"Bless you bless you bless you. Oh, and by the way—Kevin's here, Kevin knows, and Kevin is *very* cool. In case anyone wants to know."

"I'll keep that in mind." Rainey was hugely relieved; Shannon could tell through the phone. "Thanks. Talk to you soon."

Shannon hung up and gazed expectantly at Becca, who was obviously wanting to tell her something.

"That," said Becca, pressing both hands palm down on the desktop to keep them, or the desk, from flying away, "was Miss Cassandra Fitch." Dramatic pause. "She's upstairs. She was looking for you. I said you were tied up. She said don't interrupt you, she'd tell *me*—me, a mere flunky in the basement of Island Social Services—"

"She didn't say that."

"No." Becca was fairly bursting with secrets. "She *said* that Dr. Turner had just arrived for a meeting with Mr. Purcell—and that he came to a dead halt when he saw her sitting at Joan's desk. 'I might have been the ghost of his first-grade teacher,' she said." Becca credibly imitated Miss Fitch's precisely enunciated consonants. Then she sat back in her chair, hands resting quietly in her lap. Diamond nose stud and all, she looked almost prim. "Miss Fitch thought you'd want to know."

Shannon grinned. "She's got that right." Time check: 3:45. "Did she say *why* Dr. Turner had just arrived?"

"No, but she believes he was expected."

"Expected just because he called first, or expected because Purcell invited him over? That is the question . . ." Shannon drummed her fingers on the edge of the desk. "Is Purcell that sneaky? Would he summon the Gerbil at three forty-five when we're due at four?"

"You got me." Becca shrugged, twisted her mouth, and raised her eyebrows at the same time.

Jay groaned at the news but bounced back when he learned of its source. "Cassie Fitch is up there? How'd you pull that off?"

"You've got fans in high places, that's all," Shannon replied, leaning carefully back against the bookcase.

"Well, someone does, that's for sure." He glanced up at her; she watched a cloud move in and settle over his features. "I blew it with Janny," he said. "Really blew it."

"You blew it or she blew it?"

Jay frowned. "She stormed out of there like—like . . ."

"Like ice cracking on denial?" Shannon suggested, crossing her arms and hoping she didn't sound, or look, like a pompous ass. "This doesn't bring out the best in most people. More to the point, you've got plenty of time to work it out, but *we*"—she glanced at the clock on the wall—"are due in the executive suite at four o'clock *sharp*. Besides," she added, "I just talked to Rainey. Janice's already left a distraught message on her machine. Rainey's going to take care of her. You can put Janice on the back burner for the next hour or two."

"Rainey?"

"Yeah—you remember Rainey." She grinned. "She knows what's going on. I assigned her to Janice. Hope that's OK."

"She knows what's going on . . ." Jay echoed. To Becca, who was still standing by the door, he said, "And I thought she just designed books, chauffeured the dog around, that kind of thing."

Becca pushed the door all the way open. "Be glad she's on your side. If the Gerb were that smart, you'd be looking for work in Nebraska. Speaking of which . . ." She tapped her watch with one forefinger.

Jay stood up and looked at Kevin. "You want to hang out?"

"Sounds like maybe it's a good time not to be home," Kevin said.

"I can give you a ride later," said Jay. "If we all live that long."

Straight-backed and opaque, Joan was back at her desk, but the ad hoc hostess in the executive suite was clearly Cassandra St. Christopher Fitch, and just as clearly the doyenne of the board of trustees was enjoying the role. She ushered Jay and Shannon into the small conference room, to the right of the closed door bearing the antiqued brass nameplate JOHN M. PURCELL, JR. The office was nearly silent. Their shoes made only the barest whisper on the thick carpet; no sound escaped the executive director's office. At Island Social Services status was signaled less by the size of the office than by the density of the door. Counselors, administrators, and minor office heads got hollow pine. Upper management got solid oak.

Jay had left the conference room door partway open behind him. Shannon, at the corner table pouring three glasses of ice water, watched Cassie Fitch go back to close it.

Well-brought-up boy that he was, Jay was waiting beside a generously padded gray chair for the women to sit down. Cassie took the seat to the left of the one customarily reserved for the executive director. She nodded Jay toward its counterpart to the right; Shannon, after distributing water and gray cocktail napkins, sat on Cassie's left. Just before the silence grew too awkward, she brushed the immaculately polished oak lightly with the palm of one hand. "I'm *not* going to be the first to lay down a water ring on this table," she said. Then she turned to Cassie Fitch: "Does Dr. Turner know—"

"I don't believe so, no."

Shannon hoped that by the time she reached seventy-five—or was Cassie Fitch closer to eighty?—she'd be able to deliver a line like that, with a pleasure so exquisitely self-restrained that it conveyed no breath of smugness. Her answering smile was downright unsubtle by comparison.

"Did the police," Cassie was asking Jay, "ever find whoever it was who shot at your car last fall?"

With his usual deftness at evading the truth while telling no lies, Jay answered, "I don't believe they have any leads."

Shannon sneaked a look at her watch: 4:16.

"I must say," said Cassie Fitch, "I was relieved that it didn't lead to a series of similar incidents. Mind you, I am not against guns or against hunting—nearly every fall until he had his stroke my father went hunting in Maine. He wouldn't take me with him, but of course he taught me and my younger sisters to shoot—"

Shannon could imagine Arabella Fitch Roth on a rifle range, or stalking through the state forest in camouflage. Maybe she kept a pearl-handled six-shooter in her desk drawer in case irate town officials forgot their manners.

Abruptly Jack Purcell was standing on this side of the door, briskly closing it behind him. Shannon hadn't even heard it open. He was alone. For a split second his face was grave, then he was working the crowd, small as it was, smiling at Cassie, reaching across the table for Shannon's hand, nodding cordially to Jay, who had pulled his chair in to make room for him to pass.

Christ, now what? Shannon had been so preoccupied with setting up this meeting that she hadn't given a moment's thought to what would happen once it started. Here she was in the front row, willing the actors to come to life.

Jack Purcell cleared his throat, but it was Jay who spoke

first. "Before we get into this," he said, "I'd like to say one thing—if I may."

Perfect, Shannon thought, letting a long exhale slip soundlessly between her lips. His voice was low, clear, steady: just right. Purcell settled back slightly with an almost imperceptible nod: *Go ahead.*

"You know Martha's Vineyard backwards and forwards," Jay said to his boss's boss, as if there were no one else in the room. "You can guess that it's not an easy place to grow up—gay. I couldn't wait to leave. But when I came back three, three and a half years ago, I didn't stop to think that it wouldn't be an easy place to be a gay adult either. It's not that I wasn't warned—" he smiled over at Shannon "—but, well, my father was sick, my sister's marriage was in serious trouble, and ISS was advertising for a youth services director. I guessed I could figure the rest out when I got here. What I want to say is," he said, drawing an audible breath, "is that I've made some pretty major errors of judgment, and I've been less than honest with just about everybody, including myself, but in my work, in my dealings with ISS clients, and their families, and every young person on this island, I have done nothing to betray the trust that they, and you, have had in me. Mistakes, sure. Even two or three failures. But there's no, well, no smoking gun out there. If you're worried about that—and if you are, I don't blame you—please, don't be."

Shannon gazed out the window behind Jack Purcell, at the late-afternoon light playing in the new oak leaves. What paints would she use to convey the flickering light, the rustling breeze? Maybe if she made a mental list of every shade of green she'd ever heard of she could keep the lump from blocking her throat. Not that anyone would notice if she started to cry: Jay Segredo and Jack Purcell were so intent each on the other that the link between them would resist all but the loudest distractions.

"That being said," Jay continued, his voice still steady, "if you think the agency would be best served by my resignation,

I will resign."

And, Mr. John M. Purcell, Jr., thought Shannon, *if you accept this offer, I have licked my last stamp, lifted my last finger, housed my last family, and made my last phone call for this sorry excuse for a human services agency.* The lump gave way a little.

After a long, very long, terrifyingly long pause, the executive director glanced down at the table then back up at Jay. "I don't believe that will be necessary, Mr. Segredo—Jay," he amended, a little embarrassed by his own formality. "However, there are certain issues that should be addressed—"

Unless Shannon was much mistaken, Jay had relaxed a bit. "There are," he agreed, "certain discrepancies in the Youth Services conference and staff development budget . . ."

At 5:06 Becca Herschel lifted her jacket off the coat rack. Some dishevelment on the second shelf from the bottom of her bookcase—mostly bound journals that had overflowed her boss's office—caught her eye. Dumping her jacket on the desk, she went to straighten them up. Of course she had to check the top two shelves as well, and to reshelve several books that had slipped out of alpha order.

5:13. She retrieved her jacket and slipped into it. Her desk was clear. Her daybook was open to Wednesday. She had already completed the first two tasks on her reminder list.

5:15. She grabbed her oversize, overstuffed handbag, switched off the overhead lights, and stepped out the door, closing it behind her. For a moment she squinted at the half-open door to her boss's office. The lights were still on. She rapped twice and leaned into the room.

Kevin had given up pretending to study. He was sprawled in one of the conference chairs pretending to read *Sports Illustrated.* He looked like a four-legged spider.

"I could give you a ride home," she said. "It's not out of my way. I've got to hit the liquor store anyway."

"Nahhh," he said, not looking up. "I mean, thanks, but I think I'll wait." He glanced up at the clock. Becca looked at her watch. They both said 5:18.

"Me too," said Becca. "I've run out of things to do. Mind if I wait in here?"

"Be my guest," Kevin replied, gesturing vaguely toward the other chair.

Silence fell, like a curtain that leaves a little light peering through at the bottom. One of Becca's housemates liked Harpoon I.P.A. Another preferred Sam Adams Boston Ale. As far as she was concerned, beer was beer, and she couldn't remember which she'd brought home last time. Damn it to hell, what was the matter with her? Mind like a sieve—couldn't remember anything one day to the next.

Her mother was always telling her father he had a mind like a sieve.

Which was it, Sam Adams or Harpoon? One of them liked pale; the other couldn't stand it. Which the fuck was which? Why the fuck was she always the one who had to decide, when she couldn't stand beer and would rather drink wine? She wished there were a bottle of chablis in the fridge right now. Whichever one she picked was going to piss someone off. Life sucked, life really sucked. If anyone bitched, she was going to tell them to buy their own fucking beer.

"If they fire Jay," she heard herself say, "I'm quitting."

"If they fire Jay," said Kevin, "I'm gonna burn this building down."

"Good idea," Becca said. "I'll help."

Of one mind, they slapped each other high fives and settled back to wait. 5:25.

At 5:53 they heard voices at the top of the stairs. Ordinarily you couldn't hear people talking at the top of the stairs, but the building was nearly deserted and sounds were echoing in the concrete and metal stairwell. The voices bubbled, the voices were tumbling one over the other, around and around, like laundry in a dryer. One was male, one was female, and neither Kevin nor Becca could understand a word.

Someone landed with a thud at the bottom of the stairs. "Hah!"

"You stupid dyke, you could have killed—"

"You were fucking brilliant! I can't believe it! You're better than Sir Laurence Olivier, better than Peter O'Toole—shit, you're even better than *Diana Rigg*."

That was, without question, Shannon. Becca looked at Kevin. Kevin looked at Becca. Neither one moved a muscle. 5:57.

"Jesus. Someone's here." Jay.

"The cleaning lady?" Shannon.

"I don't think so." Jay flung the door all the way open. The knob banged against the wall. "Jesus," he said. "Your mother's going to kill me."

"She's already killed you once," said Shannon. "How many times can she kill you? But while we're on the subject of violent death, you listen to me, buddy. If you ever, *ever* pull another stunt like this, I am not, I really am *not,* going to bail you out again, because you know why? I'll tell you why. I was afraid we were going to lose. I was so goddamn rotten fucking afraid—" She choked on her own in-rushing breath and stopped. She stared at Jay as if she'd never seen him before. He stared back, wondering what was going to happen next.

Shannon Merrick burst into tears. Her knees started to liquefy. Jay held her up. Becca and Kevin helped. Six o'clock on the nose.

6:15. "We're in no shape to go home," Jay decided. "Supper at Linda Grease, my treat."

"Awww," said Shannon, sprawled bonelessly in a chair but mostly recovered, "let's charge it to ISS."

Becca burst out laughing.

CHAPTER TWENTY

Steve DeKuyper really didn't care that his photographs were going to appear in the next issue of *People*. "I'm not a photographer," he said. "I'm a reporter." He seemed genuinely peeved that the car crash on the North Road was taking him away from his Steamship Authority story, his folksy up-island town government stories, his guess-what-the-idiots-at-the-county-commission-have-done-now stories.

Steve didn't even seem to care that the political reporters from inside the Beltway and upstate New York had stolen his story. "What's the matter with these people?" he asked, as Leslie used the office microwave to heat the croissant she'd bought on Main Street and he shuffled through the sections of the *Boston Globe,* the *New York Times,* the *Cape Cod Times,* and the Falmouth *Enterprise* on the kitchen table. "They don't care about who, what, when, where, and why. All they want to do is embarrass this congressman they don't like."

"And your problem with that is . . . ?" Leslie inquired, a little too tartly. She'd been trying to persuade herself that Steve was putting on an act, that he was concealing furious disappointment at being robbed and hanging on to secret hopes of a byline in the *New York Times.* But with Steve what you saw really was what you got. He had lived on Martha's Vineyard for more than twenty of his forty-nine years, which was long enough for anyone to convince himself that ambition was useless and apathy a virtue. She had to get out of here;

she really had to get out of here.

"It's like your page three story," he was saying. "Think how it would appear in the *Globe*: VINEYARD DEALS SETBACK TO BEST-SELLING AUTHOR. Period. Nothing about who used to live in the house, and what's happened to her since—or who used to own the house, or how the two are connected. You got that. It's a good piece."

"Thanks," said Leslie, removing her pastry from the microwave. *You should have seen the leads that got away.*

Back at her desk, she read the story through one more time on her screen—always a dangerous practice when the page was ready to be electronically transmitted to the printer and Production would kill her if she made any changes. It wasn't bad, really; it just didn't say anything that hadn't been said before. Her phone rang: a regular source at town hall had gotten wind of serious cost overruns on a controversial computerization project; some people wanted to keep it under wraps until the deadlines for both the *Chronicle* and the *News Beacon* had safely passed, but her "old guard" source wasn't averse to leaking the news in time to hit this week's papers. She was still scribbling away when Shannon Merrick walked through the front door, trailed by her dog, whose toenails click-click-clicked on the bare wood floor.

Shannon saluted with the manila envelope she was carrying and swerved in her direction; Pixel had paused to wheedle a biscuit from Classified. Without a by-your-leave, Shannon dropped into the extra chair and settled the envelope across her knees. Leslie managed to catch her eye and point forcefully at the phone's mouthpiece. "Ten minutes," she mouthed, one forefinger in the air.

"No prob," Shannon murmured. She rose and headed for the back hallway, whistling for Pixel to follow.

Ear still pressed intently to her phone, Leslie still couldn't help noticing that Shannon didn't pause to exchange greetings and news with anyone back in Production. No, she was on a mission: Leslie heard human footfalls going up the stairs, followed by the bounding of a large dog whose nails needed clipping. Shannon had come to see the editor in chief?

Later, when Arabella Roth buzzed her from the second floor, Leslie almost begged off. The town government story looked promising, very promising, but it was going to be a bitch to verify enough details in time to make page one, and it was Chet, not Arabella, that she needed to run it by, Chet who would tell her if it was worth pursuing on such short notice—Chet who would give Laura the bad news that she had to redo the front page. But blowing off the publisher was never a good idea. "I'm on my way," she said, grabbing a notebook and two pens. She checked the nearest wall clock: thirty-five minutes, nearly forty, since she'd told Shannon ten. Shannon must have left.

Laura was standing over one of the graphics guys. "Try lightening the screen," she said. "Ten percent is enough."

"You're gonna lose detail," he warned.

"We don't have to recognize the faces," Laura said, well on the way to exasperation. "What we want is the numbers in the chart."

"The Queen Mother's calling," Leslie interrupted. "Shouldn't be long. You seen Chet lately?"

"No," Laura snapped. "He's pulling his usual Wednesday down-the-rabbit-hole trick. If he's upstairs, kick him down here."

It was clearly a bad time to mention her possible front-page story.

Chet's office was at the front of the building, overlooking the Beach Road. When people commiserated that his mother the publisher got the harbor view while he was stuck sucking up auto exhaust and asphalt, Chet retorted that Martha's Vineyard was more about traffic than about sailboats. "On top of that," he'd been known to say, "you wouldn't believe what goes on at that gas station. I could write a novel. Maybe I will." The office door was closed, but Leslie could see the editor in chief's blurry shape through the textured glass. She knocked. Pause. "Come in," he called.

Chet was, as usual, seated at his computer, but Leslie couldn't see what he was doing because his monitor was backside to the door, all its cords and cables exposed for visitors to see. It had not always been so. One hectic Wednesday the previous summer Laura had stormed into his office, furious that fifteen minutes' worth of buzzes and rings had gone unanswered, and caught him at his terminal racing virtual stock cars, complete with very loud sound effects—revving engines, squealing tires, the works. He'd been so startled that his virtual car had hit the virtual wall with an impressive crash. The very next day he had rearranged his office. Now he had plenty of time to minimize whatever he was doing before anyone got too close. "Heads up," said Leslie. "Laura's putting on the warpaint. Better get down there quick."

Chet looked hurt. "Half an hour ago she told me she didn't want to see me downstairs till I finished the editorial."

"What are you writing about this week?"

"Oh," Chet sighed, "tempted though I am to write about the man in the blue dress—I must write about that SSA report, of course." He made a point of looking at the screen, which Leslie couldn't see. Was he writing his editorial or playing NASCAR with the sound off? "Of course I must not gloat when I point out that the report confirms the worst suspicions we have voiced, and voiced frequently, in the last six months—the suspicions, I might add, that their well-paid flacks have been protesting with such *vehemence*. The Vineyard is becoming a more vehement place, Leslie," he said, shaking his head.

"If you don't get downstairs pretty soon," she advised, "the newsroom will be awash in vehemence."

Still shaking his head, Chet Roth rose to his feet. "Thanks for the warning. Nice work on that story about Alice what's-her-name, by the way. I even read the McAuliffe profile. Well done. You make them sound like real people, not like those paragons of virtue that I'm always reading about but never get to meet. I've told you ten times and I'll tell you again: you should think about going into feature writing." Having come around his desk, he grasped the edge of the door a few inches above Leslie's shoulder.

She must have looked stricken, because he hastened to clarify: "Not for the *Chronicle!*" he said. "Not that Natalie doesn't do a fine job—a heroic job—considering what she's got to work with, but you could do with more scope, don't you think? Sunday magazine features, *The New Yorker . . .*"

"Don't I wish," said Leslie, somewhat relieved. "Oh," she interrupted herself. "Something's come up at town hall—Tisbury town hall—I've got to ask you about, but right now I've got to see Arabella. "

"*Don't* keep the Queen Mother waiting." He grinned slyly. "I'll be downstairs."

Once she heard him thudding down the wooden stairs, she rapped lightly on the publisher's door. In response to the brisk "come in," she entered, already apologizing for the delay, explaining that Laura had asked her to rouse Chet—then she almost stumbled on Pixel, who was nosing hopefully at her jacket pocket.

"Pixel!" warned Shannon, who was sitting at the left hand of Arabella Roth.

Leslie couldn't believe her eyes. Shannon had been conferring with the Queen Mother? Shannon had been conferring with the Queen Mother for *forty minutes*? "Sorry," she said.

Arabella smiled and gestured toward the leather chair at her right. "Have a seat," she said. "How are things downstairs?"

"It's Wednesday," said Leslie, sitting down but not settling into the chair. "What can I say? I was mostly done, then this hot tip came in from Tisbury town hall—it could go either way at this point." She acknowledged Shannon with a nod. What was Shannon *doing* up here?

"I promise not to take up too much of your time," Arabella assured her. She slid a memorandum across the table, turning it so that it reached Leslie right side up. Leslie noted that it carried the elaborately intertwined letters of the Island Social Services logo and that it seemed to be a press release: "FOR IMMEDIATE RELEASE," line space, today's date, line space, "For more information, contact: John M. Purcell, Jr." The head honcho his very own self is the press contact? This must be big. But Leslie couldn't read further without taking her eyes off Arabella Roth's face, which would be rude because Arabella was still talking.

"It seems that a power struggle of sorts has been going on at Island Social Services," she said, with a brief but almost *affectionate* smile in Shannon's direction. "It came to a head yesterday. The press release before you is the result. Do go ahead and read it. I've yet to meet a reporter incapable of reading and listening at the same time."

Leslie read:

Dr. Jerome R. Turner, director of Family Services at Island Social Services, will take early retirement effective October 1, 1998, John M. Purcell, Jr., ISS executive director, announced this morning. . . .

Leslie couldn't suppress a big grin. Her perseverance in the matter of Terrence Randolph had brought the wrath of Dr. Turner down upon her and the *Chronicle*, and Dr. Turner had never apologized for his intemperate invective, never mind his appalling errors in judgment. Randolph's public humiliation and subsequent departure had only hardened Turner's excuse for a heart. After Jay Segredo's car got shot at, he'd refused to make a public comment. How much would it have cost him to say, "I am relieved to learn that Mr. Segredo was not seriously injured"? Leslie thought Dr. Turner was a pretentious, vindictive, arrogant slimeball, and she knew that Shannon loathed him even more than she did. She beamed at Shannon;

she beamed at Arabella. "How sad," she said.

Shannon chuckled. "I hear no one wants to help organize his retirement party."

"Miss Merrick," said the *Chronicle* publisher, leaning slightly forward, "why don't you explain some of the background? You know it *much* better than I do."

"Sure," Shannon said. She caught Leslie's eye. "This is deep background, very deep background. Not that it won't be all over the island by Friday, but it's not for publication, OK?"

"OK," Leslie sighed. "Another Pulitzer Prize–winning story down the tubes."

Shannon managed to look sympathetic.

"OK, so tell me." Leslie made a point of pushing her notebook and pens away. "The internal tape recorder is off."

"Dr. Turner, it seems, has been harassing Jay Segredo in petty ways for quite a few months," Shannon said. "Recently the harassment crossed the line into behavior that was unprofessional, unethical—behavior that put people at risk. One of Dr. Turner's clients is Wayne Swanson. Mr. Swanson's violent history is well known to the court system, the police, and, of course, Dr. Turner. As you know, Mr. Swanson was married to Jay Segredo's sister. Mr. Swanson blames Jay for the disintegration of his marriage. He is, need I say, pretty much alone in his opinion. He was arrested last fall for shooting off a handgun in Jay's front yard—"

"Not to mention," Leslie interrupted, "persistent rumor has it that he was the sniper who took a shot at Jay's car on the Edgartown–West Tisbury Road."

Shannon's expression was downright mysterious. "It would not," she said, "be inconsistent with what we know of Mr. Swanson."

Shannon Merrick speaking in double negatives? Only press secretaries and lawyers spoke in double negatives. *Does that mean we can expect an indictment in the near future?* Leslie wondered.

"Anyway," Shannon was saying, "the case was continued

and *Mr. Swanson* was sent off-island for psychiatric evaluation and treatment for alcoholism. When he left, there were several restraining orders out on him—involving his ex-wife, their two younger children, and Jay. The restraining orders are still in force. Early last week he returned to the island. Dr. Turner knew when he was coming, and knew when he arrived. He didn't communicate this to Women's Resources. He didn't communicate this to Janice Swanson. Late last week Jay asked Dr. Turner about Mr. Swanson's whereabouts, Dr. Turner told him, more or less, that it was none of his business, and none of his sister's business. When they heard this in Women's Resources, they went *up in the air,* let me tell you. They were calling for the Gerbil's head by last Friday."

"Gerbil?" Arabella said aloud, tasting the word.

"Sorry," Shannon said. "Dr. Jerome Turner is known to some of his, uh, colleagues as Gerbil." She looked a little embarrassed. "Gerbil Turd."

"Ah." Arabella clearly relished the nickname.

"Meanwhile," Shannon went on, "you'll remember that Dr. Turner was among those who fought hardest against Jay's appointment?"

Leslie nodded. "It wasn't clear why either," she said. He had enough egg on his face by then, didn't he? He should have retired discreetly to wash it off."

"Their relationship has not improved," Shannon said. "Dr. Turner is Jay's supervisor, so he writes Jay's performance reviews. Each one has put Jay on the low end of 'adequate,' which his co-workers think is ridiculous. The first time around, Jay tried to work it out. No go. So he took it to his boss's boss, Jack Purcell. The revised version put him in the middle of 'superior.' Dr. Turner didn't get the hint, because he did the same thing the next year, and the next."

"Not a rocket scientist," Leslie muttered.

"To make a long story short," said Shannon, obviously enjoying herself, "Dr. Turner was looking for a weapon, and

Wayne Swanson handed over a pretty good one. Jay's gay. Since he moved back to the island . . ."

Leslie saw Shannon's lips moving, talking, smiling, but she couldn't hear a word. Leslie's face froze. Shannon had been right, Shannon had been right all along. *Again.* When Leslie was sure that she wouldn't start shrieking like the Wicked Witch of the West—*I'm melting! melting!*—she let herself begin to relax. Hearing returned.

". . . seems he even encouraged Mr. Swanson to play detective," Shannon was saying, "without technically violating the terms of the restraining order, of course."

"*Turner* encouraged *Swanson* to play detective?" Leslie asked. The consummate stupidity of this momentarily overwhelmed her exasperation.

"Yeah," Shannon said. "However, the good doctor tipped his hand Monday. Jay bit the bullet, so to speak, and came out to Purcell yesterday, not realizing that Turner was already in deep—" she glanced at the *Chronicle* publisher "—mud up to his eyeballs with the big boss." She pointed to the press release. "You have before you the deceptively simple consequence of a convoluted combination of coincidences."

Leslie skimmed the rest of the release: a summary of Dr. Turner's history with Island Social Services, mention of several articles published—the most recent in 1979—and his intention to play more golf and spend more time with his family. The last paragraph before the ISS boilerplate quoted Mr. Purcell as saying that a search committee was being formed to find a new Family Services director. Among those already appointed was Shannon Merrick, who had agreed to serve as the committee's vice chair.

"Not chairman?" Leslie inquired, a little too sweetly.

"Nah," said Shannon. "The chair has to have 'standing in the field.' The vice chair gets to do all the work."

"So," Leslie began, addressing the publisher this time, "how much of this goes into the paper?"

Arabella Roth pointed at the press release. "That should

suffice," she said. "Off the record, it might be noted that no one is quite sure what Dr. Turner plans to do. He is said to be rather upset. The possibility of an anti-discrimination suit has been mentioned. It can't have been a pleasant experience to find himself checkmated so very neatly." She regarded Shannon with glowing admiration. "One might even say 'brilliantly.'"

Shannon Merrick was *blushing.* "I didn't—" she began.

"But you *did,*" Arabella insisted. "My sister was waxing *rhapsodic,* and as you and I both know, my dear, Cassie is not the world's most effusive woman."

Leslie's stomach was starting to growl; she could feel claws appearing on her tongue. "I'll take care of it," she said, rising to her feet with the press release in her hand. "I've got this Tisbury story to follow up on. Thanks for filling me in."

Shannon glanced at her watch. For a moment Leslie thought she was going to say something, but she didn't. "See you later," Leslie said.

"Later," Shannon echoed, as Leslie closed the door behind her.

Chet Roth was sitting at Laura's terminal, writing heads and cuts for the Steamship Authority story on page five, when Leslie went by. "Jim Everett from the Tisbury fincom returned your call," he told her without looking up. "Sounds like you've got a live one."

Shannon Merrick was out creating stories that Leslie couldn't cover, and now her boss was chatting up her sources for her? Leslie barely bit back a snotty retort. As it was, her "I'm *so* excited" sounded so disgruntled that Chet's fingers paused over Laura's keyboard.

"The Queen Mother must be in a bad mood," Chet said.

"The Queen Mother's not in a bad mood at all," Leslie said, arrested in her flight toward the solace of her desk. "The Queen Mother is ebullient."

"There's a word you don't hear very often," mused Chet.

"Maybe I could work it into one of these cutlines?" He studied the screen. "Guess not. All the guys in these pictures have the sourest pusses this side of Bill Clinton's legal team. What's Queen Mom ebullient about?"

"Some bloodless coup at ISS."

"So *that's* what Auntie Cass came by about at eight o'clock this morning," Chet said. "I didn't think it was about tennis."

"Auntie Cass" came by at eight o'clock this morning? Why didn't you tell *me that Auntie Cass came by at eight o'clock this morning?* Leslie was not happy.

"What's up at ISS? Is it a story?"

"It's a press release," Leslie replied, rattling the paper in her hand. "Just the facts, ma'am. It seems the Family Services director was trying to blackmail the Youth Services director, but it blew up in his face. Something like that. The upshot is that the Family Services director is taking early retirement, effective October 1."

"Oho!" said Chet, a big grin on his face. "Dr. Jerome Turner, am I right?"

"You are right."

"Man must be eight feet tall. He stood over me in my own office and swore to sue you, me, and the Queen Mother herself into bankruptcy, and I tell you, for a minute there I thought we'd made a big mistake about your friend Randolph. And did Mr. Doctor Turner *ever* call to apologize for the terrible names he called me? Not once. I won't be sorry to see him go." He ran his hand over his hair. Not a gray strand in sight. "I hope they don't say that about me when I retire."

"No way, boss," Leslie reassured him, her own spirits almost restored. "Now I better get down to this story before—"

"So who was he trying to blackmail? Jay Segredo?" Chet chortled. "Dr. Einstein he's not. As far as Jack Purcell's concerned, Segredo walks on water."

"Supposedly," Leslie said with feigned nonchalance, "Segredo is gay."

"Supposedly," Chet chuckled, "the pope is Catholic."

Leslie didn't rip the press release to shreds. She didn't run screaming from the newsroom. She went to her desk, sat down, and rapidly punched in the number for the interviewer in New York. When she hung up the phone, she had an appointment for 1 p.m. Friday. Should she drive or should she take the train? The Steamship Authority reservations desk settled that question by booking her Camry on the 1:15 ferry Thursday afternoon. She could stay at her parents' Thursday and Friday nights. Whatever it took, she was getting off this rock if it was the last thing she did.

Jay was lying on the sofa contemplating the high ceiling of his living room, which was more or less what he had been doing since dusk. The sofa faced the cold, empty fireplace, its back to the rest of the living room. The whole house was dark except for the light he'd left on in the kitchen. Beyond his feet was the huge window whose curtain he had been too lazy to pull when he got up an hour or so ago for his second beer. The bottle, still half full, sat on the floor beside him. The slider door was open just enough to admit a cool, clammy breeze. Nothing else moved. By the glowing red numerals on the clock by the phone it wasn't even eight thirty: too early to go to bed.

He wasn't sleepy; he just didn't want to move.

For the last forty-eight hours, he reflected, he had been *on, on, on.* From the moment he called Shannon on Monday night till he got home this evening at quarter till six: *on, on, on, on.* Even the most grueling workdays usually had some blowing-off-steam time built in, some forget-about-work time, but not today, and not yesterday either. Yesterday and today there had been no casual conversations. Casual conversations did not begin with "Do you have a minute? We have to talk."

People really had been amazing. Starting with Becca, and Kevin, and Rainey, and Shannon, of course, though Shannon was so routinely amazing that he wasn't amazed anymore.

Shannon could have said "I told you so" about a dozen times but hadn't, not once. Now *that* was amazing. *If anyone drops dead of a heart attack, it's going to be because you said it out loud.* And she had been right about everyone—even his mother, who hadn't fainted away or even tried to change the subject, though Jay didn't think she'd taken it all in either. Everyone except Janny. True, Janny hadn't dropped dead of a heart attack, but since she stormed out of the hospital cafeteria yesterday she'd hung up on him three times, the third time after screaming, "You stay away from my kids or I'll get a restraining order!"

That one had left him shaking. When several deep breaths didn't help, he'd knocked on Becca's door, jerked a thumb toward the second floor, and gone up the stairs to the Women's Resource Center. Jack Purcell's memo about the impending retirement of Dr. Jerome Turner had just reached the desk of director Evalina Montrose. "Shut the door," she said when he stepped into her office, "and tell me what you know about *this.*"

So he'd told her, start to finish. She wasn't surprised that Jay was gay, and she wasn't surprised that Janice had flipped out. "You do remember," she said delicately, "that Janice asked to be removed from Shannon Merrick's house?" When Jay nodded, she went on: "What you don't know is that she sat right where you're sitting and told me that, rather than stay there one more night, she'd move back in with Wayne and take the kids with her."

Jay leaned back in his seat. His fingers slid into his hair, his palms absorbed the throbbing at his temples. "She wouldn't—Do you think she would have gone that far?" he asked.

Evalina pressed her two hands together and gazed intently at her thumbs. "At the time I took the possibility pretty seriously," she said. "There are definitely some issues there."

Evalina hadn't been pleased when he told her about Kevin, Wayne, the rifle, and the Marlboro butts, but she hadn't read him the riot act either. "You *know* what you've got to do," she said. "Do it."

So he had a lunch appointment with Edgartown police chief Flores for tomorrow at 12:15. Flores was a relatively unflappable guy. More important, he and Jay had played varsity basketball together in high school. Maybe Jay could beat the rap for withholding evidence and corrupting a minor. Probably the evidence would be enough to get Wayne indicted, or at least brought in for serious questioning.

Jay raised his head enough to see its reflection in the window, above the sofa's armrest, above the tips of his own toes. *Yecchh.* He fell back and felt around for his beer bottle. Found it. Took a draught. Lukewarm but not all that bad. *Tomorrow is the first day of the rest of your life,* he thought. *Tomorrow. Not today. Today is gone, in the can, history. Time to put today to bed.*

Except that his mind couldn't muster the authority to direct his feet to hit the floor and propel him toward his bedroom. So he stayed where he was, gazing at the ceiling, pretending to contemplate the last forty-eight hours but really just spacing out.

Until headlights moved up the driveway, winking on and off through the trees until they came to a rest next to his Volvo. One car door slammed, and then another. Hushed voices and muffled laughter followed, like kids trying to *very quietly* make breakfast on Christmas morning. Another slam. *Whatha fuck . . . ?* Jay was mildly curious about what was going on out there. Maybe his landlord-neighbor was in the middle of a hot date. Jay resumed staring at the ceiling and thinking about going to bed.

Outside the gravel crunched, closer and closer. "You think anyone's home?" one voice stage-whispered.

"His car's here, isn't it?" retorted another voice, less subdued. "What happened to those damn sensor lights? Shouldn't they have come on—"

Abruptly the deck, the gravel walkway, the scattered

daffodils on the little lawn were bathed in stark light by crisscrossed beams from facing corners of the house. "Yeow, I can't see!" said the first voice. "Don't shoot!"

The second voice choked on a laugh; the first voice giggled.

Jay recognized the voices. As uninvited guests went, these weren't bad, but he wasn't at all sure that he was ready to deal. *Like I have a choice?*

He raised his head enough to watch them come up the stairs, carrying—what the hell was it, a coffin? No—not unless two people could carry a coffin with one hand each. It was draped with a dark blanket from one end to the other.

They navigated the screen door with no trouble. "Anybody home?" Shannon called, not too loud.

Jay resigned himself to his fate. "Yeah," he said. "Over here."

"Christ!" Giles gasped. "Give me a heart attack, why don't you?"

"You guys," said Jay, his stocking feet hitting the floor with a thud, "are breaking into *my* house. Don't give me any crap about heart attacks."

Giles turned to Shannon. "It's him!" he cried, at the same moment Shannon hit the dimmer switch by the door. The chandelier—a modern fixture of four concentric circles suspended from the high ceiling and hanging about eight feet above the floor—came on full strength. No one could see a thing. Shannon brought the light down to about twenty-five watts. Giles surveyed the room. He nodded toward the easy chair by the telephone. "There," he said.

They set their burden down so that it rested against the chair back. It stuck out beyond the arms about a foot on each side. Shannon straightened the blanket that covered it. Against his will, Jay was dying of curiosity. It had to be a painting. The question was, which one of them had done it? "C'mon, kids," he said. "I told you to leave the ISS sign *alone.*"

"It's the door to the Gerb's office," Shannon said, deadpan. "His nameplate's still on it."

Jay relented. "Gimme a hug, you bad girl," he said, laughing. "There was dancing in the halls all over Island Social Services today. Women's Resources ordered pizza from Louis', and Connie got *two* bottles of champagne on the way back from picking it up . . ."

They slapped high tens with fair-to-middling accuracy, then Shannon threw her arms around Jay, singing, "Ding dong, the wretch is *dead!*" and spun him around a couple of times. Then she got serious. "How you doing?" she asked, without stepping back.

"Not bad," he conceded, "considering. People have been pretty awesome—"

"How about Janice?"

"Ouch," said Jay.

"Yeah?" Shannon prompted.

"She's probably signed up with the Traditional Values Coalition by now." Jesus, that hurt. Like one of his arms had been lopped off, and the ghost feeling came from where his sister ought to be.

Shannon knew. She squeezed him hard around the middle. "She'll come back," she said.

"You think so?"

"I think so."

"*Your* sister didn't."

"*I* didn't care if she did or not."

"At least Kevin's cool."

"Kevin's *very* cool. Tell me one thing," Shannon said. "Everyone's dying to know, but I won't tell a soul."

Jay braced himself.

"Are you going to put in for the Gerbil's job?"

Jay looked at her blankly. "You aren't serious."

"That means no?"

"It means no."

"Good," said Shannon. "It's going to drive Dr. Turd right over the edge. Word has it he's telling his buds that he was undone by your ambition and your friends in high places."

"Oh, *right!*" Jay snorted. He would have said more, but Shannon cut him off:

"Besides, if you put in for the job, I'd probably have to resign from the search committee—"

"Why the hell would you do that?"

"Conflict of interest," Shannon said, raising her eyebrows as if he were unusually dense and then slipping into atonal song: "We are fam-i-ly."

Coffee smell reached their noses at almost the same instant. "I love you program people," Jay said. "When the going gets tough, the tough make coffee. So," he glanced toward the kitchen, "are we going to have an unveiling?"

Giles was opening cupboard doors. The third one proved the charm: he extracted a box of sugar and set it on the counter, beside three identical ceramic mugs. Shannon looked at him for guidance. "Go ahead," he said, without looking up. Then he started opening drawers, probably looking for spoons.

"In the corner," said Shannon. "Left of the stove."

From all this Jay inferred that Giles, not Shannon, was the painter. The tension in the room, already considerable, was rising, but it wasn't coming from him. That was a relief. Since yesterday morning, every time he entered a room where other people were present, his stomach had started to spin like a basketball on the rim of a hoop. Shannon drew the blanket off the painting and draped it over the back of the chair.

The painting pounced. It grabbed him round the throat and before he could struggle it settled over him like a revelation, an awareness that was not quite part of him but would become so soon, that might cause others to see him differently for a while, until they all got used to it. If there had been a chair behind him, he would have collapsed into it.

Of course he knew who it was, and where it was, and even when it was: the night following the day late last August when a brisk southwest wind banished the sultry summer air and on the street, at work, everyone smiled with the exuberant knowledge that September was truly coming, the summer people would leave (most of them), the workload and the traffic would drop, the island would soon be theirs again. It wasn't the merry month of May that islanders celebrated most enthusiastically, it was the bracing month of September. That night it had been at least an hour past midnight when Jay finally said, "I should be going," and Giles said, "You could stay if you wanted," and for some reason, maybe the coming of September, his guard had dropped, and he had.

The painting was beautiful. The light in the painting was September light. He looked at the painting and thought, *I have never seen myself sleep.*

"We could move it over there," Shannon said softly, nodding toward the fireplace.

They moved it. Two mugs of coffee had appeared on the hearth. Jay had visions of the painting smeared with soot and stained with coffee. "It'll get dirty," he said.

Shannon ran her left forefinger along the bricks and held it out to show him. It was clean. She and Jay set the painting down. Jay sat on the edge of the sofa. Shannon studied the painting, squinted, then moved it a bit to the right. She sat down too, and slouched back against the cushion. "It's all there," Jay said in wonder.

"I'd rather paint than be painted any day of the week," Shannon said, reaching for the coffee. The black one was hers; the one with cream wasn't. "Believe me, no sane person wants to live with a painter, or a novelist, or a songwriter—"

"Is that why you're single?" Jay ventured, suddenly curious.

"No," Shannon snapped, then relented almost immediately. She sipped her coffee, watching the painting through the flickering steam. "There are women interested in me," she said lightly, "and there are women I am interested in, but at the moment the twain are not meeting."

Jay listened to the silence and gazed at himself on the hearth. *Not a care in the world,* he thought, although he knew better. "You're going glib on me," he said. From behind a finger traced the edge of his neck; a hand rested on his right shoulder. Jay shivered.

Shannon gazed at the painting. "Yeah, I am," she said at last, leaning forward to return her mug to the hearth. "Sorry." She looked at Jay and noticed out of the corner of her eye that Giles was standing behind the sofa. After a moment's consideration she laced the fingers of her hand through the fingers of Jay's left. "I'm not sure I'm going to like the new you," she said with a wry smile. "This is the first time in six months that you've noticed."

Jay lifted his right hand, palm up. Giles rested his own right hand on it for a moment then started tracing Jay's fingers with an exquisitely ephemeral touch. Jay remembered to keep breathing, but that touch was jumping across space to caress his cheek, his jaw, his throat—except that he could still see the hand hovering above his own hand. *Jesus.*

"I woke up," Giles said. His words shimmered quietly in the still air and then disappeared. "I was cold. I got up to close the window, and I looked . . . I didn't even know what I was feeling. That morning I started sketching. Over and over. It was shit, it was dead, it was nothing. Day after day I tried pencil, pen and ink, colored pencil, watercolor, acrylic—I even tried modeling clay."

Jay knew in his gut what came next. He would have said it out loud but the words had spikes and couldn't move without tearing his throat. He waited, his mind's eye watching a projectile moving in very slow motion toward his right front tire.

"After Columbus Day," Giles said, "I was a mess. Only God, the Devil, and Shannon Merrick know what a mess I was. Shannon's begging, pleading, screaming at me: Paint, you fool. Goddammit, paint! I don't give a shit how much it hurts to paint, it's a shitload better than drinking."

"I didn't say that," Shannon protested.

"The hell you didn't, girlfriend." Giles dropped a kiss on

the back of her head. "I remember every single word. It was my mantra for weeks. I painted and painted, I went to work, came home in the middle of the night and painted some more. I didn't know what the fuck I was doing. Finally I painted myself into a corner. It dawned on me that I loved you a lot. Believe it or not, I really hadn't figured it out."

No one moved, or spoke. Jay's eyes never left the painting, and finally the painting put words in his mouth. "How," he asked, "can you guys take something like *that* and hang it up in public where anyone can see it?"

"Hah," Shannon said. "Don't ask me. I'm the one who hasn't painted anything worth hanging in six years at least."

"Because," said Giles, "most people don't have a clue what they're seeing."

Another while passed, and finally Shannon said, "If I leave, do you promise to behave?"

"Probably not," said Jay.

"In that case, I'm going home," she decided out loud. "I'm wasted." She rose and stretched her arms up toward the ceiling. "If your truck's still in my driveway next Monday, I'm calling the cops."

"It's a deal," Giles said.

Shannon got as far as the sliding door then turned back. "You want me to call you in sick, or do you want to do it?"

Jay snorted. "You do it. Just don't be so graphic that I have to walk in there Friday with a paper bag on my head."

Shannon laughed. "I promise," she said, and slid the screen shut behind her.

They listened to her feet clattering down the steps and crunching across the gravel, listened until the Subaru's engine turned over, settled into a steady, undermuffled rumble, then vanished down the road.

AFTERWORD

If you sensed that these events took place slightly before the present day, you're right. Prices that were astronomical in 1998 now seem unbelievably low, cell phones are ubiquitous, and more people have high-speed Internet connections now than then. But chapter 10 took place in the funky old county airport, which by 1999 had been replaced by the sprawling and soulless new one. In theory, fiction writers can do whatever we want. I thought of plunking the old airport down in the middle of 2004, 2006, or 2008, but that threw too many other things out of whack. Turns out these events took place in the mud of a particular time as well as the mud of a particular place. In 2004, 2006, or 2008 the story would have unfolded differently, as it would have unfolded differently in Boston or Brewster or on Nantucket.

Martha's Vineyard does exist. For some people it's here year-round; for others, it winks into existence around Memorial Day and disappears by mid-October. None of these events happened on that Martha's Vineyard, in 1998 or any other year. But if any of the characters in these pages managed to make it to the real Martha's Vineyard, they'd almost certainly recognize the place.

ACKNOWLEDGMENTS

It takes a village to raise a book. Words need readers the way plants need water and sunlight. Almost three dozen people read *The Mud of the Place* in its various drafts. Some of them live on Martha's Vineyard, some of them don't, and some of them I still haven't met in person. They helped bring this story to life. Thank you all. Thanks especially to Bronwyn Becker, Cathleen Jasper Vincent, Don Dale, Jeannette Cézanne, Kathie Gibbs, Nancy Leverich, Mike Mason, Patty Blakesley, Sara Fogg Crafts, Susan Robinson, and William Stewart for their comments and support, written and otherwise. Bou W. offered counsel and insight that improved chapter 11. Susan Klein not only tells wonderful stories and writes great blurbs, she's an ace catcher of typos. So is Sally Noonan, who read the second-pass proofs. Thanks to Marilyn Kerr for the Black Bush, chocolate chip cookies, and many writerly gatherings in her kitchen, and thanks beyond thanks to Wendy Palmer, who has probably read more of and heard more about *Mud* than anyone else on the planet.

Long time ago, Irene Zahava asked me to contribute to a lesbian mystery anthology she was editing. Do I have to kill someone off? I asked. No, she replied. The mystery anthology never happened, but the story I wrote, "Deer Out of Season," wound up in another Zahava anthology. We both thought there might be a novel in there. We were right. Here it is. Whew.

Martha's Vineyard is not an easy place to live. For a single woman to attempt to support not only herself but a dog, a horse, and a novel in progress requires a suspension of disbelief that borders on the insane. I got by with a little help from a whole lot of friends. Thanks to everyone who helped me through the Great Housing Crisis of 2002, especially Martha and Dick Mezger, who rented me the apartment, and Christina Brown and Kate Davy, who helped me move in. My Detached Retina Adventures of 2004 were made bearable by the support of, among others, Ginny Lobdell, Elaine Shabazian, Billie Aul, and my sister, Ellen Sturgis, and the Sturgis-Kopczynski family. Sara Crafts treated me to more lunches and Cris Jones to more breakfasts than I can remember or repay. Support for the arts takes many forms. My muses thank you, and so do I.

Some people moved on before I finished, or before I started, or before I knew where the starting line was. I wish I could put a copy in your hands: Rosamond T. Little, Rozzy Bennett Kramer, John Bordeaux, Thom Higgins, Brad McMinn, Betty Ann Lima Bryant, Linda Rannells Lewis Bullard, Jim Kane, Chiquita Mitchell Sturgis, Gerry Kelly, Mary Payne, Jack Reece, Virgil Peterson, Virginia Mazer, Lisa A. Barnett, Joan McGurren and Robert Shaw Sturgis. In so many ways, Grace Paley's words both inspired the novel and kept me honest while I wrote it. I so wanted to tell her the story and ask permission to use those words as an epigraph. I waited too long. Thanks so much to Nora Paley for hearing the story and giving permission on her mother's behalf. Rhodry Malamutt won't be at the first book party, but he is on the back cover, and he lives on in Pixel. Merry met, and blessed be.

Finally, thanks to the late Stan Rogers for "The Mary Ellen Carter" and to Pete Morton for "Another Train." The beginning is now.

If you enjoyed this book,
please spread the word
by telling some friends.

❁

GET FREE BOOKS

For every ten Speed-of-C books you buy,
we'll send you another one free.

You can buy ten different titles,
ten copies of one title, or any combination.

In each of our books,
you'll find a barcode and number
in the bottom right corner of the last page.
Cut out the original barcodes from
ten Speed-of-C books, and send them
to us along with your name, mailing address,
and email address.

When our next book is released,
you'll receive a free copy.
It's as simple as that.

Speed-of-C Productions
PO Box 265
Linthicum, MD 21090-0265

More Books from Speed-of-C Productions

The Curse of the Zwilling by Don Sakers
0-9716147-2-5 • 384 pages • $19.99
*It's Hogwarts meets Buffy at Patapsco University: a small,
cozy liberal arts college like so many others – except for the
Department of Comparative Religion, where age-old spells are
taught and magic is practiced. When a favorite teacher is
found dead under mysterious circumstances, grad student
David Galvin finds that a malevolent evil has awakened. And
now David, along with four novice undergrads, must defeat
this ancient, malignant terror.*

The SF Book of Days by Don Sakers
0-9716147-6-8 • 184 pages • $14.99
*Drawn from the pages of classic sf literature, here is a science
fiction/fantasy event for every day of the year…and for quite
a few days that* aren't *part of the year. From Doc Brown's
arrival in Hill Valley (January 1, 1885) to the launch of the
Bellerophon (Sextor 7, 2351), this datebook is truly
out of this world.*

PsiScouts #1: At Risk by Phil Meade
0-9716147-3-3 • 132 pages • $9.99
*In the 26th century, psi-powered teenagers from all over the
Myriad Worlds join together as the heroic PsiScouts.*

Order through your favorite bookstore, online retailers such as
Amazon.com, via our website (*www.scatteredworlds.com*), or mail
orders to Speed-of-C Productions, PO Box 265, Linthicum, MD
21090-0265. For mail orders, please include $4 per book for shipping
& handling.

More Books from Speed-of-C Productions

Gaylaxicon Sampler 2006
0-9716147-8-4 • 114 pages • $4.99

Sample the work of thirteen writers from across the spectrum of gay, lesbian, bisexual, and/or transgender science fiction, fantasy, and/or horror. Includes big names and small, much-published veterans and promising beginners, Lammy and Spectrum Award nominees and winners, past Gaylaxicon Guests of Honor, and fresh new names.

QSpec Sampler 2007
978-1-934754-00-9 • 132 pages • $4.99

Originally prepared as a giveaway at Gaylaxicon 2007 in Atlanta, this volume is available at a nominal charge as a sampler of the fine work being done by GLBT writers in SF, fantasy, and horror.

Act Well Your Part by Don Sakers
0-9716147-7-6 • 189 pages • $14.99

A beloved gay young adult romance, back in print for its adult fans as well as a new generation of teens. At first Keith Graff dislikes his new school. He misses his old friends, and despairs of ever fitting in. Then he joins the school's drama club, and meets the boyishly cute Bran Davenport....

Order through your favorite bookstore, online retailers such as Amazon.com, via our website (*www.scatteredworlds.com*), or mail orders to Speed-of-C Productions, PO Box 265, Linthicum, MD 21090-0265. For mail orders, please include $4 per book for shipping & handling.

The Scattered Worlds Universe of Don Sakers

Dance for the Ivory Madonna
a romance of psiberspace
by Don Sakers
0-9716147-1-7 • 460 pages • $19.99
Spectrum Award finalist; 56 Hugo nominations
*"Imagine a **Stand on Zanzibar** written by a left-wing Robert Heinlein, and infused with the most exciting possibilities of the new cyber-technology." -Melissa Scott, author of*
Dreaming Metal, The Jazz

A Voice in Every Wind
two tales of the Scattered Worlds
by Don Sakers
0-9716147-5-X • 108 pages • $7.50
On a world where meaning lives in every rock and stream, and every breeze brings a new voice, one human explorer stands on the threshold of discoveries that could alter the future of Humanity.

Weaving the Web of Days
a tale of the Scattered Worlds
by Don Sakers
0-9716147-0-9 • 113 pages • $7.99
Maj Thovold has led the Galaxy for three decades, a Golden Age of peace and prosperity. She is weary and ready to resign, but she faces one last battle: a battle on the strangest battlefield known: a web of living tendrils that stretches across interstellar space. A web where Maj's enemies wait, like spiders, for their prey....

Order through your favorite bookstore, online retailers such as Amazon.com, via our website (*www.scatteredworlds.com*), or mail orders to Speed-of-C Productions, PO Box 265, Linthicum, MD 21090-0265. For mail orders, please include $4 per book for shipping & handling.

The Scattered Worlds Universe of Don Sakers

A Rose From Old Terra
a novel of the Scattered Worlds
by Don Sakers
0-9716147-9-2 • 263 pages • $17.50
Jedrek left the Grand Library and his work circle eleven years ago. Now a crisis in uncharted space brings the circle back together. Soon, Jedrek and his friends are at the focal point of a clash of cultures, and the only thing that can save the Galaxy is one modest group of Librarians.

The Leaves of October
a novel of the Scattered Worlds
by Don Sakers
0-9716147-4-1 • 304 pages • $17.50
Compton Crook Award finalist
The Hlutr: Immensely old, terribly wise...and utterly alien. When mankind went out into the stars, he found the Hlutr waiting for him. Waiting to observe, to converse, to help. Waiting to judge...and, if necessary, to destroy.

Order through your favorite bookstore, online retailers such as Amazon.com, via our website (*www.scatteredworlds.com*), or mail orders to Speed-of-C Productions, PO Box 265, Linthicum, MD 21090-0265. For mail orders, please include $4 per book for shipping & handling.

Printed in the United States
138364LV00003B/104/P